SYLVIA'S SECOND ACT

SYLVIA'S SECOND ACT

Hillary Yablon

PAMELA DORMAN BOOKS | VIKING

VIKING
An imprint of Penguin Random House LLC
penguinrandomhouse.com

A Pamela Dorman Book/Viking

LIBRARY OF CONGRESS CATALOGING-IN-PUBLICATION DATA
Names: Yablon, Hillary, author.
Title: Sylvia's second act : a novel / Hillary Yablon.
Description: [New York] : Pamela Dorman Books/Viking, 2024.
Identifiers: LCCN 2023033690 (print) | LCCN 2023033691 (ebook) |
ISBN 9780593493618 (hardcover) | ISBN 9780593493625 (ebook) |
ISBN 9780593832240 (international edition)
Subjects: LCGFT: Humorous fiction. | Novels.
Classification: LCC PS3625.A335 S95 2024 (print) | LCC PS3625.A335 (ebook) |
DDC 813/.6—dc23/eng/20230929
LC record available at https://lccn.loc.gov/2023033690
LC ebook record available at https://lccn.loc.gov/2023033691

Printed in the United States of America
1st Printing

DESIGNED BY MEIGHAN CAVANAUGH

This book is dedicated to my mother, Lorna Yablon.
It is also dedicated to my father, Alfred Yablon, the kind of
man who would have insisted I put my mom first.

One

I admit it. I have fantasies. Of course I do. Who doesn't?

If I were to make a list of my own fantasies, the ones that pop into mind would be the following:

To be a runner. I turned sixty-three last month; I'm sure my body would be in for quite the shock. But, boy, would I just love to wake up and pull on a pair of those adorable running shorts I see the girls in these days. I actually thought about getting into it after my daughter, Isabel, joined the cross-country team in high school. I thought we'd go for mother-daughter runs, but somehow things were always too busy. Izzy had a million activities. I was always in the car, driving her somewhere, like all the other Connecticut housewives.

I used to fantasize about leaving Connecticut. Even just for a night. Taking the train into Manhattan and trying one of those "hot new places" people were always taking about. Having a glass of wine at the bar and then . . .

Okay, the truth is that I fantasized about that almost every day after Izzy left for college. Now I fantasize about going back there and leaving this dreadful Florida retirement community my husband, Louis, insisted we move to. Boca Beach Gables, BBG for short. Don't get me wrong. It's very nice. Very pretty, very upscale, very pink. But I hate the sun. I hate the humidity. I hate the way the days feel stretched out and empty. I have never felt so alone.

I fantasize about what it would have been like if, instead of marrying my husband right after college, I'd had a career abroad, somewhere vibrant. Like London.

I fantasize about taking a bat and swinging it in Belinda Teller's Botoxed face. That may be because Belinda is currently sitting on top of my husband with no clothes on. She is facing me. Because I am an avid fan of *Sex and the City* (I've seen it from start to finish six times), I know that Belinda is in reverse cowgirl position.

For a moment, I fantasize I'm in reverse cowgirl with Marcus, our spin instructor. That's the best thing I can say about BBG—their staff is excellent. Marcus is gorgeous. I pretend I don't know how to adjust the bike seat so he'll help me. I can almost feel his hands on my lower back right now . . .

Shit. I must have gotten caught up in this fantasy because I don't hear Louis and Belinda trying to get through to me.

". . . Sylvia!" Louis is calling. "Jesus Christ, Sylvia! Say something."

But I'm frozen. I can't move my mouth. So instead, I look to the left and catch my reflection in the mirror above the dresser. To be honest, I think I look quite good. As much as I hate it, the Florida sun has given my fair skin some color. And I've just gone to the hairdresser. She convinced me to go a little more beachy and added highlights to my shoulder-length hair.

I'm wearing the linen pants and cotton blouse ensemble that has become my uniform down here. I keep telling myself it's classy and functional but deep down I feel boring and frumpy. I love clothes. But there's something about shopping in South Florida that makes me feel old. Like I'm one step closer to white sneakers and track pants.

I run a hand through my hair and frown. Where was I? Right. I'm standing in the bedroom of my ocean view condo staring at Belinda Teller's naked body. She is now sitting on the bed *next* to my husband instead of on top of him. Louis has the sheets around himself.

Typical. He's always been selfish.

"Oh my god, Sylvia. This isn't what you think," Belinda says as she shivers a bit.

"Oh, that's a relief," I say. "Because I thought you were having sex with my husband. But maybe you're just playing bridge. Only with no clothes. And no cards."

Belinda blinks. I can't stop staring at her enormous boobs. They're quite perky and, from what she told us at last month's Ladies' Wine Night, freshly redone by the best surgeon in South Florida.

"How long are you planning to sit there naked?" I ask.

"It's just . . . I'm so sorry, Sylvia. But would you mind?" Belinda's voice trails off and I follow her eyeline and look down. I'm standing on her bra. Instinctively, I bend down and pick it up. It looks like a small tent. I toss it to her.

"Thanks," Belinda says as she puts on the bra. Naturally, it's sheer, and somehow her nipples look even bigger beneath the black lace.

"You do the Brazilian?" I have no control over what comes out of my mouth. It gets worse in stressful situations. Plus, Belinda is now standing up and I have a full frontal view. "I ask because I was watching the episode of *Sex and the City* where Carrie can't decide what she thinks of men who want a completely bare pussy."

Louis looks positively scandalized. "Sylvia!"

"What? I can't say pussy? You're the one having sex with a woman you know I hate."

"You hate me?" Belinda looks surprised. "I thought we were friends."

I want to hit her. But instead, I glare. "Get out."

"You're right! I'm sorry! I just, um . . . I just don't know know where my clothes are."

Of course she doesn't. As if on reflex, I drop to my knees and start looking under the bed for her clothes.

Louis crouches down next to me. "Sylvia." He swallows. "I'm so sorry. You don't have to do this."

"Just help me find her damn clothes." My voice is muffled as I flatten myself on my stomach and squirm farther under the bed.

Louis sighs and gets up. From my vantage point, I see his and Belinda's feet padding around the room. "Louis," Belinda whispers. I don't hear what else she says, but I see Louis's feet leave the room.

It's dark under the bed. The carpet is gunmetal gray—hardly my first choice—and I can barely see anything. My arms are outstretched and I'm swimming them slowly over the floor. My hands finally hit something that is lacy and obscenely small. "I think I've found your underpants," I call as I slither back out from under the bed.

Before getting up, I glance over my shoulder. The coast is clear. I covertly turn Belinda's thong inside out so I can see the label printed on the waistband. Size zero.

That bitch.

I drag myself to my feet and hand Belinda her panties. "All right. Now get out."

Belinda pulls them on and nods. "I just need my dress. Or if you want me gone, maybe I can borrow something of yours?"

"We both know my clothes won't fit you."

"Don't be silly! We're practically the same size."

"I'm six inches taller and thirty pounds heavier." My voice is flat.

Belinda waves a hand as though we're just girlfriends at lunch fishing for compliments. "You've got a gorgeous figure. I'd die to be tall and athletic like you."

She's lying. She loves being tiny and feminine. I am sick with jealousy over her flat stomach. The last thing I need to see is her swimming in my clothes. And I'd sooner die than watch her walk out in one of Louis's big T-shirts like this was some frat house.

I swallow. "Let's just find your dress. Where do you think it is?"

"On the ceiling fan." Louis says as he walks in from the living room. He's still only wearing his boxers and looks short of breath. "I tried using a flyswatter to get it down. But the dress is really tangled up there."

I blink. "I'm sorry. Did you say the ceiling fan?"

Louis nods. I blink again. How did I miss that on my way into the bedroom? And, seriously? Just how passionate was this lovemaking session? Louis has a bad back. Since when did he turn into a sexual acrobat? I must still be staring at them, because Louis clears his throat and finally says, "I may have to call building maintenance to get it down."

A shot of humiliation jolts through my body. "Louis, I can take a lot. But I would rather be set on fire than have Derek from building maintenance come up here to retrieve Belinda's dress from our ceiling fan. Get me a goddamn hanger."

Belinda's eyes widen. But Louis is stone-faced. The only other time he's seen me like this is when I was in labor. He quickly obeys, grabs a hanger from the closet, and gives it to me.

Mustering whatever ashes of dignity I have left, I square my shoulders and walk into the living room.

Sure enough, just above our couch, Belinda's sundress is tangled around the one purchase I bought for our prefurnished condo: the Big-Ass Fan. It's really called that. They're very chic. Oversize, hand-carved wood. Gives our place a Bali-like feel. Now, of course, it's more a brothel-like feel.

Belinda and Louis—both of whom are still in their goddamn underwear—stare as I gingerly step onto the armrest of the couch to reach the dress.

"Careful, Sylvie," Louis says.

"Do not call me that. Do not ever fucking call me that again," I say through clenched teeth as I try to angle the hanger just right so that I can pull down the dress.

I miss.

I take a breath and steady myself as I fling the hanger forward again. I grab hold of the dress and slowly untwist it from the fan's blades.

Louis is impressed. "You got it! Wow!"

For a moment, I'm quite impressed with myself, when—

I fall off the couch. Belinda and Louis rush over. "I'm fine," I say as I rub my leg. "Nothing's broken."

"Let me get you some ice," Belinda says as she quickly scoops up her dress. I close my eyes a moment as I hear *click-clack, click-clack, click-clack* . . .

I open my eyes. I look up and stare at Belinda rushing through my apartment in high-heeled sandals. I lean my head back against the couch and start to laugh.

"What's so funny?" Louis asks.

I point to Belinda as she wraps ice in a hand towel and heads toward us.

"Look at her," I wheeze. "She's like an aging stepmother in porn."

Louis glances up as Belinda comes trotting over in her heels, bra, and panties.

I'm laughing and laughing. Belinda glances at Louis. "Did she hit her head?"

This makes me laugh harder. Belinda looks truly worried as she kneels in front of me to give me the ice. Her massive bosom presses against me. God, these boobs. I cannot get away from them.

And so I give in. I cup her breasts. "Oh!" She jerks backward, shocked.

But I don't let go. I squeeze them like I'm shopping for fruit. "Wow," I murmur. "Much more natural than I thought."

Belinda is so flustered that she jumps up and puts on her dress as quickly as possible.

She then grabs her purse and runs out of the apartment.

When the door slams, I look at Louis. My voice is deadpan. "If I'd known she was homophobic, I would've felt her up sooner."

Louis just stares. "You sure you're okay?"

"No, Louis. I'm not okay. I just molested my husband's mistress."

"She's not my mistress, Sylvia. It was this one time. I swear. Let me explain—"

"Get dressed first."

Louis looks down at his boxers and then quickly heads into the bedroom. I massage my sore leg for a moment.

Louis returns wearing pants. As he hastily pulls on a shirt, I lean my head back against the couch and take him in. He's a good-looking man. Six feet, two inches. Daily golf and tennis have kept him trim. His hair went gray twenty years ago, but he's still got plenty of it. I can see why other women want to have sex with him.

Finally dressed, he looks at me and exhales. "Sylvia, I'm sorry. So, so sorry."

"Do you love her?"

"Of course not. This really was an accident."

Why do men say such stupid things? This whole situation is just so pathetic that it's almost funny. I start to laugh again until I realize that maybe it's me who's pathetic. Louis and I haven't made love in . . . I've lost track. Have we done it since moving down here? I'm racking my brain, trying to figure it out, when I hear Louis's voice cutting in and out . . .

". . . and so when I found out we lost it all . . ."

Maybe the first week? We must have. How could I not know this?

". . . and I think I'm in shock, Sylvia. Don't worry, though. We're paid through our dues until the end of May down here. So I'll figure something out. The lawyers said . . ."

"What?" I look at Louis. I realize he's talking about something important.

"I said that the lawyers think they'll be able to recover some of our savings. It just may take a little while."

"What lawyers? What are you talking about?" I'm rubbing my forehead.

"I just told you, Sylvia. My retirement account was mismanaged by the investment firm I hired last year."

"What does that mean? I thought we chose a low-risk plan for our portfolio."

"We did," he says as he reddens. "But I took a chance. I didn't tell you because I knew you'd be nervous. But the returns were out of this world. And their reputation was great and . . . shit. I screwed up." He looks down.

"Louis," I say very slowly. "Is all of our money gone?"

He nods, his face dark and heavy. "I just found out last week. I've been scrambling to see how bad it is and I remembered Belinda had a big position at J.P. Morgan before she retired. And so I was talking to her about things and she introduced me to a lawyer and then I guess I was feeling pretty broken and one thing led to another . . ." His voice trails off.

"So let me get this straight. We lost everything. Belinda gave you a shoulder to cry on and an attorney to call. And that—accidentally— led to sex?"

He nods. "Don't worry. I'm going to make sure we're okay."

I look at him for a long time. I know I should feel sad and probably a little scared. But all I feel is a deep, deep relief. I know exactly what I'm going to do.

"Louis," I say. "I'm leaving."

Two

After I left my condo, I headed straight to Evie's. She took one look at my face and insisted we start drinking immediately. Evie's my only real friend at BBG. We met my second week there and instantly bonded. That was only a year ago, but it seems like we've known each other forever. She and I have the same birthday. She just turned seventy. Apparently she's turned seventy for the last few years. But I pretend not to know that. What do I care? For a woman who uses a cane—she has arthritis in her knees—one would be a fool to underestimate her. When her husband, Henry, was alive, he used to call her the General. That makes me think they had a good marriage.

"What did they feel like?" Evie asks as she takes a long sip of her cosmo. We're at Moonlight's, Boca's trendiest bar. "Were they hard? Semi-hard? Did you squeeze them or just stroke them like petting a cat?"

She's talking, of course, about Belinda's boobs. I ponder my answer as though trying to describe the meaning of life. "I gave them a good squeeze," I finally say. "And then I just kind of held on to them."

Evie throws her head back and laughs. A group of people nearby turns and looks. It's 5:00 p.m. and happy hour is in full swing. We're lucky to have gotten this booth. But then again, we've been here since 2:30, when the place was mostly empty except for the dedicated alcoholics at the bar.

I finish my drink—maybe my third?—and let out a long breath. Evie watches me carefully and then turns serious. She runs a hand through her short, blond shag. People often mistake her for Jane Fonda, and I know this thrills her. She has a certain glamour that's hard to describe. Even her cane is somehow stylish rather than geriatric.

"Sylvia, I'm sorry this happened. But what are you going to do?"

Before I can answer, a new waiter approaches. He's young, in his late twenties, and handsome in the way that everyone in their twenties is. At least to me. "Hello, ladies. Your server, Cassie, just clocked out. I have the pleasure of taking over your table. Another round?"

Evie nods. "You bet. That's why we Ubered here."

"You Ubered? That's amazing."

"What's amazing about it? That two old ladies know how to work a smartphone?" Evie's eyes narrow.

"No," the waiter stammers. "I mean, it's just so great that you're so hip and . . ." I feel sorry for him.

But Evie cracks a smile. "I'm just fucking with you, dear."

Now the waiter's eyes go wide. He stands there, not sure what to do. Evie has that effect on people.

Evie pats his arm. "Go bring us our drinks." He nods, looking dazed, and walks away.

I laugh, grateful for this light moment. "What would I do without you, Evie?"

"I'm more interested, Sylvia, in what you're going to do now that you've discovered your husband is a cheating shit who lost all of your money."

I let out a breath and look at the ceiling. The truth is, whatever relief I felt before has given way to a deep panic.

But I try to stay calm. "Maybe things aren't that bad," I finally say. "I don't know what's going to happen with my marriage, but financially speaking, Louis said he would sort things out. And it's not like we're actually broke. The hair salon took my credit card today. I've had no trouble at the grocery store or getting gas for the car. So, really, it just sounds bad. But it's all going to be fine."

Evie shakes her head. "Get your head out of your ass. Things are bad. But things were bad before. You were stuck in a life you hate."

"That's not . . . entirely true." But even as I say it, I know Evie is right. My life is a mess. My husband makes me sick. We have no money. Our credit cards will eventually run out. And I have no idea how much cash—if any—is left in our account. My eyes fill with tears.

"Oh, Sylvia," Evie says as I begin to cry.

"I just don't know how I could have been so stupid," I sob. "Louis always handled the investing. But I paid the bills and kept track of our budget until he retired and we moved down here. He transferred everything online and it just seemed easier to let him handle things. He's an accountant after all!" The tears are pouring hot and fast now. "I'm such a cliché. I'm one of those stupid women you see on a miniseries and don't feel sorry for because you secretly think what's happened is their fault."

"That's not true." Evie rubs my arm as she speaks.

I put my head in my hands and weep. The same people nearby turn and look at us. I start hiccupping. I've always been an ugly crier. Of course this is also the moment the handsome young waiter returns with our drinks. He slips them wordlessly onto our table.

Evie hands me my cosmo. "Sylvia, there's a silver lining here: it's the kick in the ass you need to get your life in order."

"Kick in the ass?" I moan as I gulp my drink. "More like a bullet to the head." I finally get control of my breathing and dry my eyes with some Kleenex I've dug out of my purse.

Evie takes my hand in hers. I'm surprised by the intensity of her grip. "A bullet to the head is cancer or ALS or finding out your child overdosed on some designer drug you've never even heard of."

I stare at my friend. I know she's talking about her son, and she never talks about her son.

I swallow. "Evie, I—"

"My point, Sylvia," Evie says as she cuts me off, "is that you're at a fork in the road. There's two ways to go. Drown in self-pity or use this opportunity to take control of your life. I'd kill to be sixty-three again. You have so much time ahead of you and I'll be damned if I'm going to let you waste it."

I've never heard her talk like this. It concerns me. "Evie, you have time, too. You're very youthful. You Uber!"

But Evie looks down at the table. She folds a cocktail napkin in thirds, drawing the crease down tight. She then stares at her hands a moment. I've never heard her play, but apparently she was a brilliant piano player. Her fingers are still long and graceful. But the skin is thin and wrinkled, crisscrossed with time.

"You can stay on my sofa for now. You've had a terrible shock. But then you will rise like the strong woman you are and conquer the day. Maybe you'll travel the world. See France and Argentina and New Zealand."

I take another sip of my drink. "I've always wanted to travel," I confess. "Louis never liked to. He hates to fly. And he hates hotels. Who hates hotels? All those fresh towels and little bottles of shampoo. We were supposed to go to the Amalfi Coast before we moved down here. But Louis had a nightmare that our plane crashed, so he canceled the trip and we went to the Jersey Shore instead."

I push my hair out of my face and think about how angry I was that day. I'd spent three months learning Italian. My daughter, Isabel, helped me download an app onto my phone. I was getting quite good.

I can feel myself getting all hot and furious again. My eyes fill with fresh tears. I finish my drink. As if on cue, our waiter brings another round. "On me," he says as he smiles at me. "I hate to see a beautiful woman cry." Evie nods approvingly as he walks away.

I blink back my tears. I like being called beautiful. Even if it's by someone younger than my daughter who's aiming for a good tip. I pick up my drink.

"Wait," Evie says. She then holds up her glass to toast. "To seeing the world. You are a free woman with your health and a passport."

I nod. That's true. I renewed my passport for Italy. It's crisp and official-looking. I've been keeping it with my jewelry because I like to look at it on special occasions. I take a long sip of my drink and, ignoring the fact that I have no money, I get lost in a fantasy. I am on a jumbo jet. I'm wearing one those casually elegant travel outfits I read about in *Vogue*—a lightweight cashmere sweater, Donna Karan trousers, ballet flats. I have *The New York Times* peeking out of my Goyard bag. I've just misted moisturizing spray over my face because everyone knows cabin air is drying. The stewardess brings me champagne and I say, "Thank you, darling."

"Sylvia." Evie's voice cuts into my reverie and I realize I'm drinking from a now empty glass. Wow. That one went down fast. I'm a little dizzy.

"Are you okay?" Evie looks concerned. But I nod. I'm better than okay. I'm traveling around the world. I feel fabulous. I feel first-class. I feel free.

I vomit.

WELL, THERE'S CERTAINLY something youthful about tossing one's cookies in a bar. It's the next morning and I'm lying on Evie's sofa staring up at the ceiling. Thank god she doesn't have a fan.

I gingerly sit up. I'm not sure what hurts more—my pounding head or my throbbing back. Or my ego. I cringe and curse the fact that despite my alarming level of inebriation, my memory of last night is shamefully intact.

It was like no one had ever seen a person throw up in a bar before. Well, maybe no one's seen someone my age do it.

"Sylvia," Evie calls. I hear her cane lightly tap against the floor as she enters the living room. She wears a kimono robe over her pajamas and looks way too fabulous for having just spent the night drinking. Then again, we were kicked out of the bar before 6:00 p.m., so I suppose she got a good rest.

"Evie," I moan. "How on earth are you not hungover?"

"I'm a WASP, dear. I can handle my liquor."

I force myself up to a full sitting position and run my hand over the silk pajamas Evie leant me. Evie sits in the chair next to the couch and turns on the TV. It's only 5:30 a.m., but she has Max, so she easily queues up an episode of *Sex and the City* for us. The opening credits always cheer me up. I start bobbing my head in rhythm. But the movement makes me queasy. The morning sun is just beginning to peek its way through the curtains.

"How's your head?" Evie asks as she hands me a glass of water and two Alka-Seltzer tablets.

"It hurts. As does my stomach. And I cannot stop these waves of humiliation." I drop the tablets into the glass and watch the water fizz.

"You had good reason to drown your sorrows. The bouncer thought so, too."

I wince. Jesus. Who knew they even had bouncers in Boca? But as soon as I barfed, a bouncer came over and carried me out so the waiter and bussers could clean up.

"He was very nice," I concede.

She pauses the episode of SATC and turns to me, nodding. "He ferried you out like a princess. I can't believe he actually knew who Belinda was."

"I know," I say, and recall how in a mortified, drunken stupor, I told the bouncer everything. While Evie called our Uber, he kindly sat with me on the pavement and said he'd seen Belinda there before, looking for men.

Evie shakes her head. "Belinda's poor husband. I keep trying to figure out if she cheated on him before he got Alzheimer's."

"You and Henry knew them when they moved down here. Were they happy?"

"Hard to tell. Edward was a bit of a blowhard and Belinda was always Belinda. Botox and boobies."

Evie and I sit in silence for a moment. All at once, I feel sorry for Belinda and ashamed of myself. It must be awful seeing one's husband suffer like that. Should I have been more evolved? Instead of forcing Belinda out of my apartment, should I have taken her aside and said in a compassionate but firm voice, "Belinda, while this doesn't excuse your behavior, I know you must be grieving the illness of your own husband and that's why you were in bed with mine"? What would Jesus have done? Of course, I'm Jewish. But I suppose Jesus was, too.

Evie seems to read my mind. "Sylvia," she says. "Belinda may be having a rough time of it. But she doesn't get a free pass just because her husband is sick. And nothing changes the fact that Louis cheated. You still have to move forward."

I sigh. I know she's right. "But first can we finish our episode?"

Evie hits play on the remote. SATC starts up again. We lean in and escape our lives as Carrie, Samantha, Miranda, and Charlotte discuss cunnilingus over brunch.

Three

I left Evie's and am now sitting on the floor in my condo next to the bed—I can't bring myself to sit on the actual bed—and stare at my passport in my jewelry box. I bring it to my nose. I love the way it smells. So fresh and crisp. I put the jewelry box and passport in a small tote bag and zip it up. My big suitcase is open next to me on the floor. I'm nearly finished packing and I'm trying to sort through my magazines. I keep them in a bin next to my bed. There's *Vogue, Town & Country, Elle, W,* and a random assortment of European fashion magazines. I love to get lost in the glossy pages. Sometimes I use a magnifying glass when I read them. Louis always made fun of me. I thumb through my pile and put just five of my favorites into my suitcase and continue packing. There's not much more to do. I'd gotten rid of most my winter clothes when we moved down here because we knew the condo would be considerably smaller than our old house. And who needs scarves and gloves and winter coats in Florida? Isabel and Bunny—Izzy's mother-in-law—took what they wanted and then I donated the rest to a women's shelter.

Hmm. I wonder if it's cold up north yet. I let my eyes blur and can almost see the apricot-hued leaves flutter in the autumn wind. I can't help but yearn for one of my cozy sweater-coats and find myself checking the weather back in Connecticut on my phone when I get a text message. It's from Louis. **Is it okay if I'm early?**

I make a face. I had asked him to please be out of the condo between 1:00 and 4:00. I figured it would be easy because he has his weekly tennis match and then beers with the guys. But I glance at the time and see it's only 2:15.

I type back, **How early?**

He responds right away. **Now?**

I feel a rush of irritation. I don't respond for a moment. Another text message dings. **I'm standing outside our door.**

I grit my teeth and get up. I walk briskly through the condo and go to the front door. I open it. Louis is holding a dozen tulips. "Hi."

I cross my arms. "What happened to your match?"

"I skipped it. Instead, I went for a long walk and thought about how much I love you. Your favorite." He holds out the bouquet.

I stare at the gorgeous flowers. They look expensive. "I thought we were broke."

"I stole them from a funeral home."

Despite myself, I laugh. Louis has always been funny. He looks me in the eye. "I'm so sorry, Sylvia. So, so sorry."

"You can't just bring me flowers and expect everything to be okay."

"What else can I do? Rob a jewelry store? Hold up a chocolate shop?"

"Oh, Louis. This isn't a flowers and earrings and truffles kind of thing."

Louis shifts on his feet. I realize he's still in the hallway and step aside so he can enter the condo. After I close the door, we both just stand in the foyer a moment. I finally reach for the flowers. "Well, these shouldn't go to waste." I head to the kitchen to put them in water.

Louis follows me.

"Are you really packed up?"

I nod. He lets out a breath. "You staying at Evie's?"

I nod again. Louis looks at me. "So I basically got flowers for myself?"

I shrug. "I guess I could take them to Evie's."

"How much does she hate me?"

"If it makes you feel better, I don't think she ever really liked you."

He smiles sadly. "I know. How come? Everyone likes me."

It's true. Louis is one of those people. "I think she knew that things were off between us."

Louis shakes his head and puts a hand over his heart. "That's not true, Sylvia. I love you. I've loved you every day for forty-three years."

"We've only been married forty-one years."

"Yes, but we dated for two years before that."

Louis looks triumphant. I raise a brow. There's a passion in his voice that I haven't heard in a long time.

"What can I do to make this right? Because I'm not giving up. You are everything to me. I know I screwed up. I thought I was doing a good thing with the money and I'd surprise you but then it was a disaster and I got scared. I should've told you the truth. Instead, I tried to fix it without you finding out and that led to an even worse decision. That day with Belinda was a one-off. Temporary insanity."

I'm still standing in the kitchen and lightly hold the countertop for support. Louis has said everything I could ever want to hear. He sounds passionate and honest. My head whirls.

Louis comes closer and gently takes my hand in his. "And I'm not an idiot, Sylvia. I know you're not happy here. I forced us to move. I honestly thought it would be great. That you'd love it."

"But I told you point-blank that I didn't want to move."

"I thought if you tried it, you'd change your mind."

"How come you canceled our trip to Italy?"

"What?"

"You knew how much I wanted to go. You knew how much I planned. But you just canceled it like it was nothing."

Louis looks thrown. "Why are we talking about that?"

"Because that trip to Italy is a metaphor for everything that's happened. It's like I'm an afterthought and you do whatever you want. You went behind my back and lost our money. You cheated on me. Sure, you're saying all the right things now. But how can I believe any of it?"

Louis's jaw twitches slightly. He opens his mouth, then closes it. Something inside me flinches.

Is he—

Is he *annoyed* with me?

I narrow my eyes. I know this man too well. He's biting his cheek and looking over my shoulder. Which is exactly what he does when he's trying not to lose his temper.

I pull my hand away from him. The sudden movement surprises him. He clears his throat and speaks slowly. "Look, Sylvia. I hear you. You feel taken for granted. And I apologize for that. But things will be better."

"I want a divorce." The words are out of my mouth before I can even think. But as soon as I say it, I know it's the truth.

"Don't be stupid," Louis snaps. "We can't get divorced. We can't afford it right now."

"Then I'll wait until we can. For now, I'm moving out."

"And do what? Jesus, Sylvia. This isn't some episode of *Sex and the City* where you go shopping and get a makeover and start a whole new life. You're not a young woman. You have no money. You have no skill set. What's your big plan? Live on Evie's couch until she drops dead?"

I slap Louis across the face. He looks stunned.

His cheek is bright red and he stares at me like I'm an alien. "What's the matter with you?"

"The matter with me? You're the one—"

"Knock knock. Yoo-hoo! Louis? The door was open." I stiffen. It can't be. It just can't.

But it is.

Even Louis looks horrified as Belinda enters the kitchen and stops short. She sees me and freezes. She turns to Louis. "Your text said to come. That she was packed up."

Louis grits his teeth. "I said *not to come*. That she would be here packing."

Belinda looks honestly confused as she takes her phone from her purse and looks at the screen. She squints.

"Belinda, did you read your phone without your glasses again?" Louis's voice is tight. I turn and look at Belinda. She blushes and puts her phone away.

I finally speak. "Louis. Why are you texting her at all?"

But as soon as I ask the question, I already know. I swallow. "This wasn't a one-time thing."

Louis just looks at the ground. I shake my head. I am so stupid.

Before I can respond, our home phone rings. Everyone jolts. It rings again. Louis is standing right next to it. As if on autopilot, he picks it up.

"Hello?" He pauses and then lets out a breath. "Isabel, nothing's wrong." Another pause. "I'm not sure why Mom hasn't been answering her cell phone. She's probably busy."

Louis looks at me pleadingly. I know that the last thing he wants is for me to tell Isabel what's going on. I hold out my hand for the phone.

Meanwhile, Belinda sneaks out the front door.

I gesture again to Louis. *Give me the phone.* But instead, he speaks quickly into the receiver. "Mom and I are actually in the middle of something. Can we call you later?"

Unbelievable. I walk out of the room and into the bedroom. I take a deep breath and pick up the receiver next to the bed.

"Hi, Izzy." There. I've joined the conversation.

"Mom? What's wrong? Why aren't you answering your cell?"

"Everything is—" Louis's voice is quick and sharp but I interrupt him.

"I'm sorry, honey. I'm a little out of sorts at the moment."

"Did you go to the doctor?"

"It's nothing like that. It's just . . . well, it's a little hard to explain. But nothing for you to worry about."

I can hear Louis's voice tighten on the phone as he tries to change the subject. "How are you, honey? Todd and the girls okay?"

"I made partner and the twins were kicked out of preschool. Todd thinks it's our fault. That we work too much and the girls are acting out." Her voice is calm, but I detect just the faintest underlying quiver.

Louis and I are both silent a moment. I finally speak, "Izzy, that's wonderful about your job. We're so proud of you. Don't worry about the preschool. There's plenty of places for the girls to go."

I can almost hear Louis smiling a little through the phone. "Your mom's right. And I like that my granddaughters are rambunctious. It shows spirit."

"There is no other preschool," Izzy blurts. "This is the only dual-language immersion, Reggio-inspired school in the area. I know you have no idea what that means but it's important. The girls need to be there in order to get into the right kindergarten. Everyone will be ahead of them." Izzy's voice is getting higher and higher.

"Just breathe, honey," I say. "I'm sure it's very competitive out there. But it will all work out. You can even do one of those private pods if you have to. Hire your own teachers. I was just reading an article about that in the *New York Times*."

"I don't want my girls to be the weird homeschooled kids!"

Louis sighs. "Maybe the school overreacted. Was it really so bad?"

"Everly threw a bottle of bubbles at a little boy's face and then Emerson head-butted him. I called the pediatrician and she referred me to a children's psychologist. She then asked if the girls see any violence at home." Isabel's voice breaks and she starts to cry. "It was humiliating. As if we're some trashy couple on daytime TV who hit each other."

Louis says something soothing when I interrupt, "Maybe the other kid deserved it?"

Isabel sniffles. A beat of silence. "Mom, is everything okay with you?"

"Your mother's fine, honey."

I make a face into the receiver. If Louis speaks for me one more time, I may actually kill him. In fact, I'm a little worried about how easily that thought sprang into my head. All at once, I feel a powerful urge to get as far away from here possible. For everyone's sake.

"Isabel, honey. Would you like me to come for a visit? Help with the girls while you get things settled?"

Louis exhales sharply. "Sylvia, that's not a great idea right—"

But Isabel cuts him off. Her voice is high and childlike. "Oh, Mom! Would you?"

Four

As I sit in the Uber that Evie ordered for me, I look out the window and watch the palm trees fade into dark silhouettes beneath the setting sun. It's been three hours since I left my condo with my luggage. Once I told Evie everything that happened, she and I decided I should head directly to the airport before I lose my nerve. Truthfully, I suspect we're both a little worried about the trouble I might get into if I stay another day. Slapping Louis felt a little too easy. And although it would feel quite good in the moment, I would prefer not to murder the father of my child. I don't think I would do well in prison.

As though reading my mind, my phone beeps. It's a text message from Louis: Please come back.

I delete the message and put away my phone. I know Louis didn't believe I would really leave. But as Evie said, this isn't about him.

This is about me. And so I let out a long, cleansing breath. As my Uber exits the highway toward the Fort Lauderdale airport, I silently recite my mantra for this trip:

I will not:

Tell my daughter that her father is a cheating lying bastard.

Beep!

Another text message. I take out my phone and glance at it: This is ridiculous. Stop behaving like a child.

I start typing back furiously but then stop and mentally cleanse myself with:

I will not:

Get into a text message war with Louis.

Google "How do I dispose of a body?"

Google "How sympathetic is a jury to a 60-something-year-old woman?"

MY UBER DRIVER PULLS UP to the American Airlines terminal and takes out my suitcase. As I take my bag and turn to head into the airport, a skycap approaches.

"May I check your luggage for you, ma'am?"

"No, thank you," I say. "I need to purchase my ticket."

I wheel my luggage into the airport and get in line. Evie was kind enough to offer to buy my ticket. But there's only so much I can ask of my friend. And so as I wait to be helped, I continue my mantras:

I will:

Remain calm and remember that everything we go through is part of life's journey.

Remain serene and remember that one's hardships are one's teachers.

Remain centered and remember that nothing is as bad as it—

Oh, fuck.

"What do you mean, my credit cards have been canceled?" I am now standing at the ticket counter and staring at an American Airlines representative. Her nametag says "Marjorie." She has steely eyes and not a single smile line on her face. Even her blackberry lipstick looks mean.

"I'm sorry, ma'am," Marjorie says. But she doesn't sound sorry at all. She glances behind me at the growing number of people in line. "Perhaps you should step aside and discuss this with your bank. I'm sure there's a reason."

"The reason, Marjorie, is that my husband is a world-class asshole." The words spill out of my mouth before I can stop them.

Marjorie lifts an eyebrow as though I'm wasting my breath. But I don't care. I am so angry that my skin pulsates. "He's a manipulative, philandering bastard. I'm sorry. I'm sure you don't care about my personal problems. Why should you? You look at me, just another South Florida retiree wearing dry-clean-only clothes and think, 'What problems could this woman possibly have other than chipped toenail polish?' Well, Marjorie. My problem is that my husband is right. I'm a fool. I can't leave him. I can't even leave the state of Florida. You see, Louis doesn't want me visiting our daughter. He's terrified I'll tell her about how he mismanaged our money and slept with the roving whore of Boca Beach Gables. And so he canceled our cards. It's my fault. I handed over my life a long time ago. I'm old. I'm useless. Louis wins, I lose."

She looks at me a long beat as I try to catch my breath. Baring my soul to a stranger is oddly liberating. As I try to reorient myself, I realize that Marjorie has picked up my Mastercard and is now typing away on her computer.

I'm confused. "I thought you said my cards were canceled."

She keeps typing away. "You have miles, don't you?"

I smile sadly. "We're only silver club members. Our miles aren't sufficient for a same-day flight."

She hits a few more buttons on her keyboard. She doesn't smile but suddenly she's not looking so mean. "Your miles seem plenty sufficient to me." With a final click, the printer next to her computer revs up and spits out a boarding pass and luggage ticket.

Marjorie hands them to me. She then takes my suitcase, tags it, and heaves it onto the conveyor belt. "Gate F4. You board in an hour. Next?"

She is now looking behind me, waiting for the next passenger. But I don't move. I can't stop staring at this wonderful woman. I love Marjorie.

"I don't know what to say," I humbly begin. "You've restored my faith in—"

"Ma'am?" Marjorie says. "Could you move it along, please?"

Well, I suppose not everyone is comfortable with emotion. I can certainly respect that.

And so I give her my most solemn nod and head toward security.

GOD, I LOVE AIRPORTS. I know most people hate them. The lines. The delays. The overzealous security check wherein a stranger wearing latex gloves runs her hands up and down my backside is not exactly my favorite thing either. But I love the whirring of suitcase wheels moving down the corridors. I love seeing families headed somewhere together, the little children carrying chocolate-milk boxes. I love the young couples with their backpacks lying on the floor of an abandoned gate asleep on each other's shoulders.

I take all of these things in as I practically float toward my gate. En route, I see New River News. I'd love a magazine and a bottle of water and maybe some chocolate-covered almonds. But then I remember that I'm now officially broke. In fact, I bite my lip and wonder, just how much money do I have?

I quickly leave the newsstand and enter the ladies' room. I go into a stall and lock the door. I was feeling so good but now my hands shake as I hang my purse on the stall door and take out my wallet. I slowly count off the bills. Eighty-eight dollars. I open my change purse. A quick glance tells me I've got forty-seven cents. I close my eyes a moment. Eighty-eight dollars and forty-seven cents.

I take another breath and steel myself. I refuse to have a panic attack in an airport bathroom. Things will work out. In fact, thanks to my new favorite person in the world, Marjorie, things *have* worked out so far. I glance at my watch and realize that it's almost time to board. I take a deep breath and straighten my blouse.

I exit the stall and go to wash my hands at the sink. As I do, I catch another glimpse of my watch and wonder how much I can get for it. It's a lovely piece. Vintage Cartier. White gold with tiny diamonds on the face. I start to perk up. It must be worth a few hundred at least. I will get through this. I will.

As I walk to my gate and get in line to board, my phone beeps. It's Louis: **Call me ASAP**.

I stick my tongue out at the phone just as the boarding agent takes my boarding pass. My eyes meet hers, and my face flames. I try to casually put my tongue back in my mouth. She doesn't bat an eyelash. "Seat fourteen A. Enjoy your flight."

As I make my way down the walkway to the plane, I hit dial on my phone. Louis picks up mid-ring. "Sylvia? Where are you?"

"Getting on the plane." My tone is curt as I enter the cabin and find my seat.

"Isabel called and said you left her a message that you're arriving at JFK just before midnight."

"That's correct. I told her to leave me a key. I'll let myself in and go right to the guest room. Anything else you want to know?"

"How did you pay for a ticket?"

"Right. Thank you for canceling our cards, Louis. That was very mature. I used miles."

He's silent a moment. I can hear him thinking aloud. "Well, how are you going to pay for a car to Isabel's?"

"Evie downloaded Uber onto my phone. She's sharing her account with me. I'll be paying her back as soon as I'm able. I have to go now, Louis. The plane is getting ready for takeoff."

"Wait! Sylvia, what are you going to tell Izzy?"

I make a face. Of course that's what he's worried about.

"I'm going to tell Izzy the truth."

"But the truth makes me look bad."

"Yes, well, whose fault is that? Goodbye."

I hang up and turn my phone all the way off. I then lean my head back into my seat and close my eyes. Goodbye, Florida.

Five

My eyes adjust to the crisp, white ceiling. I try to snuggle a little deeper into the pillow and realize there are about ten pillows of various geometric shapes and sizes around me. All in complementary shades of white. I'm in Isabel and Todd's guest room. I arrived here around 2:00 a.m. and collapsed into bed.

I glance at the ivory clock on the nightstand and see it's now 7:30 a.m. As sunlight peeks through the white shutters, throwing a glaze along the white walls, I remember a tedious conversation I recently had with my daughter as she debated between the paint colors "glacier" and "igloo." I peer at the paint and try to think about which she chose but give up. If I know Isabel, she probably convinced the company to custom-make a new shade of white.

I feel heavy with exhaustion. But I stretch my arms and realize my granddaughters must already be up. I tilt my head, waiting to hear the padding of their little feet. Hmm, nothing. Unusual. The guest room is tucked away on the first level, all the way in the back by the garage. But the acoustics are such that I can hear everything when I stay here, despite the enormous five thousand square feet of space.

Anyhow, as I crane my ears, I still don't hear anything. I'm about to force myself out of bed but then see a card on the opposite nightstand along with a small carafe of orange juice. This wasn't here when I arrived. I smile to myself and realize Isabel must have slipped in quietly after I'd fallen asleep. I also smile to myself thinking that I have a daughter who owns a carafe. I kept a nice home, but Isabel takes it to a new level. I used to worry about her perfectionism.

Sometimes I still do. But perhaps she's just driven, I think, as I scooch to the other side of the bed, knocking pillows over in an avalanche. I pick up the card.

Hope your flight was okay. Todd and I are taking the day off and making it a long weekend. We'll be out with the girls so you can get some rest. See you back at the house for brunch.

Wow. Isabel hasn't taken a Friday off in . . . Has she ever taken a Friday off? For years, she worked seven days a week at her law firm. Todd's the same at his computer company. They still haven't even taken a honeymoon. And their wedding was five years ago. The girls typically spend every weekend with either a babysitter or Todd's parents, who live twenty minutes away.

Something must really be wrong. I remember how distressed Isabel sounded on the phone yesterday. She actually cried. I bite my lip and am about to worry but then find that I'm just too stocked up on worry right now. Which makes me worry more. My head hurts.

Stop it, I tell myself. I am here to help my beautiful granddaughters get though whatever rough stage they are in. I am here to help my brilliant daughter feel good about her promotion. I am here to help my dear, sweet son-in-law with whatever he needs. And I am here to forget that I ever helped my husband's mistress find her underpants.

I OPEN MY EYES AGAIN and look at the clock. 10:30 a.m. I feel like a new person as I hear the clang of dishes from the kitchen. And the smell! I can practically taste the fresh bagels and steaming coffee.

And so I swing my legs out of bed and hurry into the adjoining bathroom. That's funny. The drain in the sink is a bit stuck. I jam my fingernails beneath it and crack it up just enough. I'm surprised Izzy doesn't have a plumber here at this very moment. I shrug and quickly wash my face and brush my hair, taking a moment to appreciate my new highlights once again. I really do look more youthful. And the layers around my face make me look a little thinner. Of course, that could be the lack of proper food and the absence of alcohol-induced bloating. Either way, I'll take it.

I swipe on some lip gloss and dab concealer under my eyes. I quickly sift through my suitcase and select my heaviest slacks and a cashmere sweater. I'm a tad underdressed for October in Connecticut. But Isabel and I have the same build. I can always borrow something if I'm too chilly.

Once, during a visit here when no one was home, I snuck into Izzy's closet and tried on one of her Armani suits. It was a gorgeous midnight blue and fit perfectly. Well, it was a little tight across the rear, but that's not necessarily a bad thing these days. I then pretended to preside over a board meeting in the dining room. I've never told anyone that. Not even Evie.

I let out a breath and call out, "Good morning!" as I practically skip down the hall. I didn't realize just how much I was looking forward to seeing my daughter and granddaughters.

"Grandma!" I hear as two giggling masses coming thundering to meet me. I kneel down and wrap my arms around Everly and Emerson. Their soft honey-colored curls tickle my nose.

I get to my feet and let them drag me toward the kitchen. I love feeling their pudgy hands grip my fingers. "Did you girls go on an adventure this morning?" I ask.

Everly swings from my hand as Emerson talks a mile a minute. "We went to the park. Then we went shopping. Mommy and Daddy bought bagels. And Lulu and Grampy brought wine. Grandma, what's a whore?"

My mouth drops open. I'm about to ask where she heard that word, but we've just entered the kitchen and I am stunned silent as I take in the scene. On the white marble island lies a feast for twenty: bagels, spreads, smoked fish, fruit, pastries, coffee, and juice. And then, just beyond the kitchen in the dining room, Isabel, Todd, and Todd's parents, Bunny (a nickname for Betty; I have no idea why) and Marty, sit at the oversize glass and chrome table.

I reflexively take a step backward into the hallway. I had no idea Isabel was planning a surprise brunch. She hates surprises. She knows I hate surprises. But I smooth my hands self-consciously over my pants and try to shake it off. This is nice, I tell myself. This is your family.

Isabel rushes over. "Emmy! Enough! You and Everly go watch TV."

"More TV?" Emerson is agog and Everly practically hugs herself.

Isabel is a sergeant about screen time, but right now, she nods. The girls are delighted as they trot off into the den.

Isabel then turns and hugs me. "Morning, Mom. How are you feeling?"

"Good, thank you. What a lovely surprise to see everyone." And it is true. Really. I don't want Izzy to think I'm ungrateful. So I smile, walk into the kitchen, and pick up a mug. But as I pour some coffee, I can't help but think it's a little strange that everyone is still seated at the table. Shouldn't they come over and say hi? No one is even looking at me.

No one, that is, except for Izzy. She's staring. "Everything okay, dear?" I touch my face self-consciously.

"Oh, yes. Good, good. How are you?"

"Um, fine." *You just asked me that.* I take a sip of coffee and look her over. At thirty-four, she's a very pretty young woman. She grew into her looks, which was difficult as a teenager but certainly better than the alternative. She has the same thick, wavy hair as me. Her eyes are dark like her dad's and she has extraordinary lashes. But right now, her skin looks puffy, and so I peer more closely. She senses I'm examining her and immediately turns away.

"Everyone is excited to see you. Shall we go into the dining room?" And then, out of nowhere, Izzy hugs me again. That's odd.

I'm about to ask her what's going on when Todd enters the kitchen and kisses my cheek. "You look amazing." He squeezes my arm.

Okay, now I'm worried. I put down my mug. I'm proud of my brilliant and accomplished daughter and son-in-law. But one thing they are not is affectionate. Between the antiseptic guest room and this white and metal kitchen, it's safe to say that my daughter has the decorating sensibility of the Third Reich. This lack of warmth permeates other aspects of her life. There's a reason she's known as the

Terminator at her firm. How one gets that reputation in patent law, I have no idea.

And Todd. Well, Todd is a computer whiz. He's sweet and soft-spoken and can talk passionately about light-speed travel for hours. He's tall—six foot, five inches—and self-conscious about his height. He isn't particularly coordinated and is always having to tell people that no, he doesn't play basketball.

"All right," I finally say as I look from Izzy to Todd and back again. "What's going on?"

But before either can respond, Bunny enters the kitchen and rushes me like me a linebacker. "Oh, Sylvia! You poor thing! That Louis is a disgrace!"

Huh? I try to untangle myself from Bunny's whirlwind of fluorescent lipstick and too much perfume. But she's holding me tight and whispers in my ear, "Marty and I know people. If need be, we'll take care of that disgusting whore."

"Okay, Mrs. Soprano. Let's take it down a notch," Marty says as he enters the room and gently pulls his wife off me. "Hi there, Sylvia. We're so sorry to hear about your troubles."

I stare at Marty. I actually like him very much. He has a kindly way about him, which is interesting because he's the longtime attorney to one of the most notorious mafia families in New York.

I must have been silent a long time, because Bunny is elbowing Marty, who looks from Todd to Izzy and back again. "You didn't tell her we know?"

"Know what?" It's like an icicle has run down my spine. I turn to Izzy, who looks at Todd, who looks at the ground.

If one more person cannot meet my eyes, I will scream. "Tell me what," I repeat.

Marty's eyes are full of feeling as he pours me a glass of water.

But Bunny takes the glass. "She needs something stronger." She then dumps the water and reaches for the wine and pours me about twenty-four ounces of chardonnay.

My voice is tight. "Would someone please tell me what's happening?"

Izzy lets out a breath. "Dad called me and Todd last night and told us everything. Bunny and Marty were over for dinner. I was upset and so they overheard."

Bunny's nostrils flare. "Believe you, me. As soon as I got the gist of what happened, I called Louis myself. Did you really squeeze that woman's boobs?"

I drink the entire glass of wine. I then sink onto one of the barstools. It's metal and cold and hurts my butt. "So let me get this straight. Your father waited until I was on the plane and then he called you? And told you everything?"

Todd and Izzy look so uncomfortable. This makes me hate Louis even more. Marty clears his throat. "Bunny? Let's go check on the girls."

But Bunny stays put. She puts an arm around me. "With the right makeup and some new clothes, Sylvia, I'll have Louis begging you to come back."

I look at Bunny's lilac yoga pants with a diamanté logo and can't believe my life has come to this. Bunny gives my shoulder a final squeeze. "I'm here for you." She then mercifully leaves the room with Marty.

Now it's just Isabel, Todd, and me. I look at Izzy and ask, "What did your father say?"

Izzy glances at Todd. "He said that he made some bad investments and that he met a woman and you caught them in bed. I sort of blanked out but I think there was something about a ceiling fan and groping."

Todd swallows. "That about sums it up."

"What a lousy thing to do." My face is on fire and a tear leaks down my cheek. Louis has always been consumed with what people think of him. So I understand him getting a head start on his side of the story. But why mention the ceiling fan? Or the groping? Was it just to humiliate me?

Izzy bites her lip. "For what it's worth, Mom, I think he'd had a lot to drink. I called him this morning and he seemed surprised that we talked at all."

"Oh," I say, and wipe my eyes. I want the wine but instead reach for a black and white cookie. I take a violent bite. Crumbs spray onto the counter and I see Izzy flinch. Shit. I try to sweep the crumbs onto a napkin but they scatter onto the gleaming white floors.

Todd stops me from cleaning. "Izzy can live with a few crumbs. It's good for her."

I put down the cookie. "I just hate that you found out like this. I came here to help you. And now we're talking about my drama."

Izzy grabs a sponge and wipes up the crumbs. "Oh, Mom. It's not your fault. Todd and I are furious with Dad."

I can't help it. This makes me feel a little better. "You are?"

"Of course! How dare he be so irresponsible with your future? That was money you were supposed to live on for the rest of your life. Frankly, I'm disgusted." Izzy throws the sponge into the sink.

I see Todd look away a moment and feel a pang. He's always adored Louis, who has treated him like his own son, insisting Todd call him Dad. This must be terrible for him.

"You guys don't have to be angry with him. We haven't been

happy for some time. This is life. People get divorced all the time." I smile bravely.

But Izzy looks horrified. "Mom, forget the divorce. You and Dad are in real trouble. You need a sustainable plan to recover your funds. I already have someone at the firm looking into it. I don't know how much we'll be able to salvage, but we need to try. Todd and I are going to talk to Dad about returning to work."

My head starts to spin. Izzy's talking a mile a minute.

Todd holds up a hand. He's always been good in a crisis. "Let's relax a moment. The good news is that you and Dad are paid through till end of May at the retirement facility. Including meals, which is great. So you have a place to live and food to eat. Izzy and I can help out with incidentals."

"But I don't want to live in Florida." My voice feels small. Like I'm the child here.

Izzy takes a slow breath. "Mom, we know this is awful for you. Dad is clearly having a crisis. It's gross and tacky. So how about this: Stay here for a few weeks. Give him a good scare. Let him think he's lost you. Then you can go back to Florida and work everything out."

"Are you out of your goddamn minds?"

Their mouths drop. It's not often that I curse aloud. But I am agog. "Isabel, I understand your father and I are in an unusual situation. So perhaps a divorce isn't the best option right now. But I am not returning to Florida. Nor am I going to play games in order to give your father something to think about."

Izzy pats my shoulder as though trying to rub sense into me. "But what choice do you have?"

"I'll get a job. Same as your father." As soon as I say this, I start to perk up. Of course that's what I'll do. Why didn't I think of that sooner?

I hate the way Todd and Isabel are looking at one another right now. Todd clears his throat. "Doing what?"

I'm about to respond when Izzy shakes her head. "I know this is hard to hear. But there's a price for having lived a life of leisure."

I flinch. "A life of leisure? That's what you think I had? Because there was nothing luxurious about going to the grocery store and picking up dry cleaning and packing your school lunches. Who do you think vacuumed every night after dinner? Who did the laundry? Who took you to the library and helped you check out books every time you had a term paper? I don't remember having a staff. Sure, we had a housekeeper once a week. Anna was lovely. But who do you think scrubbed the toilets when your father had too much dairy at dinner?"

"I get it," Izzy says. "But, Mom. You've never worked aside from a few wedding planning gigs a decade ago. How do you expect to get an actual job? You can't put 'drove my daughter to lots of cross-country meets' on your resume."

"Jesus," Todd mutters.

Isabel turns on Todd, fury making her dark eyes flash darker. "So I have to be the bad guy here? You're the one who said we can't let her live in one of her fantasylands."

I feel slapped. I turn to Todd. He reddens. I can see him searching for what to say but this time I hold up my hand.

"I understand getting a job at my age isn't easy," I say stiffly. "But people do it all the time. I can work retail at the least. God knows my life of leisure taught me how to fold an item of clothing."

Izzy sighs. "So you'll get a job at the Gap making minimum wage? Be on your feet ten hours a day?"

"Yes. I'm in excellent shape." Then, an afterthought. "Knock on wood."

"And where will you live? Because while we love having you here, our guest room isn't a long-term solution. As much as I would love your help with the girls, they *will* go back to preschool."

"I wouldn't dream of burdening you," I say coolly. "I'll get an apartment. Now if you'll excuse me, this interrogation is over."

My heart is beating so fast that I'm scared if I stay another moment, I will collapse. And so without a word, I walk out of the room and back down the hall.

As soon as I enter the guest room, I shut the door. I barely get it closed before tears pour from my eyes. I sink onto the bed and try to shake Isabel and Todd's faces from my mind. They were staring at me with such naked pity. And something else. Something worse.

Exasperation, I realize. As though I somehow deserve this. A fresh wave of sobs chokes me. I have never felt so mortified. I put my head between my knees and try to steady my breath. Can it get worse?

"Sylvia?"

I look up and see Bunny. She's holding a large metal toolbox of sorts and a bottle of wine. "Oh, you poor thing!" Before I can stop her, she's sitting on the bed next to me. She puts the box on the floor and rubs my back. "I could just kill Louis." Then, lowering her voice. "Marty and I do know people. We're *connected*."

I wipe my eyes and laugh a little, feeling a rush of fondness for her. I've always judged Bunny rather harshly. Sure, her lipstick is a little too heavy and she wears clothing that belongs on a slender teenager rather than her chunky sixty-five-year-old frame. But who am I? The fashion police? Let's be honest. I've been wearing different shades of beige for the last year.

"I don't even know who I am anymore," I say.

"I understand," Bunny says.

And with the look she gives me, I believe her.

She then shakes her head. "I overheard your conversation with

Todd and Isabel. I'm so disappointed in them. You can come and stay with Marty and me for as long as you need."

All at once, I want to cry again. "Oh, Bunny. That is so kind. I couldn't impose, though."

"Nonsense. We're family." She then picks up her toolbox and opens it. The entire contents of Nordstrom's cosmetics department spill out. "Marty has plenty of divorced friends. Have you met Harold? He's lovely. He'd die to take you out."

Bunny is already sweeping shadow across my eyelids. And I let her. There's something so soothing about the soft bristles touching my skin. She keeps talking and talking and I'm not really sure what she's saying. But I don't care. I keep my eyes closed and let my mind go blank.

OKAY, MAYBE BUNNY WENT a little far. But I suppose that's what happens after a bottle of wine. We've been in the guest room for over an hour. It's actually been quite fun. When she finally picks up her handheld mirror, I gasp.

"I had no idea blue eye shadow could be so vivid." I can hear the slur in my voice as I keep talking. "Bunny, is it bad that I've consumed more alcohol in the last week than I have in the last year? Wow. Is that gold eyeliner beneath the shadow?"

"It is! And it's normal to be drinking too much, Syl. You're going through a trauma. Which is why you have to be gentle with yourself. Now take a look at what I've done. Your bone structure is to die for. Do you see how I did a more subtle face and lip to balance the dramatic eye?"

I peer closer at my reflection. The turquoise eye shadow surrounds what I imagine is supposed to be a smoky gold and black cat-eye.

But I can see what Bunny means by a more subtle face. The apricot blush is less iridescent than I imagined. The bronzer she layered on top, however, gives me a unfortunate yellow pallor. I look like I've been embalmed by a Las Vegas showgirl.

I look up from the mirror and smile at Bunny. "I feel beautiful. Thank you."

"You have to experiment with colors. Really blend a few to find the right shade." Bunny then puts her toolbox on the floor and lies across the foot of my bed, propping herself up on an elbow. We look like two teenage girls having a sleepover.

"So what do you think, Syl? Marty and I know plenty of men. It would do you good to have some fun."

I raise a painted eyebrow. "And by fun, you mean sex?"

"Have you been with anyone besides Louis?"

I flush and look away. Her eyes go wide.

"I knew it! You have! Marty owes me fifty bucks."

"You and your husband have a bet on my sex life?" I should probably be a little offended. But, oddly, I'm flattered.

Bunny grins. "Marty thinks you were a virgin before marriage. I can see why. You come across all classy and reserved. But men are blind. I can see the wild child beneath your slacks and sweater sets. I bet you have a whole drawer of silk panties that you never wear but tell yourself you're buying for special occasions."

My mouth drops open. "How could you possibly know that?"

She laughs and looks at my suitcase. "Come on. Show me."

"You want to see my underwear?"

"Just the good stuff. La Perla. Agent Provocateur." She winks. "Maybe some trashy Victoria's Secret?"

I gasp. It's like she's a spy.

Bunny giggles. "Like I tell Marty. I know people. Now show me."

As I get off the bed and go to my suitcase, I think about the last time I bought something special. It was about a month ago. Evie convinced me to go to Saks. There was an exquisite little teddy on a mannequin. God, I think, as I bite my lip. It now seems a fortune. $150. Evie couldn't believe I bought this kind of stuff. She laughed and laughed and then decided to buy one for herself. The next day, she told me she wore it around her apartment all evening. I lied and told her that I did, too.

I take the teddy out of my suitcase and unwrap it from its tissue paper. The tags are still on. I hold it up.

"Ooh!" Bunny squeals. "It's fab! The perfect amount of naughty and nice." She strokes the black satin bodice, her fingers traveling lightly over the red lace trim.

"It's hard to find red lace that's done right," I say, as though I'm an expert in underpants. "Gosh, this is a beautiful piece. What's wrong with me? Why haven't I worn it?"

"Good question," Bunny says.

"What if I put it on and look ridiculous?"

Bunny shakes her head. "Nonsense. In fact, put it on. Right now."

I laugh. But Bunny narrows her eyes and stands up. She is not going to let this go. But I have my pride.

"Bunny, I appreciate what you're doing. But I am not putting on a teddy in the middle of the afternoon in my daughter's guest room."

"Sylvia, I don't give a shit what time or day it is. You are sexy and young. I won't let Louis make you feel like you're not. Now put on the goddamn teddy." She puts her hands on her hips. "Or I will."

"Bunny, let's calm down. We've had a lot to drink . . ." Bunny pulls down her pants.

My eyes go wide. Does everyone over sixty now do the Brazilian, I wonder, as I look at Bunny's bare thighs in her bikini-cut panties?

They are cotton and cute. Pink with little hearts. I think about the high-waisted nude briefs I'm wearing and feel sad.

But Bunny isn't wasting time. She pulls off her velour sweatshirt and snatches the teddy from my hands. She rips off the tag and is about to put it on when I cry out.

"Okay! You win! I'll put it on."

She smiles triumphantly and waits for me to get undressed. I turn my back to her and slowly take off my clothes.

"You don't have to be so modest, Syl. God knows you're in better shape than me."

"Never," I say on reflex, even though it's true. Bunny has a chunky tummy and large, heavy breasts. But there's something undeniably sexy as she stands, unabashed, with her hands on her hips, waiting for me.

I slip the teddy over my head and finally turn to her. She claps her hands. "It's gorgeous," she breathes. "You're gorgeous."

I can't help it. Maybe it's the wine. But I do feel gorgeous. Bunny reaches out and touches the silky material along my lower back.

"I have to get one," she says.

"You do. It's better than I thought."

Bunny keeps petting me. I start to giggle. It tickles. She does it more and I giggle harder and harder when I hear—

"Mom?"

Oh, fuuuck. If only I had a time machine. I would travel back and lock this door.

I slowly turn and see Isabel standing in the doorway. Her face has a funny look on it as she takes in the scene: Bunny, still in her bra and panties, stroking my body as I giggle in a teddy while wearing an obscene amount of makeup.

"This isn't what you think," I say, and walk toward her. Oops. I accidentally knock over my wineglass.

"Shit!" I cry out, and Bunny quickly throws a blanket over the spill.

Normally, Isabel would have a heart attack. The wine we've been drinking is red. But she barely glances at her bleached-oak floors. "I'll come back later," Isabel says as she backs out to the hall and then quickly shuts the door.

Her footsteps echo as she scurries away from the room. Bunny looks at me. For a moment, we're silent.

"Sorry. My daughter's kind of a prude. I guess she got that from me." I sit on the bed and let out a breath. This whole day is like a weird dream.

Bunny sits next to me and puts her hand on my thigh. "I have feelings for you, Sylvia."

Or a twisted nightmare.

Bunny caresses my leg. I'm frozen.

"Don't worry. Marty knows and is totally okay with it. I never sleep with other men."

"That sounds reasonable." My voice is thick. I stare at Bunny's fingers now massaging my thigh. I have no idea what to do. On the one hand, I want to leap onto the ceiling. On the other, Bunny is a surprisingly good masseuse and this feels rather soothing.

God, I'm drunk.

I gingerly stand up. "Bunny, thank you for the makeover and the kind words and the offer of hospitality. I'm truly touched."

I'm hoping if I keep this light and polite, it'll be like it never happened.

Bunny smiles and starts getting dressed. Her tone is equally casual. "Of course, Syl." As she pulls on her pants, she adds, "And we're serious about you coming to stay with us. We have plenty of room and would love to have you."

THIS EYELINER IS LIKE CONCRETE. It's been about forty-five minutes since Bunny left. I've taken a shower and now stand at the sink trying to scrub my face clean. I've used facial cleanser, lotion, Vaseline, and then more cleanser. I now inspect myself in the bathroom mirror and see a tiny bit of gold still glued to the corner of my eye. As I try to scrape it off my face, I wonder: Could I have sex with a woman?

There's an episode of *Sex and the City* in which Samantha dates a stunning lesbian named Maria. For a moment, I fantasize that I'm now a stunning lesbian. I wear tailored vests and visit Georgia O'Keeffe art exhibits. Is that offensive? Would a lesbian hear this and think I'm stereotyping?

I just can't get anything right.

I stare at my pale face and let out a breath. What a day. I had no idea about Bunny. Or Marty. Maybe that's why they have such a healthy relationship. They keep it spicy. And the truth is, I'm complimented. It's nice to be desired. And their home is large and lovely. I'd be quite comfortable. I could stay a few weeks while I get a plan underway for my future. But then I imagine walking into their living room and catching them in a contortionist position from *The Joy of Sex, Volume 14*. I'd stop short and apologize, all flustered. They'd smile and ask if I wanted to join.

Oh god. That would be . . . nope. I just can't go there. I pull my robe around me tightly and walk back into the bedroom only to find Isabel sitting in the armchair by the window.

"Mom," she says when she sees me. "We need to talk."

"Of course," I say as I sit down on the freshly made bed. The comforter is pulled tight and I can smell the bleachy scent of Bona from where the wine spilled on the floor. Gosh, she must've cleaned this entire room while I was in the shower.

"Isabel," I begin. "What you witnessed between Bunny and me was just two women having had too much to drink. It was totally innocent and—"

"Let's talk about that later." Isabel makes a face that says by "later" she means "never."

I nod. "Okay, then. What do you want to discuss?"

"I want to apologize for how I sounded earlier in the kitchen."

Has Isabel ever apologized before? I clear my throat, now moved. "Oh, Izzy. I know you didn't mean to be cruel. This was a terrible shock for all of us."

"I'm not apologizing for what I said, Mom. I'm apologizing for how I said it. I know I'm harsh. But I don't know how else to be. Especially with you."

"Especially with me?" I echo.

She sighs. "You say you're going to get divorced and be independent. But it's all a fantasy. You don't know how to live on your own and I'm worried you're going to get yourself into an even worse situation. The responsible thing to do would be to return to Florida. Even if you and Dad sleep in separate bedrooms and lead separate lives, fine. That's none of my business. But you going on about getting a job and finding an apartment is ludicrous. It's a pipe dream. You don't know how to be on your own. For instance, do you even know how to apply for medical insurance? Dad has you both under his plan. If you leave him, what will you do? You're two years away from Medicare."

"My job will provide medical insurance."

Isabel practically leaps up out of her chair. "What job? There is no job. And even if you get some position at Chico's or J.Jill, they're not going to give a retail associate medical insurance. Jesus, Mom. Do you know how dangerous it is to be your age and not have medical coverage?"

Before I can think of how to reply, Isabel starts pacing as though in a courtroom. "Ten years ago, you took up ballroom dancing. You went to two classes and decided it wasn't for you. And then you thought you'd sculpt. You converted my childhood bedroom into an art studio that never saw clay. You thought about writing a children's book. You thought about opening a cake shop. Then there was the wedding planning business. Laura Eliot still doesn't speak to me five years later."

"She was a bridezilla. She took time away from my other clients. In fact, I had to give up my other clients in order to handle her."

"That's the job, Mom. Handling bridezillas is the whole fucking art of it."

My face flames. I knew Isabel was still angry about Laura Eliot, her best friend from forever ago. After Isabel got married, I realized that I'd done quite a bit to help her very expensive planner pull off the whole affair. It was kismet. I had been wanting to find something to do professionally. Several of my friends' daughters and girls in the neighborhood hired me—I offered a very reasonable rate—and I was good at it. I enjoyed it. I still remember my clients—Sydney, Madison, Grace, and Toni. And then my last client, Laura Eliot.

By the time Laura got engaged, my confidence had grown and I had a great reputation. Even Isabel was impressed. I remember one day in particular. Izzy and I were shopping together and I noticed a gorgeous Armani shift dress. It was professional but chic. Izzy had loads of fancy suits in her own closet and encouraged me to buy the dress for myself to wear to the wedding. She said, "Mom, you're really good at your job. You've earned something fabulous."

But I couldn't. It was just so expensive. I remember saying, "Maybe after I finish Laura's wedding. It'll be my little treat."

Laura was set to have one of the most beautiful weddings imaginable. The local paper was doing a feature on it. I knew it was going to further my career to the next level. Unfortunately, Laura underwent a personality transformation during the course of planning this wedding. She'd call me at least forty times a day. She threw a tantrum at the dress fitting. She threw a tantrum at the tasting. She threw a tantrum on my front lawn in the middle of the night and the neighbors called the police. It was exhausting, and frankly, I felt I had no choice but to terminate our arrangement.

I explained this to Isabel. But she was furious. When I think back, maybe she was right.

After all, Laura was the client. And after word got out, no other bride wanted to hire me. Plus, Laura sued me for breach of contract and my attorney advised that I pay compensatory damages to avoid a more expensive litigation. So, really, the whole thing ended up costing me money.

Louis, I have to say, was very supportive.

I say as much to Isabel now, in her guest room, all these years later.

She stares at me before letting out a breath. "Of course Dad was supportive. He's always enabling your delusions."

"Wedding planning was a real career, Isabel. Not a delusion."

"Fine. Not a delusion. But definitely a failure."

I open and close my mouth. I feel a stinging in my eyes.

Isabel notices and stops pacing. "Look, I don't want to fight. I love you. You've had a horrible couple of days. So let's just stop talking about things like wedding planning and jobs. Stay here for a few days.

A few weeks. And don't worry about helping with the girls. I've spoken to an agency and hired a nanny to start full-time Monday until I sort out their preschool situation. I took your suggestion and found someone who can keep up with their language immersion and get them started on phonics."

"I'm not sure I said to do that, exactly. And I'm happy to help you."

Isabel shakes her head. "I don't want you to help me. I want you to help yourself. Look, I don't mean to sound mean. But I just need you to acknowledge that you aren't going to go out and get a job and start a whole new existence. This is not an episode of *Sex and the City*. You life is not West Village brunches and high-heeled shoes. Your life is Sylvia Fisher and you live in Boca Raton with your husband, Louis. Do you understand what I'm saying?"

I stare at Isabel's face. Gosh, she looks so old all of a sudden, and I realize that she's never going to understand me. But I don't want to fight anymore either. So I nod. "I do, Isabel. I understand."

Isabel closes her eyes a moment. She then leaves the room. After she shuts the door, I get up and lock it. Still wearing my robe, I sit back down on the bed. I need silence. I need to think.

Six

It's all going to work out.

It's not enough to just think this, however. I need to take action.

I spent all afternoon and evening in the guest room in total silence. Like a monk. I needed to flush the alcohol, shame, and anger out of my system. No more carrying on. Isabel made several points that I couldn't shake. I don't want to treat my life as though it's some big joke. I must take myself seriously. What is it I really, truly want?

To remember what it's like to enjoy sex. To live in London for a year. To find a sunscreen that blends well into my skin . . .

To move to Manhattan and restart my wedding planning business.

I smile to myself. That's exactly what I want to do.

And so now it's just after 10:00 p.m. and everyone has gone to sleep. I've crept into Isabel's office to borrow her laptop and a legal pad.

I'm sitting at the kitchen table eating a peanut butter sandwich. It's completely dark except for the glow of the computer screen and a candle I've lit and placed in the middle of the table as a symbolic gesture to show that I'm "burning the midnight oil" as I research. I feel a thrill of excitement in my stomach, not unlike the first kick of a baby. Something is growing inside of me. A new life.

And this move isn't some flight of fancy. No. It will take thought, preparation, and careful execution. I am capable of all these things. I take a thick bite of my sandwich and then type the following into a search engine: *WHAT DOES ONE NEED TO MOVE TO NEW YORK CITY?*

Results spill down the screen. I scroll and click various links, opening up web pages: Rently.com, Craigslist.com. I begin reading and reach for the legal pad and a pen. I write carefully at the top of the page:

List for Sylvia's Move

1. MONEY

I underline it three times and begin the subcategories of:

A) *Rent, first and last month. $6000*

B) *Groceries and incidentals, one month. $1000*

C) *Initial emergencies. $500*

The emergency category is something I've come up with on my own. I feel quite good about it. What if I'm in an accident and sprain my ankle? What if my refrigerator breaks and I lose a week's worth of meals? What if Louis cancels my cell phone? Hmm, how much is monthly cell service? I chew my pen a moment and think. Louis signed us up for a family plan. Hopefully he won't be able to cancel the plan without canceling his own phone. Then again, he could work something out with the carrier company. I have to anticipate everything.

I take another bite of my sandwich and keep writing and reading and then writing some more. There's even a blog by someone who documented their entire move to New York!

Granted, this person is twenty-two years old and just graduated from Stanford with a degree in microfinance. But, still. I can use her experience as a blueprint.

I try to get comfortable on Izzy's minimalistic chrome kitchen chair and settle in for a long night.

THE NEXT MORNING, I wake up full of nerves around 5:30. One thing is clear—before I can move to New York and restart my career, I need money. Too jittery to stay in bed, I leave Isabel's house and start walking.

It's brisk and blissfully not humid as I turn down the main drag of downtown Ainsebury and head into Café Beaux Mots, the suburb's trendy coffee shop. It just opened and I snag a corner table by the window.

A waitress drops off a menu. "Coffee?"

I smile, am about to order a double latte but stop short. My eyes bulge. Six dollars for a regular drip! Nine dollars for something fancy.

I swallow. "I'll just have hot water and lemon to start."

The waitress nods and leaves. I let out a breath. Was life always this expensive?

On that note, I reach into my purse and take out my phone. I dial Evie. It rings only once before she picks up.

"Sylvia. I got your texts. I cannot believe all that happened." Evie's voice is full of awe and laughter.

Before bed last night, I sent Evie a long message detailing everything from brunch to Bunny to my conversation with Isabel. I figured it was just easier to write it all out than have to relive it by saying it aloud.

"I know." I half smile. "It was quite a day."

"I'm rather enchanted by Bunny. But no offense, dear, it sounds like your daughter is a bit of a tyrant."

"No, Evie." I shake my head, growing resolute. "Izzy has a point. I've had plenty of grand ideas over the years but I never saw them through. This time, however, is different. I know what I want to do."

I straighten up in my chair as the waitress drops off my water and lemon. I feel pleased to have ordered something so responsible.

Ooh. Is that cinnamon?

I peek over at the next table where a group of early morning cyclists chat and refuel.

They've ordered glazed cinnamon rolls and French-press coffee. My mouth waters. I can't stop staring as I squeeze my lemon.

"Sylvia? Did I lose you?" Evie's voice cuts in.

"I'm here."

"So I suppose this means that you traveling the world like we discussed falls into the 'grand idea' category?"

"Oh, Evie. I would love to travel. But, yes, doing so with no income and no savings seems a bit far-fetched." I take a sip of my hot, lemony water. Delicious, I tell myself.

Evie sighs. "Well, that's too bad. Because I would've come."

I straighten up in my chair. "You'd consider leaving Boca?"

"After Henry passed, I was planning to. I never had any real friends down here." Evie pauses, her voice dry. "I've been told I'm difficult to get along with."

I smile. "You're the most misunderstood person I know." I then tilt my head. "But you stayed? How come?"

"I didn't know where to go. Then you moved here and life was somewhat bearable again. But now you're gone and I'm telling you, Sylvia, I feel like I'm sitting around waiting to die. It's depressing the shit out of me."

I can't imagine Evie as depressed. She's too spunky. She also dresses beautifully and never leaves the house without lipstick. Even to exercise.

In fact, right now I imagine my friend standing in front of her bedroom closet deciding whether to do water aerobics or tai chi today. She picks up her bathing suit but then puts it down. She instead chooses those adorable magenta yoga pants she just bought. She puts them on and admires her slim figure, but then, suddenly, her face falls. After tai chi, what's next?

Another iced tea? Another chopped salad? She sits down on her bed and starts to cry . . .

"Sylvia? Hello? Do I keep losing you?"

I wipe my face and realize it's me who is crying. "Evie, come with me," I blurt out.

"Come where? I thought you weren't going to travel."

"I'm moving to New York. That's my big plan, what I was going to tell you. I've thought it all through. You have to come. We'll be roommates and take on all of Manhattan together."

Why didn't I think of this sooner? It's perfect! I wish I could see Evie's face as she takes this all in.

But she's silent. I clear my throat. "Evie?" Still, nothing.

I take a deep breath. "Evie, before you say no, just think about it. I did quite a bit of research. All we need to get started is roughly seventy-five hundred dollars each. Even less if we live in Queens," I hastily add.

I know I'm speaking quickly. But I want this to sound reasonable. I want Evie to come.

I didn't realize how much I wanted it until right now. I squeeze my eyes shut.

What if she says I'm delusional? I open one eye. Shit. I just can't hear that again. "Sylvia," Evie finally says.

My stomach tightens. "Yes?"

"We cannot live in fucking Queens."

Seven

I can't believe it. It's going to be just like *Sex and the City*. Naturally I would never say this aloud. All I mean is that Evie and I are both fans of the show, so why shouldn't we shop at sample sales and drink mimosas and wear fabulous shoes?

Of course, Evie can only wear flats with her cane. And my knees are sometimes an issue.

But there are plenty of fabulous yet sensible shoes on the market. In fact, that's fitting. Fabulous yet sensible. This is my new mantra.

It's just before noon and I've taken an Uber to a questionable part of town. I'm walking down the sidewalk searching for an address that didn't pop up on the Google Maps. I hug my purse tightly to my chest and turn down an alleyway.

I have to stay grounded but I'm bubbling with nerves. Evie and I were on the phone for an hour making plans. We're going to meet Monday morning in Manhattan. That gives me the rest of today and tomorrow to come up with $4,500 and then slip away from Isabel's without alerting her to anything dramatic.

Evie offered to loan me the money I need. But I was firm. Absolutely not. She may be financially comfortable in Boca, but this is a big move for her as well. Her social security goes a lot further in Florida than New York. Besides, taking a loan goes against the very spirit of what this journey is all about: making it on my own.

Yes, $4,500 is a lot of money. But I have a plan.

As if on cue, I see my destination. A tiny sign in the window reads "One Stop Pawn." I peer through the black metal bars gating the front door and see a middle-aged man behind the counter.

I wave at him. He gestures for me to look to my right. Ah. A doorbell. I push the button. The buzz vibrates beneath my fingertips.

After a moment, another buzz, and the sound of the security gate unlatching makes my heart thump. I enter the store.

PAWN SHOPS ARE DEFINITELY not the stuff of fantasies. More like a healthy dose of reality. I'm standing at the jewelry case examining the artifacts of people's lives. How sad and scared these people must have been. Never once did I imagine standing in a back-alley pawn shop hoping that the answer to my problems would lie in the hands of a man named Joey.

"You can lay each piece out on the counter," Joey says as he wipes his magnifying glass.

As I carefully arrange my jewelry, I can't help but stare at the pieces for sale. My eye goes straight to a yellow diamond engagement ring. It's enormous. Easily five carats and the cut is exquisite. In fact, it feels like I've seen this ring before.

Laura Eliot.

My stomach drops.

This isn't her ring, I remind myself. She had a yellow diamond that she then demanded be exchanged for a pink diamond after reading a quote from some celebrity that said yellow diamonds are passé.

Joey picks up the first piece and puts it under his scope. He twists a piece of his beard while he works. I have a feeling this is going to take some time. I quietly take a step back. But I can't stop staring at the yellow diamond.

Laura Eliot.

For whatever reason, the fact that Isabel brought her up is staying with me. I don't care about the art studio or the bakery or the ballroom dancing. I accept that those were a little frivolous. But it's the wedding planning that got to me. Izzy saw how talented I was. In fact, she was going to be Laura's maid of honor and saw Laura's progressively horrifying behavior firsthand . . . I even tried to talk to her about it. But Izzy was working a zillion hours a week at the firm. She just shrugged it off and said, "This is the job, Mom. It's her day."

The thing is, Laura made every day her day. She would arrive at my house at 7:00 a.m. and not leave. She and her fiancé had moved back in with her parents—right down the street from me—six months before the wedding while their new home was being renovated. At first, this was ideal. We could pore over magazines and catalogues and travel to appointments together. It allowed me to give Laura the personal attention I wanted to lavish on my brides.

And so Laura began to open up. She didn't want the traditional country club wedding that her parents were pushing. She wanted something people would "ooh" and "ahh" over. I did some research and found a fabulous venue. It was a spa and inn in New Hampshire where the ballroom was a gorgeous, modern barn with a retractable ceiling. Everything was falling into place. I was already booking new clients because the press was spectacular. The local paper was doing a spread on it under the heading of "Off the Beaten Path Luxury Weddings."

Laura became such a presence at our house that Louis grudgingly joked about charging her rent. She accompanied me to the grocery store. She stayed for dinner. She came to my yearly mammogram. It got a little intense. Especially when she showed up to my aunt's funeral. In Chicago.

I ignored the tantrums. Yes, Laura's behavior was alarming. But I figured once she was married, it would all be over.

And then it happened.

Three a.m. on a Tuesday, six weeks before the big day. Laura set my lawn on fire. How, one has to wonder, did it come to this?

Well, she was ringing the doorbell and I told Louis that we couldn't let her in. I had hit my limit. We had to draw a boundary. He more than agreed. We ignored the doorbell and hoped she'd go away. I put the comforter over my head to drown out the noise.

About ten minutes later, we started to smell smoke. We ran to the window and saw Laura lighting matches and dropping them onto our lawn. There was an empty bottle of vodka in the bushes. It was madness. She was glaring up at me, her long blond hair hanging in strings around her face like in a horror movie. I thought we were going to die. I clutched Louis. He called 911.

Later, at the police station, we were asked if we wanted to file charges. Louis said yes. But I convinced him not to. "Let's not make this any worse than it already is." I was trying to be kind.

Laura was released after only an hour. Her mother was friends with the mayor's wife, so I guess she made a few phone calls . . .

Anyhow, later that afternoon, I told Laura I could no longer be her wedding planner. I felt my safety was at risk and that she should seek therapy. When I told Isabel what happened, I expected her to be on my side.

But that's not how it went at all.

I close my eyes and am transported back to my kitchen. Isabel stands there, her eyes full of judgment. "What did you think this job was?"

"I thought it was planning a wedding. Not enduring arson."

"Jesus, Mom. Do you know how many times my boss has thrown a cup of steaming coffee at my head?"

"What?! Have you reported him to HR? That's completely unacceptable."

Isabel just laughs, her voice dark. "HR is for people who can't cut it or who don't really want it. What I do is learn to dodge the coffee, get a rag, and mop up the floor. Then I apologize profusely for whatever I've done to make my boss so upset."

And with that, Izzy turned and left the room.

I felt so confused. Is that really what one has to do in order to make it in the world?

Surely not. But Izzy wouldn't speak to me for weeks. I figured she just needed time to cool off. After all, Laura kicked her out of the wedding and stopped speaking to her.

I tried to tell Izzy my side of the story, but she wouldn't hear it. Because that's the other thing. Laura managed to convince people that she was the victim. I had stressed her out so much that she'd resorted to taking Ambien and Ativan in order to sleep. She claimed she wasn't fully conscious when she set our lawn on fire. She was a poor, vulnerable bride who was pushed by her money-grubbing wedding planner to have a lavish, over-the-top wedding. And it was the stress I had caused that drove her to drugs.

I still get shaky with rage when I think about it. Money-grubbing?

I had yet to see a single dollar of payment for my services. But, somehow, Laura won. All the brides who were booking with me withdrew. I was forced to pay Laura thousands of dollars just to avoid a bigger lawsuit. She then hired Verena Simmowitz, one of my competitors in town. Verena didn't know up from down about the details of this event. But I had a private meeting with her and gave her all of my notes and contacts.

And the paper still ran a story on Laura's beautiful wedding. The focus was "Laura's Emotional Journey." Verena got credit for all of my work, was featured in *Luxury Brides*, and has now opened an agency on Madison Avenue.

And I'm currently in a pawn shop selling my tennis bracelet.

I let out a breath. No. I cannot be bitter. I just hate that a tiny part of me realizes that Izzy was right about something. I heard through the grapevine that Laura never calmed down. The morning of her wedding, she punched Verena in the face and broke her nose. But Verena got some ice and moved on without missing a beat. A month later, she visited a top plastic surgeon and looks better than ever.

I finally turn away from the yellow diamond ring. Enough, I tell myself. No more living in the past. I must stay positive. And so as I look around Joey's shop, I note that despite its location, the place itself is quite nice. Neat and organized.

I then glance at my jewelry and remind myself that this is all just stuff. I've never been a fancy jewelry person. In fact, I always felt like I was playing dress-up when I wore the platinum necklace Louis wanted me to wear to business dinners so clients would know he had the money to spoil his wife. So, really, being here isn't so much depressing as it is cleansing. It's all about attitude.

And so I take a deep breath and try not to look too desperate as

Joey continues examining my jewelry. He's a quiet man, in his fifties. And according to the reviews on the internet, he has a reputation for being fair.

Did he just yawn?

I'm sure not. He's probably just stretching his mouth. I try to peek at what he's writing down in his little notebook, but he's being awfully private about things.

Is it hot in here? Sweat trickles down the back of my neck. I unbutton my cardigan and catch my reflection in a small mirror behind the counter. How many other privileged women have stared into this same mirror? After Madoff and the other crooks? And how did those women turn out?

Images from the nightly news of women in fur coats picking up food stamps flash in my mind.

I feel tears behind my eyes. No matter how hard I try, I just can't get it right. It's the Laura Eliots of the world who win. Not the Sylvia Fishers.

I close my eyes a moment and will the tears to flow back inside my head. No more crying. No more self-pity. No more binge drinking and underpants parties. I must face reality. And my reality is Louis, Boca, and Belinda.

I let out a breath. I'm finally about to speak when Joey takes off his glasses and looks at me.

"I can give you ten thousand dollars."

TEN THOUSAND DOLLARS. Ten *thousand* dollars. Ten motherfucking thousand dollars!

I've never used the word "motherfucking" in my life. But I want to shout this from the rooftop as I walk up Isabel's driveway and enter the house through the garage. I slip into my room. It's after lunch and the girls are napping.

I put my purse on top of the dresser and sink on to the bed, giddy. *Ten thousand dollars.*

Where do I even put this much cash? In my suitcase? A duffel bag? One of those steel briefcases with a handcuff handle that I secure to my wrist?

Okay, Sylvia. This is not an Al Pacino movie. I am not actually carrying ten thousand dollars in cash. I open my purse and take out the cashier's check that Joey wrote me. He offered to wire the money directly into my account but I realized that unless I want to split this money with Louis, I'm going to have to open my own checking account.

I can hear Izzy and Todd in the kitchen cleaning up. I haven't spoken to anyone since yesterday. I hate feeling that there's tension between us. And after my trip down memory lane with Laura Eliot, I feel even more unsettled. Sure, it's been years. I thought Izzy and I had moved past it. But the fact that she brought it up shows me that she's still angry. Which, truthfully, hurts. She's my daughter. She should be on my side.

"Mom? You decent?" Isabel's voice jolts me into the present as she knocks on the door.

"Give me a sec. I'm just trying on bikinis with the neighbor, Mr. Curtis."

"Very funny," Izzy says as she opens the door and enters. "You look happy. What's up?"

I realize that Izzy is right. There's a smile on my face as I feel the cashier's check in my hand. I discreetly slip it back inside my purse and look at my daughter. The truth is, I'm desperate to tell her about my day. I want her to be proud of me.

But I can already see the hesitant, almost fearful expression in her eyes. And so I shrug and say, "I'm going to visit my friend Evie for a few weeks."

"Doesn't Evie live in Boca?"

"Yes," I lie. "But now she's in New York visiting relatives and asked if I'd like to join her. She knows the situation with your father, and I think she'd like the company as well."

I look away. I'm a terrible liar, but my plan is to tell Isabel and Todd the truth after I'm settled. They'll be so impressed once they see I've become a success. I'll have a career, an apartment, a whole new life.

"Mom? Are you listening to me?"

I wince a little. Izzy's voice is so much softer in my head. "I'm sorry. I'm just a little tired. You were saying?"

"I think it's great you're going to see your friend. When are you planning to go?"

"Monday morning. If you don't mind, I'd love to use your laptop computer to sort out the arrangements."

I bite my lip. Will Isabel think it's strange that I want to go online?

But instead her face washes with relief. "Of course! In fact, why don't I just give it to you? My office ordered me a new one."

"Are you sure?" Wow. My very own computer. This day just keeps getting better.

"I'll grab it," Isabel says.

As she goes to leave the room, I realize something. "Izzy, wait."

She turns. I lower my voice. "I know this is a lot to ask, but I'd prefer that your father didn't know I was going to stay with Evie. I just need a little space for myself to think about things."

Izzy nods. "I understand. Mum's the word. God, I'm almost jealous. I'd love to go to New York and let Todd handle life for a few days."

I blink, surprised.

Izzy blushes a little. "It's not like I'm going to do it."

"Izzy, is that really true?" I try to read her face. "You want to leave?"

"Of course not," she says, waving a hand. "I just got a promotion. And my children will be fine. I signed them up for a junior coding class, too."

I'm about to say something when she cuts me off. "Mom, all is great. Perfect, even. You enjoy yourself with Evie. Dad can suffer a little. Now come on. You'll need some cold-weather clothes. You can borrow from me. You know how much I love to declutter."

As Isabel heads out the door, I feel a bit of whiplash from this conversation. But I'm getting a computer, clothes, and the quasi support of my daughter. Surely that's a sign. And so I stay quiet as I follow Isabel into her room, because the thing is, I've decided that she was both right and wrong yesterday. Sure, I've made choices that didn't work out. But I don't live in Boca Raton anymore. I don't live with my husband, Louis, anymore. As for my age? She's absolutely right. I'm sixty-three years old. And you know what? I've got my whole life in front of me. New York: here I come.

Eight

It's been one disaster after another. We've been in Manhattan more than a week and we're still staying at an Airbnb in Harlem, which sounded hip at first but has, in reality, been a little slice of hell. It's not the "entire place" but, instead, a "shared room." At least it only costs seventy-six dollars per night. Evie and I have spent all day, every day, searching for apartments in every neighborhood on the island but have come up empty. I can tell Evie's starting to lose hope. She's barely said a full sentence since lunch. In fact, she didn't even eat lunch. She sat silently next to me on a park bench while I ate a hot dog from a street vendor.

I knew I needed a plan to lift her spirits, which is why I'm now leading her into the women's apparel section of Bergdorf Goodman. If anyone loves beautiful clothes, it's Evie.

"A little dream shopping," I say brightly. "We try on but don't buy anything."

Funny enough, it was Isabel who introduced me to the concept. After my move to Boca, she came down to visit and saw how depressed I was. She said she had just the cure: She took me to the designer shops at Bal Harbour and we spent the afternoon playing dress-up. I asked her when she started doing this and she admitted it was in high school when she'd get stressed about finals.

It's funny when your children surprise you.

I smile a moment at the memory, then turn to look at Evie. I gesture for her to follow me to the Prada section. There's a violet silk pantsuit that would look smashing on her. I pick it up, then float over to Balenciaga where I see a black A-line cocktail dress with horseshoe buckles at the waist. It's love at first sight.

"Let's try these on," I breathe to Evie as I clutch the hangers.

Evie reaches out to touch the clothes but then yanks her hand back as though she might get burned. "No," she says. "It's depressing. And makes me feel stupid. I accept that I need to budget. But I am not going to act like I've never bought a designer outfit before."

My heart sinks. But I don't want to argue. So I turn to put back the clothes when I hear a man's voice. "Don't you dare."

I turn and look over at the most beautiful person I've ever seen. He's small, maybe five feet, four inches tall, and incredibly thin. But somehow this works for him. His smooth skin glows with youth and fabulous products. His eyes are full of feeling. A matrix of green-gold depth.

The young man takes the hangers from my hands and looks soulfully from me to Evie. "If I don't see you ladies in these outfits, I might die."

I look at Evie and smile, hopeful.

But she narrows her eyes. "We can't afford these clothes. There's no sale to be won here, dear."

"I don't work on commission. My name is Reese. I'm the manager of the personal shopping department and I have to stay late tonight to unpack the new inventory. I've been asking the universe all day to bring me two fabulous women to model the clothes and it seems like my prayers have been answered."

I swallow. "Are you asking us to stay and try on all the new clothes?"

"I am."

I nearly reach out to hug him when Evie's voice cuts in, sharp. "What's the angle here? Are you fucking with us?"

I glance sideways at Evie. I've heard her curse plenty of times. But it's always done with good humor. This is different. This is crass.

Reese seems to sense Evie's frame of mind and speaks more plainly. "I overheard you ladies talking by the elevator. From what I gather, you just moved here and things are not going well. That's interesting to me. I've never met two women of a certain age moving to Manhattan versus out of it."

Evie lifts a brow. "Women of a certain age?"

Reese lifts a brow back. "Mature, sophisticated women."

"Sylvia and I are grandmothers trying to live like thirty-year-olds. Don't you think that's ridiculous?"

"It's marvelous."

Evie looks him up and down. "Why are you being so nice?"

"My mother died last month."

"I'm sorry," I say, breaking into the discussion. I put a hand on Evie's elbow to signal that her interrogation is over.

But she shrugs me off. "Yes. It's very sad. I still don't understand why you want us to try on clothes we can't buy."

"When my mother was in the hospital, I brought her something new every day. An Hermès scarf. Tom Ford sunglasses. Why bring sunglasses to someone in the hospital? Because they were fabulous.

I'm not a doctor or a priest or a social worker. I don't adopt animals. But I love to make people feel beautiful."

I see Evie opening her mouth to say something snarky again.

"Enough." My voice surprises even me. But I meet Evie's eye and hold it. "It's enough," I repeat quietly. I then turn to Reese. "My name is Sylvia Fisher. Thank you for such a generous invitation. I would love to stay."

I stick out my hand to shake. Reese takes my hand and kisses the back of it.

AND SO HERE I AM NOW standing in the store's decadent dressing room—larger than the apartments Evie and I have seen—wearing something from Dolce & Gabbana's newest evening collection. It's a metallic body-con dress with a plunging V-neck. My breasts have never been so exposed. They also have never been so suctioned and lifted. I don't know what this dress is made out of, but NASA should start recruiting from the high fashion industry.

I pivot in front of the three-way mirror as Evie and Reese whistle yet again. "When I die, I want to be buried in this. Can I put that in my will?"

"I don't see why not." Reese hands me a glass of champagne. He's brought up a tray of food and champagne from the store's in-house café and sets everything down on a large side table.

I take a sip of the champagne. God, that's good.

"I'd love a refill, Reese." Evie holds out her empty flute. Reese obliges.

After we all headed to the dressing room, Evie apologized for being a "goddamn stick in the mud" and vowed to change her attitude. Or at least try. I glance over at her. She's relaxing on a plush chaise in a pair of thigh-high leather boots and a mod dress from Roberto Cavalli.

"So what's the plan for an apartment?" Reese pops a quiche into his mouth.

I take one as well and chew slowly, savoring the buttery crust and delicate flavors. Is that sage? I should cook with sage. It sounds so romantic. I take another bite and lose myself in a fantasy. Evie and I have been invited to a gala at the Met. I'm wearing this exact dress. My hair is swept up in a chignon but the wind blows a few tendrils around my face. I reach to brush them away when a handsome stranger intercepts my arm. He holds it gently. "Don't. The wind is dancing with you. You must dance back."

I look at this man. A youngish Harrison Ford. He's wearing a tuxedo and smells like cinnamon and whiskey. "I want to make love to you. Right here, on these steps."

I laugh but realize that he's serious. "Won't we get arrested?"

He looks heartbroken. I try to stay positive and suggest, "Maybe we could make out a little here? And then go somewhere more private?"

His face instantly blooms. He takes me in his arms. From out of nowhere, there's music in the air. We sweep across the pavement. It's as though I've never had arthritis. The man's hands move slowly down my back and rest on top of my tush. He brings his face toward mine and I can feel the tickle of his almost-beard against my cheek. My body tingles all over when . . .

"Sylvia! Earth to Sylvia."

I turn to Evie, flushing. "Sorry! What did I miss?"

There's a light on Evie's face that I haven't seen since we arrived in the city. I feel a surge of hope as she gushes, "Reese was just explaining that we've approached the apartment hunt all wrong. We shouldn't be looking for rentals. We need to find a sublet."

"What's the difference?"

Reese smiles. "There's plenty of wealthy people who don't want to sell their apartments but have to leave for a short-term job transfer or family emergency. They tend to ask for reasonable rents. You get a nice place for a set amount of time while saving up for something better."

"When you say 'plenty of wealthy people,'" Evie begins slowly. "Exactly how many do you mean? Is there a special real estate section for sublets? How nice a place are we talking about?"

Evie and I lean forward as Reese talks.

"TWO TALL PEPPERMINT TEAS, PLEASE." Evie and I are now at Starbucks, part of our nightly ritual. After Reese gave us a tutorial, Evie insisted we begin investigating these sublets ASAP. I couldn't agree more. I glance over at Evie. She's been on her phone since we left. She's a woman on a mission. It's nice to see her so motivated.

The cashier rings me up. I smile at him. "This is a new card, so tell me if it's not activated correctly."

I insert my pristine Visa debit card into the chip reader and wait.

Next to me, Evie looks up from her iPhone and rolls her eyes. "You just used the card here this morning."

"I know. But I like to pretend it's the first time all over again."

The cashier hands me the receipt and our teas. I happily tuck the slip of paper into my wallet as Evie and I then make our way to the restroom.

As we wait for the bathroom, Evie types and swipes some more. "I've bookmarked seven listings. I'm emailing the owners and setting up appointments for us. We start the search at nine a.m."

The sound of a toilet flushing makes Evie look up. She wrinkles her nose. "Maybe we should start at eight a.m. The sooner we're out of this situation, the better."

"I feel like our luck is about to change," I say confidently as the bathroom door opens and a respectable-looking young woman exits. I give Evie a thumbs-up. See? A good omen.

This morning, we used this Starbucks restroom after a tubby businessman with a newspaper tucked beneath his arm exited. I still feel nauseated from the memory. But what other choice did we have? It beats the bathroom situation at our Airbnb.

And so with a deep breath, Evie and I enter what has become our personal restroom. It's a single, handicap-accessible bathroom with a large sink. I glance over and see that the paper towels have been refilled. Another good omen.

Evie and I put down our teas and begin our evening ablutions.

I line an area on the floor with two layers of paper towels and then remove a toiletry bag from my purse and place it on top of the towels. Evie places her kit next to mine.

We both take our toothbrushes and squeeze toothpaste onto them. We take turns at the sink brushing and rinsing.

As Evie starts to floss, I pluck a few Mustela baby wipes and reach beneath my blouse to wipe my armpits down. I then run a fresh wipe over my neck and chest.

Evie squirts her Clinique facial soap into her hands and carefully massages her face, taking care not to splash water on her sweater as she rinses. She offers me some of her collagen-boosting night cream. I swipe a bit under my eyes.

I then go to the toilet. Evie turns her back so that I can pee in semiprivacy. I squat and try to squeeze every last drop out. Not touching the toilet has become my daily butt-enhancing exercise. But I still hold the handicap rail for support.

I flush and move to the sink to wash my hands. Evie takes a turn peeing.

We then repack our kits and straighten our clothes and pick up our teas.

We exit the bathroom, leave the Starbucks, and head up to the light at 110th Street. While we wait to cross, Evie turns to me. "If you had told me that we'd be peeing in front of each other and cleaning up like homeless women, I would have said you were crazy."

"Oh, come on. It's like we're college girls all over again." I try to keep my voice light but know that Evie always gets like this before we enter our Airbnb.

We silently make our way down the hallway—we're on the first floor—just as Constantine, a fifty-two-year-old tourist from Greece, exits the communal bathroom. He's smoking a cigarette and wearing nothing but rubber flip-flops. His woolly chest hair is matted with water and Mambo cologne, a truly unfortunate sensory combination for the rest of us.

He smiles at us. "Kalinikta."

"Good night," Evie and I murmur back as we try not to look down, hurry into our room, and lock the door. Evie turns on the overhead light, illuminating a space not much bigger than our closets back in Boca.

I put my purse on the top bunk—yep, we're sleeping in bunk beds—and wait for Evie to take a seat on the lone wooden chair. There is no table. Just a chair. She needs to sit down in order for me to have enough room to open my suitcase to get my pajamas.

"Evie," I say as I change into pajamas. "If you want to go back to Florida, I understand."

I climb onto the top bunk and stay on top of the blanket. I arrange my coziest sweater around my pillow. Neither of us trusts the linens here. I finally lie back and peer down at Evie as she now has enough room to get herself ready for bed.

"I know, Sylvia. And, again, I'm sorry for being such a downer." Evie moves carefully around the tiny space so that she doesn't slip. "I feel guilty because I'm higher maintenance than you."

"Oh, Evie. It's okay. I want an elevator, too. Plus, you're being such a good sport. I know that you can afford more than I can right now."

I bite my lip. I know Evie has more flexibility with her finances right now. Although not as much as I imagined.

"It's not just the elevator, Sylvia." Evie says as she eases herself into her bunk and lies against the pillow that she's likewise wrapped with one of her sweaters. "I need a real apartment. Because if I see another 'converted one-bedroom' that's the size of a closet, I may jump out the window. Only I can't because there's probably bars over it."

I laugh. But Evie just sighs. "Here's what I want: A functional kitchen. Not a hot plate and mini fridge. Two bedrooms. The fact that we've been sleeping in bunk beds makes me feel ridiculous. And I want a bathroom that's big enough to use the toilet and close the door at the same time."

I swallow, suddenly depressed by this list of luxuries. I'm not sure these are reasonable expectations. And I really don't want Evie to give up. So I try to stay positive. "The sublets sound promising."

I can hear Evie nodding against her sweater-covered pillow. "Let's hope."

Nine

I feel dirty. It's the next morning and Evie and I are in the back seat of a taxi—the first we've allowed ourselves since arriving in New York—and I touch my head self-consciously.

"Does my hair smell?" I ask.

Evie wrinkles her nose. "What?"

"My hair. I think it smells bad." I sniff my fingers again and then hold them out to Evie.

Evie slips her oversize Chanel sunglasses down her nose to look me in the eye. She's decked out in full Jane Fonda mode: black pantsuit, the Valentino flats she saves for special occasions because they hurt her bunions, and her movie-star sunglasses.

"Sylvia, we've been through a lot this past week. We help each other pee. But I draw the line at smelling your fingers. I'm sure your hair is fine."

But my stomach flips with worry. "Neither of us have had a proper shampoo in nearly a week, Evie. We probably both smell awful. No one is going to rent us their apartment."

I dig my compact from my purse and open it to survey my appearance. My hair is twisted into a low bun. I'm wearing my Eileen Fisher topper jacket over a pair of black crepe pants. Evie and I both thought it best to dress up for today's itinerary of sublets. We want to look like responsible, classy women a person can trust with his or her home.

Of course, all that goes out the window if we smell like dog food.

As though reading my mind, Evie pats my hand. "We smell fine. Besides, the French go months without washing their hair. Who's more chic than the French?"

I snap my compact shut. "Don't talk to me about the French and their natural oils. Maybe we're too old for natural oils. Maybe we're all dried up. Maybe we're too close to dying to smell good anymore. Maybe—"

"Jesus Christ, Sylvia." Evie whispers, cutting me off. "Our cab driver is eating a barbecue brisket sandwich."

Oh. I look up and see that our driver is indeed gnawing away at an oozing, meaty sandwich. Evie rolls down her window. I do the same. We're both quiet a moment.

"Sorry, Evie. I don't know how I missed that."

"You're nervous. I am, too. This apartment we're about to see sounds perfect and neither of us wants to be disappointed."

I sigh. "Two bedrooms, an upgraded kitchen, a real living room . . ."

"An elevator, a doorman, a bathroom with shower and tub," Evie continues. She then clears her throat. "The price is a little high but we could probably swing it if we cut back on other areas. And I'm hoping the owner will negotiate. He only has two days to find subletters."

I'm about to respond when my cell phone rings. I see that it's Louis. My finger hoovers over the Ignore button, but I answer at the last minute.

"Hi, Louis."

"Sylvia! Hi. Hello. Thank you for answering."

I shift in my seat, annoyed with myself. I shouldn't have picked up. But I always do things that make feel worse when I'm nervous. I grit my teeth.

Evie shoots me a look. *Are you okay?* I shrug back, *Yep.* I clear my throat. "What do you want, Louis?"

"It's so nice to hear your voice. How are things?"

I don't say anything. Instead, I look out the window. We've exited the highway and are now stuck in traffic on Sixty-Second Street. I love Manhattan in the morning. People dressed for work walk briskly down the sidewalks. Soon I'll be one of them. I'll carry a smart handbag and wear the kind of outfit that takes me from day to night if I have a dinner meeting.

Or a dinner date.

I close my eyes a moment and imagine I'm out with a bulldog of a man. A district attorney, perhaps. He wears a suit to work but sweatpants on the weekends. He has a thick, masculine neck and a booming laugh. I imagine we're in his apartment. He pulls me down onto his BarcaLounger so that I'm straddling him. His runs his hands up and down my back so hard that I'm worried he's going to rip my Brunello Cucinelli blouse.

"Sylvia," he whispers. "You drive me crazy. I need you. Right now."

Honk!

I realize that I'm staring lustfully out my window at another taxi driver. He winks at me and honks again.

I turn away and hear Louis calling my name. "Sylvia? Hello? Are you there?" Even Evie is looking sideways at me with raised brows.

I fan my face and clear my throat. "I'm here, Louis."

"So Isabel, Todd, and the girls are okay? Everyone's good?"

"They're fine." I then narrow my eyes, remembering. "Of course, things would be better if you hadn't gotten drunk and filled them in our private problems. My daughter now has to live with the image of her mother molesting your mistress."

I feel my face prickle with humiliation all over again.

"I'm so sorry, Sylvia. I'm ashamed of myself for doing that. My therapist says it was a cry for help."

"A therapist?"

"I've been going twice a week." Louis's voice suddenly explodes across the line as he talks a mile a minute. "BBG has an excellent mental health policy. We get twenty-five free sessions a year with our membership and living fees. And so I've been seeing the resident psychologist on staff. Rebecca—that's her name—is actually hoping that you might join me for couples counseling when you return."

I speak slowly, trying to process all of this. "Good for you, Louis. I'm happy you're in therapy. But I won't be returning to Florida."

"I know you aren't happy down here. But we need to sit tight and get our finances sorted out. Once we do, I'm happy to consider moving elsewhere. We'll have a fresh start."

"This is the problem, Louis. You never listen to me. I'm having a fresh start right now. In fact, I've never felt so fresh."

As if to prove a point, I take a deep breath and nearly throw up from the odor in this taxi.

Who eats barbecue at 8:45 a.m.? I lean my face out my open window and try to calm down.

Louis, meanwhile, changes tone. "What are you doing for money? Are Todd and Isabel supporting you?"

I stiffen. "That's none of your business."

"You have food and housing down here. It's selfish to ask them for help, Sylvia."

Evie, who's been eavesdropping, can't help herself. "What an asshole," she mutters.

I stare at my hand. I'm gripping the phone so hard, I worry it might break. "Louis," I say slowly. "How dare you. Last I checked, this entire mess was your making. But just so you know, I'm supporting myself."

"How?"

"I have a job."

Silence on the other end of the phone. Even Evie looks at me. I lift my chin my little. I know I don't technically have a job. But I'll get one.

Louis finally speaks. He sounds stunned. "Doing what? Where are you, Sylvia?"

"I'm exactly where I've always wanted to be. Goodbye, Louis."

I hang up the phone. Evie takes off her sunglasses. "Good for you."

And just like that, the taxi driver pulls up in front of a respectable-looking apartment building. Our stop. My hands are still shaking as I step onto the sidewalk.

I wait for Evie to carefully slide out and join me. She puts her hand on my arm. "Are you okay?"

I look around the lovely neighborhood and nod with fresh resolve. "I'm better than okay. I'm about to rent my first apartment without a man. Let's go do this, Evie."

I turn and head into the building. Evie follows.

. . .

WELL, I CAN SEE why people stalk sublets. Evie and I entered the building, walked through the lobby—there's a lobby!—and went up the elevator. We are now standing in front of unit 424. The door is slightly ajar and there's a half dozen people milling around.

Evie stands there, her face pained. "Oh, Sylvia. We're never going to get this place. The owner will get multiple offers." She shakes her head. "I feel so stupid. I thought he'd negotiate with us."

I narrow my eyes. "Evie, have a little faith."

I then square my shoulders and stride into the apartment. Sure, there's a lot of people here, mostly in their thirties. All impeccably dressed. Their handbags and suits suggest they have either fabulous jobs or parents who help with the rent. But I will not be deterred. This is my new home. I am in it to win it, as the young people say.

I walk through the open-concept area. The kitchen is small but high-end. There's even a gleaming stainless steel juicer. I've always wanted to juice. And the living room furniture is modern but tasteful. A gorgeous leather couch and the biggest flat-screen TV I've ever seen. I start to smile. It's perfect. Evie and I will host foreign film nights here. Not that I watch a lot of foreign films. But I could start. We'll drink Barolo and serve something exotic like ratatouille.

Evie comes up beside me. "The rent is six thousand dollars a month." Her voice is soft and almost apologetic.

I turn to her. "What? I thought you said it was just a tad over budget."

She reddens. "I thought we'd be able to negotiate."

"Negotiate?! Evie, six thousand dollars is literally double our budget." I try to keep my voice low, but I feel gutted.

83

"I'm sorry. I just wanted this place so badly that I thought . . ." Her voice trails off.

I open my mouth but then close it. I see that Evie feels terrible. And I certainly know what it means to get lost in a fantasy. I then hear the *tap tap tap* of Evie's cane and see that she's making her way back toward the front door.

I hurry to catch up with her in the small foyer. "Evie, don't go."

She looks at me. "I'm sorry, Sylvia. I shouldn't have brought us here. Look at all these people. I'm such an idiot."

"You're not an idiot, Evie. You're an optimist. And you know what? So am I." I narrow my eyes. "Evie, we are going to get this apartment. Follow me."

I stride into the middle of the living room and point to the TV. "Is this high-def?"

My voice is loud and cuts through the low chatter. Everyone turns to stare at me. Evie slowly comes up beside me. She tries to catch my eye, but I just smile and wait for . . .

"I bought it last month," a young man says as he approaches us. "Hi, I'm Raphael Hunter. Owner of the place."

I put out my hand. "Sylvia Fisher. And this is my friend, Evelyn Neiss." Raphael shakes my hand and then Evie's.

I smile at him and lower my voice. "Is there someplace we can talk?"

Raphael looks a little confused but leads us down the hallway to one of the bedrooms.

We enter. I nod appreciatively. It's large enough for a king bed and a dresser. "Is the other bedroom the same size?" I ask.

Raphael shakes his head. "It only fits a queen. But it does have its own bathroom."

I tilt my head and look at Evie. "Well, Evelyn. What do you think? Is a queen bed sufficient?"

Evie stares at me. "Um, yes?"

I turn back to Raphael. "I can see a lot of people are interested in this place."

He nods. "I have to move to London for a year to head up a new division of our firm. It's a promotion, which is great. But I have to be there next Monday, which is tough. So I've made the place quite reasonable."

"Yes," I say. "Six thousand a month is reasonable on a relative scale. But do you know how difficult it is to get the stench of marijuana out of a leather couch?"

"Excuse me?" Raphael tilts his head as though he didn't hear me correctly.

"And that's just the smoke. There's also spilled bong water, which is quite nasty. My daughter once threw a party at our home in Connecticut when we were out of town. The whole house was ruined. Bong water on my bedroom carpet. In the living room, my favorite ottoman had a purple vomit stain on it that never came off. The floors were sticky even after a professional cleaning service came. Twice. The paint on the walls was chipped. My piano was broken. I had several antique vases that shattered. There was food left out for days and we developed a rodent problem."

Raphael looks revolted. "What exactly are you saying?"

I smile softly. "I'm saying that Evelyn and I are the only people offering to take care of this place in the manner it deserves. We are the only people currently in your apartment over the age of thirty-five. We've dedicated lifetimes to maintaining a home and all that it entails. We have experience, early bedtimes, and the only drugs we take are for arthritis."

Out of the corner of my eye, I can see Evie's face start to shine. Raphael, meanwhile, is hanging on my every word.

And so I summon my most maternal voice and continue, "The only catch is that Evie and I are admittedly on a different budget than perhaps you were hoping for. And so I have to ask you, Raphael: If your home is your first major investment, is it worth it to accept a little less rent for a lot more peace of mind? Because the people out in your living room may be able to pay more than us. But they will throw parties. They will drink liquor. They will take drugs. They will forget to do their dishes. God knows if any of them actually even own a vacuum, whereas Evelyn and I have experience with Dysons and steam mops. Have you ever used a steam mop? It's one of god's miracles. And your floors are so beautiful."

A long beat as Raphael absorbs all that I've said. He looks from Evie to me and then back again. He finally asks, "Can you swing five thousand a month?"

I smile. "Let's call it four thousand and your place will be even better than when you left."

THE GOOD NEWS IS THAT my apartment strategy of presenting ourselves as responsible women of a certain age worked.

The bad news is that it wasn't on Raphael's gorgeous apartment.

As soon as he heard $4,000 a month, he gave Evie and me a tight smile, shook our hands, and said he'd be in touch. I wanted to barricade myself inside the master bedroom and take a shower, but Evie reminded me that posting bail would put a serious damper on our budget. So we left.

We then spent the following eight hours looking at sublets. But, like I said, my strategy worked. Not on Raphael's place or the following three sublets we then saw. But number five was a home run.

And instead of paying the asking price of $3,500 a month, we negotiated down to $2,750. Under budget!

So what if it's in a six-unit, walk-up building? We're on the first floor, which means stairs aren't an issue. Of course, the bathroom window is eye level with the building's dumpsters. But at least there's a window. And it feels like destiny that we're in the West Village. There's leafy trees on the block and all the buildings have those stone steps where we can sit and people-watch on warm Sunday afternoons. As for our actual apartment, there's two bedrooms. Well, one real bedroom and one "bonus" room with a brand-new futon that's quite comfortable. Evie volunteered to take it, but I really don't mind a small room. I already have a thousand ideas of how to make it "cozy chic."

The owners, a lovely young couple moving to Spain to teach at the University of Madrid for a year, were kind enough to let us move in immediately. As in today. They'd already packed their things and had been staying at their family's home in New Jersey. So, really, it was fate that we met.

Now it's Tuesday evening just after 6:30 p.m. I'm putting together the first bedroom I haven't had to share with someone in over forty years and thinking about mood lighting. Maybe I can buy a few of those hanging lanterns. They won't take up space, I think as I smooth a comforter over the futon and fluff the pillows. There's a small dresser that doubles as a nightstand. The floors are a blond wood and the walls are a joyful lemon color.

I walk into the living room to unpack the rest of my clothes in the hallway closet—there's a hallway closet!—and notice that there aren't any paintings or prints on the walls. Instead, the owners decorated with books and clocks and maps of the world. Evie and I will definitely spice things up a bit. Don't get me wrong; I love to read and it's always convenient to know what time it is. And geography is likewise fascinating. But if we're living in Manhattan's West Village, we're going to need some pizzazz. Samantha from *Sex and the City* moved downtown and I know she didn't decorate her love nest with cartography.

But I'm not complaining. This place is perfect. The couch is new. There's a TV on the wall next to several rows of built-in shelves. The kitchen is tiny but has enough space to cook simple meals. There's an old-fashioned card table Evie and I can dine on. And despite its unfortunate view, the bathroom's shower has excellent water pressure. The lighting isn't too terrible and there's enough counter space. In fact, I'm about to go and take a much-needed shower when I hear a pop. I swivel around to see Evie in the living room with a bottle of Veuve Clicquot. Mist rises from the open bottle like a little cloud of heaven.

"I was saving this for a special occasion," Evie says as she walks into our kitchen and opens cabinets, looking for glasses. She finds some champagne flutes and pours us each a drink.

She raises her glass. "To you, Sylvia. You were magnificent today."

I flush and try to wave off the compliment. But Evie shakes her head. "Every place we went, you got better and better. I've never heard you so confident. Now let's get ready. I'm buying celebratory dinner."

Oooh. Our first night out on the town. I clasp my hands around the glass of champagne and ponder a very serious matter. "What shall we wear?"

"DO YOU THINK we overdid it?" I ask Evie as I tug at my silk leopard-print blouse that's just sheer enough to see my bra. I bought it on a whim during one of my fancy lingerie sprees and had intended to keep it folded in tissue paper with the tags intact, per usual. But something came over me this evening when I was unpacking. I saw this beautiful top and realized that I don't want to be in a box anymore.

"Overdid it how?" Evie asks as she scans her menu.

It's just after 8:00 p.m. and we're at Wild One, a hip seafood restaurant with the best cocktails in town according to an app Evie swears by. So far, I'm not disappointed. The dining room is airy and sexily lit. There's a live piano player behind the bar. The crowd is a diverse mix of beautiful people that makes me feel self-conscious and old. I say as much to Evie right now as I hunch forward and try to hide behind the menu.

"Is there an age limit on wearing animal prints? Do I look like one of those sad women who competes with her daughter by getting a belly button ring? Can you see my nipples in this blouse?"

"Breathe, Sylvia."

I open my mouth to take a breath but immediately feel compelled to start talking again. "I'm just so worried that—*ummph!*"

Evie reaches across the table and puts her palm against my mouth. My eyes go wide with shock. I try to say something but she pushes her hand more firmly. I glance around, my face flaming.

"No one is looking at us." Evie says. "Now, tell me. Where did the confident Sylvia from earlier today go? I love that woman. Can you please bring her back?"

I nod. Evie takes her hand off my mouth and sits back in her chair just as our drinks arrive. I grab my frothy cocktail and take a long sip. It's sweet and spicy and I'm definitely going to need at least two more of them.

Evie peers up at the waitress. "We'll start with the scallops and jalapeño-seared tuna. Do you think my friend and I look silly dressed up like this?"

Evie gestures to my outfit and then hers. She's wearing a tuxedo shirt tucked into a pair of buttery black leather pants.

The waitress surveys us a moment and then looks down at her own outfit: Her mini apron is tied over a pink tutu. She wears laser-cut tights, combat boots, and a vintage Neil Young T-shirt. She finally answers, "I don't understand the question."

Evie smiles. "Exactly. Thank you, dear." The waitress leaves.

Evie leans forward. "Sylvia, take a minute to appreciate all that's happened in the last week. You left your cheating husband, you stood up to your daughter, and you've moved to New York. You did all that and now you're wondering if you're too old to wear animal prints? Cut the shit, my friend. The only thing you're too old to do is sit around wasting time."

"Oh, Evie. I want to be the confident person I was earlier. I want to be her all the time," I confess as I start poking my fingers with the prongs of my fork. "But I'm terrified. What do I do about work? Can I really be a wedding planner again? I mean, how does that even happen?"

Evie thinks a moment, then brightens. "Call Reese. He already said he'd be happy to refer you to all the brides who come to Bergdorf's for a wedding dress."

I shake my head. "The brides who shop at Bergdorf's want top-tier planners. Not some old lady who planned some suburban weddings nearly a decade ago."

"Don't forget, Sylvia, that I need a job as well. So if sixty-three makes you an old lady, then seventy-seven must make me hopeless. Is that what you're saying?"

My jaw drops. Evie has never admitted her age. I knew it was seventy-something, but I didn't realize she was tiptoeing toward eighty. God, she looks good.

Evie reads my mind. "Genetics. My mother was a beauty queen. Did I ever tell you that?"

I shake my head.

She laughs and takes a long drink. "It will all work out, darling. It really will. Hell, we already found an apartment. Now we'll both find jobs and be glorious successes. I'm sure of it."

"That's easy for you to say. You have nothing to prove."

"What you mean, Sylvia, is that I have no one." Evie puts down her drink and stares into space a moment.

She's not laughing anymore. I've never really thought about how lonely her life must be. Within the last two years, she's lost both her husband and her son. She has a grandchild but he lives on the West Coast. Evie sends gifts, but her daughter-in-law has made it clear that she doesn't want any reminder of Evie's son in her life. I only know this from the various gossips who've been at BBG as long as Evie. The truth is, I've never asked her about any of it.

Even now, I tread carefully. "I'm sorry, Evie. You're just so strong that sometimes I forget you've lost so much."

"Yes, well. When you get to be a certain age, I suppose we've all lost something. God, this piano player is total shit."

And just like that, I know the subject is closed. So I turn and follow Evie's gaze behind me to where a young man, maybe in his late twenties, plays a popular song on the piano. I can't place it but I know I've heard it on the radio . . .

"It's Coldplay," Evie says. "He's not in the right key. And his timing is off. But look at all those tips in his jar. It's a shame when we stop demanding quality."

Evie's fingers start moving up and down the side of the table. As she plays, it's like her hands go back in time. Her crooked knuckles and papery skin are replaced by long, graceful fingers that move masterfully through air. I know she was a professional pianist for a number of years and then transitioned into teaching music at a local college in Boston before moving down to BBG about seven or so years ago. But from what I heard, she played for fun at dinner parties and such while down in Boca. And then, all of a sudden, she stopped.

I realize I never asked her about this. And so I clear my throat. "Why did you stop playing piano, Evie? The arthritis?"

"I stopped when Julian overdosed."

Oh. Maybe the subject isn't closed. I'm not sure what to say and so I let Evie continue playing piano along the table. When she finishes, she lays her hands flat. Neither of us speaks.

The waitress drops off our appetizers and second round of drinks. Evie and I both reach for ours. Her eyes are dry but, right now, the saddest eyes I've ever seen. Like there's no more tears left for her grief. She lets out a breath. "When we lost Julian, I stopped doing the thing I love most. Henry did, too. He gave up golf. How silly is that? Our son died, so I donated my piano to a local elementary school and Henry donated his clubs to his best friend, Arthur. And that was it. It's almost funny."

"It's not funny at all, Evie."

"No. No, I suppose it's not." Evie looks away a long moment and then meets my eye. "Tell me more about that bride from hell, the one who set your lawn on fire."

"Laura Eliot? Why?"

"Didn't you hand her wedding over to some colleague of yours? Didn't she benefit greatly from your hard work and hardship? It seems like this woman might owe you a favor."

I sit with that a moment. Perhaps Evie is onto something. I start to slowly nod to myself. I then glance down and see Evie's hands still on the table. I grab them and hold them tight. "I'm so happy we did this."

She squeezes back. "Me, too."

Ten

Okay, don't say it. Do not say that Verena owes all of this to you, I think as I shift on the lilac sofa in the chicest waiting room I've ever seen. A receptionist named Miku smiles at me from behind a carved oak desk. Her silky black hair is highlighted with streaks of purple and pinned in a crown of braids.

"It'll be just a few minutes, Mrs. Fisher. Can I offer you something to drink? Cappuccino? Pellegrino? Aloe juice?"

I grimace. Gross. BBG started serving aloe juice at the gym. Everyone said it boosted collagen and helped with constipation. But I say none of this. Instead, I smile back at Miku. "Nothing, thank you."

Miku returns to her computer just as the phone rings. She answers in a throaty voice that belies her tiny frame. "Verena Heart's office. This is Miku."

I shake my head. Six years ago, Verena Heart was Verena Simmowitz, a forty-seven-year-old wedding planner with an office in a Connecticut strip mall, sandwiched between a dumpy nail salon and DK's Donuts. Now her office is the third floor of a Madison Avenue brownstone on Seventy-Second Street.

I was so inspired by my dinner with Evie last night that I sent an email to Verena asking if we could meet. I sent it just before midnight to the email address on her website. I wasn't even sure she'd respond, but I woke up to a message saying that I could come by this morning. And so here I am, at 9:00 a.m., sitting in her office waiting room. Everything is so beautiful that it makes me want to cry. The seating arrangements, all done in shades of purple, surround a Baccarat crystal and bronze coffee table in nineteenth-century neoclassical style. It's the real deal. Not a knockoff. I know this because I used to read *Town & Country* in what feels like a former life.

As an espresso machine whirs and whistles in the distance, I inhale. The air smells like hand-picked coffee beans and almond biscotti. I gaze at the walls, which naturally showcase Verena's most impressive weddings. There's one at the Plaza, one in the Hamptons, and of course a giant black-and-white photo of Laura Eliot tossing her bouquet.

My throat tightens.

I try to shake it off. This is ridiculous. This is ancient history. But then I see the framed cover shot of *Luxury Brides* next to Laura's picture and my face grows hot with rage.

Stop it, I tell myself. This is not Verena's fault. She didn't steal the job. I handed it to her. Sure, when *Luxury Brides* turned Laura's wedding into their cover story, they credited Verena instead of me. But it would've been strange if Verena had corrected them by saying, "It was Laura's former planner, Sylvia Fisher, who put all of this together. I only took over last minute because Laura and Sylvia are currently involved in a lawsuit."

Actually, would that have been so hard to say?

Okay, I'm not being fair. Verena was in the right place at the right time. She's also talented and hardworking. So I look around once more and remember my mantras: I am the architect of my own success. My mistakes don't define me. I can't make everyone happy; I'm not a jar of Nutella.

"Are you fucking kidding me, Dan? You ask me this now?"

My eyes fly open. I turn and take in a young woman, in her early thirties, painfully thin. She has just entered the office with a young man. He is already apologizing. "Please, Ashton. Just hear me out."

But Ashton walks away and plops herself on the periwinkle love seat across from me.

She takes out her phone and buries her face in it, trying to shut out the world.

Dan looks at Miku, who gives him a slight nod. She quietly picks up the phone on her desk and whispers something into the receiver. I try to eavesdrop but am distracted when the door opens again and another man, around my age, enters. He's on the shorter side, maybe five foot seven, and has a long-distance runner's physique, which makes sense given his "NYC Runners' Club" shirt and Adidas track pants. He's bald, wears glasses, and looks like he reads the real newspaper, not the online version. There's something very decent about him that is unfortunately ruined by his scowl.

He looks from Dan to Ashton and sighs. "Why am I here again?"

"Thanks for being so supportive, Dad." Ashton looks up from her phone and glares at her father. "I asked you to come to one appointment because I thought maybe you'd like to be a part of this wedding. But if you're going to complain the whole time, then just go. Do you have something to add, lady?"

I startle. "I beg your pardon?"

Ashton turns her glare to me. "You just rolled your eyes."

I see her father smirk. Dan stares at his feet as I swallow and try to think of something disarming to say when I'm saved.

"Ashton, Dan! So lovely to see you. And Mr. Morris, a pleasure." We all turn and see a young woman in the doorway between the main offices and the waiting room. She smiles warmly and asks, "Can I offer anyone anything while you wait for Verena? She's just finishing up at a vendor."

They all shake their heads and look at the ground. Sheesh. I'd forgotten how some weddings feel more like funerals. But I shake it off as the young woman turns to me and asks, "Sylvia?"

"That's me!" I answer brightly and leap out of my seat. I wince. I seem eager. Too eager.

But the young woman just smiles and extends her hand. "I'm Verena's assistant, Molly." She then points to the wireless earbuds young people wear these days like earrings. "I was on a crisis call with a flower vendor. So sorry to keep you waiting. Let's go on back. Love your shoes, by the way."

I follow Molly through the doorway, feeling a thrill as I sneak a look at my faux snakeskin Diane von Furstenberg kitten heels. I don't know why, but I want Molly to like me. She can't be older than twenty-six, but she has the air of someone who majored in astrophysics while making ends meet as a supermodel. Her black-and-cream Chloé dress matches her onyx-rimmed Prada glasses, and she has clearly mastered the art of high heels. I feel my spider veins flare up just looking at the lean curves of her calves as she escorts me down the corridor. But I force myself to walk taller. I'm here to get a job.

We pass a conference room, a kitchenette, and an office suite. Molly opens the French doors to the suite and I see a workstation that is as complicated as a strategic missile operation's HQ. Molly's desk, complete with the largest Apple computer screen I've ever seen, is covered in pink, yellow, and green sticky notes. There are giant calendars mounted along the walls, each with color-coded pushpins tacking on names and numbers and pictures of all things wedding and beyond—from roses to zebras. I stare, slack-jawed.

Molly notices and explains. "Verena likes to have pictures so that the brides can visualize their big day."

I nod as though this makes total sense despite the fact that I'm staring at a photo of Charmin toilet paper. What on earth could this mean?

Hmm. Perhaps the bride has insisted that the venue's lavatories be outfitted with quality toilet paper for the guests?

I gesture to the door behind Molly's. "Is that Verena's office? I'm so looking forward to seeing her after all these years. When will she be back?"

"That is her office. But she's out and then unfortunately tied up for the rest of today." Molly sits behind her desk and motions for me to sit in the single straight-backed chair across from her. Just as I do, her cell phone beeps. She looks at it and sighs. As she types a reply, she asks, "So, Sylvia. You and Verena used to work together. Tell me about that."

"We didn't work together so much as near one another." I pause a moment. Molly is still typing. I hate when people do this. Louis does this. So does my daughter. I take a deep breath and politely wait for Molly to finish.

But Molly waves a hand. "Keep going. I'm listening. Just have to handle a quick dress-fitting fiasco."

I grit my teeth and try to keep my voice pleasant. "Well, like I was saying. We worked near each other in Connecticut. We were colleagues." I perk up a little. The word "colleague" makes me feel professional. "As Verena knows, I have extensive experience with different types of weddings and, of course, brides. In fact, I can tell you about some—"

"How charming," Molly interrupts, finally finished with her phone. "You were the neighborhood wedding planner."

I flush. "Not quite. Well, sort of. My clients were local. But I planned weddings all over the, um, Northeast." Molly gives me yet another smile. Is she patronizing me?

I clear my throat. "I don't mean to be rude, Molly, but when will Verena be here? I had hoped to talk to her personally."

"Verena is extremely busy. I handle all of her preliminary interviews. The good news is that we are looking for a second assistant. The bad news is that we have so many candidates."

"I see." I tighten my lips.

"But don't be discouraged. I think it's inspiring you would be willing to restart as an assistant. And when I read your email about how you and Verena have known one another for years, we wanted to be in touch immediately as a courtesy."

"A courtesy?" Unbelievable. Verena is having her assistant kiss me off. I feel slapped. "What does that mean? Is this a pretend interview?"

"Of course not. We would never waste your time." Molly says, now serious. "In fact, let's begin the formal interview. In a few words, describe your greatest professional strength."

"Well," I begin, "I've always been good in a—" Beep!

Molly's phone interrupts me. "Keep talking. I'm listening," she says as she texts.

Fuck her. I tuck a strand of hair behind my ear. "My greatest professional strength is telephone etiquette. And, apparently, my greatest professional weakness is impulse control."

I get up, reach across the desk, and pluck the phone out of Molly's hand. She stares at me, stunned. "What are you doing?"

"I'm tired of staring at your forehead while we speak. It's rude, disrespectful, and, frankly, a little bizarre. I certainly hope you don't treat clients like this." Molly opens her mouth, but I shake my head. "Do not interrupt me. While I appreciate the courtesy interview, I expected the actual courtesy of Verena seeing me herself. I'll find my way out. Take care."

I place Molly's phone on the desk and walk out of the office. I head back down the hallway and out into the waiting room, where Ashton now stands with tears pouring down her face.

Dan tries to put his arms around her. "I'm sorry, Ashton. I didn't mean anything by it."

But she pushes him away. He looks helplessly at Ashton's father, who just shrugs and flexes his feet, presumably to stretch his calves. Oy.

I glance at Miku, who is now ushering a middle-aged couple back toward the conference room. I hold the door open for them. Miku nods *thanks* and tells the couple, "I'll make your lattes and Molly will be right with you." Her voice is chipper, but it's obvious she's trying to clear the waiting room as the three of them disappear into the inner office area.

I close the door behind them just as Ashton's father sighs. "Jesus, Ashton. Dan was just trying to help."

Dan nods. "You're so stressed. I thought a beach wedding would be romantic. Just you and me. We can forget all this stupid wedding stuff."

Ashton sucks in a breath so sharp, I worry she's dislocated one of her jutting ribs. "All this stupid wedding stuff," she repeats. Her voice is tight and low. "I guess I'm stupid, too. Just a stupid uptight crazy bridezilla because I give a shit about the difference between roses and peonies and want this one day to be really fucking special."

Before Dan can respond, the door opens and closes with a *whoosh!* Ashton is gone. Dan sinks back onto the love seat. He looks at Ashton's father. "Frank, what do I do?"

Frank shrugs. "Clearly my daughter has made a choice about what your wedding should look like. You are not part of that choice. Get used to it. That's what marriage is."

"Just because your marriage is lousy doesn't mean theirs will be," I blurt before I can stop myself.

Both of them turn and look at me. Frank opens his mouth as though to say something but instead gets up and storms out of the office just like his daughter.

Dan looks so helpless. I can't help myself. I sit beside him in the love seat. "Can I be honest, Dan?"

Dan blinks, clearly thrown by a stranger practically sitting in his lap. These seats are smaller than I thought, actually. But I press on. "Do you love this woman? Do you want to spend the rest of your life with her? And her father?" I add as an afterthought.

Dan blinks again. "Who are you?"

"I'm Sylvia. And this isn't my first wedding rodeo. I want to help, dear. But I need to know—do you love her?"

Dan lets out a long breath. "I do. Very much." He looks at the ground. "She's not usually like this. She's just having a hard time right now. Her parents are getting divorced. It's so fucked up." He pauses. "Sorry for cursing."

I smile inwardly. This boy is polite. I pat his arm. "No need to apologize. It is fucked up that her parents are getting divorced in the midst of you getting married. But that's life. I recently walked in on my husband having sex with another woman. It was awful. They were just so . . . naked."

I wince at the memory.

Dan looks unsure of what to say. I clear my throat. "I realize that was 'TMI,' as my daughter would say. But my point is, children shouldn't get caught in their parents' cross fire. It's not fair. This is a day Ashton has dreamed about since she was a girl and now it feels joyless and filled with tension. Can you see how that might make her feel?"

Dan's eyes go wide. "That's why I thought we should elope. Go somewhere drama-free."

"What a lovely and thoughtful suggestion. But Ashton wants a wedding. For her to give that up because her parents can't get along is sad."

"What do I do?"

I look at the deep bags under Dan's eyes. "Have you tried talking to her parents?"

"And say what? You're ruining everything? Your daughter turns on the shower because she doesn't want me to hear her cry? That she went from being the kindest, most down-to-earth girl ever to now telling waitresses to fuck off because they put too much ice in her water?"

"Yes. Well, a version of that. You need to be honest with them."

Dan shakes his head. "Maybe we should postpone stuff. Get married after her parents sort out their mess."

"When's the wedding?"

"In two months. But Ashton's made no decisions. It's like she wants this wedding so badly but sabotages things. I don't even know if she has a dress."

My face falls. Dan notices. "You have the same look Molly and Verena get. But then they smile and tell me not to worry. Is this normal? Does Verena just magically put together a wedding even if the bride hasn't chosen a single thing? My sister says we're in trouble. I honestly have no idea. What do you think?"

I sigh. "I'm sorry, Dan. It sounds like things are complicated. But Verena is a talented planner and if she says not to worry, then trust her. This is part of the job." I pat Dan's arm one final time. "Find Ashton. Apologize for suggesting that you elope. Explain that you understand why she wants this day to be special, and then promise that you'll do whatever it takes to help her. You are her rock. And she is yours. Because that's what marriage is—two people promising to support, to love, and to be there for each other. She is not alone. In fact, say that twice. 'Ashton, you are not alone.'"

I let out a breath, a little hypnotized by my own speech, and watch as Dan slowly repeats my words to himself. His face starts to shine and I feel that particular rush of relief and excitement when the world suddenly makes sense. I slowly rise to my feet. I am a wedding planner. This is what I do.

I'm feeling so pleased, in fact, that it takes a moment to register someone calling my name.

"Sylvia Fisher? Is that you?"

I turn around and come face-to-face with Verena.

"What are you doing here?" she asks as she stands in her office foyer. She then looks at Dan, who is still talking to himself. "Is everything okay? Where's Ashton?"

Dan smiles. "She had a breakdown and ran off. But I know how to help. Thank you, Sylvia. I'm going to do exactly what you said."

Dan rushes out, leaving me and Verena alone. She stares, bewildered. "My god, it's been so long. You look terrific. What just happened with Ashton and Dan?"

My face darkens. "Just stop, Verena. I know you had Molly give me the kiss-off. It's fine. It was presumptuous to assume that you'd help me out in the first place. And as for what just happened with your clients? You're welcome. Again."

I leave the waiting room and walk to the elevator. I punch the button. It opens.

I step on and realize that I'm shaking. I have never told off so many people in such a short span of time. My brain and body are on major ass-kicking overload. I feel twenty feet tall.

As I get out of the elevator and exit the building, I stride down the tree-lined sidewalk like an Amazonian warrior. I am fast and furious and would roar aloud if I were one notch less self-aware. Plus, I'm not sure I know how to roar.

"Sylvia! Please, stop!"

I turn. It's Verena again. Her once frizzy auburn hair has been polished into a perfect bob. She tries to smooth it down but is still panting. "I have no idea why you were in my office. I would've asked Molly but I literally ran down the stairs to catch you. And we both know how much I fucking hate exercise."

I briefly remember a time years ago when I once asked Verena to join me for an aerobics class. She cracked open a Dr Pepper, lit a cigarette, and laughed. I suddenly feel so confused. I try to read her face. "You really don't know why I'm here?"

Verena exhales. "Look, Sylvia. I've become one of those annoying people who's always busy. But seeing as how you just saved me a couple hours worth of premarital counseling for Ashton and Dan, let's go back to my office. If nothing else, I'm dying to hear what's going on."

VERENA LEANS BACK in her ergonomic chair and shakes her head admiringly. "Good for you, Sylvia. Screw that guy. Most people wouldn't have had the balls to leave their husband after all those years."

I blush at the compliment. We're now back in Verena's office. Her proper office, that is, which is shockingly monk-like. Her glass desk is bare except for a laptop computer, a notebook, and a pen. I sit across from her on a simple leather chair. There's a bank of windows on one wall that offers a tranquil view of treetops. You'd hardly know we were in a city. The other three walls are bare. No shelves, no whiteboards, no magazine displays. There are no rugs and no lamps. The only other thing in this room is a mini fridge, which is behind Verena's desk.

Verena turns to open the fridge and takes out two glass bottles of IBC root beer. She offers me one. I accept it, smiling. "I remember your affinity for soda."

Verena twists off her bottle cap. "It's better than my affinity for vodka. So, tell me. What about having your marriage fall apart inspired the desire to reignite your career as a wedding planner?"

I bite my lip. "I hadn't quite thought of it like that."

Verena laughs. "Don't be embarrassed. I love it. Look at me. I've been married four times. The first two don't count, as I consider them moments of temporary insanity coupled with crippling alcoholism. But the latter two happened during sobriety and confirmed my deepest suspicion—I am not marriage material."

"Surely that's not true."

"Oh, but it is. I have a deep fear of intimacy. And self-sabotaging tendencies. But that's between me and my overpaid therapist. What's always been true is that I love weddings. The shoemaker with no shoes."

Verena's eyes gleam. I can't help but laugh and sip my root beer. The fizzy sweetness makes me feel childlike in all the best ways. Like I'm tasting a carnival or running through the sprinklers on a hot summer day. I take another sip. Sure, money and success have made Verena shinier. Her teeth are bleached. Her skin has the glow of hundred-dollar creams. She's still chubby, but the extra weight makes her look younger. And she carries it in what can only be custom-made suits and Chanel flats. Her look is at once refined yet approachable. I imagine clients feel taken care of when they're with her.

She tilts her head to the side and asks, "Yes?"

"I never know you had a drinking problem. Or were divorced." I wince a little. I didn't mean to be so blunt.

But Verena smiles. "It was a lifetime ago. The black hole of my twenties and thirties. When we met, I was single, several years sober, and in my forties." She pauses a moment. "You were always kind to me, Sylvia. Other women in town thought I was an overweight weirdo with a big mouth. No husband. No kids. I'm the youngest of six. I hustled all of my nieces and nephews, forced them to let me do their weddings for nearly no money in order to build a name. And then you gave me Laura. That was a gift. I always wondered why you cared enough to find her a planner. Why not just let her wedding fall to pieces?"

"I'd known Laura for years. She was my daughter's close friend. I couldn't abandon her."

"Bullshit."

"I beg your pardon?"

"You didn't want *Luxury Brides* to cancel their coverage of it. You hoped it'd be redemption. All those clients who disappeared after the Laura fiasco would read it and call you back."

I'm about to disagree but then sigh. "I suppose that's true. At least partly. But that's not quite how things turned out."

"No, it isn't." Verena glances at her watch. "Look, I can't blame Molly for not passing along your email to me. Her job is to make my life easier and that means vetting every person who writes to us looking for a job. I need another assistant who can continue making my life easier, and there are just too many people who are more experienced than you at this point."

I want to argue, but I've just taken a big sip of root beer. I try to swallow but my throat is tight. My eyes heat up with tears. This is ridiculous. Do not cry. Do not dare cry. I am a professional.

"Are you crying?"

Goddamn it. A tear leaks down my face. I swipe it with my hand. "I have allergies."

Verena watches me a moment. "I have allergies, too." She takes a tissue pack from her monogrammed Louis Vuitton tote bag and hands it to me. "I wasn't finished. Yes, there are people applying with more experience. And so it was only natural for Molly to dismiss you. But I like you, Sylvia. More than that, I trust you." Verena looks over my shoulder, as though seeing through the wall into Molly's office. "I already see Molly sharpening the knife that she'll inevitably stab in my back. She doesn't realize she's doing it. But every young person I hire eventually sells me out to go off on their own. Most of them fail. Why? Because they don't have grit. They expect everything to be Insta-fucking-perfect because that's the world we live in. But I want grit. I want loyalty. I want the person who finds out her husband is a cheating bastard and walks out to start anew." Verena now looks me squarely in the eye. "So here's my offer: Seeing as how you already made a connection, I'll put you on as my temporary assistant for Dan and Ashton's wedding. If all goes well, I bring you on as a full-time assistant."

My mouth hangs open. I can barely breathe. And so I wipe my eyes and search for the right words to express my gratitude.

But Verena holds up a hand. "Cards on the table: Ashton's parents are in the middle of a nasty divorce. Her mom signed up for a poetry workshop and started sleeping with the instructor, who is all of thirty-one years old. Same age as Ashton. Naturally, Ashton's father is furious. It's ugly. So there's that. Also, the pay sucks. Because you're starting on a trial basis, there's no overtime and no health insurance. My brides have access to us twenty-four hours a day. That's part of what I offer. It's how I've built my business. And so I don't want to hear about crazy brides or family dramas or lawns being set on fire. Whatever happens, you handle it. Can you do that?"

I let out a breath. "I can. I will." And then, unable to help myself, "I do, Verena."

Eleven

I t's official. I'm employed. It's been four hours since I've accepted Verena's offer and I'm sitting here in the conference room while Miku figures out how to split Molly's office into two workstations. I was terrified Molly would resent my presence. But when she returned, she gave me a big hug and said she couldn't wait to be officemates. Then she promised to take me to the next sample sale she hears about that features Jill Stuart because I would sell a kidney for one of those car-wash skirts.

Of course, I'm keeping Verena's knife-in-the-back comment in mind. Yes, Molly enjoys having a little power. I could tell by the way she asked me to fetch the lunches this afternoon.

But I didn't mind. I loved walking over to the deli on Third Avenue. I loved telling the man behind the counter that I was placing an order for my coworkers. I had purpose. And petty cash.

Verena treats for lunch if we eat at the office while working.

And so it's off to a great start. This conference room is somehow both large and intimate. There's eight chairs total around the walnut table: three on each side, one at each head. I sit in the center on the left side. Behind me is a low console with bottles of water that are flanked by two small vases of hydrangeas. An elongated black pendant light shines from above. On the table, I've lined up my phone, my iced coffee, my trusty legal pad, and two pens—one black, one red—so that I can make notes while working my way through Dan and Ashton's wedding file, which Miku printed and organized in a dark purple binder. I read through each page carefully, immersing myself in all things Dan and Ashton. First, the clip of their engagement announcement in the *New York Times*: they met while building yurts in Peru, dated for one year, and got engaged on top of Mount Kilimanjaro.

Adventurous and altruistic, I write. This makes me think about Dan's idea of eloping—they do sound like the kind of couple who would elope. Or, at the very least, get married while white water rafting somewhere in Norway. But perhaps that's what the honeymoon is for.

I dive back into the biographical section of the file. Ashton is an only child. She grew up in Old Westbury, a posh part of Long Island. Her father, Frank, works in finance and commutes to the city. Her mother, Nina, is an interior designer who has worked all over the world but has recently slowed down to pursue other creative endeavors. Like poetry.

My stomach drops. I feel guilty for my rude remarks to Frank. I owe him an apology. To be fair, I didn't know his wife was sleeping with someone as young as their daughter. How would I feel if Belinda were thirty years younger? Just knowing she's thirty pounds lighter than me makes me homicidal.

I return to reading: Dan works in marketing at a lifestyle company that specializes in vegan apparel and Ashton teaches restorative yoga while studying to be a social worker. Lovely. But I can't imagine that the two of them can afford an apartment on East Eighty-Fifth Street. Turns out, the condo is Ashton's parents' pied-à-terre. They gave it to the couple as an engagement present. I shake my head. You really do need wealthy parents to live in this city. Either that or forty-plus years of expensive anniversary and birthday jewels to pawn.

The section on Dan's family is more straightforward. He grew up in Wilmette, a nice Chicago suburb. He has an older sister. His parents are happily married and predictably intrusive, according to Verena's commentary. Well, at least they live eight hundred miles away.

As for wedding details, the date is set for December seventeenth, two months away. The venue is the ballroom at the Plaza Hotel, which surprises me. A hotel wedding is too stuffy, too indoors, for this couple. But. The fact that there is a venue is a win. And from what I can see, it's our only win. Dan wasn't joking. There's nothing else: No color theme, no bridal party list, no menu, no cake, no flowers, no music. No dress.

How can there be no dress? The best part of any wedding is the dress. And from what I heard earlier, Ashton is desperate to have a perfect wedding. And yet she's made no decisions. Something is very wrong here. I put down my pen and think aloud. "What is going on with this girl? Where is her mother?"

The question hits me like a reflex, and I feel instantly embarrassed. Why am I so quick to judge Nina and defend Frank? Because he was cuckolded? Sure, I can relate to being cheated on. But maybe Frank was a lousy husband. Maybe he stopped noticing when his wife got a new haircut. Maybe he dismissed her desire to travel, telling her that the Jersey Shore was really no different than the Mediterranean, and then rolled his eyes whenever she wanted to try a new restaurant.

I narrow my eyes. Maybe I don't owe Frank an apology. This poetry teacher might be exactly what Nina needs. So what if he's young? Samantha from *Sex and the City* fell in love with a younger man. A gorgeous model with a giant heart. And cock.

I flush. When have I ever used the word "cock"? But there is something thrilling about it.

Something powerful. I can't resist saying it out loud in the glass-walled privacy of the conference room, albeit in a low voice. "I wonder if Nina's poet lover has a giant cock."

The door opens and Ashton's voice cuts through the air like acid. "Ask her yourself. She'd love to tell you all about it."

I whip my head around and see Ashton, escorted by Miku, enter the conference room.

Note to self: Next time, sit facing the door.

Miku, mercifully, remains neutral. She looks me in the eye. "Verena called Ashton and let her know you would be joining the team. Verena is still out with another client. Let me know if either of you needs anything."

My face is a furnace as Miku leaves the room and Ashton slumps into a chair across from me. "My mom loves talking about her new sex life. It's really awesome." She pulls her hair into a loose ponytail. She wears baggy workout clothes and her face is even paler than before.

"I'm sorry," I say quietly. "I didn't know anyone was coming."

"Clearly."

I take a deep breath. I've had this job for less than an afternoon.

I cannot lose it. And so I offer Ashton my warmest smile. "Let's start over. It's nice to formally meet you. I'm Sylvia."

I extend my hand to shake, but Ashton just rolls her eyes. "So. Dan really likes you. But my dad hates you. And I think I hate you, too."

"Well. I suppose we have nowhere to go but up." I try another smile.

Ashton scowls. "Why did Verena hire you?"

"Do you want to get married?"

"Excuse me?"

I lean across the table. "My entire job right now is your wedding. But I cannot in good faith push you into something if I don't believe you truly want it."

"You mean if I call everything off, you don't have to deal with me."

"The opposite. I'm desperate to help you." I sigh. "When my daughter was engaged, we spent hours looking through magazines, cutting out pictures, and debating things like trumpet versus mermaid. Lace versus silk. We even made pro and con lists for the ball gown. And that's just dresses. We tasted cakes at four different bakeries. We smelled every flower. What I'm trying to say, Ashton, is that you've done none of the fun wedding stuff. How come?"

Tears float behind Ashton's eyes. But she stubbornly lifts her chin. I press on. "Dan seems lovely and kind. But if you're not ready—"

"Stop! I want to get married. Okay?"

"Not okay. What are you so afraid of?"

"You're a wedding planner. Not my fucking therapist."

"A wedding planner is a fucking therapist."

Ashton startles. Gosh, people really react when women over the age of sixty curse. It's like a superpower. I take a breath and soften my voice but remain firm, remembering my mantras. I am the captain of this ship. "Why can't a bride, so insistent upon having a wedding, make any decisions? There's something going on. Talk to me, Ashton. I'm a stranger. But sometimes strangers are the best listeners."

Ashton opens her mouth to reply but then closes it. She looks away and stares at the wall. The fact that she doesn't storm out of the room is a victory. I bite my cheek to keep from saying anything else.

When she runs a hand through her hair, I notice that her engagement ring is simple. In fact, I don't even think there is a diamond. I tilt my head to get a better look. Nope. It's just two tiny slivers of gold braided together. Interesting. I take a moment to really look at this young woman. Despite the gray color, her face is quite lovely. High cheekbones and large, wide-set eyes. She wears no makeup. Her hair is thick and luxurious and definitely her natural color. She wears the sort of athleisure wear I see all the girls in these days, but I don't spot a designer Alo Yoga or Lululemon logo anywhere. I glance at her canvas New York Public Library tote bag that she probably got for free and realize that for someone so wealthy, there's nothing ostentatious about her.

"I can't cook," Ashton finally says.

I scrunch my brow. "Excuse me?"

"My baking is shit," she continues as though she's making complete sense and this is a two-way conversation. "I've had housekeepers my whole life and then did that laundry-service thing in college, which is embarrassing but my mom signed me up and I didn't protest. So basically I can't cook, clean, or do laundry."

I nod slowly, trying to comprehend. "Is Dan under the impression that you're some kind of domestic goddess?"

Ashton finally laughs. "God, no. He loves to tease me about the time I blew up our microwave trying to make popcorn. He says it's sexy that I don't know what a garlic press is."

I smile but am very confused. Ashton can tell. She sighs. "Look,

Sylvia. I'm not usually such a bitch. I don't even like that word. I'm just . . . Is it hot in here?" Her voice trails off. Beads of sweat bloom across her forehead.

There's a pyramid of Fiji waters behind me on the console. I grab one and hand it to her. "Thanks." She's now pouring sweat. She takes off her sweatshirt and mops her face.

Her breasts spill over the top of her fitted tank top in an uncomfortable-looking way. As though she bought a top two sizes too small, which seems odd. She opens the bottle of water, takes a tentative sip, then grimaces.

"Have you eaten enough today?" I ask gently. "I know brides are on all sorts of excessive diets, but you need to take care of yourself." I open my purse and start pulling things out. "I have a granola bar, some pistachio nuts, dried apricots . . . Oh! In the kitchen, there's half a tuna sandwich—"

"No!" Ashton cuts me off, her voice hoarse. "Please stop talking about food. I'm fine. I'm just dehydrated." She takes another tiny sip of water. It's like she's rationing her last drops in the middle of the Sahara.

My phone beeps.

We both look at it on the table beside me. It lights up with a text message. And then another. And another. All from "Louis Fisher, Fuckwit." Evie changed Louis's contact information in my phone the other day. It seemed like a good idea at the time. But now my face flames as Ashton raises a sweaty brow.

"Sorry." I stammer. "Let me put it on vibrate." My hands feel heavy and old as I fumble to unlock the passcode while the phone beeps with more messages. What on earth does Louis want? Why can't he send one long message instead of pressing Send every time he has a goddamn thought?

"Maybe you should answer it." Ashton's voice is thick, as though it's an effort for her to speak.

I finally unlock the phone and switch it to vibrate. There's no way I'm talking to Louis now. Especially when Ashton looks moments from fainting. Her face is white and her breaths are shallow. I reach for my purse and find the emergency treat, a dark chocolate Snickers that I keep in a special eyeglasses case so that it never gets mushed. "I'm worried about you. Take a bite." I tear open the bar and hold it out. The scent of caramel-coated nuts and chocolate floats into the air.

"For Christ's sake, I'm not hungry!" Ashton grabs her things and bolts out of the room.

I drop my face into my hands. Just when she was opening up to me, I go and shove a candy bar in her face. Damn it, Sylvia. Wedding planner 101: every bride feels the pressure of looking thin on her wedding day. Sad, but true. In a flood, memories rush back to me. The crazy cleanses, the fasting, my bride who only ate pink foods and therefore subsisted on a diet of grapefruit, shrimp, and strawberry jam. I may not like it, but it's my job to navigate low blood sugar and starvation-induced mood swings. In fact, it's the "whole fucking art of it," as Izzy said not too long ago.

She was right. And so I straighten up, take a bite of the offending Snickers, and force myself to give Ashton a few minutes to cool off before I find her and apologize.

My phone vibrates again. Jesus. I take another bite of the candy bar and take my phone back out of my bag. This time, I unlock it with ease. What on earth does this man want? If it's just to tell me that his therapist brought up some weird mother issues, I simply cannot . . .

My heart stops. My throat swells with panic and there's a hollow ringing in my ears as I read:

The creditors called me.

They were alerted about your new checking account.

Where did you get that much cash?

Why didn't you tell me you had it?

I logged into your bank.

I guessed your username.

I guessed your password.

You should make these things much more difficult.

I was able to drain the account.

There are more texts but my eyes blur. My chest is so tight that I can't swallow the hunk of candy in my mouth. So I spit it into my hand. The saliva-covered chocolate mush oozes down my palm. I grab my bag and phone with my clean hand and hurry out of the conference room.

I speed-walk toward the bathroom. Thank god the hallway is empty. Thank god Verena has a single-use restroom in this office. It's very serene. There's a granite vessel sink set into a marble countertop, one of those high-tech toilets that washes your tush, and just the faintest scent of lilac. The walls are black and there are two amber light fixtures flanking the mirror above the sink. I turn a corner and see the door. I tuck my phone under my arm and open the handle, desperate for a quiet place to call my bank, to call Louis, to call a hit man . . .

"What the hell?!" Ashton looks up.

"It was open," I say in a whisper as I fling the candy bar into the trash and slam the door shut with my foot. I barely notice that Ashton is on her knees, bent over the toilet bowl, which is just to the right of the sink.

"Can I please have some privacy?" Ashton coughs. She is completely oblivious to my state of my mind, which is probably a good thing.

I pretend I don't hear her and turn on the sink. I rub soap all over my hands, letting cool foam bubble up over my skin. It feels so soothing. Water rushes over my wrists and a steady stream of chocolate disappears down the drain.

"Seriously? Do you not see that I'm sick here?" Ashton lifts her head and wipes her brow.

I turn and look at her. "You're not sick. You're pregnant."

Her mouth drops. I can tell she wants to protest, but another wave of nausea seizes her. The water is still running. I grab a hand towel from a little gold basket next to the sink and soak it. Then, I kneel next to her and place it across her neck. "This should help." I sit all the way down and rub her back. "Don't talk. It makes it worse. Just breathe."

Ashton places her head against the cool, tiled wall next to the toilet. The muscles along her shoulder blades start to sink as she inhales, then exhales.

"You're really good at this." She sighs a little.

I reach for a wad of toilet paper and wipe a dribble of vomit from her chin. I then return to massaging her. It's true. Louis used to beg me for foot rubs.

Louis. My stomach drops again. How could he do this to me? Surely it's just a scare tactic. He can't really take my money. I take another deep breath. I need to get out of here. I rub Ashton's back once more and then slowly stand up.

"Where are you going?" Ashton's voice is childlike.

"You asked for privacy. We can talk tomorrow. And congratulations." I manage to smile. "A baby. How marvelous."

I open the door and am about to step out when Verena's throaty voice echoes from down the hall. "Frank! I'm so glad you're here. I'll find Ashton and Sylvia and meet you in the conference room."

Before I can register anything, Ashton somehow leaps up and yanks me back inside the bathroom. She shuts the door, this time making sure to lock it, and then slides to the ground and sits with her back pressed against it so I can't leave.

My jaw drops. "What are you doing?"

"No one knows I'm pregnant. Not my parents. Not Dan. Not Verena. You can't tell anyone. I won't let you out until you promise."

There's a rapping at the door. "Hello?" Verena's voice cuts in. "Sylvia? Are you in here?"

I open my mouth to answer, but Ashton beats me to it. "It's Ashton! I'll be out in a sec."

"Sorry to disturb you, darling. Do you know where Sylvia is?"

I open my mouth again but realize I can't answer. Why would I be in the bathroom with Ashton? We're not teenage girls at prom. This is ridiculous. What do I say?

As though reading my mind, Ashton calls out, "I asked Sylvia to grab me a smoothie from the juicery across the street."

"Great! I'll text her to meet us in the conference room. We'll see you when you're ready." We both wait for the sound of Verena's shoes to grow fainter in the distance.

I take off my blazer and fan my blouse against my chest. "Ashton, I will keep your secret until we discuss things further. But here's the plan for now: I can't arrive with no smoothie if you said I went to get a smoothie. So you go first. Tell Verena and your father that I called to let you know they didn't have the flavor you requested. I'm on my way back. Understood?"

Ashton offers a half smile. "This is kind of fun."

My head throbs. Ashton and I have gone from "I think I hate you" to accomplices in lying to my boss in a span of twenty minutes. Then again, she is pregnant and scared. And I did just give her a massage and wipe vomit from her face.

"See you in there." Ashton pulls on her sweatshirt and goes to the sink to wash up. When finished, she flashes me a thumbs-up.

I flash her one back and then nearly push her out the door. I firmly shut and lock it.

Finally. Alone. I take a deep breath and reach for my phone.

It vibrates in my hand. Shit. It's Verena. **In the conference room with Ashton and Frank.**

Shakily, I write back. **Be there soon.**

Then, I take a deep breath and dial Louis. It rings only once.

"Sylvia, don't be angry." Louis's voice is at once familiar and so far away.

"I'm not angry. I'm homicidal. Where's my money?" I clench the sink counter so hard, my fingers nearly snap in half.

"Let me explain."

"I'm done hearing you 'explain' things. Where is my goddamn money?"

"The creditors called. I needed to liquidate the account or else they would've seized it. Where'd you get that much cash anyway?"

"I sold my jewelry. You don't want the money in an account? Fine. Wire it back to me and I'll hide it under my mattress."

"You can't hide sixty-five hundred dollars beneath a mattress in New York."

He sounds so satisfied. I roll my eyes. "Yes, Louis. You've seen my account activity and have deduced that I'm in Manhattan. Bravo." I try to stay as quiet as possible but pure rage boils through me. "How could you do this to me?"

"You can't just walk away and start a new life. We have responsibilities here." Louis clucks his tongue.

I grit my teeth. I can picture him right now, standing in our living room, rolling a tennis ball between his fingers as he thinks. I'm sure he hasn't missed a single fucking day of that tennis round-robin thing he does so that he can feel twenty-five again.

Do I want to be twenty-five again?

The thought knocks me off-balance. I stare at my reflection in the mirror above the sink. My hair is matted against my head, and mascara cracks in the fine lines next to my eyes. I grab some toilet paper and lightly dab the makeup. It smears a bit, giving me a smoky look. I shake my hair out behind me. It lands just below my shoulders in a wind-blown way. Or at least that's how I'm choosing to see it.

I stand up straighter. "Louis," I finally say. "If I were twenty-five right now, I'd be apologizing to you. I'd think everything was my fault. But I'm sixty-three. You want to know the truth? I'm in Manhattan working as a wedding planner. And I don't care if you and Isabel think I'm ridiculous. In fact, I've decided that it's none of my business what anyone thinks of me."

I'm breathing hard. I cradle the phone to my ear and wet another washcloth. I untuck my blouse and wipe under my armpits and beneath my breasts. Thank God for menopause. No amount of sweat scares me now.

"Sylvia," Louis says slowly. "No one is calling you ridiculous. Just come to Florida and we'll talk. I can give you your money then."

"Are you *extorting* me?"

"You owe me a conversation."

"I owe you nothing!" I practically spit. "When I walked in on my husband of forty years being straddled by another woman, I felt less betrayed than I do now. How dare you take from me? All you do is take and take and take."

My shirt now sticks to me in wet patches. Oh, fuck it. I take the blouse off and shove it in my purse. I fan myself dry and can't help but admire my new "old bra." I bought it three years ago at Saks but took the tags off this morning. It's a deep mauve silk with lace scalloping along the straps and bust. I'm wearing the matching, scoop-bottomed underpants. Not a thong—I'm not a sadist—but the seamless cut creates a smooth silhouette beneath my skirt. I narrow my eyes. I am never going back to sagging beige *anything* again.

"Sylvia?" Louis's voice cuts into my ear. "Hello? Did I lose you?"

"Yes," I answer.

And just like that, I hang up.

I take a deep breath. I'll have to sort out my cash situation later. Verena, Ashton, and Frank are waiting for me. And so I slip on my blazer and button it up over my bra. Hmm. This is actually quite sexy. I turn to my side to make sure I look decent. I almost smile. Time to get to work. I take another deep breath, open the bathroom door, and walk right into Frank.

"Oof!" I drop my bag as we bump shoulders. My snacks, wallet, phone, makeup . . . everything spills to the floor. Mortified, I drop to my hands and knees and start shoving things back in my purse.

"Here," Frank says as he hands me my blouse. He's on the ground as well. "Thanks." I stuff it into my bag.

We both stand up. It's awkward. "I didn't realize anyone was waiting," I finally say and try to read his face. Did he hear anything while I was on the phone with Louis? No. He couldn't have. I was so quiet. But why is he just standing there? And why won't he look me in the eye? Sweat starts trickling down my back again. I'm about to unbutton my blazer but mercifully catch myself. Good gracious, I can't even imagine . . . The thought of flashing Frank—or anyone—makes me laugh aloud.

That gets Frank's attention. He finally looks at me. I push a smile onto my face and put out my hand. "I apologize for how we already met. I'm Sylvia, Verena's new assistant."

"Frank, father of the bride." He shakes my hand. For someone with such a small and wiry frame, his hands are quite large. His nails are neatly trimmed and he sports one of those enormous runner's watches that computes heart rate, gravitational force, and a host of other diagnostics. His glasses are a little smudged. I almost reach out to wipe them but catch myself.

I blush and step to the side. "The restroom's all yours. And I'm sorry about earlier. I shouldn't have said anything about your marriage."

I bite down hard on my lip. Shit shit shit! I was supposed to pretend that never happened.

I wait for Frank to snap at me. But instead he offers the same half smile I saw earlier on Ashton's face. "Sounds like we've both got lousy marriages." Frank steps around me and enters the restroom.

I wish the earth could literally swallow me whole. My brain blurs with all the personal information Frank now knows: I pawned my jewelry, my family thinks I'm ridiculous, I walked in on my husband being straddled by another woman—

"Sylvia!" Verena's voice shocks me back to reality. She's down the hall, ushering me toward her with a hand. "Let's go. Miku is running an errand at the florist, so I need you to prepare a tray of coffee and tea for this meeting."

I feel suddenly drained by this entire day. Like someone turned my battery off. But I have no choice. I force myself forward.

Twelve

When Isabel used to have panic attacks before her final exams, she would wake me up at 2:00 a.m. and beg me to sit at the kitchen table and play Worst-Case Scenario. Poor Izzy. She was always so high-strung. She got diagnosed with IBS at age twelve and I have always done whatever I could to help her. And so we played a lot of Worst-Case Scenario, a game I once read about in, of all places, *Glamour*. It's supposed to show you that what you fear isn't really so bad. And so as I stand here in the office kitchen organizing a tray with French-press coffee, herbal teas, and sliced fruit from a platter that Miku orders daily, I try it out.

Bad thing that happened: Louis took all of my money.

Worst-case scenario: My paycheck from Verena doesn't cover my expenses. Evie's cash runs out and she hasn't yet found a job. We're evicted and forced to return to the Airbnb. After a week of washing up at Starbucks, we surrender to the Airbnb's bathroom. Evie slips on the slimy floor and cracks her head. She dies. Devastated, I wander the streets of New York until I'm delirious. I accidentally-on-purpose step in front of a subway train and kill myself. A mother and her young daughter witness this. The young girl is forever scarred and turns to drugs. Her parents sell their home to pay for rehab but . . .

Boiling water splashes my hand. I've overfilled the teapot. I blow on my fingers. Let's just move on.

Bad thing that happened: Ashton is pregnant and I've promised not to tell anyone.

Worst-case scenario: Verena finds out that I knew and fires me for not telling her. I have no income. Our cash runs out. Evie and I are evicted and . . .

I bite into a grape. I will not go down this imaginary road to hell again. Let's try a new game: Best-Case Scenario.

Bad thing that happened: Frank knows about my dreadful personal life.

Best-Case Scenario: Frank and I commiserate over cheating spouses and bond. One day, at a cake-tasting appointment, I make a witty but not bitter joke about Louis and Frank laughs. He offers to take me running. I meet him at Central Park. I'm wearing a pair of flattering, matte-black jogging tights. Somehow I have incredible endurance. We're jogging and chatting and the breeze blows my ponytail out behind me. After a couple of miles, we stop and buy one of those giant pretzels from a food vendor. We sit on a park bench to eat. Frank wipes salt from my chin. His fingers lightly graze my lips and he leans in gently . . .

I eat another grape. My cheeks flame and I feel a flutter of excitement inside my chest. Best-Case Scenario is a much better game. Of course I don't actually desire Frank. This was just a meditative exercise. I pick up the tray and head toward the conference room. Thankfully, the door is open just enough so that I can squeeze through without rebalancing the tray. But as soon as I walk in, my excitement evaporates. On one side of the table, Ashton sits next to Verena with her arms crossed. She flicks her eyes at the enormous catalogue of bridal gowns Verena has spread open between them and scowls. "I don't want to look like a fucking cake topper."

Why is this bridezilla back? Where did the other Ashton go? I want to say something but remember that Verena is in charge. I put the tray on the table, take a seat in a chair across from them, and wait for a cue before speaking.

Ashton glances at me briefly but says nothing. Verena keeps her attention focused solely on Ashton. "We're not choosing your specific dress, darling. I just want to get a sense of the shape and style you prefer before we have another appointment."

I tilt my head slightly. Verena is a portrait of patience. You'd never guess that the previous appointments were disasters. According to the notes, Ashton made the consultant cry at the first, had a raging fight with her mother at the second, and stood Verena up at the third. But Verena is completely composed as she flips pages of the catalogue before stopping. "Oooh! This would look dynamite on your lean figure. Don't you agree, Sylvia?"

Verena turns the picture around. I peer at a willowy model wearing a skintight trumpet gown with a corseted back. I bite my lip. Ashton may not gain much weight over the next two months, but she's going to need something that doesn't feel quite like bondage.

"Maybe a dress with more flow," I suggest.

"Are you calling me fat?" Ashton glares.

My jaw drops. I find Ashton's eyes and try to communicate: *You are pregnant.* She looks away.

"Ashton," I say with meaning. "Remember how we discussed things earlier?"

"Not really," she says coolly.

I look at the table, unsure what to do. Verena notices and reaches for a piece of pineapple. "What did you discuss earlier, Sylvia? Catch me up." Her tone is casual, but I hear an underlying edge.

Before I can respond, however, the door opens and Frank enters. "Sorry about that. Got caught on the phone. What'd I miss?"

Ashton folds her arms. "Sylvia thinks I'm too chunky to wear a fitted dress."

Frank slides into a chair next to Ashton. He knits his brow. "What?"

"I certainly do not!" I blurt. Damn it. I can't lose my cool. But blood pounds in my ears as I sit here and look at their faces across the table. It feels like a parole hearing. I look at Ashton. "I did not, in any way, imply that you are heavy. That would be preposterous. I merely suggested that you should think about what we discussed earlier."

"So I'm a liar?" Ashton turns to Verena. "I'm not getting a good vibe here. I don't want Sylvia on my wedding."

My eyes bulge. Frank cuts in. He puts a hand on her arm. "Honey. I'm sure Sylvia is a great wedding planner."

Ashton shrugs his arm away. "How would you know what a 'great wedding planner' even is? You're only here because Mom and I aren't talking." Ashton's eyes start to fill. "But even when you're here, you're not really here."

"That's not fair," Frank says quietly.

"Well, I don't think it's fair that you spent the last twenty minutes outside on the phone. And now you're going to spend the rest of the time looking at your watch. God forbid you give me one full day. Story of my life, huh?" Ashton wipes her eyes with her fists, like a child.

There's a moment of silence. I look at Frank. His ears are bright red as he fiddles with his watch, but then catches himself.

Verena cuts in calmly as though none of this drama were happening. "Frank, we were just looking through this catalogue of dresses. Would you care to take a peek?"

She slides the catalogue toward Frank. Grateful to have something to do, he turns the pages. "These look really nice. Very white . . . and fancy." His voice is so earnest.

"I hate them all," Ashton snaps.

"Of course you do," I say with frustration.

Frank and Ashton startle. Verena shoots me a warning look. But I don't care. I may have promised Ashton that I'd keep the pregnancy a secret, but I did not promise to pretend it doesn't exist. Besides, what do I have to lose? She's already fired me.

"Ashton," I say firmly. "We both know why you're having such a hard time with this wedding. And it has nothing to do with your parents and their private lives."

Ashton opens her mouth, but I keep going. "I am very confused. Less than an hour ago, I was meeting with a sweet young woman who had a terrific sense of humor. Where did she go? I want to plan *her* wedding."

I look at Ashton meaningfully. But her face is still frozen. Frank likewise stares at me.

Even Verena seems lost. "Sylvia," she says slowly. "Again, what are you talking about?"

I reach across the table and close the catalogue. "Big white dresses just aren't going to cut it. Based on our earlier meeting, I strongly believe that Ashton is a nontraditional bride trying to have a traditional wedding. This is where all these problems and frustrations stem from." I soften my voice and look at Ashton. "I suspect part of you thinks the wedding needs to look a certain way and you haven't given yourself persmission to think outside the box. The Plaza Hotel? Glorious, but so not you." I see Verena's face and hastily add, "Of course, we can transform the ballroom into anything we need it to be. But let's make sure the rest of your wedding details feel authentic. Starting with the dress. I know your past appointments haven't gone well, and that's why we're here with a catalogue. But let's try again. My dear friend Reese works at Bergdorf's. I'll ask him to meet us there tomorrow morning to shop."

Verena interrupts sharply. "Sylvia. There's at least a two-week waiting list for bridal appointments in Manhattan. Let's not promise anything we can't confirm."

I shake my head. "That's my point. I don't think we should schedule a bridal appointment. Why limit Ashton to an actual wedding dress when she so clearly wants something different?"

Verena squints slightly. Ashton stops sniffling and Frank, God bless him, looks just utterly confused. "What do you mean, 'not an actual wedding dress'?" he asks.

I take a breath. "Reese is the manager of Bergdorf's personal shopping department. He has access to all the latest designer gowns. So I say let's skip wedding dresses and open our minds. J. Mendel, Tadashi Shoji, Naeem Khan . . . so many divine options. And here's the added bonus—Ashton can wear the dress again in the future."

Ashton's eyes start to brighten. Verena nods slowly and Frank, well, poor Frank. He stares as though I'm speaking another language. To be fair, I feel my college-level French swirling up over my tongue and can't help but add, "And, naturally, we'll take a look at Givenchy, Balmain, Akris. Tu seras si belle, Ashton." I look off into the distance like a great auteur. "Off the top of my head, I see you in bohemian rapture, something flowing and feminine. Silk chiffon, perhaps a little lace. Floral appliqué if it's done right. A little beading, a tiered skirt. Something with structure but also, as I said earlier, *flowing*." I make sure to hit this last word hard and catch Ashton's eye.

This time, she doesn't glare. "That sounds really . . . nice." She folds her hands together and looks down at her lap. Her face relaxes and she finally starts to resemble the human being I met earlier. I glance at Verena and see her start to smile. Even Frank exhales. Goose bumps tickle my forearms. I did it.

VERENA SMILES AT ME as we walk back to the office after saying goodbye to Frank and Ashton at the elevators. "That was magic, Sylvia. No, not magic. Genius."

We enter her private office. She sits behind her desk and I sit in the chair facing her.

Even when I sit, I feel like I'm floating.

I try to shrug modestly. "Oh, please. It was nothing."

"Nothing? You did in one day what Molly and I failed to do in six months." Verena pops open another IBC root beer. She offers me one. "No doubt a whiskey moment. But this is all I got."

"This will do just fine." I take a long drink and fight the urge to kick up my feet.

Verena's office now makes sense to me. Just a desk and a view. A person could really think in here.

"How'd you come up with the 'nontraditional' bride bit? And don't tell me it was nothing." Verena leans forward on her elbows. "I hate when women don't take proper credit for their work. I have yet to hear a man say, 'Oh, it was just an accident that I came up with nuclear fusion.'"

"Well, I didn't exactly solve nuclear fusion."

"So not the point, Sylvia."

I smile. "Trust me. I feel good about what happened earlier. It's all I can do to not call my daughter and give her a play-by-play. I really needed that win."

Verena tilts her head slightly.

I flush, then clear my throat. "It was the benefit of having fresh eyes. I could see Ashton more clearly."

"And what did you see?"

I saw her puking in a toilet after smelling food and thus knew she was pregnant.

Obviously, I can't say that. I shift in my chair.

"Everything okay?" Verena gives me an odd look.

"I'm just thinking about how to answer."

"It's not a trick question. This is a learning opportunity for me."

I want to tell Verena everything. But if I betray Ashton's trust, I'll never get it back. And I must pull off this wedding. Without my cash cushion, the pressure to succeed so that Verena hires me full-time makes my stomach knot.

"I saw her canvas tote bag," I finally say. "I saw her soap and water skin, product-free hair, and workout pants that she's probably worn since college."

"Right," Verena agrees. "I saw all of that, too. She's down-to-earth. And so I once suggested we look at a consignment shop for a bridal gown. She hated that idea." Verena wrinkles her nose. "She really hated it."

I nod. "Oh, I bet. Ashton isn't a thrift-store girl."

Verena leans forward. "That's what I mean! How did you know that?"

I start to smile. "Ashton could have easily turned down her parents' luxury apartment and moved to the Bronx or Queens or wherever young people live these days when they can't afford Manhattan. But Ashton likes a nice life. Maybe a part of her feels embarrassed by it, but she's not a martyr. She wants a big wedding. Yet she also wants it to be unique. More than that, she wants it to mean something. This is a special time for her."

But Verena shakes her head. "How'd you know that she'd want a fancy dress? That's the part that confuses me. It's not like you were talking about going to some new age designer who makes clothes from recycled tires. By the way, I literally had Molly research that."

I giggle. "Recycled tires?"

Verena nods grimly. "I was desperate."

I giggle more. "It's so creative. She could wear the seat belts as straps."

Verena starts laughing, too. "I swear to God, Sylvia, I would've put a muffler on a veil and streaked Dan and Ashton's faces with motor oil if it got the job done. I'd get ahead of the press—and their mothers—by releasing a photo shoot of the wedding as an avant-garde statement on marriage in today's fast-paced world."

My eyes are bright. "So poetic! 'Our Journey Together Begins Now.'"

Verena snorts. I nearly spit out my root beer. We're both laughing when Verena's phone buzzes. She looks at it and rolls her eyes. "A guy I met at a party is texting to see if I want to have dinner. Is it old-fashioned that I want him to actually call?"

"I haven't dated in over forty years, so maybe I'm not the one to ask. I guess it just depends—how hungry are you?"

Verena laughs again. "Good question. I'm quite hungry." She starts texting back. "But I also have standards. I'm writing that this is a one-time pass. All other social inquiries must be made via live phone call."

"Or postal service." I can't help it. This is fun.

Verena nods. "Yes! Love it."

She types quickly. I want to lean over to see what she's writing but catch myself. Despite this girlfriend moment, I am her assistant. In fact, is this my cue to leave? Or will she dismiss me formally? Unsure, I sit and wait. Verena's cheeks flush as she types. Her lips move as she reads aloud to herself. She looks like a teenager, and I can't help but wonder: Do I want to date again? Could I date again? Of course, I'm not even divorced. That didn't stop Louis, though.

I'm about to speak when Verena looks up. "Sorry, Sylvia. You can go for the day. I'm looking forward to hearing about tomorrow."

"I'll update you as soon as the appointment is over. One quick question." I force a casual tone. "When are paychecks distributed?"

Verena puts down her phone. "Every two weeks, on Fridays. Why? Do you need an advance?"

I swallow, taken aback. "What?"

Verena takes out a checkbook from her desk. "I know what it's like to leave your husband. I've done it four times. How much will tide you over?"

I'm about to protest but then stop. I close my eyes a moment. "Just the first two weeks should be fine."

"I'll give you a month." Verena picks up her pen and starts writing.

"I really don't need that much—"

"Are you planning to run off and leave me hanging?"

"Of course not."

"Then take the money. I trust you." Verena hands me the check. "Besides, after today? I need you."

"Thank you," I say quietly.

"It's my pleasure. And I'm happy to help with a loan if things get really bad. Just ask."

I look at Verena's face and know instantly that she means it. But there's only so much I can accept. "This advance is sufficient. Thank you again."

She nods. I smile, feeling a rush of gratitude.

Thirteen

Evie narrows her eyes and turns around from her vanity table. She wears a pale pink dressing robe and spritzes Chantecaille's Darby Rose perfume on her wrists. "Careful, Sylvia. You're turning Verena into a saint."

"She gave me a job, an advance, and then offered me a loan. Who does that?"

"The mafia."

I laugh and reach down to massage my foot. It's just after seven o'clock and I'm finally home sitting on Evie's queen-size bed. It's the only proper bedroom in this apartment and Evie insisted that if she were to take it, she would pay sixty percent of the rent. I tried to argue, but she was firm. The bed has a simple metal frame and the quilt is silver with light blue stripes. There's a three-drawer dresser that doubles as a nightstand and a child-size desk across the room that Evie has transformed into a vanity. She's put a standing face mirror on the edge of the desk and sits in a metal folding chair that we found in the basement storage area. She covered the seat with her plushest pashmina and looks like a queen on a throne as she turns back around to resume applying her makeup.

I watch her in the mirror's reflection a moment before crossing my other leg to massage my other aching foot. I walked more than forty blocks after leaving Verena's office. I had intended to take the bus but wanted to call my bank. I make a face, remembering the conversation.

"What if he weren't my husband?" I asked Jerome, the third manager I was transferred to. "What if he were a stranger who hacked into my account and stole the money?"

"That would be different, Mrs. Fisher." Jerome's English accent made me feel like a schoolgirl who failed long division. "Then we would call the police and recover your funds as a courtesy."

"But you can't do that now?"

"This wasn't a breach of security. This is a marital dispute. I strongly suggest you contact an attorney."

Something rustled in the background on the phone. "Are you eating?"

"I beg your pardon?"

"I can hear you chewing." My voice felt tight. I pictured him sitting at his desk devouring something obnoxious, like pasta salad with too much vinegar. I'd be one of the stories he'd tell his wife about later. Some sad woman who didn't have a clue.

And so I dropped my phone into my purse without saying goodbye, and walked the rest of the way home. It was chilly and gray outside. I was still wearing only my bra and blazer but welcomed the cool wind on my neck. Verena had saved me. Her check was more than money for food. It made me tingle with hope. Someone believed in me enough to pay me in advance. I kept saying that to myself as I walked and walked, soaking in the city. I inhaled flowers from a corner bodega and the warm, salty air streaming from a pizza parlor. Once I got downtown, I zigzagged down side streets and tried to count how many vegan bakeries and clothing boutiques promised explicitly to be cruelty-free. I wondered why we couldn't all adopt that motto.

When I finally arrived at the apartment, I was humming even though things were still catastrophic: my cheating husband had stolen the money I needed to survive.

"Evie," I say, my voice a little heavier as I shift forward on her bed and put my feet on the floor. "Maybe we shouldn't go out tonight."

"You got a job. What's not to celebrate?"

"Well, let's see. First, I'm going to be broke in a month. Second, I can't afford to sue Louis to get my money. Third, the bride whose wedding I'm planning is secretly pregnant and may, at any moment, go completely sideways on me, which would end my career before it even starts. Are you applying false eyelashes?" I've never seen Evie apply false anything.

"I'm trying them out." Evie painstakingly places each "lash" along one eyelid as she speaks. "I was at Sephora today. They have very good deals, much better than the department stores. Chin up. All you've told me are a list of problems that *could* happen. Today, everything is perfect."

"Why aren't you more freaked out? You don't even have a job."

Evie looks at me. She wears one set of eyelashes and I have a hard time focusing as she talks. "We have to celebrate the victories. Today was a good day."

I put my head in my hands. "In the morning, I'm asking Verena for a loan."

"Absolutely not." Evie pulls off the eyelashes and blinks a few times before giving me a hard look. "She hasn't even offered you a full-time position."

"This is a trial period. She needs to know I can do the job."

"She wouldn't have put you on an impossible wedding if she didn't think you could do the job, Sylvia. Leave it at that."

"But she can solve all my problems."

"No one can solve all your problems. Isn't that what brought you to New York in the first place?"

I know Evie's right. My shoulders sag. "What am I doing here?"

"What are any of us doing here?" Evie holds my gaze a moment before picking up a basket of lipsticks. She starts opening tubes, looking for the right color. "Henry and I went through our savings paying for Julian's rehabs. Ten years of private treatment centers, sobriety coaches, wellness retreats. We paid and paid and then he died. He left his family with nothing. When Henry passed, I tried to give Amanda the life insurance. She didn't take it. I then insisted it be used for Oliver's education. She relented. I thought that would mean I could be in their life." Evie pauses a moment. "I haven't heard from them in two hundred and seventy-three days. Money doesn't solve everything."

Evie finally decides on a lipstick. It's a deep ruby red. As she applies it, I walk over and put a hand on my friend's shoulder. "I cannot fathom the pain."

Evie blots her lips. "Between my social security and a small pension, I had enough money to live in Florida. But here in New York? Not quite as comfortable. But I'm not 'freaked out,' as you asked, because I feel more alive right now than I have in too long a time. Today, I have money for rent, food, and false eyelashes that, in fairness, I'm returning. So come on. Get dressed. We must celebrate your first day of employment."

I smile a little. "But we just celebrated getting an apartment yesterday."

"You're goddamn right we did."

IT TAKES US TWENTY MINUTES to get to West Tenth Street. Evie insisted we return to Wild One.

I didn't think my feet could take another walk and so Evie let me borrow a pair of her Hogan sneakers. She got them during an online flash sale, but I now understand why people might pay $400 for sneakers. I'm walking on a cloud of black patent leather. I changed out of my crumpled suit and into black cigarette pants, a cashmere turtleneck the color of sand, and Evie's shiny black puffer jacket. I'm feeling very rock and roll. I put my hair in a loose French twist and wear chocolaty pink lip gloss.

We turn a corner and see the restaurant's sign. A line of people spill onto the sidewalk. I stop in my tracks and look at Evie. She's wearing red Hogan sneakers, also from the flash sale, white jeans with a thin red belt, and a gold sweater. She has on a red trench coat and dangling earrings. She taps her cane impatiently on the ground.

"Let's go, Sylvia."

I gesture to the line. "We'll never get in."

But Evie doesn't listen. She charges forward. I have no choice but to follow. People make room when they see her cane, and soon we're in front of the hostess stand where a young woman holds a clipboard. She looks like a robot from those science fiction movies about lonely billionaires who live in dark mansions with man-made supermodels for servants. Her hair is pulled into a severe bun and she wears an ear mic. I'm already afraid of her. But as soon as she sees Evie, her eyes flicker with something resembling warmth, and she gestures for us to follow her inside.

My mouth hangs open as she leads us through the restaurant, which is packed with the same type of crowd as yesterday: young and beautiful. Of course, everyone under the age of fifty looks young to me. But Evie and I are definitely the oldest by at least a decade. Or two. Despite all this, the hostess leads us to a table in the center of the restaurant. It's the best seat in the house. Evie slips off her coat, hands it to the hostess, and sits. In a fog, I do the same. The hostess whisks away our coats and leaves us with menus.

I stare at Evie over the candlelit table. "What just happened?"

"I came earlier after you called me about your new job. Told them we'd be here to celebrate. Surprise." Evie hangs her cane on the side of the chair and smiles.

I smile back, touched, and open the menu. "I'm not trying to be a buzzkill," I start carefully. "But I can't spend eighteen dollars on a cocktail. And before you argue that we need to celebrate, just being here is celebrating. Literally inhaling this air makes me feel like I'm cartwheeling across the sky."

Evie looks at me a moment. I'm worried she'll protest, but instead she picks up her water. "Water is very hydrating, much better for our skin."

A waiter arrives. He sets several plates onto our table and explains. "Toro tartare, our signature caviar dish, and a salad of roasted beets, goat cheese foam, and walnuts. On the house. Enjoy."

My jaw drops again. Evie starts to nibble, a smile dancing across her lips. "This is delicious."

I stare at her. "What kind of job did you tell them I had?"

"Wedding planning." Evie's mouth twitches some more. "And

that you were always looking for places to cater your more discern-
ing clients' events."

"Evie!" I nearly choke.

"I'm kidding." Evie rolls her eyes playfully. "I was on a walk and
came to ask about a reservation. The owner happened to be here. He
and I hit it off and chatted about life, New York, music . . . Have you
tried the beets? They're heavenly. Now tell me everything. Start
with the bride puking and how she held you hostage in the bathroom. I love that part." Evie takes another bite of food and looks at
me expectantly.

"Back up," I say as I try to read Evie's face. "What do you mean,
you and the owner hit it off? Romantically? And yes. I just ate a
beet. I officially believe in God now."

Evie laughs. "Oh, please. The owner is lovely. From Hong Kong.
A gentleman who I'm sure only dates women between the ages of
thirty-five and fifty, which isn't completely gross but certainly not
in my range. Speaking of, I can't believe Ashton's mother is dating a
thirty-one-year-old poet. Hmm. I changed my mind. That's my favorite part. When do you meet Mom?"

"I don't think she and Ashton are speaking." I sigh. "Poor girl.
And poor, poor Frank. I can't imagine what I'd do if Louis were
sleeping with someone Isabel's age."

"Would it really upset you that much more?"

"Wouldn't it upset you if Henry cheated with someone Julian's
age?" I cringe. I didn't mean to bring up Evie's son.

But Evie waves it off. "If Henry were sleeping with a woman our
son's age, I would've set him on fire."

I nod. "Exactly."

Evie holds up a hand. "I'm not finished. If Henry were sleeping
with *anyone* besides me, I would've set him on fire."

"I know the feeling."

"Do you, Sylvia?" Evie leans across the table. "Please don't take this the wrong way, but you don't seem that upset about Louis and Belinda. I'm sure you feel betrayed. I don't want to minimize it. And, granted, I've only known you since you moved to Boca, so I don't know your history together. But when did you stop loving him?"

I feel like a gust of wind just knocked me over. Evie puts down her fork and shakes her head. "I'm sorry. I shouldn't have phrased it like that."

"No, it's okay. I just . . . Up until that day with Belinda, I wouldn't have said that I didn't love him." I look off into the distance and let my eyes blur so that all the people become fuzzy. "But I do hate scented candles."

"Pardon?"

"Some time back in the eighties, someone must've told Louis that women like to be seduced by scented candles. He was always stocking up. Any time the house started to smell like an apothecary, I knew he wanted sex. Jasmine, rosemary, sandalwood. Fucking patchouli." I make a face. "It was so cliché. And if we ever started making love without some honeysuckle infusion suffocating us, he'd pause to get a candle and act like he was doing me a favor. It drove me bananas."

Evie picks up the candle on the table. The flame flickers. She blows it out. I laugh. "Regular candles are okay."

"I wasn't taking any chances."

I sigh. "What makes me sad is that I never told Louis I hated them. I doubt he'd have cared. But I never really told him anything. And that's my fault."

Evie takes a bite of beet. "Careful. He's still a prick. He took your money and is using it as a manipulation tactic to summon you back to Florida."

I frown. "He hates not getting what he wants."

"So do I. But I've learned to handle it without being a complete shithead. Seriously. Fuck Louis and his fucking candles."

A young couple next to us looks over with raised eyebrows. Evie lifts a brow back. I want to laugh but can't. A fresh wave of rage runs through me just as the waiter returns with another round of food. "Mahi mahi wonton tacos and grilled octopus, my personal favorite." He leaves.

I look at Evie. My voice is deadpan. "Just when I was desperate to stab something." I pierce a piece of octopus and bring it to my lips. It smells like garlic and charred wood, in a good way.

Evie reaches for her cane. "You enjoy. I need to pop to the ladies' room." She gets up and walks away.

As I watch Evie disappear down a side hallway, I chew the octopus but barely taste it. Why didn't I tell Louis that I hated candles? Why didn't I ever have a goddamn opinion? No wonder Louis thought he could just take my money and I'd do nothing. I nearly vibrate with rage. And so I take a long breath, hold it for five seconds, and then exhale for a count of ten. I read somewhere that this breathing technique is how snipers lower their heart rate before pulling the trigger. I do it two more times. As I push out every last breath, my shoulders start to drop and I lose myself in a fantasy: I'm back in Boca. It's the middle of the night. I slip onto the grounds of BBG wearing black cargo pants, a black T-shirt, and a black vest with secret compartments for things like a flashlight, various tools, and, of course, weapons. I enter our condo and tiptoe into the bedroom. Louis and Belinda are asleep in bed. Unsure how to wake them, I go back into the hallway, close the bedroom door, and kick it hard.

It flies open.

They bolt upright in bed and gasp as I stand in the doorway like the perfect combination of Pam Grier and Angelina Jolie.

"Oh my god!" Belinda screeches.

"Sylvia?" Louis exclaims. "You look unbelievable."

I pull out a pistol. "Give me my money."

Louis looks from the gun to my face and nods. "It's in my golf bag." I gesture for him to move. He obeys.

Belinda, meanwhile, hugs the covers around her naked body. "Sylvia," she starts. "This isn't what it looks like."

"Oh, shut up. You can have him. All I want is my money." I turn my back on her and wait for Louis to shuffle through the closet and find the bag.

He finally does and takes out an envelope. "It's all here."

I snatch it and count the bills. He stands there dumbly and runs his hand through his hair. He's about to say something when Belinda interrupts. "I've called the police!"

Louis and I look at her. She's clutching her cell phone. I walk over. She hides under the blanket. Sirens wail in the distance. Without another word, I escape through the bedroom window. I have a long rope in my vest that I hook around the small balcony railing and then rappel down the side of the building. Below, a motorcycle waits with a key in the ignition. Louis leans out the window and watches, slack-jawed, as I hop on. Just as I start the engine, the opening scales to Gloria Gaynor's "I Will Survive" burst into the air.

That's odd. I haven't ever put a soundtrack to my fantasies before. But I go with it. In fact, I'm now flying on my motorcycle, racing through the night, my cash tucked into a zippered pouch inside my vest. I feel the weight of it against my chest.

God, this music is good.

I realize that it's not in my head. It's in the restaurant. I look around and see people swaying to the melody at their tables. It's like a concert. There are no vocals but we don't need them. The piano is vibrant, colorful, full of feeling. I crane my neck. Where's Evie? She'd love this.

I get up and head back toward the bathroom to get her. But when I make it to the bar where the platform and piano are, I stop.

My eyes bulge. It's her. It's Evie. At the piano.

I put a hand on the bar to steady myself. Goose bumps shiver up my spine as I watch Evie's fingers fly across the keys. Her entire body moves while she plays and her eyes are half-open, half-closed, as though she's in a different world. It's like a time machine up there: at the piano, Evie is ageless.

As the song comes to an end, people clap. Evie smiles and leans into a mic. "If you'll indulge me, this evening I am dedicating all songs to my roommate, Sylvia, and myself." She finds me and winks. "Turns out, we both got jobs today."

More applause and good-natured laughter. People then return to their meals and Evie begins to play something contemporary. In fact, I recognize it as the Coldplay song we heard yesterday evening. I shake my head with awe. She was right—that other player was total shit.

I return to my table and watch Evie play. I stay completely present. I don't need to be Pam Grier or Angelina Jolie or any other ass-kicker in tight clothes. I'm Sylvia Fisher, and for the first time in maybe forever, I'm exactly where I'm supposed to be.

Fourteen

The next morning, the air is crisp. I pull the navy peacoat I borrowed back from Isabel around me as I walk up Fifth Avenue. I can't believe it's been less than two weeks since I was at Izzy's house. It feels a world away. I feel a momentary pang. Izzy's called me three times in the last two days and I haven't called her back. In her voicemails, she said that Dad told her I got a job in New York. She sounded confused and angry. Not my favorite mix.

Especially when I've got such a big day ahead of me. And so I take a deep breath and check my phone. It's 10:01 a.m. Bergdorf's rises before me like a fortress. I push through the heavy doors and smile at the security guard. He nods back. I arrive with the first wave of customers and turn slowly in a circle so that I can soak in the magnificence of this store.

In the handbag section, snakeskin clutches with jeweled handles are arranged in little cases next to feather-trimmed chapeaus. A mannequin with only a torso wears Chloé sunglasses and a Lanvin quilted cross-body bag. The scent of luxury leather feels warm in my nose. The music is light and airy and mixes with snippets of conversations in various languages as tourists and locals chitchat and shop.

From a distance, I watch the entrance and see Ashton enter through the front doors. She looks like a cross between a homeless person and a celebrity. Her long hair is windblown and wild beneath a newsboy cap. She wears baggy jeans and a hooded sweatshirt. She doesn't have a coat but wears fingerless gloves. She clutches her New York Public Library tote bag to her body like her entire life is packed up inside. Only her shoes give her away—a pair of baby-blue retro sneakers, the ones Madonna collaborated on with Reebok. I make a mental note—Ashton likes shoes.

She doesn't see me. I watch her for another moment. She wanders over to a nearby cosmetics counter. A salesperson offers her something but she shakes her head. She crosses to a different counter and picks up a lip gloss. She puts it down without opening it.

"Ashton," I finally call as I walk over to her. I'm about to lean in for a hug but instinctively stop myself. Instead, I clasp my hands together with a small clap. "I'm so happy to see you. How are you feeling?"

She chews her nail. "I woke up starving, ate a bagel, and then threw up. Is that normal?"

"Unfortunately, yes." I'm about to make a pregnancy joke but notice the worry in her eyes. "How far along are you, dear?"

"Maybe ten weeks? When do I know if something isn't normal? Like, I've had a little spotting." Her cheeks redden. "Sorry. But you're the only one who knows. Well, you and Google. But Google is scary."

I frown. "Have you been to your OB?"

She shakes her head. I'm about to respond when we're interrupted by Reese's musical voice. "Sylvia!"

I turn and see Reese striding toward us. He's dazzling in a Zegna copper-colored suit with just the faintest check pattern. He's shorter than both Ashton and me and yet somehow is able to sweep us both into his arms and double-kiss our cheeks in a way that makes me feel like royalty.

He steps back and takes Ashton's hands in his. "You are heavenly. This is going to be such fun."

I shake my head. Reese is barely thirty and yet has the grand air of someone who has navigated the world. I suppose escaping from Iran at nineteen, hiding above a barbershop in Turkey, and then befriending an American businessman who took on the seemingly impossible task of securing legal papers for him to come to America could make any person seem impressive. I escaped from Boca and feel like Wonder Woman.

Reese smiles. "I've already pulled several gowns. Shall we get started?" Ashton looks at the ground. Her face is grim.

Reese is about to say something else, but I put a hand on his arm. "Reese. We are so grateful that you made this time to see us. But something has regretfully come up. Would it be possible to return later this afternoon?"

This gets Ashton's attention. She looks at me, confused. I hold up a hand, *one moment please,* and wait for Reese to check the leather appointment book he pulls from his breast pocket. Such class. "Come back any time after one p.m. I'll make myself available."

"Perfect. Thank you." I meet his eye and he gives a small nod before pivoting and walking away.

Ashton watches him go. "Why'd you do that?"

"Because you need to see your doctor." Ashton's eyes widen at my tone. I soften. "I'm sure everything is fine, but neither of us is going to feel good about shopping until you get checked out. Do you have an OB?"

"Dr. Bickman. I've been seeing her forever. I was going to call last week but then didn't. I don't know what's wrong with me, Sylvia. You must think I'm so stupid."

"Oh, honey. All I think is that you're scared." I look at her pale face. "Would you like me to call for you?"

She nods gratefully and hands me her phone. I find "Bickman" in the contacts and dial.

A receptionist answers. "Dr. Bickman's office."

"Hello. I'd like to make an appointment for Ashton Morris. She's newly pregnant and would like to confirm that everything is okay."

"How about next week Tuesday?"

"How about today?" My voice is firm. "She's had some spotting and is very worried."

"I see." The receptionist pauses a moment. "Is eleven too soon?"

"We'll be there." I hang up and hand Ashton back her phone. "Let's go."

I FEEL DIZZY AS ASHTON paces the perimeter of the exam room, which is just big enough for an exam table, one chair, and a counter stocked with medical supplies and a foot-pedal sink.

Ashton refuses to sit down. I offered to stay in the waiting room, but she begged me to not leave her. And so I'm sitting in the lone chair while she walks back and forth over and over and over. She wears nothing but a paper gown that she's managed to secure quite well with the flimsy tie. I press my fingers together and stare at the gray wall. This feels very strange. I never even went to one of Isabel's prenatal appointments.

Speaking of Isabel, my phone rings again. I peer at the screen, see it's Isabel, and press Ignore. This is the second time she's tried me since I've been in this waiting room. Her calls are getting more frequent. But now she won't leave a message. I silently curse Louis. He probably made me sound unstable. And he'll know Isabel will want to talk me out of having any kind of job. I can practically see her sitting at her computer composing a litany of why my new life is doomed. There might even be footnotes.

My phone rings yet again. Ashton glances at me, and I finally just turn it to vibrate and put it back in my purse. I offer a wry smile. "I'm only this popular whenever we're together."

Ashton raises a brow. "Are you sure you don't need to answer it?"

"No. It's just my daughter."

"It sounds like she really needs you."

"Please. She's worried that I'm going to need her." Ashton looks at me with new interest. I shake my head. "Let's not get into it. How are you doing?"

Ashton scoots onto the exam table. She crosses her legs like a child. "I'd rather talk about your daughter. You guys must be close. You said her wedding was what made you want to become a wedding planner. You visited all those bakeries and made those pro and con lists about the ball gown." Ashton wrinkles her nose. "My mom wants to make a pro and con list about anal sex. Her boyfriend is literally my age and she wants to be 'in the know,' as she puts it, 'about what a young man might expect.' How come you don't want to talk to your daughter? Are you in a fight?"

Do young men expect anal sex? Is that a thing these days? Do older men expect it now, too? "I'm sorry," I finally say. "This situation with your mom. It must be hard."

Ashton looks away.

I lean forward. "I didn't see anything about your wedding party in the notes. Do you have bridesmaids? I'm only asking because I think it might be helpful to have a good girlfriend to talk to."

"My best friend, Tati, lives in Japan for work. She's the maid of honor. No other bridesmaids. Dan and I want to keep things simple."

"I really like Dan," I say.

"Me, too." Ashton smiles a little.

"May I ask—why haven't you told him about the baby?"

"We've talked about having kids, but he doesn't seem that excited. Or at least, he doesn't seem like he wants them right now. I'm scared he's gonna freak. And I can't handle it if he does."

"Ashton," I say gently. "Part of why this feels scary is *because* it's a secret. Not the other way around. And it's okay if Dan is nervous. When my daughter was pregnant, her husband, Todd, bought a rifle. He had never even seen a gun before. People do all sorts of things when they receive life-changing news."

"But I don't want Dan to buy a gun." Her voice quivers.

I almost smile. "I think you can't worry about what Dan will do. Give him a chance to surprise you. And support you," I add.

She runs her hands through her hair and tugs on it. "But I already know he's gonna be upset. We talked about kids. We wanted to wait a few years. And I can't even make roast chicken."

Now I do smile. "Oh, honey. We discussed this. You don't need to be some kind of domestic whiz to have a child."

"But I want to be a domestic whiz! Or, at least, I want to be able to make grilled cheese without starting a fire. Seriously. That happened. Dan keeps two fire extinguishers in the kitchen. One is backup. I'm hopeless. You impressed my dad, by the way. He liked your dress idea. I'm pretty sure my mom will hate it, though. But whatever."

My head whirls. How does one start a fire from making grilled cheese? Was it a stove-top fire or in the toaster oven? As for Nina, I've already been brainstorming a plan to get her on board with the nontraditional theme. I'm about to fill Ashton in, but we're interrupted by the door opening.

"Ashton, terrific to see you. And such exciting news!" Dr. Bickman smiles as she enters the room while wheeling in a sonogram machine. She's in her late forties and has dark, intelligent eyes. She wears her white coat over a snazzy orange dress. "I see you brought Mom. Hello there."

I stiffen as Dr. Bickman looks at me and extends her hand. I shake it and clear my throat. "I'm actually Ashton's—"

"I wanted to bring my mom in case anything's wrong," Ashton blurts quickly. She shoots me a look.

Okay. I guess I'm "Mom" today.

"Of course," Dr. Bickman says. "Let's take a look. Lie back and put your feet in the stirrups as though we're doing your pap."

As Ashton gets into position, Dr. Bickman takes the wand off the sonogram machine and unrolls a condom to place over it. I must look confused because she smiles at me and explains. "This early, we do a transvaginal ultrasound. Ready, Ashton? One, two, three."

Dr. Bickman inserts the wand and Ashton's breath catches for a moment while I stare into space, not quite sure what to do. I never thought my job description would include something so intimate. Then again, I've already endured arson and public shaming as a wedding planner. I suppose being part of an ultrasound is actually quite lovely.

I hear my phone vibrate again and feel a twinge of guilt for ignoring my real daughter while sitting here with my pretend one. I look at Ashton's face. She's squeezing her eyes shut. Her hands are little fists. I quietly get up and go over to her. I take her hand in mine.

"Is everything okay?" she asks me.

I turn to the doctor, who smiles. "Everything looks perfect. From the measurements, I'd say you're ten weeks and two days. Your due date is May twelfth."

"What about the spotting?" Ashton's voice is tight. She's still only looking at me.

Dr. Bickman's voice is like a warm compress. "Very normal. If there's ever heavy bleeding, call immediately. But everything here looks great. Take a look."

Ashton slowly brings her eyes to the screen. I do, too. It's fuzzy, but I see something flashing. "Is that the heartbeat?"

Dr. Bickman nods. "It sure is."

My face tingles all over. I look at Ashton, who is now mesmerized by the screen. Dr. Bickman prints two photos, removes the wand, and stands up. She tosses her exam gloves and hands both Ashton and me a photo. "Congratulations, again. The girls at the desk will schedule your next appointment." She turns to me and winks. "Nice to meet you, Grandma."

After she exits the room, Ashton and I sit quietly. She stares at the photo in her hand. "I'm sorry, Sylvia. I was too embarrassed to say that you were my wedding planner. I can't believe this is a tiny human."

"Your tiny human," I say softly looking down at my copy. "Yours and Dan's. You made this little being together."

Ashton nods. "I'll tell him. Maybe this weekend. I want to do it during a calm and relaxing moment. Just the two of us."

"That sounds perfect." I smile. "Do you still feel up to shopping?"
Ashton stretches her hands above her head. "I do. I really do."

My phone vibrates yet again. I feel a sudden pang. "You get
dressed, dear. I'll wait outside."

Ashton nods okay.

I leave the room. I walk quickly down the corridor, exit through
reception into the hallway, and stand next to the elevator bank. I
take a breath, make sure the hallway is empty, and then answer the
phone. "Isabel, I love you. But I don't want to hear a word of judgment. I don't want to hear a list of my failures. You may not like what
I'm doing, but I'm your mother."

Without realizing it, my eyes fill up. I'm clutching Ashton's ultrasound photo, and all at once, I'm flooded with memories of Isabel as
a baby. Her tiny shrimp fingers. Her soft belly.

Her ferocious scream.

I swallow and soften my voice. "You've always had such ambition,
such a sense of direction. I admire you, Izzy."

Silence.

"Izzy? Are you there?" I look at the phone. It's still connected.

"I'm here." Isabel's voice is flat. "You're right. I don't like what
you're doing."

"Why on earth not?" I try to sound upbeat.

"Because it doesn't make any sense. You're too old to be doing
this."

I feel punched. "I'm too old to be living my life the way that I
want?"

"Do you know what it sounds like when I tell people at work that
my mom moved to New York? That she and another senior citizen
are roommates? First, they think I'm joking. Then they say, 'That's
so cute!' It's not cute, Mom. It's delusional."

"It is not!" I shoot back. "I have a paycheck and a client. I'm already working on a wedding, thank you very much."

"I thought you were just going to New York and staying with a friend. Not inventing some fantasy life and have a total mental breakdown."

"Why are you taking my good news and turning it around? And I'm *not* having a breakdown. If anything, it's a breakthrough!"

"Jesus Christ! Do you hear yourself?"

"Do *you*?" I cry out. "Ever since I left your father, you've judged me. Do you know what people say when I tell them that? It certainly isn't 'That's so cute.'" My voice shakes. "Isabel. You don't know half of what your father has done. I have to go now. I'm at work."

I hang up and shove the phone back into my purse along with the sonogram photo. My whole body feels hot. I stare at my reflection in the elevator mirror. I am sawed in half by the break in the doors. My own daughter has no respect for me. My phone starts vibrating angrily again, but I ignore it and lift my chin. There's nothing ridiculous about what I'm doing. Sure, I'm at a gynecologist's office with someone I met only yesterday. But this is the job. In fact, I feel quite proud of myself. My hands are still shaking as I smooth down my hair and button my coat. There's a savage feeling inside my chest and I don't try to tame it. Instead, I step a few inches to my right until my reflection is in one piece. I can do this. I can plan a wedding. I can plan a *spectacular* wedding.

Fifteen

For the next few days, nothing brings me down. I've been working nonstop since we left the doctor's office last Thursday. Ashton and I returned to Bergdorf's around 2:00 p.m. and had the most glorious time with Reese trying on dresses. We finally settled on a gown by Lela Rose called the Glitter Firework Gown. The name alone sold us. Ashton looked radiant in the soft layers of turquoise silk that cascaded to the ground with swirling bursts of silver and gold beading. The deep V-neck and short bow sleeves would provide support for her growing bosom, and the flowing A-line skirt would keep her belly from feeling squeezed. I could not have dreamed up anything more elegant. This dress will be with Ashton forever.

As we were walking out of Bergdorf's, it was dusk. The sky was a deep indigo backdrop behind the buildings. I asked Ashton to join me for a celebratory nonalcoholic sparkling drink at a nearby café.

We took seats at the bar and I peered deep into her eyes. "Ashton.

Forgive the dramatic tone of my voice. But we have seven weeks and three days until your wedding. It's crunch time."

She nodded, then bit her lip. "How much do you think my mom will hate that dress?"

"She won't hate it at all. What makes you say that?"

Ashton shrugged. "She doesn't really do 'nontraditional.'"

I popped a salted almond into my mouth. "That dress is stunning. Sure, it's not a typical ball gown. But it's also not that brown leather catsuit you tried on." Ashton smiled a little. I patted her leg. "It's okay to want your mom's approval even though you're mad at her. It's exactly how I feel about my daughter." Ashton looked up at me. I blushed. "Sorry. I keep oversharing here."

She shook her head and took a sip of her fizzy drink. "I want to hear this. It makes me feel more normal. Why are you and your daughter mad at each other?"

I shrugged. "It's too long a story. Family is complicated. But she's your mother and you have a lot going on. Maybe after you talk to Dan about the baby, you might consider talking to her, too. She'll be ecstatic. And she could rejoin the planning. Instead of saying nontraditional, we'll say unique." I winked.

Ashton looked at me a moment. "I know you're right. But for now, let's just keep the planning between you and me. It's crunch time, after all."

I smiled. Maybe part of me was relieved. We had a lot of work to do.

TRUE TO HER WORD, Ashton let me lead the way. We had a meeting that next day, Friday, at the Plaza Hotel to get a feel for the venue. Because of last-minute notice and other events being set up, we could only take a short walk through their famed Terrace Room, where the ceremony and reception would take place. Everything was so lavish. The high ceilings, the marble fountain, the gilded chairs.

"It's just so . . . big," Ashton whispered. That familiar dread hooded her eyes.

"Don't worry." I said. "You'd be surprised by what some flowers can do."

I swept Ashton out of the hotel and brought her to a downtown florist who was in Verena's contacts. I reminded Ashton again that the hotel space was just, in fact, a space. It was our job to bring the warmth. And so we chose yellow tulips and burnt-orange roses. The florist would work with the hotel's coordinator to arrange green floral walls around the perimeter of the room. I promised Ashton that it would feel like the Swiss countryside meets a Napa winery.

Ashton smiled for the first time that day.

We then spent the rest of the afternoon in the conference room at Verena's office working through the list. We selected bronze centerpieces for the table. We chose music for the ceremony and reception. Miku brought us a late lunch, but it went untouched because we were so focused. We made decisions on everything from table arrangements to the fold of napkins. I saw Molly gaping at us from outside the conference room's glass walls. I pinned magazine photos and note cards on a giant whiteboard. I drew sketches and made notes and taped up lists. Ashton looked a little dizzy by the end of the day but didn't complain once. I finally sent her home to relax. Plus, she promised that she was going to tell Dan about the baby.

Once again, she kept her word. I was just slipping into bed Friday night when she sent me a video of Dan reacting to the news. He was silent for a full minute. He squinted, ran a hand through his hair, opened his mouth, closed his mouth, and then finally nodded.

"This makes total sense," he finally said before starting to smile.

"Are you going to buy a gun?" Ashton blurted out.

I laughed aloud. But then I bit my lip, waiting for Dan's response.

"Ashton," he said. "I don't really feel comfortable having a waffle maker in our place. Why are you asking me about firearms?"

I smiled when I heard Ashton giggle. "I love you."

And then the video cut out and I fell into the deepest, most luxurious sleep. No more secrets.

IT'S SATURDAY AT 1:00 P.M. and I'm shopping for shoes. And potentially glittery sneakers.

Isabel keeps calling me but I've gotten used to hitting Ignore. I'm busy. Ashton and I spent the morning back at Verena's office poring over pictures and websites of footwear until I shut it all down. "Let me do some recon while you're at alterations," I decided.

And so we went over to Bergdorf's for Ashton's dress-fitting appointment. I dropped her with Reese, who promised to make sure that the seamstress would allow for the appropriate amount of give in the dress. I then took the elevator down to the shoe department, and now I am slowly making my way around the perimeter displays before venturing deeper into the salon. My eyes go wide when I see a beaded leather high-heeled sandal.

As soon as I pick it up, I see a familiar face. It's Frank. He's wearing a navy windbreaker with a pair of gray-and-white-striped workout pants. He stares at me through his slightly fogged-up glasses. "I think you might be a witch."

I squint, not quite sure how to respond. "The broomstick kind? With the large nose and horrible wrinkles?"

He laughs. "The good kind. The women who can wiggle their normal-size noses and make everything okay."

"Are you talking about that television show *Bewitched*? From the seventies?"

"To be fair, they did make a movie with Nicole Kidman."

I turn the shoe over in my hand. "I'll take a compliment where I can get it. What do you think of this shoe for Ashton?"

I hold out the sandal. Frank shakes his head. "I don't like the beads. Seriously, what did you do? Ashton is now the happiest I've ever seen her, despite the morning sickness." He swallows. "I can't believe she's having a baby."

I put down the shoe and clasp my hands together. "I'm so glad she told you. Congratulations! You must be so happy."

He grins. "I already volunteered to babysit. But I'm not sure I meet her standards." He grins again, then grows quiet. "Ashton filled me in on the other day. What you did. That was above and beyond. I wanted to come and say thank you in person."

"You're very welcome." I smile and meet Frank's eye. A moment passes. Neither of us says anything. I look around the store but feel Frank's eyes still on me. My neck grows hot.

Why is he just standing there? I smooth down my pleated-front trousers and think about my underpants. Pink lace hipster briefs. Seemingly simple but surprisingly effective against gravity. I pretend to dust something off my shoulder so that I can peer at my tush. It does look higher and rounder than ever before. I glance back at Frank. He's still looking at me. My neck now flames. Why on earth am I thinking about my body? It's not like Frank is some Adonis. He's my height and probably weighs less. He doesn't even have a tush.

I clear my throat. "Frank, would you like me to escort you to Ashton's dressing suite where she's doing her fitting? So you can see the gown? It's fabulous."

"I'm sure it is." He points to a display table toward the center of the salon. "I like those shoes over there. Did you really walk in on your husband being straddled by another woman?"

I follow Frank's eyeline and see a simple pair of heels in a pale gold. My eyes widen. "Those are lovely. Let's check them out. And yes, I walked in on my husband in the reverse cowgirl position with a woman I cannot stand."

Frank follows me toward the shoes. "I walked in on my wife taking a shower with her thirty-one-year old boyfriend. I'm not sure what position they were in, but they were definitely fucking."

I wince sympathetically. "I'm sorry about your wife. Did you have a good marriage?"

Frank bursts out laughing. "I can't figure you out."

"What do you mean?" My face starts to tingle.

"You asked if I had a good marriage. The answer to that is obviously no. My wife was cheating on me."

"I realize that. I just meant did you think your marriage was good before the affair happened? Because as betrayed as I feel by Louis, I'm wondering if our relationship had started to fizzle and I just didn't notice."

Frank's face darkens. "No way am I letting Nina off the hook because I didn't buy enough flowers. Have you slept with anyone yet?" My mouth drops. Frank sighs. "I'm sorry. That was probably too forward."

I try to stop my face from burning. My voice is nearly a whisper. "Have you? Been with someone else?"

Frank reddens. "I tried. I let one of my divorced buddies convince me to go to some trendy new bar. It was horrible."

"Going to a bar was horrible?"

"I ran into one of Ashton's high school friends."

I suck in a breath. "That must have been humiliating."

"You really just say whatever comes to mind, don't you?"

"I beg your pardon? You're the one asking about my sex life like we're girlfriends in a *Sex and the City* episode."

His lips twitch. "Well, we are shoe shopping at Bergdorf's. So. Which one am I? Charlotte? Carrie?"

My eyes widen. "You like that show? Louis hated it. And you're definitely Miranda. Definitely."

Frank raises a brow. "This guy, Louis. No taste. *Sex and the City*? A complete classic."

I cross my arms. "Are you making fun of me?"

Frank's smile disappears. His face grows serious and he puts a hand on my arm. "Not even a little bit."

I'm about to say something but I'm distracted by the weight of his hand on my forearm. It feels warm. I glance down. He does, too. We both stare at his hand and I'm about to say something when I see an eccentrically elegant woman heading toward us. She's nearly six feet tall and her voice thunders across the salon. "Frank, hello!"

Frank's hand drops from my arm. "Nina," he whispers, looking stunned.

My jaw drops. This was not how I intended to meet Ashton's mother. I shoot Frank a look. But his eyes are a liquid black as Nina now stands in front of the sofa. Frank barely nods a greeting and buries his face in his cell phone.

Nina sighs. I stand up and tuck a strand of hair behind my ear.

Before I can introduce myself, Nina's eyes sweep over me. And so I let my eyes do the same and try not to blanche in shock. I was expecting someone small and curvy with a Botoxed face and helmet hair. But Nina takes my breath away. She's long and lean, with a bright smile and a deeply tanned face. She's in her sixties and doesn't try to hide it. Her curly gray hair swirls down her back. She wears a crocheted sweater tucked into tight riding pants that show off her gorgeous legs. She has the well-bred demeanor of someone who took archery as a girl and still hunts for pleasure. Even the dirt on her knee-high leather boots doesn't look dirty.

She extends her hand. "Forgive my surprise. You must be Sylvia. I was expecting someone my daughter's age when Verena told me that so much progress had been made by her fabulous new assistant."

My face falls. Nina notices and laughs. "Don't you dare! I'm delighted to meet a mature woman. One less child I have to deal with." Her eyes flick to Frank for a moment. Then she smiles back at me. "Nina Levinson, pleasure."

I shake Nina's hand. "Sylvia Fisher. And I'm delighted that you're delighted. The wedding really is coming together beautifully. Ashton is such a lovely girl."

"Yes, she is. So long as you're not her mother," Nina says with an eye roll.

"Oh, give me a break," Frank mutters.

Nina stiffens. I pretend not to have heard and instead lean in and lower my voice. "I have a daughter, too. I can understand the sentiment all too well."

Nina's eyes brighten. "And is she married?"

"Yes! With twin daughters, four years old."

"Oh, how marvelous. I always wanted a big family."

Frank snorts. "Since when?"

I can practically feel his blood boiling. Nina bites her lip, then lifts her chin. "Frank, I know you hate me right now. But this is not the place."

"What are you doing here?" Frank doesn't look up.

Nina explains calmly. "I called Verena to check in on the wedding and she mentioned that Ashton was getting her dress fitted. As her mother, I wanted to be here. So if you could exert just an ounce of self-control and not shit all over this moment, I would be very grateful."

Frank stands up. "Exert self-control? That's a funny concept coming from you."

Nina reddens and gestures to me. "Please, Frank. I'm sure Sylvia already knows more than she ever wanted to about our personal lives."

My face is plastered with a too-big smile. "Why don't we just—"

But Frank cuts me off. "Yep. I told her about catching you fucking poetry boy in the shower. But I haven't filled her in yet on the sauna, the wine room, or the library. I was exerting some self-control."

Nina's jaw drops. "You are such an asshole."

"And you are such a hypocrite." Frank practically spits.

"All right, that's enough. Everyone take a deep breath and stop talking." My voice rises and I catch a few stares from passing patrons. But I ignore them and look meaningfully at Frank. He makes a face but takes a breath. Nina does, too. As I exhale, I can't help but wonder if it's even safe to have sex in a sauna. What if someone gets heatstroke? And the library and wine room? Just how big is their Long Island home? Of course, Louis and I had a library at our house back in Connecticut. But it was more like a living room with a really nice bookcase.

I blink a few times and reorient myself. "Nina, I'm thrilled you're here. Frank, I understand you're angry. But let's focus on what's important. Your little girl is getting married and having a baby. Two incredible life events."

I look from Frank to Nina and smile warmly, like a friendly teacher or psychotherapist. Sure, Nina cheated and lied and Frank still has a murderous look on his face. But still, a baby. How can anyone not be happy about that?

Frank shoves his hands in his pockets but nods. "Fine."

I wait for Nina to say something, but she isn't reacting. I glance over at Frank and see that he's watching her, too. He narrows his eyes and a new grimness settles in around his mouth. "Ashton didn't tell you," he finally says. He doesn't sound smug. His voice is neutral, almost flat.

Nina's back goes rigid. Two dots of red burn on her cheeks. "She most certainly did not. If you'll excuse me, it sounds like I have some things to discuss with my daughter." She whirls around and heads for the elevators.

A thud of panic bursts in my stomach. My entire New York life passes in slow motion before my eyes. Ashton will be furious that I spilled the news to her mother. I can't let Nina get to her first. I catch a glimpse of her cascading hair as she weaves through the crowds toward the elevator bank. I have to stop her.

Frank's hand is on my elbow. "Let's go."

Together, we race ahead. But Nina is fast. She navigates around a group of tourists like a ballerina while Frank and I get caught in their throng of shopping bags.

"Excuse me, excuse me," I keep saying as we try to untangle ourselves.

When we get to the elevators, Nina is gone. Frank points to the stairs. We push through the double doors and fly up the concrete steps.

"Where am I going?" he asks charging ahead of me.

"Two flights up! Level four!"

I'm panting and wheezing while Frank takes the stairs two at time like a mountain goat. I really must take up running. When we get to the top, my hair sticks to my face in sweaty patches.

"Are you okay?" Frank asks.

I shoot him a thumbs-up because it's easier than talking. I shove my hair out of my eyes and open the door. I somehow get a second wind and jog across the marble floors and around the vestibule to the personal shopping department. I knock on the door.

Reese opens the door and smiles grandly at Frank and me. "Sylvia! You are not only beautiful and brilliant but also psychic! We just finished. And this handsome gentleman? Father of the bride, I assume?"

Frank looks a little dazed. "I'm Frank. Is everything okay? How's Ashton? Is her mother here?"

Frank and I both peer around the sumptuous suite. The soft lighting throws a glaze over the limed oak walls. There are several seating options arranged throughout the room, all done in shades of mauve and rose. Art deco side tables hold silver bowls of hard candy. On the far side of the room is a sliding mirrored door that opens to the rest of the suite. I suck in a breath and turn to Reese. "Is Ashton back there? Is her mom with her? Why don't I hear anything?"

Reese looks at me with a curious expression. "We soundproofed these rooms after a rather unfortunate incident with a diplomat. But there are no mothers here. I take it this is a good thing?"

I lean my back against the door to close it and nearly weep with relief. "We're trying to manage some family dynamics. Frank, why don't you go with Reese so that you can see Ashton? I'll be right behind you."

Frank follows Reese across the room and behind the enormous

sliding mirrored doors. As soon as they disappear from view, I let my feet sink into the plush carpeting and quickly dig through my purse for my compact and hairbrush. I dust some powder over my face and give my hair a few quick brushes. I then head over to the sliding doors and push them apart.

My mouth falls open. Ashton stands resplendent on a pedestal. Her hair is piled on top of her head in a loose bun. A few pieces escape in that perfect way, as though Reese brought in a wind machine so that we might just believe Ashton descended straight from the clouds like a Greek goddess. Her arms look long and delicate. Her collarbone is wide and her skin glows against the silver and gold firework detail.

Ashton beams at us. "Ta-da. What do you think?"

"Oh, Ashton. It's perfect." I feel my own eyes mist as Frank dabs his with the sleeve of his windbreaker.

"I can't believe my little girl is getting married." Frank turns to me. "Every dad must say that, huh?"

"Only the best ones." I smile. "Take some photos. Enjoy the moment."

Frank takes out his phone. While he and Ashton take a selfie, Reese comes over to me and lowers his voice. "What's going on? Should I have my team on some kind of alert for Ashton's mother?"

I sigh. "Yes. I need to speak to Ashton before she sees her."

Reese walks over to the far wall where there's a black house phone. He picks it up and turns away so that he can speak discreetly. Meanwhile, I bite my lip and look at Ashton's laughing face. She strikes silly poses and Frank snaps photos. The two of them are having a ball. How am I going to confess that I spilled the news to Nina?

"Sylvia! Sylvia, I need you! It's urgent."

I turn to see Reese hang up the black phone. Frank and Ashton are still in their own world. I walk over to Reese. His lips are tight.

I read his face instantly. "She's on her way." He nods. "Did you lock the door behind you?"

"I though it locked automatically." My eyes go wide. Oh, shit. Shit shit shit.

Reese is already across the room. I run to catch up but we're both too late. It swings open. Nina steps inside and nearly tramples us on her way over to where Ashton and Frank are still taking photos.

Ashton sees her mother first. "Mom? What are you doing here?"

Frank puts down his phone and looks at me. There's a wild beating in my chest. I try to sound cheery. "Nina, so glad you could find us. Would you care to take a seat?"

I gesture to the rolled-arm sofas around the pedestal. But Nina ignores me and glares at Ashton. "I came to see my daughter in her wedding dress. But when I went to the bridal boutique, they had no record of you. Someone called someone who told me to come down here. What on earth are you wearing? And when were you going to tell me about this baby that you're too young to have. Have you not heard of birth control?"

Ashton's face blanches. Frank steps between them. "Jesus, Nina. It's not like she's some knocked-up teenager. Take a breath."

Nina's eyes flash. "Do not tell me how to breathe. Ashton, take off that ridiculous dress. It's not even remotely appropriate for a wedding." She spins around to me. "Is this a joke? I thought you were supposed to be some sort of wedding guru. She is not walking down the aisle in some trashy dress."

My mouth hangs open. How is this the same woman I met in the shoe department? I want to say as much but instead grasp for composure. "Ashton wanted something modern and fresh. She loves this gown. It's couture," I can't help but add.

"It's horseshit." Nina puts her hands on her hips.

Even Reese looks slapped. He clears his throat and comes forward. "Madame, Sylvia and I are discussing how to add a train and matching veil. This will be very bridal, very elegant."

Nina ignores him, keeping her eyes locked on Ashton. "And you told everyone about this baby but me? Your wedding planner knows before I do? Do you have any idea how that makes me feel?"

Ashton just looks away. I can see her lip trembling but she bites down on it.

Frank sighs. "Come on, Nina. This isn't about you. This is about us having a grandchild."

Nina throws up her hands. "You know what? You're right. It's up to Ashton who she chooses to have in her life." She smooths down her sweater and plucks her sleeves. "Seeing as how I'm not needed for anything, I'll let Sebastian know that I'll be joining him for his poetry conference in Europe. We'll be back in time for the rehearsal dinner."

Ashton's mouth drops. "So that's it? You're just going to leave?"

"Yes." Nina turns and walks out of the room.

We all stare after her, dumbfounded. Did that really just happen? Reese steps respectfully out of earshot. Frank looks lost for words. I glance at Ashton. Her eyes are dry, but her face has gone dark, as though a heavy curtain has swept away the sun.

I put a hand on her arm. "Your mom is just letting off some steam."

Ashton looks at the ground. "How did she find out about the baby?"

I wince. "Ashton, I'm so deeply sorry. I thought she—"

"I told her, honey." Frank cuts in. "I didn't realize that she didn't know. I'm so sorry. Can I still take you to lunch? Cheer you up?"

Ashton's voice is faraway. "She didn't even ask when I was due."

Frank's face falls. I speak quietly. "Oh, Ashton. She's just in shock. Give her some time. And lunch is a terrific idea. May I make you and your father a reservation?"

Ashton shakes her head. "I want to go home."

Reese steps forward and picks up the bottom of the gown. "Let me escort you to the changing area so we don't lose any pins. When you're finished, I'll take the dress and the seamstresses will work their magic." Reese turns to me. "Sylvia, Frank. Pleasure to see you both." Reese sends me an air-kiss, gives a firm nod to Frank, then assists Ashton through another set of sliding doors.

Frank and I leave the suite. As we walk back toward the elevators, neither of us says anything. Frank pushes the down button.

The elevator opens. Several people get off. Only Frank and I get on. I push the lobby button.

Frank breaks the silence. "Goddamn Nina," he mutters.

"Goddamn Nina," I softly agree. "Thank you, Frank. For covering for me regarding the pregnancy."

He shrugs. "It's no big deal. Makes sense that I would've told her. God, she looked so hurt."

"I'm so sorry. I'll make sure Ashton is okay."

Frank looks at me. "You really care about my daughter."

"Of course I do."

Frank is still looking at me. But now his gaze is making my breath slow down. I once again notice the intelligence in his eyes. I feel myself inhale slowly when, suddenly, he leans forward and kisses me. His tongue is opening my mouth and I feel a volt of electricity dart through my body.

The elevator doors ding open. Frank pulls away. We both step off onto the main floor. I lean against the wall for support. My lips throb and I feel almost dizzy. My god. I forgot what it's like to really kiss someone.

Frank clears his throat. "Would you want to go out some time?"

I swallow. My voice doesn't feel like my own. "That would be lovely. But I'm quite sure Verena has a no-dating policy with regards to our clients. You're an excellent kisser."

Frank moves closer to me. "Thank you. How about tomorrow evening we meet for dinner to discuss wedding details?"

My neck is hot. "I'd love your input on the seating arrangements."

"I live for seating arrangements."

I can't help but laugh. Frank smiles. "Tomorrow. I'll pick you up at seven."

Sixteen

I have a crisis with Ashton, and yet here I am standing in the "Intimate Care" aisle at a Duane Reade three blocks away from Verena's office so that I can peruse bikini wax products.

You don't have time for this, Sylvia, the voice in my head warns.

I rub my forehead. The voice is right. I don't have time for this. But as soon as Frank left, I called Verena. I briefly explained that we had a "Nina situation" and she said to come directly to her office.

And so that was the plan. I flew out of Bergdorf's and half walked, half trotted my way uptown. But I couldn't stop tasting Frank. I felt like the heroine of a Danielle Steel novel. I'd never been so aware of my body.

As I hustled up the city blocks, I couldn't help but wonder: Would Frank kiss me again? Of course he would. But for how long? All night? Like teenagers? Would I slip my hand in his pants? Would he slip his in mine?

As soon as the notion of Frank's fingers inside my underpants entered my head, fear pierced my spine like an ice pick. Sure, I have great panties. Gorgeous lace and satin numbers. But that didn't matter. I was frozen on the corner of a sidewalk seeing nothing but flashes of Belinda's perfectly groomed bikini area. And then I remembered Bunny's crotch was likewise smooth as a supermodel's. Did Nina wax, too? Probably.

As cabs whizzed by, I looked down at my feet. I felt shamed by my own shaming. I shouldn't wax for some man. And yet a little part of me wanted to. I remembered that episode of *Sex and the City* when Carrie visited a sadist to get the full Brazilian. I laughed and laughed but remembered thinking it might be fun to at least try it. Of course, I never made an appointment. Sex with Louis stopped inspiring me so long ago.

And then, like a sign from the gods, the actual sign for Duane Reade popped into view. I crossed the street, detoured inside, and am currently scanning hair removal kits with names like Kopari Coconut Melt Mini and Flamingo Body Wax. I choose a name that seems familiar: Sally Hansen's Insta Wax Strips for Face & Bikini.

Just feeling the smooth, orange box in my hands makes my groin pulse. I squint beneath the store's fluorescent lights and see myself on the cover of my own erotica paperback. I'm wearing a man's button-down shirt that has been torn open. My hair has fresh highlights. The title reads, *Sylvia Burning.*

My phone beeps.

I reach into my purse and see the text is from Verena, wondering where I am. Shit. I rush to the register, pay for the wax, and shove it into my purse. I hurry out of the store and race down the block to Verena's. Just knowing that it's in there makes me feel like I can fly.

As I push open the heavy doors to the building, I force all thoughts of Frank and vaginas out of my head. I have a job to do. When I enter the waiting room, Miku is handing out champagne to a very handsome gay couple and their mothers. I nod a quick hello and slip through the door and head straight down the hallway toward Verena's inner office. I'm thinking about how to bring her up to speed in a confident, "I've got this" manner when a shrill voice assaults my ears.

"When will she be back?"

How odd. That sounds like Isabel. I let out another breath. I really need a good night of sleep.

"Oh, this is so marvelous. Good for her!"

Okay, that was definitely Bunny's voice. I lurch forward and push open Verena's door. My heart drops.

Isabel and Bunny sit in the two straight-backed chairs in front of Verena's desk. Isabel stands up as soon as I enter. She wears skinny jeans with a cropped military jacket and scuffed ballet flats. Her hair is pulled into a too-tight bun. Bunny stands up, too. She wears Fendi logo yoga tights with a matching, off-the-shoulder sweatshirt that makes her look like a retired rugby player. She waves at me, her French-manicured nails glinting beneath the overhead lights.

Verena sits behind her desk. She sips a root beer. "Your family stopped by."

I feel like bursting into hysterical laughter.

"Mom? Seriously? What is going on? And why haven't you returned my calls?" Isabel puts her hands on her hips. I notice that her military jacket is missing a button. "I've been so worried," she adds accusingly.

Bunny rolls her eyes. "Isabel, please. Your mother is a grown-up. Syl! I'm so happy to see you, love." Bunny envelops me in her arms and whispers in my ear, "I'm so proud of you."

After she releases me, I stand there a moment. Staring at my daughter. "How did you find me?"

Isabel bites a fingernail. "I used the Find My Laptop app on my phone. It pinged from here."

I glance behind me through the door into Molly's and my shared office. The laptop sits innocently on the desk. I turn back to Isabel, then try to read Verena's face. "Verena, I'm so sorry if this disturbed your day. Allow me to officially introduce you to my daughter, Isabel, and her mother-in-law, Bunny."

Verena waves a hand. "Don't be so formal. It's fine. I'm happy to meet your family. Do you want a moment with them before we discuss what happened between Ashton and Nina?"

I shake my head. "No. This is a pressing matter." I look at Isabel and Bunny and use my most professional voice. "I'm sorry to do this after you've come all this way. But I'm in the middle of work. May we make a plan to see each other later?"

Isabel sighs and turns to Verena. "Do you know what happened last time my mom was a wedding planner? She got sued. Did she tell you that?"

Verena smiles calmly. "Why don't you want your mother to succeed?"

Isabel looks slapped. "Excuse me?"

Verena puts down her soda. "It's a simple question. Why are you trying to humiliate your mother? She's honest and decent and damn good at her job. That really seems to bother you. I'm wondering why. I'm sure she is, too."

Isabel's eyes flash. "I'm not trying to humiliate her! I'm trying to save her." She turns to me. "You don't just get to move to New York and be happy, Mom. Life isn't some fairy tale where you get to change everything and be someone else." Her voice cracks.

I wince and take a long look at her. Her bun is coming undone in the center. I can see the concealer cracking beneath her eyes. There's a pimple she scratched into a bloody scab on her chin.

"Isabel," I say softly, my heart suddenly breaking. "What's going on?"

She shakes her head. "Look, I realize I'm overreacting. But I can't handle everyone in my whole life having a crisis."

"I'm not having a crisis," I say, slowly. "But what do you mean by 'everyone in my life'?"

Isabel looks from Bunny to Verena to me. Her face reddens and she grabs her bag. "Just forget I even came. Clearly you've got it all figured out." Isabel storms out of the room.

As soon as she disappears from view, Bunny sits back down in her chair. She wrings her hands together and I see one of her nails is chipped. Her lipstick doesn't match her eyeshadow the way it usually does and her smile is only half-lit. She's tired.

I glance at Verena, unsure what to do. She offers me a small smile, then picks up her phone. "Sylvia, I need to make a call. Why don't you and Bunny take a moment. I'll be back in five."

She gets up and walks out of the office. As soon as she's gone, I sit down beside Bunny. "What's going on?"

"Todd lost his job." Bunny's voice is blunt. But I can hear the pained undertones of a worried mother.

"Oh my god, that's awful." I narrow my eyes, gripped by a sudden fury. "Those idiots. Todd is a genius with computers. He turned that company around, made it profitable. People have no gratitude."

"He quit."

I arch forward with surprise. "When? What happened?"

"Two weeks ago. He left for lunch on a Wednesday and never

came back. They called and called but he didn't answer his cell. His boss, Raj, finally called Isabel at her office Friday morning. Izzy freaked. Todd had told her he was working from home because the offices were being fumigated."

"Oh, Bunny. That's just so . . . bizarre. What did Todd say?"

Bunny shrugs. "Nothing. Izzy called Marty and me. We came straight over. But Todd said nothing. He acts like it's perfectly normal to lie to your family and quit your job."

"Is it a midlife crisis?"

"He's thirty-fucking-five years old!" Bunny explodes, her hands jutting into the air. "Louis is having a midlife crisis. You're having a midlife crisis. Todd has not earned a midlife crisis!" She inhales sharply. "Oh, shitties. Sorry, Syl. That came out wrong."

I pat her knee gently. "I'm quite flattered that you'd call this a midlife crisis. It makes me feel young."

Bunny shakes her head, her eyes fierce. "What you're doing is not a crisis. When Izzy said you moved to Manhattan and had a roommate, well, it sounded like a crisis. But this is different." She gestures to Verena's office. "This is real. You have a job. I'm so impressed."

I feel a glow of warmth spread over me. "Thank you, Bunny. That means a lot. Louis has been, well, awful. And I'm really trying here."

Bunny nods. "I can't even imagine everything you've been through. That's why I didn't call about Izzy and Todd. I didn't want to burden you."

"It's never a burden."

"But it is. Jesus, Syl. Our kids' lives are a total shit show. Todd and Izzy sleep in separate bedrooms. The girls notice the tension and are acting out. Their new pod teacher stopped coming."

"Izzy must be out of her mind."

Bunny nods grimly. "Beyond. And Todd refuses to look for another job. With Izzy's promotion, she makes enough money to support them and he felt, how did he put it, like 'his soul was withering beneath the environmentally friendly lights' at his office."

I crack a smile. "Izzy always loved Todd's poetic spirit."

"Well, she sees no poetry in this. She's livid. I don't blame her. I was so ashamed. My son has never been a liar."

I nod sympathetically. "Izzy can be tough to talk to. Don't be too hard on Todd."

Bunny softens a moment. "At first, Marty and I were worried. What happened? Why would he just leave so irresponsibly?" Bunny then shakes her head, frustrated. "But he has no explanation. And now with the girls free all day, he says it's fate. He's meant to be a househusband and spend quality daddy time with them. But what that really means is calling me and asking for help while he does cosmic yoga on TV. I'm tired. Those granddaughters of ours do not stop moving. They don't color. They don't play Barbies. They ride their wiggle cars through the house like Formula One drivers. They take apart appliances. The new Dyson is currently in seventeen pieces and I have no idea how to put it back together. And of course Izzy and Todd don't have a broom. They never thought to get one. What kind of society do we live in when young people forget to keep a simple broom in their homes?"

I look at Bunny's tortured face and can't help but giggle. She's had a fleet of housekeepers since I've known her. I can't imagine her sweeping up rogue Cheerios. She seems to sense what I'm thinking and starts to giggle, too. "I lasted a day. I have a cleaning service coming now."

"Doesn't Izzy have a housekeeper of her own?"

"They all quit, dear. Your daughter is a bit of a tyrant. She checks for dust like a health-code inspector."

I sigh. "Oh, Bunny. I wish Isabel didn't feel like everything needed to be perfect all the time. I used to think it was a good thing. She's so organized and ambitious. But I wish she didn't feel responsible for everything. It makes her mean. And she's not mean. Well, sometimes she is. But I don't think she intends to be."

Bunny pats my knee. "I remember when Todd first brought her over for dinner. She was funny and sweet." She pauses a moment. "Well, not exactly sweet. But good-hearted. Marty and I could tell she cares about people."

"She does care. Too much." I sigh. "She probably doesn't like having a husband who's out of work and kids who aren't being groomed for a PhD at Oxford."

"No, she does not."

I look at Bunny's washed-out face and feel a pang of sadness. I miss her glittery shadows and showgirl bronzer. "You're a saint, Bunny. An amazing mother and grandmother. I feel like a total shit. I'm not helping at all."

She straightens up. "Don't! You're living your best life. And don't feel too sorry for me. Marty helps out. We kind of enjoy it in a masochistic, partners-in-crime kind of way." Her eyes start to glint. "We play little pranks on our kids. Like, sometimes I hide Izzy's phone charger and watch her tear madly through the house."

I can't help it. I laugh. "What else?"

"Marty keeps eating Todd's locally sourced almonds from some Vermont farm. It's silly. But it drives Todd bananas. Marty doesn't even like nuts."

I snort. Bunny does, too. She wipes her eyes and exhales. "And we're treating ourselves to a vacation this spring. A hotel we've always wanted to visit on Mykonos. There's a fabulous restaurant, the suites are to-die-for. And the nude beaches. We cannot wait!"

The door opens and Verena enters. "That sounds heavenly. We'll have to get the name of it for our more exotic honeymooners."

Verena stands in front of us and meets my eye. "All set?"

I nod. "Absolutely."

Bunny takes the hint. She stands to say goodbye. As I get up to give her a hug, I accidentally kick over my purse. I watch in horror as my bikini wax kit tumbles out and rolls over to Verena's feet.

She kneels down to pick it up. "At-home bikini wax? My god, Sylvia. You're braver than I thought."

Bunny's eyes go wide. "You met a man!"

The blood evacuates from my face. I take the box from Verena and shove it back into my purse. "Don't be silly. I just want to freshen up."

Bunny can't stop inspecting me. "I don't believe you! What's his name?" She sits back down.

Verena goes to sit behind her desk and leans forward. "Yes. Do tell. Someone new or an old flame?"

I stammer. "Someone new." Shit. That's not good. I clear my throat. "I mean, someone new but also old. An old friend."

"You're planning to fuck him?" Verena crosses her legs.

I flinch at the word "fuck." I, Sylvia Fisher, have never really fucked anyone. Even my ears feel hot as I try to think of what to say.

"You should wear that little teddy you modeled for me," Bunny says thoughtfully.

I could melt of embarrassment. I glance at Verena for a reaction. But she's not registering anything strange about me trying on underwear with Bunny. Instead she asks, "What's his name? This city can be small. Maybe I know him."

"No, no. He lives in . . . New Jersey." I swallow and start speaking quickly, like a person who just committed armed robbery.

Verena looks at me. "Why are you being so cagey? Is he married?" She starts to smile. "I should have guessed. It's totally normal to try on the role of cheater after what you've been through. And don't lie—it's deliciously satisfying, right?"

"He's divorced, thank you very much!" My whole face is hot and I forget I'm even lying. "I would never cheat," I add.

"It's not cheating if you're the one who's single. Yes?" Verena looks at Bunny for confirmation.

But Bunny shakes her head. "I'm with Syl on this."

Verena shrugs. "All I'm saying is that if you aren't married, you're not cheating."

"Do you really sleep with married men?" I can't help it. I don't want Verena to be that kind of person.

Verena clears her throat. "Forgive me. I didn't mean to sound so cavalier. I don't go out looking for married men. But if I happen to meet someone and later find out that he's married, it's not on me to feel guilty. Now stop deflecting. I want to hear more about your new beau."

"Yes," Bunny agrees after a sideways glance at Verena. "Where did you meet?"

"My roommate, Evie, is a whiz at computer stuff. She signed me up for Facebook and Instagram and some other app things. She found him. We went to high school together. He lives in Princeton and is a professor. Math. Some kind of multivariable summations." That's the trouble with lying. Once I start, I can't stop. "He used to help me with geometry."

Stop talking, Sylvia. My tongue feels heavy.

"Princeton? Wow. Impressive." Verena clicks on her computer. "Let's look him up. I'm on their website."

Fuck.

Bunny has gotten up and is peering over Verena's shoulder. "Which one is he, Syl?"

I swallow. "He's actually on sabbatical. He wrote a book about the mathematical beauty of the world's natural wonders. We're meeting up for a bite. I'm sure nothing will happen. I just wanted to feel sexy so I bought the waxing kit. It's stupid. I'm not the sexy type."

Verena and Bunny look at me for a moment. Bunny then leaves Verena's side and comes over to where I'm standing. She takes me by the shoulders and looks directly in my eyes. "You are beyond sexy."

Verena nods. "She's right. You're gorgeous, Sylvia. Any man, especially some geeky math professor, is going to feel like the luckiest guy in the world."

"I can't remember the last time I had sex with Louis. Isn't that pathetic? I can't even remember the last time Louis kissed me."

Verena winks. "It's like riding a bike."

I blush and think about Frank. That's true. It was pretty easy.

I look at Bunny and wait for her to say something outrageous but sweet when she leans forward and kisses me squarely on the mouth.

After a moment, she releases me and smiles. "You've still got it, babe. Now, I'll go and deal with Izzy. Don't worry about a thing. Great to meet you, Verena. Ciao." Bunny leaves the office.

I stand there, stunned. I slowly turn to look at Verena.

Verena looks pretty stunned, too. "So," she finally says. "Very supportive family you've got."

Seventeen

T hankfully, the rest of the meeting with Verena was all business. Neither of us mentioned Bunny's kiss, which suited
me just fine. Instead, I brought Verena up to speed on the
Ashton-Nina situation and promised that I would handle things. We
both agreed that Nina not being around would allow Ashton and me to
finish planning the wedding without interference. I just needed to
manage the emotional fallout Ashton was certain to be experiencing.

And so after assuring Verena that I had a plan—Reese has already
texted me, "Operation Shoes is Complete"—I hurry up Park Avenue
to Dan and Ashton's apartment and am ushered into a marble lobby
by a uniformed doorman. As I zip up the elevator to the twenty-
second floor, I can't help but laugh. Evie and I are living like fresh-
out-of-college kids compared to this.

When Dan opens the door, the first thing I see are shoeboxes.
There are mountains of them against the walls lining the foyer.

"Dan, so lovely to see you." I take in his tired but sweetly handsome face. He's wearing jeans and a Chicago Cubs T-shirt that's splattered with something brown and a little syrupy. "How are you? Ashton is here, yes?"

Dan lets out a breath and runs a hand through his hair. I see more brown splatter on his arm as he nods. "She's in the bedroom. She came home from the dress fitting with a pork tenderloin. She's been crying and cooking all afternoon."

I follow Dan's eyeline and see the discarded heap of dirty dishes on the kitchen's center island. Remembering that Nina is an interior designer, I have to assume this beautiful apartment is her work. It's been modernized with floor-to-ceiling windows and an open concept floor plan.

The kitchen is a chef's dream except for the fact that it's a complete disaster right now. There's a discarded hunk of meat on the counter that looks half-raw. There are bottles of sauces and spices spilled everywhere and a large pan overflowing with some kind of brown, lumpy sauce, which explains the stains on Dan. As I walk toward the mess, I'm overwhelmed by a tangy odor that I can't quite place.

Dan notices my wrinkled nose. "Ashton called it culinary fusion." He picks up a stained recipe book and reads, "Barbecue roast with deconstructed seaweed crisps."

"That must explain these." I squint at a baking sheet containing little burnt green balls. "They look . . . interesting."

"They look like cat shit. At least, that's what Ashton says. I don't know. I've never had a pet. It's Nina's fault. Every time Ashton fights with her, she embarks on some *Iron Chef* project." Dan tosses the recipe book back onto the counter.

I smile sympathetically. "Family can make us do crazy things. But before we say anything else, congratulations on the baby. It's such wonderful news. And more than ever, now is the time to stay focused on the good stuff."

Dan's face brightens. "You're right. I'm really stoked about the baby. Terrified, too. But everyone says that's normal. And my mom will help. She's one of those people who is very excited about grandchildren."

I clear my throat. "Do your folks have a good relationship with Ashton's parents?" I can't help it. I'm curious. Besides, this is important data for me.

Dan puts the dishes in the sink and pours soap onto them. His face looks slightly pained as he chooses his words. "My mom has tried to be friends with Nina. But they're really different."

I wait for Dan to say more, but he doesn't. And so I gesture to the sink. "Well, your parents have certainly taught you well. I like a man who helps with cleanup." I pat his arm. "And don't worry about Nina. That's what I'm here for. You said Ashton is in the bedroom?"

Dan nods and reaches for a large sponge. "She was crying and cooking and I was about to get out the fire extinguisher when the doorman told us we had a large delivery. Two men came up with dollies. There must be twenty-five pairs of shoes here. Ashton's mood definitely improved." Dan looks at me and grins a little. "For what it's worth, you really know my girl. She actually smiled when she saw these boxes."

I say a mental thank-you to Reese for sending them so quickly. I knew doing a pep talk over shoe shopping would help my chances of breaking the bad mood. Ashton may not care about clothes or handbags or jewelry. But she does like shoes. And when I texted Reese the request to send over as many as possible, he came through.

I look back at Dan and smile. "Do you mind if I go join her? And don't worry about these dishes. I'm happy to help before I leave."

Dan almost looks offended. "You can't clean our kitchen, Sylvia!"

I shrug. "I'm a wedding planner. I've cleaned worse."

He shakes his head. "By the time you ladies come out, you'll see what magic I can do. Bedroom's down the hall, on the left."

"Thank you. And in case I forget to say this, Ashton is a lucky woman."

Dan puts on some hot-pink dishwashing gloves. "I try."

I laugh and head toward the bedroom. I knock on the door. "Ashton? It's Sylvia. I'm coming in."

I open the door to a massive primary bedroom and see Ashton sitting in the middle of the floor surrounded by shoes. Her hair is in a loose ponytail. She wears a simple white T-shirt and a pair of capri cargo pants. She's arranged the shoes in circles around herself and sits like a yogi looking at stilettos, heeled sandals, glittery sneakers, cowboy boots, a pair of combat boots—not really sure why Reese sent those—flip-flops with rhinestones, Mary Janes, and traditional peep-toe pumps.

"Wow," I breathe as I glance from the swirling display of shoes to the rest of the bedroom. Behind Ashton is a low platform bed with a white quilted leather headboard. To my left is a small seating area with a Mark Rothko print on the wall. To my right, a bank of windows offers a glittering view of the city. I focus back on Ashton and survey the display of shoes. "Have you tried any on yet?"

She looks up at me. Her eyes are a little glassy. "I wanted to see them all first." I carefully step over the shoes so that I can arrange myself on the floor next to her.

"Good plan. How are you doing?"

She reaches out to run a finger over a metallic, chunky-heeled pump. "My mom would hate these." She then looks at me. "Don't worry. I'm not going to cancel the wedding. It's not fair to Dan and his family. And it's not fair to our baby."

I smile, surprised. "You've grown up a lot in the last few days."

She rolls her eyes. "Well, not that much. Did you see our kitchen?"

"Would you like me to send you some simpler recipes? Because for what it's worth, your baby does not need to eat deconstructed barbecue seaweed. We can start simple. With something that doesn't require fire. Maybe mashed bananas."

"You mean banana pudding?"

"I mean you take a banana and mash it."

Ashton laughs. I do, too. I reach forward and grab a pair of leopard-print sneakers emblazoned with glittery stars. "I had no idea Reese would be so liberal with the choices. Shall we weed some of these out? I'm thinking it's a no for these sneakers. Also the combat boots. I can start a reject pile."

"Toss the combat boots. But I love these." Ashton snatches the sneakers from my hand. "For the reception."

I make a face. Ashton raises a brow. "I thought you were supposed to support all my choices."

"I'm here to guide you. If you want comfort, go with flat sandals to change into for dancing. Because trust me, in ten years when you look at your pictures, you don't want to see yourself wearing sneakers with your wedding dress." I wince. "It's like when brides insist on black nail polish because they want to be edgy. It's not edgy. It's ugly. There's a difference."

Ashton's mouth drops open. "I thought we were going for nontraditional."

"Yes. But we must maintain standards." I turn to look out the windows a moment. The evening sky blurs into a starry tableau as I drift back in time. "My daughter insisted on Converse sneakers for her reception. You think it's cute, but then the shoelaces come undone and it just looks wrong. She didn't listen to me. I told her, 'Isabel, you can wear sneakers every other day of your life. For once, have a little fun. Go for cowboy boots if you want to be different.'"

"And her entire wedding was ruined?"

I glance at Ashton. Her lips twitch. Unreal. She's making fun of me. I cross my arms. "She tripped and fell into her cake."

Ashton gasps. "Oh my god! Was she okay?"

"Yes. Thankfully. But she was just mortified. They had just wheeled out the cake. Everyone was seated. She and Todd, her husband, were going up to do the cutting ceremony when she tripped. She reached out to grab something. Half the cake came down on top of her."

A giggle escapes Ashton's lips. She claps a hand over her mouth. "Sorry. It's not funny. It's awful."

"It was awful. Everyone started to laugh and she grew angrier and angrier."

"What happened?"

"Bunny, her mother-in-law, and I whisked her to the bathroom and helped her clean up. Thankfully, her dress was strapless and the cake was white. So we really just had to wipe a bunch of whipped cream off her shoulders and back. The rest of the cake kind of slid off the satin bodice. It wasn't perfect but it was manageable. I was actually impressed." I remember Izzy's fierce expression in the bathroom mirror. "After cleaning up, she redid her makeup, used paper towels to blot her hair, then told me and Bunny that she wasn't going to let some 'stupid cake ruin her special day.' She also told us that if anyone laughed again, she would punch them in the face."

Ashton eyes are wide and bright. "Wow. Isabel sounds scary. In an awesome way. Are you still in a fight with her?"

As I think of how to answer, I hand Ashton a pair of glittery heels. She wordlessly puts them on, stands up, and walks across the room in them. Even with her loose cargo capris, they look stunning.

I let out a breath. "I love those. Now, try the Jimmy Choo feather cocktail sandals in gold. I would consider knee-replacement surgery to be able to wear them. And, yes, Izzy and I are in a fight. Well, maybe not. I don't really know. She's just very angry with me."

Ashton sits down and reaches for the Jimmy Choos but doesn't put them on. She looks at me. "Why? You seem like the best mom in the world. Unless you're one of those Jekyll and Hyde people. Great at work, awful at home."

"I recently left my husband after finding out he was unfaithful." I begin.

Ashton nods. "Dan told me. You walked in on him naked with another woman."

My cheeks burn. I forgot about my overshare with Dan at Verena's office that first day. To be fair, I didn't know at the time that I would ever see these people again. I swallow. "Right. Then as you can imagine, it was quite a shock for Isabel."

"Of course I can imagine! I know all about it."

"Well, Izzy is having a tough time. She thinks I should go back to Louis and work it out. She doesn't like the idea of me on my own. She thinks I'm too old to be independent."

"That's ridiculous. You're not even old."

I want to weep. Instead, I smile softly. "Thank you, dear. But in my daughter's eyes, I'm ancient and useless."

Ashton shakes her head, vehement. "Call her. Invite her for a girls' night. Make her see you as someone who isn't just her mom. I'd die to have my mom treat me like a real person."

I tilt my head. "How does your mom treat you?"

Ashton looks away for a moment. "Like someone who owes her something."

My heart feels crushed. What a sad thing to say. I'm about to reach over to comfort Ashton, but she turns toward me so suddenly that I'm knocked off-balance.

"Call her, Sylvia. Do it. Right now." Ashton grabs my purse and hands it to me. I look at her, totally baffled.

"Isn't it me who was giving you family advice?"

"Sometimes I like to be the smart one. Call her and then let's try on more shoes."

I hesitate a moment. Is Ashton going to sit there and listen? She holds the Jimmy Choos in her hand and stares at me. I suppose so.

I dial Izzy's number and try to keep my breathing steady. Voice-mail picks up. As soon as I hear the beep, I force a calm, loving tone. "Izzy, it's Mom. I don't like how we left things today. I know you're probably back in Connecticut already. But I'd love to make a plan so that we can have some special time just us. Call me. And I love you." I hang up and sigh.

Ashton smiles, pleased, and puts on the Jimmy Choos. "These are the ones."

The high-heeled satin sandals are embellished with gold sequins. A whimsical ostrich feather hangs from a tassel down the front of Ashton's foot. "Those are definitely the ones," I breathe. "Would you like to try any others just for fun?"

She stares at me like I've got three heads. "I want to try on every single pair of shoes."

She looks at her watch. "Unless you need to be somewhere."

I look at Ashton's sweet face and feel a rush of fondness for her for considering my time. I rearrange myself on the floor and smile. "I have nowhere to be. I'm even looking forward to seeing those sneakers now."

Ashton winks. "I'll double-knot the laces."

"Deal."

. . .

I GOT HOME FROM ASHTON'S last night after eleven. Evie was still working and so I took a long shower, got into my coziest pj's, and climbed into bed. Before falling asleep, I sent Evie a novella of a text detailing the day's events. It was actually quite soothing to write everything out. Nina. Frank's kiss. Isabel's anger. Lying to Verena. Bunny's kiss. Shoe shopping and bonding with Ashton. By the time I hit the Send button, it was as though the entire day unlatched from my shoulders, and I fell deeply asleep.

When I wake this morning, I get out of bed and change into a cotton polo shirt and a pair of drawstring pants. I go into the living room and find Evie already sitting on the sofa still wearing her python-print silk pajamas. She's reading her phone, her brow knitted above her rimless glasses. She doesn't notice me at first.

I clear my throat. "Morning, Evie."

She looks up and sets down her phone. Her brow unfolds and she takes off her glasses. "Sit. I'm dying to know: Who's the better kisser?"

I laugh and sit on the floor and tuck my feet beneath me with my back against the sofa so that Evie can stretch out on the couch. "I'm not sure if Bunny's kiss counts."

"Was there tongue involved?"

I think a moment. "I don't know. Maybe by accident?"

"It counts, then," she says matter-of-factly. "God, Nina sounds like a total psycho. Who treats their child that way? Isn't she afraid of being cut out of Ashton's life?"

"I'm not sure Nina's mind goes there."

Evie's cheeks are pink. "I've been stalking Oliver on Instagram. He's in his first year at Pratt."

"The art and design university? In Brooklyn? That's one of the best in the world. It's fate that you're both here."

"Well, sort of." Evie's eyes shine, but her face reddens again. "I probably should have told you this, but I was a little embarrassed. Part of why I was so thrilled to move to New York with you is because I wanted to be in the same city as him. Even if we don't see each other, it's just nice to know we breathe the same air." She pauses. "That sounded revoltingly sentimental."

"It sounds like a grandmother. Why haven't you told him you're here?"

She looks away. "I don't want to bother him."

I stare at her, confused. "You follow him on Instagram. Wouldn't he recognize the name Evelyn Neiss as one of his followers?"

"I'm masquerading under a different name. I created a fake Instagram account just so I could follow him."

My jaw drops. "But why?"

Evie folds her hands. "Last summer, I promised myself that I would stop googling him and his mom, Amanda. It was too painful to know about their lives and not be a part of them." She finally looks at me and offers a wry smile. "But I'm just too good at this computer shit. If I were forty years younger, Sylvia, I would be a hacker." She takes a breath. "Anyhow, I made it through the summer and into the fall. But one day, I couldn't help myself. Long story short, I went down the cyber rabbit hole and saw that Oliver had begun his first year at Pratt. And then you had this brilliant idea of moving to New York. It *did* feel like fate. So I made up a new identity so that I could kind of be in touch."

"Evie," I start slowly. "I truly don't understand. You are not a woman of half measures. Why not just call him? Keep it simple. You're here.

He's here. Have some lunch. Or a nice dinner. College kids love to be taken to dinner. Why on earth would he say no? Nothing bad happened between you guys."

"Well, my son overdosed and died on him."

She says this so bluntly that it takes my breath away for a moment. "Surely he doesn't blame you."

"His mother does."

"That's completely unfair. You did everything you could to save him."

Evie runs a hand through her hair, her voice now weary. "I know, Sylvia. But she's the mother. I have to respect her."

"That's bullshit. Oliver is in college. He's old enough to make his own decisions." I exhale. "Just send him one message. What's the worst that happens? He says he doesn't want to see you? Fine. Then he's a shit. I'm sorry, but that's the truth. So give him a chance to not be a shit. Life is too short. You're the one who taught me that."

I feel blood thumping through my body. I'm about to say more when Evie pats my arm gently. "I'll think about it. But now I want to talk about something else. Like the hot sex you're going to have tonight. And I think you need to leave it at sex and not actually date this man. Actually, hold that thought. I need to pee."

Evie stands and smooths down her pajamas. The silk shimmers in waves over her body as she takes her cane and disappears around the corner to our bathroom.

I stand up and pace back and forth. I know that she wants the conversation about Oliver to be over. I know that it's none of my business. But as I glance at her phone lying there on the sofa, I'm seized with a wave of righteous energy. Every ligament in my body pulses and before I can stop myself, I've taken her phone and swiped it open.

I open up Evie's email inbox and go to send a message to Amanda and Oliver when I suck in a breath. There, in plain view, is a message from Amanda dated five days ago. Without thinking, I open it and read:

> Evelyn, Thank you for your message. It's nice to hear that you're doing well in New York. I'm sorry to disappoint you but nothing has changed on our end. Oliver and I do not want to be in touch. We know that you understand. Take care. —Amanda.

Tears spring into the back of my eyes. I sink onto the sofa. Of course Evie wrote to them. I'm so stupid. She was probably so hopeful, already planning which chic restaurant to go to. She must have fantasized about him hearing her play the piano. He'd gasp and say proudly, "That's my grandmother."

Then she got this awful reply. I can't stop dissecting Amanda's words. The patronizing line "We know that you understand," and the dismissive "Take care." God, they must have made Evie feel so small. How dare she.

How fucking dare she.

I have never felt such rage. It's like the Incredible Hulk is ripping through my chest, and before I know it, I'm swiping through the contacts and I land on Oliver's number. I'm about to dial but then, mercifully, realize that Evie will be able to see the outgoing call. She can't know that I snooped.

Quickly, I pick up my phone and dial Oliver's number into it. As it rings, I toss Evie's phone back onto the couch and tiptoe outside our front door to make sure Evie can't overhear me.

The phone rings and rings. I'm staring at my shadow on the wall in the cramped hallway by the stairs. Voicemail picks up. My thoughts ping back to leaving Isabel a message last night. No one picks up their damn phones anymore.

Well, maybe it's better this way. My voice feels shaky as I wait for the beep. "Oliver, this is Sylvia Fisher. You don't know me, but I'm a dear friend of your grandmother, Evelyn. She doesn't know I'm calling you, but I just wanted to tell you that . . ." I stop talking, suddenly unsure of what to say. What can I do to get him to call her back? I feel each second of silence go by in slow motion. And then, without warning, I just start talking as though I have no ability to control my mouth, ". . . You see, she's sick, and I thought you should know before it's too late. Call me directly as, again, she doesn't know I've called you. My number is . . ."

As I rattle of the rest of the message, it's as though I'm in a fugue state. When I finally hang up, I stand there a moment. I can't believe I did that.

I turn and see Evie. "Sylvia? What are you doing? Is someone out here?"

I shake my head and have no idea what to say. "Just wanted to check the weather," I blurt.

Evie gives me an odd look. "But you're standing in the hallway. Not outside."

I nod and talk as if on autopilot. "Right. That was dumb. I just got distracted. Let's go inside and talk about the hot sex I'm having later."

Eighteen

vie sits next to me in one of the spa chairs at our neighborhood nail salons. I turn and look at her blissful face. Her eyes are closed and I can hear her breathing lightly as a nail technician massages her feet. It's now after 4:00 p.m. and I've managed to keep all thoughts of Amanda and Oliver out of my head. In fact, it's as though it never happened. We've been so busy all afternoon.

After we went back into the apartment earlier, Evie wanted to see the bikini wax kit that I bought. She barely skimmed the flimsy leaflet of directions before shaking her head. "Sylvia," she said firmly. "There is no reality in which I am letting you give yourself a bikini wax in our apartment. You are going to a proper salon to have this done."

I completely agreed with her logic. The only thing is that most proper salons don't have drop-in appointments available on Sunday afternoons. We did the next best thing and found a nearby nail place that offers body treatments. Evie insisted we treat ourselves to mani-pedis before the wax.

As I look at Evie soaking in the relaxation now, I know it's the right move. We needed this. We're the only customers in here. Spa-themed music gently hums from the speakers. It's some kind of drum combined with a babbling brook. Or maybe it's a rainforest. I can't quite decide, but who cares. I sigh and feel my shoulders sink into the cushy chair. The salon is small with silver walls and hanging pendant lights. Rita, the young woman painting my toes, uses a tiny brush to wipe away any stray polish. She's not a day over twenty-two and yet has the countenance of a strict schoolteacher.

"This color is perfect," she affirms.

I look at the ruby red on my toes and fingernails and smile. I was going to choose a light pink color called Innocence, but Rita—and Evie—gave me two choices: red or red. And so I chose Pop My Cherry. Evie, pleased, went with a different shade of red called Bury the Hatchet. I wonder if the people who name these polishes have a bit of mysticism about them. I'm about to ask this aloud when Evie's voice cuts in.

"Sylvia," she says, her eyes now open and focused on me. "This is all a bit of fun, yes?

"What do you mean?"

"This date with Frank is about sex. Not romance, yes?"

My face prickles as Rita looks up for a moment. I clear my throat. "Frank is a good man and a great kisser. We're going to have some fun tonight and then, yes, if we decide to see each other again, I've already made it clear we need to wait until after the wedding. I wouldn't risk my career for a man," I add.

Evie nods. "I just wanted to make sure."

"Consider yourself assured." I flex my gleaming toes and smile. "This color is brilliant. I may have to mark it down for Ashton on her wedding day."

Rita places paper flip-flops onto my feet and stands up. "Brides love it. Classic with a splash of flirt. Let's head to the waxing station."

My stomach tightens. My arms go stiff.

Rita gestures for me to stand. "Don't be scared. I've done this, like, a thousand times. Maybe more. I can even make a heart if you want instead of a landing strip."

Evie's mouth drops. "That's fantastic." She swings her legs over the side of the chair and reaches for her cane. "I'm coming."

"I am not having a heart waxed onto my vagina." I gulp. "Maybe this is a bad idea."

Evie lifts a brow. "Don't be so negative, Sylvia. It's not your style."

THE WAXING STATION is just a tiny room behind a curtain in the back of the nail salon. I'm lying on this paper-lined flimsy table with no pants and no underpants. I have nothing covering my lower body but my hands. I look at the bare wall to my left. It's bright pink. I feel like I'm engulfed in bubble gum. I turn to my right and watch as Evie peers over Rita's shoulder. Rita stirs a pot of wax on a little table covered with bottles, tubes, wooden sticks, tweezers, and several other utensils that I've never seen before.

"Should it be boiling like that?" Evie asks.

Rita nods. "We want it super piping hot. It makes it easier to rip the hair off in a single tear." Rita demonstrates a ripping motion. I see her bicep ripple beneath her T-shirt.

"What do you mean by 'single tear'?" My voice is hoarse.

"We use hard wax," Rita explains. "No paper strips. I just spread it on, let it harden, and tear it off. Easy peasy. Okay, move your hands and butterfly your legs."

I look over Rita's shoulder at Evie. She meets my eyes. "It'll be fine. You've birthed a child."

That's true. And so I try to get the soles of my feet together but my legs won't go flat. "I'm sorry," I say to Rita. "I'm just not flexible enough anymore."

"We'll do one at a time. Here, put your left leg out straight and I'll take your right one up on my shoulder." Rita picks up my entire right leg and drapes it over her bony shoulder. She spreads hot, oozing wax from my inner thigh all the way up and over half of my groin. It's warm and gooey, like a little blanket of lava being spread on my body.

"This isn't so bad," I say to Evie. "Almost like the heating pad I use when my arthritis flares up."

Evie nods. "That's good. I like heating pads." She reaches for my hand and gives it a quick squeeze.

Rita, meanwhile, is now eye level with my pelvis and blowing on the wax. She presses it down until it forms a hard, crusted surface.

"Are you ready?" she asks.

"You said it won't hurt?" I try to smile.

She shakes her head and pulls a little tab of the wax up from my inner thigh.

"This doesn't hurt at all," I start to say as Rita tugs that tab a little harder and then yanks it with all her might. The wax flies up in a single sheet from my leg to my labia.

I bolt upright on the table.

Tears stream down my cheeks and the whole world pulses for a moment. I look at Evie. She is as wild-eyed as I am.

Rita, unfazed, pushes me back down on the table. "We need to tweeze the strays." She gets out a magnifying glass and a pair of tweezers. As she plucks hairs along my inner thighs and upwards, I try to remember my rescue breathing.

"Ow!" I shriek.

"Sorry. The ones on the lips are pretty painful." Rita peers closer. "There's only a few more."

"No. That's it. I can't do this." I swing my leg off her shoulder and reach for my clothes.

"But you're only half waxed." Rita puts down the tweezers. "Let me get you some water."

"She needs vodka," Evie cuts in. She fans her face. "We both do."

AS SOON AS EVIE AND I walk into our apartment, we move without speaking, like synchronized dancers. She gets the glasses, I grab the vodka from our little freezer. I pour two shots. Evie takes hers to the sofa and sits. I stand at the kitchen counter and throw mine back. Walking is still too painful. Heat radiates from half of my lower body.

I reach for the vodka and pour another shot. "Women are completely batshit. Who does this once a month?"

Evie sips her drink. "I think, over time, one becomes a bit numb to it. Slow down there with the vodka. Frank is picking you up in an hour, yes?"

I glance at one of the numerous wall clocks—we haven't gotten around to redecorating and the owner's love of maps and clocks still makes me dizzy whenever I try to figure out what time it is. I scan the times in Tokyo, Argentina, and Madrid, and finally find New York. It's just after six.

I sigh and take my shot over to the couch. I gingerly sit down next to Evie. "Maybe I should cancel."

Evie looks down a moment. "Maybe you should."

"That's not what you're supposed to say."

Evie starts talking quickly, like she's been bottled up. "I've been thinking. Why not postpone this date until after the wedding? Let the chemistry build. Let your job be drama-free. Let your pubic hair grow back."

I put my glass down a little more sharply than intended. "Why the sudden change in tone? You've been more excited about this hot sex I'm having than I have."

"I know. And I feel badly about it. As your friend and number-one supporter, Sylvia, I just want to make sure you don't do anything to compromise your job. I feel like we've lost focus and I would regret it if I didn't say this."

Evie so rarely looks contrite. But her eyes are wide and she's grabbed one of my hands.

I sigh. "I can't cancel an hour before he's picking me up. But for what it's worth, I understand. And even if I didn't, I would be too mortified to ever be seen with half a wax. I've never felt more turned off in my life."

Evie snorts. She clasps a hand over her mouth to cover up the laugh. But it's no use. "I'm sorry," she says. "It's just so funny. My god, just thinking about Rita chasing us down the street . . ."

It's true. Rita was so shocked when Evie and I tossed cash on the counter and sprinted from the salon. Well, sprinted as fast as Evie and her cane could go.

I start giggling, too. The whole thing is so absurd. Evie is practically wheezing.

I catch my breath and glance again at the wall clocks. "Evie, I can't cancel this dinner. It would be rude. But I can keep it platonic. I'll tell Frank the truth. He knows I'm nervous about getting into trouble with work. We'll enjoy a nice meal and get to know each other a bit. And who knows? Maybe we can take care of some wedding details. This could be a productive evening."

Evie looks at my face a long time before nodding. "I think that's a great idea."

Relief settles over my shoulders. All I really want is a fun evening out. I don't care about the sex. Well, that's not entirely true. But I can wait for it. Particularly since I don't feel like getting naked with yet another person today.

I take my vodka over to the sink and pour it down the drain. I turn to Evie. "Now that this evening is business casual, let's discuss wardrobe."

Evie is already on her feet. "What about my suede skirt? It would look great across your tush. In a dignified, professional manner, of course."

I smile as the fizz of excitement finally kicks in.

Nineteen

I don't wear the skirt. But I do borrow Evie's Veronica Beard crepe belted pants in ivory. I've paired them with a black jersey top and silver ballet flats. I'm standing in front of Evie's bedroom mirror. She sits at her makeup table and watches as I insert a final bobby pin into my French twist. I pull a few wisps of hair to frame my face.

Evie whistles. "You look fabulous. Your waist is so tiny."

I touch my hips self-consciously. "Am I trying too hard?"

"You look perfect." Evie glances at her phone. "He'll be here in a few minutes, but I have to leave for the restaurant. You're okay to wait alone?"

"I'm fine." I smile. "Go. You can't be late for work."

Evie smiles back briefly. "Good luck."

I shoot her a thumbs-up. She shoots me one back, then leaves the room.

I stay in the bedroom and press my hands together. As soon as I hear Evie open the front door and lock it behind her, nerves clutch my stomach. I pace back and forth.

Relax, Sylvia.

This is just dinner with a client. Sure, it's a client I've kissed. But Frank and I are grown-ups. I stop pacing and smooth my pants down once more. My waist really does look tiny. Because this is a platonic evening, I opted for my least sexy and yet most effective underwear: Spanx's Power bodysuit. Basically, they're super-elasticized bicycle shorts that suck in every inch of skin from my knees to my ribs and then pull everything up with the bib suspenders. It's a truly unfortunate look that should probably be marketed as a type of birth control, considering the vision is so painfully unsexy. But I am wearing a great bra—a black satin demi-cup. Of course, Frank won't be seeing it. But I needed a little something for myself. It's not every day I go to dinner with a man. Even if it is for business.

I feel my nerves again and open my phone to read one of Reese's inspirational texts. He loves to send them to me and Evie at random times. Today it's: "Eat glitter and shine all day!"

That's goddamn right.

The door buzzes. I feel like I might vomit.

But I force my legs to move through the apartment and hit the intercom. "Hi," I say into the speaker. "Be right there."

I make my way down the hallway to the stairs by our building's front entrance. I walk down the steps, push open the door, and blink a few times.

I almost don't recognize Frank at first. Rather than his usual sportswear and sneakers, he wears a suede jacket in a gorgeous shade of maple brown over a jacquard-striped sweater. His distressed trousers are cuffed perfectly over stonewashed boots. He's not wearing glasses and the effect is a bit like watching Clark Kent turn into Superman.

"Frank. My god. You look so snazzy."

Beneath the streetlamp, his cheeks flush. "You sound surprised. Too snazzy?"

"Not at all! That jacket is incredible."

He tugs at the sleeve. "I just got it." He shifts as though he's being smothered by all this nonbreathable fabric. "I just got everything I'm wearing," he confesses. "I literally walked here from John Varvatos. These pants are supposed to be fashionably broken in but they're killing my quads."

I giggle. "Don't you have any normal, nonsporty clothes?"

"I do. But I wanted to impress you."

I swallow. "Well, I wanted to impress you, too. I'm wearing the world's ugliest underwear so I look a full size smaller."

Frank's face breaks into a grin. "You look terrific. I should've started with that, by the way. Why do we always end up saying the things that most people keep in their heads?"

I grin back. "Surely it's a good thing. For once, we can say what we really think and not worry about it."

He meets my eyes. "Indeed." There's so much heat in the way he holds my gaze that I start to blush. He steps into the street to hail a taxi. "Shall we?"

Twenty

Obviously I'm not going to have sex. I'm not even thinking about sex. It's just that every time this cab driver makes a turn, he cranks the wheel so sharply that I practically slide onto Frank's lap. Frank, meanwhile, is unfazed. He's taken off his jacket and rolled up the sleeves of his sweater. His forearms are much more muscular than I'd expect given his leanness.

"Where are we going?" I ask as I brace for yet another body-slam as we veer onto the Brooklyn Bridge.

His eyes glint. "It's a surprise. A very interesting restaurant in Brooklyn."

"Fabulous."

Frank looks at me and laughs as we cruise across the bridge. "What?" I demand.

"Nothing. You're just so positive. All the time."

"Am I?" I'm about to say more but get distracted by the view out the window. The city beneath us is covered in a spill of light. "This is so beautiful."

"See? Not everyone looks out the window from a cab."

"Well, they should. Look at this view."

Frank stares out the window. "Ever since Nina and I separated and I moved back to the city, I keep remembering what it was like when I first moved here. I was twenty-one. I can't believe how much time has gone by."

"Is it the same being in the city now as it was when you were younger?"

Frank turns to me. "When I was twenty-one, I lived with three roommates in a shithole with rats. Now, I have six-month lease at The Pierre."

"Ah. But I bet you miss the rats."

He grins. "Not for a single second. But I do miss my friends. And that feeling of being happy. Of building something. I miss that."

We're both silent for a moment as the cab whizzes around.

I look at him. "I'm sorry. I just can't feel bad for you. You have twenty-four-hour room service."

He laughs just as the cab pulls over beside a brick-faced restaurant that's all lit up.

There's music and people laughing on the sidewalk outside. Frank pays the fare and slides out first. I take his hand and he gently helps me out.

As we walk inside the restaurant, he doesn't let go of my hand. His grasp is warm and strong and I feel like I'm floating as we move around people having drinks at the bar. We approach the host stand, where a middle-aged man with a lumberjack beard in a flannel shirt claps Frank on the back.

Frank smiles. "Sylvia, this is Ray. Owner of this esteemed establishment. Ray, Sylvia."

Ray bows slightly to me. "Great to meet you, Lady Sylvia. May I escort you to your table?"

There's something sweet about a being called Lady by a man who looks like he lives in a tree. The two of us follow him to a table. As we move through the restaurant, I take in the décor. It's rustic chic. Lots of wood. Each table has a little lantern on it. The ceilings are high and I see a double staircase in the center of the room leading to an upper level.

Ray leads us to a cozy corner booth. Frank looks at me from across the table. The lantern's light throws an amber glaze over the wood.

"Wow," I breathe as I look at the menu. "This looks delicious."

Frank's eye gleam. "The drinks are great. The skillet cornbread is unreal. And the ax-throwing is the ultimate."

"Ax-throwing?" I repeat, incredulous.

Frank nods and gestures to the upper level. I turn and see the walls are decorated with various size hatchets and axes. People are lined up in lanes with netting across the sides, similar to those arcade-type games where one throws a ball at a target.

These people are not tossing balls. Rather, they're hurling axes.

I turn back to Frank. My mouth is on the floor. "This is legal? Serving people alcohol and then letting them throw weapons through the air?"

Frank nods. "A new trend. It's cathartic."

"I'm sure it is. Has anyone been arrested? Or murdered?"

Frank laughs just as a waiter approaches and drops off a pitcher of beer and two frosty mugs. "Compliments of Ray."

Frank looks at the waiter. "Thanks. Can we get the cornbread, two smoked brick chickens, and Ray's famous artichoke dip to start? That sound good, Sylvia? Or did you want something else?"

"Sounds perfect," I manage. I'm not thinking about food. I'm still transfixed by the notion of what it would feel like to heave an ax through the air.

The waiter pours us each a beer and walks away. I look at Frank. "Has this been a form of post-marital therapy? Is that how you and Ray got so close?"

"Ray and I became friendly once he ran a background check on me and it came up clean. He was nervous when I brought a photo of Nina for a target."

"He thought you were acting out some revenge fantasy?"

Frank bursts out laughing. "I'm kidding, Sylvia. Ray and I know each other through a mutual friend. But I do come here often, especially since I separated. I didn't bring a photo of Nina, though. I'm not a psycho."

I take a sip of beer. It has a little kick of lemon that I love. "That's good to know."

Frank leans forward. "What happened with Louis and the bank?"

I nearly spit out my beer. "Excuse me?"

He shrugs. "We're not the bullshit kind of people. You know I heard your conversation in the bathroom that day at Verena's. I figured we could be up-front. Besides, you already know about Nina, poetry boy, and the sauna."

"Louis stole all the money I had in the world." I feel the familiar sting of tears behind my eyes. I drain my entire mug and dab my mouth with a napkin.

Frank puts a hand over mine. "I'm sorry. I try not to make women cry until the end of a date."

I smile and wipe my eyes. "It's fine. Louis is trying to manipulate me into moving back to Florida by freezing me out of New York. Can I have some more beer? And we're not on a date. This is a professional dinner. We can't have sex tonight."

My ears ring. I can't believe I said that aloud. I stare at Frank's blanched face and wait for a reaction as he silently refills my mug. When he puts down the pitcher, he takes a long pull of his own beer. "Sylvia," he begins. "I would never assume we were having sex. I was hoping for another kiss."

My face is a furnace, but I straighten up. "That sounds lovely. But I can't get in trouble with Verena. The wedding is in less than two months. If we still feel like kissing by then, I'll be a free woman."

Frank nods. "Fair enough." He catches my eye. "I hope this goes without saying. I'm happy just drinking beer and throwing weapons together. You're great company, and this is the first evening I've looked forward to in a long time."

"Thank you," I say quietly. "I feel the same."

Frank smiles. "And believe it or not, I actually do care about seating arrangements. Once you meet my mother, you'll understand why."

I lean forward. "Your mother? Do tell. Are she and Ashton close?"

He nods. "That's not the problem. My mother and her sister, my aunt Janice, have been at war with each other for over a decade. But I've told my mother that we will be inviting my aunt because her son, my cousin, and I are very close. Also, I love my aunt. She's a wonderful woman."

I take all this in, fascinated. "Why are they in such a fight?"

"None of us understand. But they're feisty. My mother threw a drumstick at my aunt's head a few Thanksgivings ago. We need to put their tables as far apart as possible."

211

I reach into my purse for a pen and my little notebook. I turn to a fresh page. "Keep talking. In fact, let's make a list of all the people who need to stay away from one another."

Frank finishes his beer. "Good idea. By then, we'll be ready for some ax-throwing."

AFTER AN HOUR-PLUS LONG dinner of the most delicious food I've had in ages—I can still taste the cornbread's buttery crumble— I've switched from beer to water so that I can keep a sound mind and beat Frank at ax-throwing.

"You said you've never done this before!" he says, astonished, as I score another kill shot.

"I have excellent hand-eye coordination."

Frank does a few lunges in his jeans. "You are full of surprises." He then pulls his leg up behind him, stretching his quads. "God, these pants are killing me. Not that it's an excuse," he quickly adds. "Clearly, you're a natural born ax-slinger."

I laugh and smooth down the pieces of hair that have escaped my French twist. "I'm a bit of a pool shark, too. Just so you're warned."

The look on Frank's face is priceless. It's the same look I'd get when I'd beat everyone at darts back in Boca. Louis was always so pleased when people would stare, wide-eyed, in shock, as I hit bull's-eye after bull's-eye. "She doesn't look like an athlete, does she?" he'd say smugly.

Hmm. Now that I think about it, that's not exactly a compliment. My face falls for a moment. Frank notices. "What's wrong?"

I release all thoughts of Boca. I love being right here, right now. We're standing in a middle lane and the people around us are laughing and chatting. The smells of beer and wood chips fill my nose with warmth. I look at Frank with a fresh smile. "Nothing is wrong. Your turn."

I step aside as Frank picks up his ax and brings both hands together over the handle. He does a few practice swings and then flips it as fast as he can at the target.

The ax slams into wood just inside the four-point zone. A very respectable throw. He gives himself a fist pump.

"Well done!" I cheer.

"You've taken me to the next level. One more round?"

I flex my shoulder blades a moment and shake my head. "I need to sit this one out. But you go. I'll watch."

"It's okay. We can take off. Maybe take a quick walk around the neighborhood before getting a cab?"

"That sounds perfect."

We head down the stairs and make our way through the crowds and out the door. After the woodsy warmth of the bar, the evening air feels crisp. The streetlights shine all the way down the sidewalks. The cafés and organic co-ops are right out of a Brooklyn hipster fantasy novel.

I look at Frank and smile. "Tonight was such fun. And so productive. The seating chart will require a bit of strategy, but I'm confident it'll work out. No airborne drumsticks at this affair."

"You really think so? Even with all our drama?"

"Every wedding has drama. Sometimes it's Romeo and Juliet— the two families despise one another. Other times, the bride's sister is jealous and 'accidentally-on-purpose' pours a glass of merlot on the bride's veil. Someone always gets too drunk. Someone else cries. It's the nature of the beast, so to speak."

Frank's face is aghast. "Why on earth do you do this job?"

I laugh and wave my hand in the air. "No one remembers those things. They become that great story you tell at a dinner party. And I really love being a part of someone's special event. It's an honor, really."

Frank looks up at the sky and then back at me. "It feels weird to be planning my daughter's wedding in the middle of my own divorce. How do you stay so optimistic when your marriage just hit the shitter, too?"

I'm about to answer when my phone interrupts. Who one earth is calling me so late?

Maybe Verena?

"Sorry," I say to Frank. "Let me get this. Could be an emergency." I dig in my purse for my phone. I don't recognize the number but answer it anyway. "Hello?"

A rustling on the other end of the phone. And then, a male voice asks, "Is this Sylvia?"

"It is. Who's calling?" My tone has gone a bit formal. Frank tilts his head and watches me.

"This is Oliver Neiss. You left a message about my grandmother, Evie."

My stomach drops straight to the sidewalk. I almost lose my balance and reach out to hold on to Frank's arm. He looks at me and mouths, *You okay?*

I force a nod as Oliver continues. "You said she's sick? What's wrong with her?" Oliver's voice catches. All at once I can hear how young he is. Half man, half boy.

I bite my lip and let go of Frank. Shit. Shit shit shit. What on earth did I do? I should put this right. Tell Oliver I'm a horrible prank caller. "I'm sorry," I begin, my voice stammering. "I shouldn't have left that kind of message—"

"How sick is she?"

I am going straight to hell.

"Why did you say not to call her?" His voice falters for a split second.

I swallow, my voice husky now. "Evie is such a proud woman. She'd be so angry that I went behind her back." At least this part is true. I take a breath. "Let's do this. I'll call you tomorrow. That sound okay?"

"Yeah, okay. Bye."

He hangs up. I stare at my phone a moment. I'm clutching it so tightly that it's imprinted with my fingertips. I catch my breath and see Frank staring at me. "What was that about?" he asks.

I pause a moment, thrown. Do I admit what I've done? Will he think I'm a lunatic?

I sigh. May as well keep up this honesty trend. "My roommate Evie's son died of an overdose a few years ago. Her daughter-in-law, Amanda, and grandson, Oliver, cut Evie out of their lives. Oliver now lives in Brooklyn. I snooped on Evie's phone and discovered that she tried to connect again once we moved to Manhattan. She was turned down very rudely by Oliver's mom. And so I called Oliver directly and told him that Evie was sick to see if he would come and see her. That was him."

I look down. "I know it's awful. But I had no choice."

"Of course you had a choice, Sylvia." Frank's voice is so sharp that I wince. "You could have done nothing. This was none of your business."

My cheeks singe. "That's probably true. But Evie is my best friend. I have no idea what it's like to bury a child. Do you?"

Frank visibly reacts.

I cross my arms. "Evie lives in that private hell every single day. Is what I did wrong? Sure. But the fact that her grandson has been instructed not to see her? That's beyond wrong. That's cruel. So stand by and nothing? I don't think so. That's just not my style."

I let out a breath and stare at Frank. He nods slowly, his face softening. "You're right. I wouldn't have done the same, but I can see your logic. I'm sorry I was so quick to judge. You're just . . ."

He trails off a moment. I wait a beat for him to finish but he just stands there, looking at me with a serious expression, which suddenly makes me feel light-headed.

"What?" I swallow. "I'm just what?"

"You're incredible," he says quietly. He holds my eyes for a few seconds while I stare back, suddenly feeling a white-hot buzz of electricity flow through me.

Before I can help it, I lean forward and kiss him.

FRANK PAUSES BREATHLESSLY between kisses. "I thought we weren't going to do this."

We've just slid out of the cab in front of my apartment. I wrap my arms around his neck and pull him toward me again. "I changed my mind," I murmur. "Are you coming inside? Evie won't be home till two. The place is ours."

I hurry up the steps to my building's front door. I can feel him behind me as he wraps his arms around my waist and nuzzles my neck. He follows me to my apartment, his hands never quite leaving my body.

As soon as we're inside the apartment, we're breathing hard.

"You're so beautiful," he says as he plants little kisses on my cheeks and lips and nose. I almost sneeze. But I distract myself and run my hands up and down his chest. God, he's so muscular. I try to ignore the fact that he probably weighs less than me given that we're the same height, and instead, I think about what a hard, toned body he has.

"Do you want a drink?" I ask.

"I want to have sex."

I look at Frank's eyes. His gaze is dark, intense. I shiver. "My bedroom is this way." Frank follows me down the tiny hallway to my little room. As soon as I turn on the light, he starts kissing me again. I'm tugging at the buttons on his jeans and he's tugging at my belt and we're headed to my futon when I freeze.

I casually push him back toward the door where the light is and flick it off.

He turns it back on.

I turn it off.

He stops kissing me. "Sylvia," he says slowly. "I don't care how ugly your underwear contraption is. I only care about how quickly I can take it off."

"I'm half-waxed."

"What?" Through the dim light sneaking in through my curtains, I can see Frank's brow wrinkled with confusion.

I sigh. "I went to get a bikini wax but it was too painful. I only did half."

Frank snorts.

I swat him. "Don't you dare!"

He throws his head back and laughs harder. "I'm strangely flattered."

"Well, I'm mortified. I can't have you see me with half a wax. We need to do it in the dark. Or with a blindfold," I add thoughtfully.

Frank laughs more. "A blindfold? Oh, Sylvia. You really are amazing. Fine. We'll leave the lights off. For now."

He pulls me toward him and kisses me again. His hands are everywhere, pulling off my belt and unhooking my pants. I step out of them and pull down his jeans so he can do the same. My whole body throbs. I take off his sweater, then push him down onto the mattress so I straddle him, completely ignoring the fact that I probably look like a member of some perverted cycling team with my bib bicycle shorts and satin bra.

But Frank doesn't seem to mind. He groans every time I shift my weight on his lap. I pull the bobby pins out of my French twist and feel my hair swirling around my shoulders like a Victoria's Secret model.

I shudder as he flips me over. Now I'm on my back and he's kneeling on the ground trying to slide off my underwear. I ache with desperation. He's pulling and yanking and grunting.

I lift my hips to make it easier. "Sorry," I say breathlessly. "They're really tight."

"I can do it." He hooks his fingers into the waistband and gives a good, solid pull when my door buzzes.

What the fuck?

I bolt upright and accidentally kick Frank in the chest. He falls backward with the Spanx in his hands.

"Shit! Sorry!" I put my hands over my mouth. "Probably a wrong doorbell. Let's ignore it. Are you okay?"

Frank coughs and sits back up. He then grins. "Mission accomplished." He tosses my underwear behind him.

I look down at my half wax. It's not exactly subtle, even in the dark. Whatever.

I don't care.

I get up and reach for Frank's boxers and pull them down. I'm practically vibrating when my door buzzes again.

Frank checks his watch. "It's after midnight. Could it be an emergency?"

I want to cry. But he's right. I scramble for my robe and throw it around myself. "Stay here. Do not move a muscle."

"Whatever you say, my queen."

Frank grins and makes himself comfortable on my futon. He tucks his hands behind his head and crosses his leg. He's totally naked and it takes all of my willpower not to fling myself on top of him.

I tighten my robe and walk quickly to the door. I jab the intercom. "Hello?"

There's a crackle, then a tear-stained voiced. "Sylvia? It's Ashton. Can I come up?"

I stare at the intercom as if it betrayed me. But I have no choice. I buzz her inside. As soon as I hear the building's door open, I sprint back to my bedroom.

"Frank," I say breathlessly. "Your daughter is here."

He instinctively covers his penis. "How'd she know I was here?"

"She's here for me. It sounded like she's crying."

There's a loud knock on the front door. Frank's face is ashen.

I pull my hair into a ponytail and force a calm voice. "Frank, everything will be fine. But there's no way out of here except the front door. So this is the plan: Sit tight and don't make a sound. I'll go and talk to her."

Frank nods. I bring a finger to my lips to indicate silence and then firmly shut the door.

I go and let Ashton inside, leading her to the couch. She wears sweatpants and a hooded sweatshirt. Her long hair is tangled and her face is smudged by tears.

I sit next to her. "Talk to me. What happened?"

"I got into a fight with my mom. Is it okay that I came here? I remembered after we left Dr. Bickman, you gave me your address and told me to come day or night if I needed you."

I nod soothingly, as if everything were normal and Ashton's father weren't lying naked in my futon ten feet away. "I'm glad you came."

She gives me a watery smile. "It was either come here or send out a mass email canceling the wedding."

My eyes go wide. "I am so happy you chose option A. Walk me through this. Why would canceling the wedding be a good idea? How does it relate to your mom? I thought she was going on a vacation."

Ashton flops backward on the couch and leans her head against a pillow so she's staring at the ceiling. "She left for Paris this morning. She posted a billion pictures on Instagram of her and her boyfriend, Sebastian. Their suitcases. Them at the airport reading poetry books. There's a photo of them kissing and I almost threw up. It looks like she's making out with her son. What's wrong with her?"

I tilt my head. "Ashton, honey. I know it can feel strange that she's dating a younger man. But what does it have to do with your wedding?"

"Because she's such a liar." Ashton leans forward and looks at me, her eyes filled with fresh tears. "In one of her posts, she wrote, 'My daughter doesn't need me to plan her wedding and insisted I take a honeymoon and pursue my poetry.' And then she wrote, 'hashtag living my best life.'"

I grimace. "That's quite insensitive. But it would have been worse than if she'd written, 'My daughter and I had a massive blowup at a bridal appointment. I behaved like a child, neglected to be happy about my impending grandchild, and have run away on a fancy vacation with my boy toy. Hashtag self-centered.'"

Ashton stares at me a moment. I start to blush. Was that too forward? I'm about to backtrack when her face screws up into a sad smile. "You really do know how to find the silver lining."

I sigh. "It makes complete sense that she would do this. What if one of her friends found that she wasn't in town right now? They all know your wedding is just weeks away. It's bizarre that she wouldn't be here. She probably guessed there'd be gossip and decided to get ahead of it by telling the world that everything is grand."

Ashton shakes her head, her voice bitter. "Who knew my mom was so savvy with social media."

I pat her knee again. "I understand why you're upset. It hurts when people pretend things aren't the way they really are just so they can look good to others. God knows what my husband's told people back in Boca. And it makes me crazy to think about what he's told our daughter."

"Do you hate him? I hate him. If that makes you feel any better."

I look at her solemn face and smile a little. "I don't hate him. Well, I do hate him. But only when I think about him. And I never go on his Facebook page."

Ashton meets my gaze. "So basically I should stop stalking my mom on the internet?"

"Yes. For your own sanity."

She sighs. "It's easier with my dad. He doesn't do social media. I have no idea what he's up to."

I burst out laughing.

"What's so funny?"

I can't help it. I laugh so hard that I cough. I put a hand on my chest and force myself to calm down. "Sorry. I can get a little punch-drunk when it's late. Speaking of, why don't you go home and get some rest. We have the cake tasting tomorrow afternoon. The best part of any wedding planning." I force a bright note of enthusiasm into my voice and stand up, hoping she'll follow.

But she stretches out on my couch. "It's so cozy here. Would it be okay if I just stayed and left in the morning? I promise you won't even hear me leave."

My door buzzes.

Ashton looks at me. "Who would come here so late? I mean, besides a crazy client," she adds with an eye roll.

The door buzzes impatiently again.

I'm starting to feel insane. I hit the intercom. "Hello?"

"Mom?"

Oh, sweet Jesus. As the buzzer vibrates under my finger, I can't help but wonder if this is what hell is like.

Ashton must notice my glazed expression because she shoots me a comforting smile. "Don't worry. I'm sure everything is fine."

There's a *thunk* from my room.

Ashton swivels around. "Is someone here?"

"Just my roommate. She's a restless sleeper," I say hoarsely. There's a knot of tension so huge in my chest that I can barely breathe. It's like a bomb is going off in slow motion and I have no choice but to continue exploding and pretend that I'm not on fire. And so I wipe my brow and open the front door. "Isabel! What a surprise."

Isabel enters the apartment. She has a small duffel bag and stands in my tiny hallway staring at Ashton. "Seriously? Is this your bridal client?"

I wince. But Ashton is all smiles and stands up. "Guilty. I'm Ashton, your mom's bride with no boundaries who comes by for a pep talk in the middle of the night."

Ashton offers another disarming smile and puts out her hand. Isabel stares at her a moment before shaking it. I lean against the kitchen counter to gather myself. Isabel wears one of those arctic high-tech fleece jackets over white jeans and a white blouse. Her hair is scraped into yet another bun. Her eyes are puffy and her nose is red.

I drum fingers on the kitchen counter. "Isabel. What's going on? Is that an overnight bag? Would anyone like a vodka?"

Isabel doesn't answer right away. She just stands there and surveys my apartment. She tilts her head at the clocks on the wall. She eyes the built-in shelves across from the couch as well as the tiny but pristine card table in the kitchen area. "This is cute," she finally says. "I got your message. Thanks for reaching out. I came to stay with you for a few days. And yes to the vodka." She drops her bag on the floor, takes off her fleece, and plops onto the couch next to Ashton.

Ashton sits back down next to her. "Vodka sounds amazing. I'll live vicariously. I'm pregnant," she says with a shy smile.

Isabel nods briefly back. "Congratulations. When are you due?"

Ashton tucks her feet beneath her. "Not till May. But my wedding's in a few weeks. So it's a little dramatic." She rolls her eyes again at herself.

Isabel shrugs. "As my mom will tell you, all weddings equal drama."

"Crazy, right? Do you usually come to your mom's place for late-night pajama parties?" Ashton flashes another disarming smile.

"I live in Connecticut. My husband, Todd, is being a complete dickhead. So I came here." Izzy's voice is flat.

My fingers tremble as I take the vodka from my freezer and turn my back to take a quick swig. The icy heat hits my stomach. I'm not sure what is making me feel the most crazy: my bride sitting on my couch, her father lying naked on my bed, or the fact that my daughter has come to me in a time of need.

I burst out laughing again.

Ashton and Isabel turn to me, both puzzled.

"Sorry," I say trying to control myself. I quickly pour two vodkas and grab a bottle of water. I place all three on the coffee table and feel as if I have no choice but to sit down on the ground next to the girls and pretend this is some kind of party.

"Izzy," I begin. "What happened with Todd?"

"Wait, Sylvia," Ashton interrupts. "Don't sit on the ground. Take my seat."

"I'm fine," I say with a wave of my hand. "I can stretch my legs." I arrange my robe carefully around my body and flex my feet.

"Great pedicure," Izzy murmurs.

I smile, say thanks, and wait for her to talk. But she glances at Ashton, who nods with realization. "Do you want some alone time with your mom?"

Another *thunk* from my bedroom.

Ashton looks at me. "Your roommate really is a wild sleeper."

I hop up. "Let me make sure she's okay. She's fallen out of the bed before."

I practically sprint back into my bedroom. I shut the door firmly behind me. When I turn on the light, I gasp. Frank is now dressed and trying to squeeze himself through the tiny window. He's straddling the windowsill. My lamp and bedside table have been knocked over.

He whispers, helpless. "I'm stuck!"

I rush over to him. My voice is feverish. "Both our daughters are out there. It's some kind of cosmic joke. What do you mean, stuck? Do we need to call the fire department?" I clutch my heart at the thought of sirens and men in uniform stomping into my apartment to extract Frank.

Frank shakes his head. "I can do it with your help. I just need a little push."

My eyes bulge. "You mean push you out the window? What if you break something?"

"I'll be fine. Or fine enough. It's less than ten feet." Frank grimaces as he twists toward me. "Just push my shoulder through. I need

224

a little force. Once my torso is out, I'll hang on to the ledge with my hands and drop down."

I nod. Sounds like a lunatic plan but I have nothing else to suggest. And so I make an *on three* motion.

Frank steadies himself.

I put two hands on his right shoulder, count softly, and then bear down, pushing as hard as I can. His shoulder squeezes through.

He somehow manages to swing his other leg out and pivot himself so that he can lower himself to the ground feetfirst. I lean out the window and watch as he drops down. He flashes me a thumbs-up and starts walking away. He rubs his tush but seems okay.

Sneaking in and out of windows is for teenagers. Not senior citizens. I dab sweat off my face and then return to the living room with my story in place.

"Sorry, girls. Turns out, my roommate isn't home. There was a raccoon on the windowsill."

Ashton and Isabel don't even glance up at my voice. Their heads are bowed together, deep in conversation.

". . . and he lied to you about quitting his job? And now just does yoga all day? While you kill yourself at the office?" Ashton's mouth hangs open with indignation.

Isabel nods. Her cheeks are pink and she's taken her hair out of its dreadful bun. She pulls at it like she did when she was a girl. "I know," she says, her voice gravelly with tears. "He says he's finding himself by re-centering. What does that even mean? And why can't he do it on weekends?"

I stare at Ashton and Isabel. It's as though I've landed in the middle of a blurry dream. My bride and my daughter are having a midnight heart-to-heart like best friends, and suddenly, I feel left out. Am

I too old to join their conversation? Should I creep quietly away and go off to sleep? I shift my weight a moment and Ashton looks up.

"Sylvia," she smiles. "I was just telling Izzy that she's not half as scary as you make her out to be."

My face flames as I once again awkwardly arrange myself on the floor.

Isabel wipes her eyes. "You think I'm scary? You can sit here if you want. I'll take the floor."

It really is an upside-down world. "No, it's fine. I meant what I said earlier. I like to stretch my legs."

Isabel stares at me, uncertain. I stare back, and all at once, her childhood face blooms before me. Her large, dark eyes squinting beneath those amazing lashes as she tries to figure out what to do. Like she's been given a map and isn't quite sure which way to hold it.

"Sit down, Izzy. It's fine." My voice is quiet. "As for making you sound scary? Let's review the facts. You showed up at my office like a federal marshal, humiliated me in front of my boss, then stomped away like a surly teenager."

Isabel sits back down on the couch. She picks at a thread on her jeans. "If you're so mad, why'd you invite me to visit?"

"Because Ashton convinced me that you needed empathy. And despite your atrocious behavior, I agreed."

Isabel looks up. I meet her gaze. Ashton looks back and forth between us. For a moment, I think she's going to get up and quietly leave. But, instead, she shifts her weight and pats Izzy's leg. "I've behaved way worse at Verena's office. Like, once I held your mom hostage in a bathroom. And she still puts up with me."

Isabel looks at us like we're crazy. "The bathroom? Why?"

Ashton shrugs. "I was having a moment."

I sigh. "You sure were. Izzy, I'm sorry you and Todd are having issues. Would you consider seeing a counselor?"

"I already asked him. He said no."

My mouth drops open.

She half smiles. "You don't think I'm the sort of person who would see a therapist."

"Last time I suggested you see a therapist to help you not feel so stressed, you told me that only weak assholes pay someone to listen to them complain."

Isabel doesn't say anything. She just leans her head back and looks at the ceiling. Ashton puts her hand on Izzy's arm again. "Do you still love Todd?"

Izzy closes her eyes. "You mean when he's not doing yoga and breaking my four-hundred-dollar Vitamix trying to make homemade almond butter?"

Ashton nods. "Yes. And I've broken a Vitamix before, too. But that's a separate conversation. Do you love him?"

Izzy sighs. "I want to kill him. Is that love?"

I impulsively stand up and wrap my arms around her.

"Mom, come on," she says, trying to wrestle free.

I hang on tighter. "I'm glad you're here," I whisper into her hair.

After another squeeze, I let her go and straighten my robe. "Let's get you some sheets and a blanket."

Ashton, meanwhile, has stood up and gathered her things. "I'm going to grab an Uber. Looks like this couch is taken."

Before I can say goodbye, Izzy blurts out, "It's so late. You can share it with me."

The three of us stare at my tiny couch. Ashton nods thoughtfully. "Maybe I can take the floor? Make a little fort?"

"Love that! Mom, where are the blankets?" Isabel is already walking through my place, opening the closets.

I stand, now overwhelmed, as Ashton fixes up the couch cushions and moves the coffee table. There's so much commotion that I don't hear the door open.

"Sylvia, darling." Evie's musical voice makes me freeze. I turn and see her by the door. She taps her cane lightly on the floor and stares bewilderedly at Ashton and Isabel. "Since when did we decide to form a sorority?"

Twenty-One

Thankfully, Evie had a sense of humor when she came home last night. After introductions were made, Evie and I retired to our bedrooms. I put on pajamas and got into bed. From there, I texted Evie every single thing that happened once Frank and I returned to the apartment and tried to have sex. I could hear her laughing madly through the wall. I didn't even think to tell her about Oliver.

It's only now, at eight o'clock in the morning, when I've just opened my eyes and reach for my phone, that I feel a sense of doom. There's a text from Oliver that simply reads, **Please let me know when I can see my grandma.**

My body aches with fatigue but my mind races. I quickly shoot off a reply, **Absolutely. I'll be in touch this afternoon.**

I put down my phone and try to stay calm. I need to figure out a way to explain to Evie what I've done. She'll understand. In fact, maybe she'll even be happy. For a moment, I relax into the warm fantasy of Evie's eyes brightening as she claps her hands together. "Thank you, Sylvia! Lying to my grandson is a fabulous way to have him back in my life."

Hmm. I'm not sure she'll say exactly those words.

I rub my eyes and sit up. At least I have until this afternoon to figure things out. One thing at a time. First, my daughter and my bride. And so I swing my legs out of bed, smooth down my pajamas, and open my door. I glance to my right and see Evie's door is closed. She must still be sleeping.

I silently pad to the living room. To my surprise, Ashton is gone. The sleepover fort has been cleared away and Isabel sits at my card table sipping tea and working intensely on her laptop. She wears black-and-white herringbone-patterned yoga pants with a matching cropped tank top. Her hair is pulled back into her usual bun, but her face looks bright when she hears me enter the room.

"Morning, Mom." She looks up from her computer and smiles.

"Morning, sweetheart. I see you've got tea. Can I make you some toast?" The question pops out like a reflex. I look behind Izzy at the kitchen counter to make sure I even have bread.

But she's already shaking her head. "I'm off carbs. How'd you sleep?"

I sit across from Izzy at the table and smile. "Great. What time did Ashton leave?"

"An hour ago. She must've heard me getting out my computer. I tried to be quiet but this place is so tiny."

I try not to be offended. "Rent is outrageous here."

Izzy nods her head and gestures to her laptop. "Totally. But I've been talking to a colleague of mine at the firm and we can likely get you out of your lease with minimal penalties. I also did research on wedding planners in Florida. I sent some inquiries on your behalf, and I'm sure Verena will have some leads. I can email her if you want. It'll be hard to say goodbye to Ashton, but she's super cool. The best part is that I talked to Dad. He loves the idea! Plus, it'll help your financial issues."

Izzy's voice is so chipper that, for a moment, I feel confused. I search her eyes for any hint of understanding but all I see is a flash of irritation. "Mom," she says slowly. "Have you been listening at all? I've solved all your problems!"

My throat tightens. My head spins. "What on earth happened between the time I went to sleep and woke up?" I say slowly, my voice shaking. "Because last night, we were discussing *your* problems. I don't have any problems. At least none that are any of your business."

"You can't be serious! Look at this place. This isn't normal—"

"How dare you!" I get to my feet, an avalanche of fury exploding inside of me. "How *dare* you even consider having an opinion on my life. You are a grown woman who showed up on my doorstep with a duffel bag complaining about your marriage. Maybe you should focus on your own issues before you start diving into what you think are mine!"

"You showed up on my doorstep not that long ago." Izzy's voice is icy calm.

I flinch, stunned with shame, as she eyes me coolly. My cheeks flush and all the anger boiling inside me comes to a standstill.

No wonder she's a good lawyer.

I take a breath and try to control my voice. "You're right. That was a mistake. I should have never come to you when things fell apart with your father. I regret it."

Now Isabel stands up. "I just don't understand why you can't go back to Dad and try to work things out. Yes, he cheated. It's horrible.

I want to barf every time I think about it. But he's sorry. I know he is. Every time he calls me, he tells me how horrible he feels."

I grit my teeth. "Why can't you hear me? I'm not even angry anymore about the cheating. Embarrassed? Yes. Betrayed? Yes. But the simple truth is that I just don't love him anymore. We fell out of love a long time ago. It happens. And aside from that, I'm happy here. Today. In my tiny apartment with the outrageous rent."

"You've been married for more than forty years. You'd throw it all away over some stupid bimbo? Without even trying to fix it? You're the one telling me to get counseling with Todd, but you won't do it for yourself?"

"You just aren't hearing me. I haven't been happy for so many years. There's no amount of counseling that will change that. There's nothing to fix. I want to move forward. What can I say to make you understand?"

"Nothing." Isabel slams her laptop shut. "Dad may have done some bad stuff. But he's not a bad man."

"I don't want you to think your father is a bad man. But he is a bad husband. A terrible one, in fact. And I just won't go backward in my life. I hope you won't either."

"What's that supposed to mean?"

"If you're not happy with Todd, try counseling. But don't stay in a relationship because it feels scary to leave."

"I am not a quitter."

Isabel glares defiantly and I realize that there is no conversation to be had here. "Izzy," I finally say, my voice now quiet but firm. "I understand it's hard when one's parent changes gears. It probably feels very uncomfortable for you. But I've spent a lot of my life devoted to ensuring you and your father's comfort. Sometimes at the expense of my own happiness. I am not resentful. But I have learned something—I am responsible for my own happiness. And so let me be super clear—I'm not going back to Florida. And I'm all done talking about it. We can either have a nice visit together or you can leave. The choice is yours."

Isabel gives me a long glare. Then, without a word, she packs up her laptop, zips on her fleece, and takes her duffel bag to the door. She opens it and walks out.

The door slams behind her. I sink back down into my chair, suddenly exhausted.

Twenty-Two

I now know what Ashton looks like during an orgasm. I take a sip of water and politely look away. I never realized cake tasting could be so intimate. It's just after two o'clock and I'm sitting across from Ashton and Dan at Darlene's Cake Shop on West 118th Street. We're at a large marble table in the corner of the bakery. There are four pieces of chocolate cake before us, each on a china plate with a little note card describing the flavors. Ashton takes another bite of the chocolate orange blossom with chili-dusted mangoes.

"Oh my god," she breathes. "Perfection." Ashton pats her nonexistent baby bump. "I seriously thought I was going to puke all over the table. But Chef Darlene is a genius."

Dan nods, his mouth full of cake. "She really is. Why have I never been here before? We should come here every day."

Ashton nods. "It's true. How'd you find this place, Sylvia?"

I smile. "I can't take credit. This is Verena's contact."

Ashton pops another bite of chocolate-covered mango in her mouth. "Why aren't you eating?"

"I had a late lunch," I say casually as I smooth down my black silk trousers and black turtleneck. For today's appointment, I wanted to wear something with a hint of French.

Darlene's Cake Shop is decorated like a patisserie with a Cajun spin. I look around at the high ceilings and bright windows, each with little orange curtains. Ribbons of buttery sweetness waft through the air and mingle with the smell of strong coffee and something else, something spicy that I can't quite put my finger on. According to Verna's notes, Chef Darlene was born and raised in New Orleans and moved to New York a decade ago. She's self-made and connected with Verena at a women's networking event.

I stare at the slices of cake before us and can tell they're something special. But after my blowup with Isabel earlier, my stomach is clenched. All the hurt and frustration has been building like water in a pipe and the pressure feels almost unbearable. Added to that is the fact that Frank has already texted me three times today asking when we can meet again. I nearly shudder thinking about it—what was I thinking? Sleeping with a client? Ashton would die.

Verena would fire me.

I shudder again but take a quick sip of water so that Ashton and Dan don't notice. I force another smile.

"It's like you two have never eaten dessert before."

Dan looks at me with wide, innocent eyes. "We're two young people in New York. We eat pretentious things like sashimi and olive oil cake. It's sad, when you think about it."

I laugh and watch Ashton take another huge forkful. "Well, I'm glad the baby likes wedding cake."

"He definitely does," Ashton affirms.

Dan freezes and repeats. "He?"

Ashton shrugs. "I've decided that I'm having a boy."

I tilt my head. "What do you mean, you decided?"

Ashton puts down her fork and speaks evenly. "After the awful morning you had with Isabel today—and considering my own mother—I've decided that Dan and I are not having daughters."

"How could you possibly know that Izzy and I had a fight?"

"Because," she explains, "I invited her to join us for this. She said she'd love to. But you showed up alone. And then, earlier, when I said how much fun the sleepover was last night, you changed the subject. And finally, no one can resist this cake. Even if you ate an entire pizza, you would make room. Which means something bad happened. Want to talk about it?"

"Ashton," Dan says with a look. "Maybe Sylvia wants some privacy." Ashton gives him a look back. He sighs. She crosses her arms.

"Ashton," I say, "Please don't worry about Izzy and me. It'll blow over. And if you end up having a girl, daughters can be such fun. Any child is a blessing. I'm so glad you insisted on a chocolate cake, by the way. Fits perfectly with our theme of nontraditional."

As if to show that all is okay and I'm not even the least bit stressed, I take a forkful of cake and pop it into my mouth.

"Would you ever date anyone?" Ashton prods.

The hunk of cake is lodged in my throat. I nod, *yes yes*, and drink water. All at once, I feel that pressure in the pipe again. But I ignore it. Instead, I pull myself up taller and summon my most professional voice. "All right, enough about me. This is about you guys. Which flavors are you loving the most?"

"Cookie crumble," Ashton declares.

"Mocha almond," Dan jumps in.

"The spicy mango," Ashton remembers. "Shit. How do we decide?"

"We have all three," comes a throaty voice. We turn our heads and see Verena enter the bakery. She air-kisses each of us, then slides into a seat next to me. "I never miss a cake tasting if I can help it." She grins and picks up a fork.

"Verena," I say with an honest smile. "Thrilled you're here. I was just going to break down the difference between cake layers and cake tiers so Dan and Ashton can understand their options. Three hundred guests give us a lot of real estate for cake."

"That's right. We're talking at least six tiers." She digs in. "God, I love Darlene. I could mainline this chocolate espresso cake." Verena swallows and unbuttons the blazer to her classic, custom-tailored suit. Her glossy hair shines expensively, and I can't help but feel a kick of pride that I work for such a force of a woman.

Verena puts down her fork and gazes thoughtfully at Dan and Ashton. "Have I missed any design talk?"

Ashton shakes her head. "We're talking about Sylvia's love life. We think it's time she starts dating."

Verena raises a brow. "Is that so?"

I pale, my voice speeding up. "These kids are teasing me, Verena. Obviously, we're not discussing my personal life. In fact, I was just . . ."

"Dad!" Ashton interrupts, waving excitedly. "What are you doing here?"

A bead of sweat drops down the back of my neck as Verena and I twist around to see Frank, dressed smartly in dark pants and a polo shirt beneath his new suede jacket, striding toward us. "Verena called this morning. She insisted that I not miss this crucial appointment."

Frank slides into a seat next to Ashton and shrugs off his new jacket. He smiles across the table to Verena and me. "Ladies. Terrific to see you both."

Verena smiles warmly. "So glad you could make it, Frank."

"Yes, super," I add, swallowing. "You look great."

Shit. The sentence pops out of my mouth before I can chase it back. I drink some water.

Does he look great? He does. But why did I say that? I feel so weird.

I glance around, but no one seems to think I did anything odd. In fact, Ashton nods happily. "You do look great, Dad. Are you headed somewhere fancy?"

Frank shrugs. "I've got to drop by the office later."

Ashton scrunches her brow. "But you always wear running clothes to your office. Isn't that why you worked so hard to be the boss?"

Frank laughs, but I see his cheeks flush slightly. He catches my eye a moment, and I feel a charge of electricity. I glance sideways at Verena to see, again, if she can sense anything. But she just smiles easily and hands him a fork. "Are you a chocolate man?"

"Who isn't?" Frank looks at the array of slices. "Catch me up on everything that's happened."

Dan grins. "Ashton has decided you're having a grandson because she's scared of daughters. And we're embarrassing Sylvia by talking about her personal life."

Frank looks at me and smiles. "Is that so? Sylvia, how is your love life these days?"

My whole face is hot. I will kill him. I will murder him with a fork.

Verena looks at me. "How was your date the other night, Sylvia? The math professor, yes?"

Things come to a screeching halt. Ashton starts to smile. "You went on a date? That's so cool! Why didn't you tell me?"

I feel something on my leg. I glance under the table. Frank has slipped off his loafer and is rubbing his foot against my leg. Oh, for heaven's sake. I move my leg and his foot falls. He raises a brow. I ignore him.

"How was it?" Ashton prods.

I look at everyone's eager eyes. Verena is the only one who looks at me coolly, as if to see how I'll handle the pressure.

I clear my throat. "Everyone. Focus. This is a cake tasting. My romantic life is nonexistent. I decided to cancel the date. In fact, I've decided to not date anyone until this wedding is over. I want to stay focused on the task at hand."

Frank raises a brow again. "That sounds drastic. Surely you can have a personal and a professional life."

"This job is very important to me," I say quietly.

He gives a simple nod just as Verena pats my arm. "I appreciate your dedication. But I would never stop you from having a life."

Ashton nods vigorously. "Seriously. I don't want to be one of those crazy brides who monopolizes your time."

Dan looks sideways at her. "You mean like the ones who show up at their planner's apartment in the middle of the night?"

She blushes. Everyone is silent for a moment. Then Frank lets out a belly roar. Dan does, too. The two of them are laughing and Verena joins in.

I pat Ashton's hand. "You can show up anytime you want." Ashton cracks a smile and everyone seems to finally relax.

Verena leans over to me. "This is going to be one of those fun weddings. I can feel it." She gives my arm a squeeze.

I feel a glow of achievement. This is exactly what I needed. Chocolate and an attagirl from my boss.

My phone rings from inside my purse. "It could be one of the vendors," I say quietly to Verena.

She nods. I take my bag and excuse myself, motioning that I'll be just outside on the sidewalk.

As I head out the door, I reach in, grab the phone, and see that it's Evie. I answer it anyway. I could use a breath of fresh air.

"Evie," I say happily. "You're going to die when I tell you about this tasting . . ."

"Oliver called me," she blurts out, cutting me off.

The phone feels like a bomb in my hand. "What do you mean?"

Her voice is breathless as she gushes. "Isn't it terrific? He's on his way over with Amanda. I'm just running over to that Italian bakery to get some cookies. I'm so nervous. Any chance you'll be able to come back soon? I could use the support."

Evie has never asked me for anything in my life. I gulp and try to steady my voice. "I'm on my way."

Twenty-Three

Okay, best-case scenario: I confess. Oliver, Amanda, and Evie are shocked but then understand that I lied with only the best of intentions. Everyone hugs and cries and it's a beautiful family moment.

I stand directly outside my apartment, wrapped in the cocoon of this fantasy. After I hung up with Evie, I said a quick goodbye to the gang at Darlene's, using the excuse that I needed to attend to some wedding details. And then my entire way here, I've played round after round of Best-Case Scenario. I lean into this family reunion fantasy for another moment before my shoulders sink.

Who am I kidding?

There is no best-case scenario for what I've done. I'm sick with fear and it takes every ounce of willpower to find my keys and enter the apartment. Evie stands in the kitchen scrubbing the already spotless counter.

As soon as I walk in, she looks up. "Oh, thank god. They'll be here any minute. I'm worried that I'm underdressed. Or overdressed. Holy fuckity fuck. I'm just so nervous." Evie throws down the sponge and sighs.

I go over to her and put my hands on her shoulders. "Evie. Breathe. First things first—you look fabulous."

And she does. She has on a long-sleeve, embroidered emerald tunic over black cigarette pants and black mules. Her makeup is perfect and she wears gold hoop earrings.

I bite my lip. "Now tell me. What—exactly—did Oliver say?"

"That his mom's in town for his birthday, which is tomorrow, and that they'd like to see me. Naturally I said of course and made a reservation at Wild One for an early dinner."

My stomach aches with guilt. I try to think of how to confess when Evie blurts out, "I lied to you, Sylvia."

I open my mouth to respond, but Evie shakes her head. "I lied about reaching out to them when we moved here. I sent a message letting them know that I moved to New York. I asked to get together. But Amanda made it clear that they didn't want to be in touch."

That familiar surge of righteous fury straightens my spine. "That bitch," I snap.

Evie looks at me. "It's her choice. I have to respect it."

"I don't understand why you say that. It's not your fault your son died."

A tear leaks down her face.

I grab her hands. "Evie, listen. I have to tell you something. I already knew that you—"

"Oh, for fuck's sake," Evie cuts me off as she dabs her eyes. "My mascara. I'm going to look like a raccoon."

"You look fine. Listen, before they get here. I need to tell you—"

"It just doesn't make sense," she interrupts again. "Something must be wrong. Why would they suddenly want to see me?"

"Because they think you're sick," I burst out.

There's a moment of staggered silence. Evie tilts her head. "I don't understand. Why on earth would they think that?"

I swallow. We're both still standing by our kitchen counter. "I'm sorry, Evie. I snooped on your phone because I wanted to get Oliver's information to see if he'd be open to a reunion after you told me he's in school out here. But then I saw that you had sent them that message. When I read Amanda's reply, I was enraged. Before I knew it, I was calling Oliver and telling him that you're sick."

I pause for a moment. Evie's face is blank.

And so I take another breath. "I'm sorry, Evie. I overstepped. But please understand that I did it because I love you and can't begin imagine what it was like to lose Julian and then not be able to see your grandson. But I realize I've now put you in a tricky situation."

I bite my lip and wait for Evie to respond. Her face is still blank. But slowly, little by little, her eyes narrow. Her neck tightens and a tiny vein pulses as she echoes. "A tricky situation? My grandson thinks I'm dying and you call that 'a tricky situation'? Are you out of your fucking mind?"

I cringe. "I'm sorry. I'll fix it."

"Goddamn it, Sylvia!" She bangs her cane on the ground. "You can't just go around inventing stories. This is my life. This is my family."

"I'll confess. Tell them you had nothing to do with it. They can't be mad at you."

"Of course they can! They've been mad at me for years!" She

shakes her head. "Jesus Christ. What did you think would happen once you told them that I was sick? That they'd come and visit? And then what?"

"I hadn't gotten that far." My voice is hoarse.

"Well, here we are, my dear. They're going to ring that buzzer any minute. So what's the big plan? I'm dying? And Oliver feels so guilty that he promises to have Sunday fucking suppers with me? And each week, I'm a little sicker? Because god knows that's the relationship I want with my grandson. Stop crying, damn it. I don't have time for you to feel bad!" Evie grips the counter, her voice rising to near hysterics.

I wipe my eyes. "What do you want me to do?"

The door buzzes.

Evie and I freeze.

I whisper, "I got this. Don't worry."

Evie glares, then hits the buzzer and opens the door, keeping it ajar for our guests.

As we wait in the foyer together, I slowly inhale for a count of two, then exhale for four.

Letting in the light, forcing out the dark. My shoulders start to relax.

Evie looks sideways at me. "I could kill you, Sylvia."

"I completely understand. But like I said, I got this."

Amanda and Oliver walk into our apartment. Oliver clutches a bouquet of flowers. Before anyone can utter a greeting, Amanda nods briefly at Evie. "Evelyn, hello. I'm sorry to hear about your health. And you must be Sylvia." Without missing a beat, Amanda swivels toward me and crosses her arms. "Oliver told me the terrible news and how you wanted him to keep it a secret. How could you burden him like that? He's been through enough."

I flinch at Amanda's hostility, which is overpowering despite her small frame. She wears a simple denim wrap dress and ankle boots. Her dark, wavy hair hangs down her back in a long, frumpy braid that I'd love to just hack off. Her face is so pinched that it makes her look every bit of her forty-something years.

Oliver stands next to her and flushes. "Mom, come on. That's not what happened."

"That's exactly what happened. I hate secrets. Your father was always keeping secrets," she says crossly.

I see Evie flinch. Jesus. This woman is a piece of work.

But I am here to keep the peace. And so I offer my most gracious smile. "Oliver, Amanda. Welcome to our home. We're so glad you're here." I turn to Oliver. "I deeply regret what I did. As you know, Evie had no idea that I reached out to you. But your mother is right. Honesty is vital. And so on that note, let me tell you truth about what's going on—"

"Are these flowers for me?" Evie cuts in, reaching for the bouquet in Oliver's hands.

She shoots me a look and I back off.

He nods, looking shy. "I didn't know what flowers you liked so I just got the most colorful bunch."

Evie examines the flowers as though they're made of solid gold. "You darling boy! You've grown up so much. Didn't I tell you he was handsome, Sylvia?"

I nod. It's true. Oliver is a gorgeous young man. Like his mother, his skin is olive-toned and his hair is nearly black. It curls at the nape of his neck. But that face. His strong cheekbones and wide-set eyes. Even the tiny dimple above his lip. It's Evie's face. And by proxy, it must be his father's face.

I glance at Evie and wonder what she's feeling. But she keeps smiling. "Love your look. We'll have to do some shopping together now that I have a job."

Oliver pulls on the cuffs of his oatmeal-colored button-down shirt. He wears it untucked over brown chinos and under a navy vest.

His eyes brighten. "What's your job?"

"I play a little piano at a neighborhood restaurant," Evie says simply.

"Your grandmother is being humble. She's the star musician at a very chic eatery. In fact, that's where you all are going for dinner, yes?"

Amanda glances at her watch. "Speaking of, can we get going? I have plans later on."

"Of course," Evie says deferentially. "Let me put these flowers in water and then we'll head out."

"Can you do them later? I really can't be late." Amanda now takes her phone from her purse and starts texting.

I want to slap this woman. I want Evie to slap this woman. But Evie just nods. "I'll go grab my coat."

She puts the flowers on the counter and goes to her bedroom. Amanda keeps texting and Oliver stands in the same spot, looking into space. I feel sorry for him. But where is his backbone? I feel like I'm in a weird dream.

I go after Evie. I quietly enter her room as she belts a trench coat. "Evie," I whisper. "I can fix this. Just let me confess. Amanda will be horrified. You can yell at me properly, really go for it. Amanda can get in there, too. You'll bond over hating me."

Evie sits down on her bed, her back hunched slightly. For the first time, my friend looks old. "I don't think that will work," she says. "Amanda will just storm away."

I want to drive my fist into Amanda's face. "Why are you letting her treat you this way?" I demand.

I wait for Evie to say something else, but she doesn't. Her sadness spills over and I feel it acutely. Like a slap to sunburned skin.

"Evie," I try again. "Amanda's using Oliver to punish you for Julian's death. It's so unfair. Can't you see that?"

"Yes," she says with a quiet feverishness. "But I don't want to pick a fight with Amanda the first time I get to see my grandson. There's a bigger picture here. You have no idea what Amanda went through with my son. I'm trying to remember that. So either help me or go away."

I swallow, moved by Evie's compassion for Amanda, and realize that I know so little about the biggest tragedy of my friend's life.

I place my hand on Evie's arm. "What do you want me to do?"

Twenty-Four

We arrive at Wild One twenty minutes later. Happy hour is as upbeat and glamorous as the regular dinner hour. The familiar swell of warmth, chatter, and amber lighting washes over the after-work crowd.

I'm still wearing my all-black ensemble when our supermodel hostess signals for Evie, Amanda, Oliver, and me to follow her to the corner table Evie requested. It's tucked away from the bar and the music. Nice and quiet and cozy. Amanda's hostility has been replaced by a general aloofness. She's been on her phone constantly, twirling the end of her braid between her fingers and typing away. She sits down and continues tapping at her screen.

I sit next to her and try to politely engage. "Work?" I ask.

"Yes," she says without looking up.

"Amanda's in real estate," Evie says proudly as she sits across from me. "The hardest working agent I know."

Amanda keeps typing. "The life of a single mother."

Evie stiffens. Oliver sinks into his seat. The mortifying silence hangs like a thundercloud above our table. No wonder Evie wanted me to accompany them to dinner.

"Evie! You goddess! How are you?" A group of regulars, male and female, bound over and take turns kissing Evie's cheek. They are all interesting and young and chic. I see Oliver admiring their tattoos and facial piercings and then looking at his grandmother as though for the first time. It's like seeing one's biology teacher at the supermarket and realizing that this person does, in fact, need to eat.

Evie smiles now at Julio, who I know is one of her favorites. "This is my grandson, Oliver. He's an artist, too," she says with a bursting pride.

"Dude. That's awesome. I'm a photographer. What's your medium?" Julio smiles at Oliver.

"I sculpt. And illustrate. But I'm just studying now," Oliver says.

"We're all studying. Students for life. Students at life. That's my motto." Julio bangs his fist against his chest. "You should drop by my studio. Evie has my info."

Oliver nods, his eyes bright. Amanda notices. I suspect she's impressed. But given the way she keeps rolling her eyes, I also suspect that she'd rather be in a Turkish prison camp.

I've never needed a drink so much in my life.

Thankfully, our server, Rachel, arrives with two cosmopolitans. She places them in front of Evie and me. "Your usual, ladies. Sylvia, chic as ever. And, Evie, you're looking extra dynamite today. Who's your boyfriend?" she asks with a wink.

Evie laughs. "Rachel, this is my grandson, Oliver. And his mother, Amanda."

Rachel smiles. "You brought the family. I love it. What can I get you all to drink? Oliver, I'm also giving you my phone number."

Oliver blushes a deep, almost purple color. Amanda finally looks up from her phone and surveys Rachel with a hard stare before turning to Evie. "Should you be drinking in your condition, Evelyn?"

Evie freezes. Rachel turns with sudden concern, "What condition?"

Oliver elbows his mom. Amanda looks like she's about to say something else, but I cut in quickly, "No condition other than being a bit sleepy today. And over fifty."

Amanda's mouth drops. "Evelyn is over seventy. Pushing eighty. And you still haven't told us exactly what's wrong—"

I interrupt again. "Amanda, have a cosmo. They're fabulous."

"They better be for eighteen dollars," she snips as she glances at the menu.

"My treat." Evie quickly smiles. "Everything is on me."

"Your money is no good here," Rachel says. She glances at Evie one final time with concern before turning to Oliver. "You look like a whiskey man. Strong and handsome. May I suggest the Burning Mandarin?"

"Sure," Oliver says shyly. He looks up at Rachel and a dark curl falls over his eye.

"He'll have a Sprite." Amanda's face narrows. "He's not twenty-one. And stop flirting with my son. You're not as cute as you think."

Rachel's mouth drops. But then, well versed in difficult customers, she swallows. "My apologies. One Sprite and one cosmo. Pronto." She walks away.

"You didn't have to do that, Mom," Oliver says hotly. For the first time, I see some proof of life. "You embarrassed me. You embarrassed Grandma. We all get that you don't want to be here. But can you please stop being such a bitch?"

Amanda's eyes fly open. I try to think as quickly as I can but it's Evie who cuts in. "Oliver," she says, and places a hand on his arm. "Don't speak to your mother that way. I know this is difficult for her."

"Don't discipline my son." Amanda glares at Evie. She turns to Oliver. "What do you want from me?"

"I want you to act like who you usually are. It's like *Invasion of the Body Snatchers* when we're around Grandma. And it's not fair. She didn't do anything." Oliver crosses his arms and glares at his mom.

Amanda's eyes fill up with tears. Evie notices and looks at me. I nod and take a long sip of my cosmo.

"Did Evie tell you guys how we ended up in Manhattan?" I ask.

Everyone turns to me, their faces blank. Amanda's eyes are still watery. But I smile and lean in as though we're all best friends and this is the greatest meal we've ever had. "Back in Boca, I caught my husband cheating with a woman who had spectacular fake breasts. I was mortified and lost. But Evie convinced me that Belinda and her boobies were the best thing that ever showed up. They got me thinking about what's important. I thought being in my midsixties meant I couldn't change the course of my life. But I was wrong. And so I made a plan to follow a lifelong dream of being a wedding planner and living in Manhattan. Evie, ever courageous, joined me. I couldn't have done it without her. And now we have an apartment, jobs, and, random but worth noting, I tried my first bikini wax the other day."

I beam. Everyone stares.

Rachel arrives and silently drops off a Sprite and a cosmo.

Oliver and Amanda both reach for their drinks and take long sips. Evie takes a large gulp of hers as well. She dabs her mouth with a napkin and shoots me a glance.

But I just keep smiling. "The point I'm trying to make is that tomorrow is Oliver's birthday. Let's toast to youth, whether it be biology or a state of mind. Let's toast to family. Let's toast to boobies and bikini waxes and anything else that reminds us that life's in session."

I raise my glass and wait. Evie just stares. Oliver, now the color of eggplant, looks at the table.

Only Amanda meets my eyes. "Boobies and bikini waxes?" she repeats. And then, without warning, she laughs. The sound is so shocking at first that no one says anything. She very nearly cracks a smile. "You're funny, Sylvia."

I clear my throat. "What's funny, Amanda, is that I never intend to be funny."

Evie holds up her drink. "To Oliver."

We all clink glasses just as a tray of food arrives. Rachel sets down plates. "Round one: bluefin tuna tartare, butternut squash fries, and truffle salmon sashimi. Enjoy."

The food looks almost too beautiful to eat. But Evie picks up a small plate and starts dishing out helpings to everyone. Oliver happily accepts and pops a piece of tuna in his mouth.

"This is amazing," he says.

"You spent nineteen years rejecting anything that doesn't have cheese melted on it. Then you come to New York and eat raw fish."

"I'm maturing," Oliver says as he eats another piece.

Amanda looks at him with such warmth. Her jaw is softer, her back more relaxed. She turns to Evie with genuine interest. "You play the piano here? How'd you get that gig?"

Evie smiles modestly. "I asked for an audition."

"What songs did you do?" Oliver asks.

"Coldplay. A little Gloria Gaynor. And, naturally, some Lady Gaga."

Oliver looks staggered. "Lady Gaga?"

Amanda finishes her cosmo and pops a fry in her mouth. "Your grandmother can play just about anything. She played the Beatles at our wedding."

Evie's face softens. "Julian wanted you guys to walk up the aisle to 'When I'm Sixty-Four.'"

"Now, he was funny." Amanda sighs. Then her expression darkens. "Except for when he wasn't."

"You mean except for when he was high," Evie says.

"I mean except for when he was dead."

Oliver mutters something that sounds like *shit* under his breath. He looks at the table. I catch Evie's eye. What is she doing?

But Evie just sighs. "I knew Julian had a drug problem when he was sixteen. We got him help but it was never enough. Then he met you, Amanda, and he cleaned up. You were so happy. The day Oliver was born, Julian called from the hospital and told me he finally understood the meaning of life. He said, 'Beauty is the electricity of pain.' It was five o'clock in the morning and I turned to Henry and said, 'He's going to start using again.'" Evie pauses to sip water. "He went to rehab before Oliver was three months old. I was so ashamed. How could he do this to his family? But he cleaned up, went home, and had a good couple of years. And then repeat. Repeat. Repeat. And then he was dead."

Evie says this last line so matter-of-factly that I stop breathing. I reach across the table to squeeze Evie's hand. But she snatches it back. "I didn't know how to help him."

"You can't be so hard on yourself," I say.

Evie's eyes are hard. "Sure I can."

An image of Isabel pops into my mind. What would it feel like if she died? My breath shortens. The agony is primal. This is my daughter. I may want to kill her, but I never want her to die.

Evie now turns to Amanda. "I know you blame me for Julian's death."

Amanda lifts her chin. "I don't."

"Yes, you do," Oliver says. His voice is flat.

Evie looks away a moment. "I've been to all the meetings that say it wasn't my fault. That it wasn't even his fault. He had a disease. I don't believe that. And yet I know it's true. Isn't that odd? To not believe something but know it's the truth."

"Oh, Evie." I can't help it. My eyes fill up. "You're torturing yourself."

She looks at me. "I think it's time we told the truth."

I flush.

Amanda looks back and forth between us. "What truth?"

Evie's voice is calm. "I'm not sick."

Oliver and Amanda both blink. "I don't understand," Oliver says.

Evie turns to him. "Sylvia lied to you. She thought she was doing me a favor. But I'm in perfectly good health. For a woman pushing eighty," she adds, looking at Amanda.

Oliver stares at me. "You lied? About my grandmother being ill?"

I swallow. "I'm sorry. Evie and I were talking about family, and I felt so angry that you guys cut her out of your lives. I wanted to do something that would convince you to see her. But I went too far. Much, much too far."

Amanda's eyes narrow. "And you were in on this charade, Evelyn?"

I cut in, strong. "No. I told Evie what I did right before you arrived. She wanted to tell you the truth but didn't know what to say. It's my fault. Completely, one hundred percent my fault."

"But why would you let us believe it, Grandma?"

Amanda throws her napkin onto the table and stands up. "Because she wanted us to visit. Even if it was under the guise of deception. Let's go, Oliver. These women are psychotic and we shouldn't—"

"Goddamn it, Amanda. Sit the fuck down." Evie's voice is so firm that Amanda, white with shock, sits. Oliver's mouth tumbles open.

I smile and nearly break into applause because this is the Evie I know.

But Evie sees my smile and glares. "This is not a happy moment, Sylvia. I'm furious with you."

I swallow. "Evie, of course. I know. I've already told you how sorry I am."

"And I've already told you that this is my family. You had no business meddling. No wonder Isabel can't make sense of you. Half of what you do is ridiculous."

I flinch, feeling slapped. Evie has never said something so cruel to me.

Evie turns away from me and looks at Oliver. "When you called and said you wanted to see me, I wondered what happened. Maybe it was your upcoming birthday. Maybe it was a song on the radio. Maybe you saw a boy and his grandmother together on the subway. I felt so happy. I was perfectly willing to forget all the times you rejected my invitations for dinner, for a visit, for a chat. But when I found out you only wanted to visit because you thought I was dying, I felt pathetic." She lets out a long breath. "I have never been so hurt. I didn't deserve to be cut out of your life. You may have been a boy. But now you're a man. And I hope to god that you start acting like one."

Now it's Evie who throws her napkin on the table and rises. She squares her shoulder, takes her cane, and walks away.

There's a beat of silence as Amanda, Oliver, and I watch her go. Then Oliver jumps up. "Grandma!" he calls out.

Evie stops. She doesn't turn around, but she waits. He jogs to catch up with her. He whispers something in her ear and she looks up at him. Then she nods, and the two of them walk out of the restaurant together.

I shift in my seat. I've been holding my breath and my body so still that all my joints ache. I feel shaky as I pick up my cosmo. It's empty. But I tip it back and try to get out any remaining drop.

Amanda does the same. We both stare at our empty glasses. "So," she finally says. "I'm not sure if I hate you or not."

"I feel the same way about you, my dear."

She nods, fair enough. "Another drink?"

I lean back in my chair. "I should think so."

Twenty-Five

I t's half past ten o'clock when I return to the apartment. I flip on the lights expecting Evie to be sitting on the couch like an angry parent. But the place is empty. I tiptoe to her bedroom but see it's also empty. Where could she be?

I drop my purse on the sofa and rub my temples. It's late and I'm drunk. After Evie and Oliver left, Amanda and I ended up having two more rounds of cosmos.

Half of what you do is ridiculous.

Just hearing the words inside my head again makes me squirm. I feel hot and dirty. I speed-walk to the bathroom and turn on the shower. Steam fills the air like a down blanket. I inhale deeply, leaning into the flowery aroma of the too-expensive shampoo Reese gave Ashton and me in a thoughtful gift basket. I turn off the shower and reach for my robe. I stare at my face in the fogged-up mirror. My features are blurry, which is exactly how I feel. I open the medicine cabinet and grab two Advil. I'm about to close the cabinet when I see the gold foil package of another too-expensive product Reese gave me—a face mask that promises to do more than a face lift. I'm tempted to use it but don't feel deserving of such luxury right now. My head pounds. I wonder if Amanda is faring any better. She was drunker than I was. I almost laugh, thinking about her pink face when she finished her last drink and let out a great big belch. "Good god, Sylvia," she slurred. "You're a terrible influence."

For whatever reason, we both found this hilarious and roared with laughter, each clutching the table to regain our breath.

When we finally settled down, I looked at Amanda and sighed. "You're not wrong. What I did was terrible."

Amanda shrugged. "I did something terrible, too. I lied about having someone to meet so we could hurry up and be done."

"I suspected," I said. "But you're not the first person to tell that lie."

"Yeah. But it's what people do that to get out of bad dates. Not ditch a dying family member."

"At least she's not really sick," I offered weakly.

"Any of us could go at any time," Amanda insisted, gesticulating in that exaggerated, drunk-person way. "I wasn't expecting Julian to die. And I never thought it would change me like it did. I loved Evelyn. She was the greatest mother-in-law a person could ask for. But I hated that she was so sad. It made me feel like I wasn't sad enough. Isn't that awful? Good god, I'm drunk. Are you drunk?"

"So drunk," I breathed.

We both stared around the restaurant for a moment. Happy hour had melted into the dinner crowd. The lights were dim and people were laughing and eating. I loved how the modern bronzed tables and black chairs looked against the concrete floors.

"I could see Carrie Bradshaw holding court at one of these tables." I sighed.

"Or Samantha with a waiter in the bathroom." Amanda grinned. "I love that show."

"My daughter makes fun of me for watching it. She says it's a stupid fantasy for an old lady like me."

"Is this the daughter who can't make sense of you?"

I winced. Amanda noticed. "I'm sorry. It sounds like you and your daughter have a complicated relationship."

"It's actually quite straightforward," I replied. "Everything is my fault."

IT'S NOW AFTER ELEVEN and I'm the one sitting on the living room sofa like a concerned parent. I pull my robe around me, run a hand through my damp hair, and pick up the television remote. It feels like a betrayal if I turn on *Sex and the City* knowing Evie is so furious with me. I settle for QVC and am instantly riveted by the toilet night-lights currently being sold. The segment's host is a woman named Moira, who looks like the world's most nurturing grandmother.

"If your husband leaves the seat up, you'll never fall into the toilet again," she promises. "Just hit the button and choose from a variety of beautiful colors that glow in the dark." She demonstrates an electric blue. "And for parties," she continues, picking up a martini. "Enhance the décor of your powder room with a disco light!" She hits a different button and a rainbow of colors strobes from the toilet seat.

"Remarkable," I whisper aloud.

I reach for my phone, about to fire off an email to Ashton asking her thoughts on colored toilet lights at the Plaza, when I hear Evie's voice.

"Sylvia. Put down the phone. Turn off the TV. Your brain has been hijacked by QVC."

I look up at Evie. Wordlessly, I turn off the TV and stand up. "Thanks," I say.

She nods and starts walking toward her bedroom. I cautiously follow. She doesn't slam the door in my face as I enter behind her, which I am taking to be a good thing. She tosses her coat and purse on her bed, then sits at her vanity and begins rubbing cold cream on her face.

I stand, unsure what to do. "I wasn't sure you'd be coming back here," I finally say.

"Where'd you think I'd go?"

"Oliver's." I shift my weight from side to side.

"After our internment at that Airbnb, I have no intention of ever sleeping in anything resembling a dormitory again."

I nod. Makes sense. I watch Evie pick up a washcloth and gently remove her makeup. She meets my eyes in her mirror and pauses a moment. "I had a very good time with Oliver. Marvelous, in fact."

I brighten. "That's wonderful!"

"It is. We went to Little Italy and had the most fabulous meal and dessert. We talked for hours and decided that no one would ever interfere with our relationship again."

I clap my hands together. "Oh, Evie. I'm so happy for you. And I think it'll work out with Amanda, too. We had drinks. I think she misses you quite a bit."

Evie turns to face me head-on. "You had drinks with Amanda," she repeats.

I bite my lip. "Was I not supposed to do that? On a scale of one to ten, how angry are you still? I really need to know."

Evie sighs. I pray silently. *Please let her say she's not angry anymore.*

"I'm not angry anymore."

I swallow and look up, hopeful, as Evie wipes the last bit of cold cream from her face.

She drops the cloth on her vanity and sighs. "I admire you, Sylvia."

"Did you and Oliver have a lot to drink?"

"I wanted to respect Amanda's wishes. We had Sprite."

I must look very confused, because Evie gets up and comes over to me. "I was angry with you. What you did was outrageous."

"And ridiculous," I blurt.

Evie nods. "Yes. Ridiculous. I'm not going to apologize for being upset. But I'm sorry for dragging Isabel into this. That was a kick in the balls."

"I suppose it's a good thing I don't have testicles." I wipe my eyes. "You really admire me?"

"More than anyone I've ever met." Evie takes my hands in hers. "I would never have done what you did. But sometimes I wish I could. You're a good person. Who sometimes does the wrong thing. But always for the right reason."

I throw my arms around Evie. "Let's never fight again."

She hugs me back. We hang onto one another and I start to feel a warm sensation, something pulsating, against my body.

"Sylvia. Your phone is vibrating." Evie sits back.

I blush and let go of Evie. I reach into my robe pocket to find my phone. My heart stops.

It's Louis.

Evie peers at his name on the screen. She looks at me. I shake my head, and this time, I hit Ignore.

Twenty-Six

Louis never left a message, and I make it through the rest of the week without major issues. At least, nothing involving botched body waxing or fibbing about a terminal illness. Of course, there was the seating arrangement fiasco on Wednesday. Dan's mother had a fight with her brother and developed strong feelings about where he should sit. Siberia was her first choice. We talked her into putting him at a faraway table by the kitchen. And so along with the notes I took during my dinner with Frank, I reorganized our original seating chart like a three-star general, complete with color-coded pushpins to identify problem areas and safety zones. Ashton was very impressed.

Then there was the photographer, who, in hindsight, I should have realized was too high-maintenance when he referred to himself in the third person. And there also was the flower-girl drama just yesterday. Every cousin with a young daughter was competing as though this were a debutante event. I still shudder thinking about the headshots I received of several three-year-old girls and one boy in full makeup. And so I suggested to Dan and Ashton that instead of the traditional flower girl, why not have flower women? Their grandmothers are alive and would surely delight in playing a role in the ceremony.

And now it's Saturday evening and I'm in the bathroom covering my face, neck, and breasts in snail mucus and bee venom. It's the luxurious Korean face and body mask that Reese procured for me. Apparently, everyone from Cindy Crawford to Elton John swears by it. Evie is at work for the evening, which is why I've decided to go topless. I examine myself in the bathroom mirror. The mask feels like Jell-O, is the color of concrete, and smells like a rainy day at the beach. I'm wearing a fancy underpants purchase from years ago—a dead-sexy pair of red silk boy shorts with a drawstring waist. My hair is piled into a bun and I feel like a queen as I head into the living room, arrange myself on the couch, and open the latest issue of *Luxury Brides*.

Tonight is a mixture of relaxation and work. I stretch my legs onto the coffee table and lose myself in an article debating the pros and cons of having a complimentary tattoo artist at one's wedding.

"Fascinating," I breathe aloud to myself as I read about how to set up a sterile station during cocktail hour.

My door buzzes.

It's nearly eight o'clock. I know it's Ashton. I try to shake off the irritation. This is the job, I remind myself. And, besides. I do enjoy her company.

I force a smile onto my face and get up. I hit the buzzer. "Ashton?" I say.

"It's Frank."

Butterflies instantly dive around my stomach. I hit the buzzer again. "Is everything okay?"

"Are you busy?"

I take a breath. I should tell him that I'm in the middle of something. I should tell him I have company. But as though an outside force has taken control of me, I buzz him in. I then look down at my slimy, bare breasts and race into the bathroom. I grab a washcloth and scrub the mask off as best I can, roughly wiping my chest, neck, and face.

I throw on my cutest robe—a black kimono with pink and green butterflies—and unknot my hair. I shake it out, then spring back to the door. I open it, out of breath.

Frank stands there in black running tights and a fitted, high-tech running shirt with little reflectors built in. "You look amazing in that robe. Can I come in?"

I step aside. He enters and I'm instantly transported back to high school. He smells like a teenager who just finished gym class. That sweaty, musty odor. I would normally wrinkle my nose but I can feel myself heating up.

I clear my throat, resolved. "I can give you a glass of water. But you can't stay."

He stares at me. "Because it's complicated?"

"Because I could get fired."

He nods. "I'm sorry. I was out and the evening sky was perfect. Before I knew it, I ran all the way downtown. But you know what? I'm not disappointed. It was worth it just to see your beautiful face."

I open my robe and let it fall to the floor.

Frank opens his mouth to speak. I put my palm over his mouth. "Don't speak," I whisper. "Or else I'll change my mind."

He immediately runs his hands over my silky boy shorts as I peel off his running shirt. He pulls me toward him and kisses my face, my neck, my breasts. "Your skin is so soft," he murmurs.

"It's the snail mucus," I murmur back.

Frank tilts his head but doesn't stop running his hands slowly over my body. He caresses my nipples. "Snail mucus?" he repeats.

"It's very in vogue." I put my hands inside of his running tights. To be honest, men in spandex is not my favorite look. But Frank's thighs are hard and muscled. And I can feel how much he wants me as he groans in my ear.

The door buzzes again.

I freeze. This is absolutely ridiciulous.

Frank groans again. "Ignore it," he says.

"It might be your daughter," I say, hoarse.

"All the more reason to ignore it." It buzzes again.

I swallow and slowly pull away. "I can't. She's my client. But I promise—no sleepovers tonight. You won't have to sneak out the window."

Frank nods *okay*, and he picks up his clothes as I hit the intercom button again and find my soothing voice. "Ashton? Is everything okay?"

I hear someone clear their throat. Then a man's voice asks, "Sylvia?"

My entire body goes rigid. I snatch my finger away from the intercom as though burned.

I feel like throwing up. It can't be. It just can't.

Frank looks at my stricken face. "Who is that?"

I don't answer. Instead, I push the button again. "Louis? What are you doing here?"

Frank's eyes go wide as Louis responds. "We need to talk."

"It's not a good time," I say, my voice growing stronger. "Call me on the phone and we'll set up a proper—"

"See you in a sec, Syl," Louis cuts in, excited. "Someone's letting me in."

I turn to Frank. He's completely naked and holds his clothes and running shoes in his hands. "Did you want to introduce me?" he asks, his mouth twitching.

"It's not funny." I glare.

"But it so *is*," he says.

"Go hide in the bedroom," I order, my head spinning, as I pick up my robe and secure it tightly around my body. "And under no circumstances are you to come out. I mean it, Frank," I add quietly.

"You have my word." Frank pads off into my room and shuts the door.

"Unbelievable," I say to myself. I don't even bother to check my appearance. In fact, as I wait for Louis to knock on the door, I feel as though I'm about to meet someone from a past life. A ghost. Certainly not someone who is technically—legally—my husband.

As soon Louis knocks, I open the door. I stare at him as though looking at an old photograph. He's tall and lean. His thick hair has grown longer and he's as tan as ever. I try to remember if he's always had little bags beneath his eyes or if he just looks older to me. He wears jeans and a blue cashmere sweater I remember buying for his last birthday. Anyone else would call him handsome. But I feel completely immune to his charm.

"You should have called," I say, my voice flat.

"I did. Last week. You didn't pick up. Have you always had that robe? It's stunning." He looks me up and down, his eyes growing dark. "*You're* stunning. God, I've been such an idiot."

"Thanks."

"Can I come in?"

I stand in the doorway and think.

"I just got off my flight and came straight here," Louis says quickly. "I've been thinking about this moment for so long."

"Where's your suitcase?" I ask as I reluctantly step aside so that he can enter.

"I didn't bring one."

I shut the door and turn to face him. "You came with nothing?"

He sighs. "I was flipping channels and saw an episode of *Sex and the City*. Before I knew it, I found myself on the way to the airport. I called Izzy and begged her to go online and buy me a ticket so that I could come see you face-to-face."

"And she did? Just like that? Without even calling me?" I am incredulous.

"She didn't want to," Louis admits. "But I convinced her."

"I see," I say slowly. "You realize you're not staying here, yes?"

Louis's face flushes. "Just for the night? So we can talk? I'll sleep on the floor," he offers.

Blood pounds in my ears. My voice is low and gravelly. "You are un-fucking-believable."

Louis blanches. "Sylvia, please. This was supposed to be a romantic gesture. I flew all the way—"

"You have no respect for me," I continue as though he weren't talking. "You need to leave my apartment right now. You can call Izzy or sleep under a bridge. I don't care."

I turn around, yank open the door, and run smack into Isabel.

"Oh, shit. Dad got here first." Isabel sighs and steps around me so that she can enter the apartment.

My face contorts but no words come out. I feel powerless with shock and barely clock the fact that she's wearing a very un-Isabel outfit: ancient jeans and a hooded sweatshirt that I recognize from her college days. Her hair is in a messy ponytail. She drops an oversize tote bag onto the floor and plops down on my couch. She's about to slip her feet beneath her but then changes her mind. She sits upright and folds her hands in her lap.

Louis wordlessly follows her to the sofa.

I stare at my husband and daughter sitting side by side on my tiny couch and feel insane. "Mom," Isabel says softly. "Can we please just talk?"

"About what?" I'm still standing in the hallway by the door next to our kitchen. I pull the belt of my robe even tighter around my waist as I glare. "The fact that neither of you called before ambushing me in my apartment on a Saturday evening? With no regard to my plans?"

Louis looks around. "What plans?"

He says this so earnestly that I want to punch him in the face.

But Isabel shoots him a look, then turns back to me. "I'm sorry. I should have called as I was driving in. I wanted to get here before Dad and tell you in person that I got him a ticket. I don't know why I didn't do it on the phone. It was stupid."

"Why would you call your mother?" Louis asks. "This was supposed to be a surprise. You loved the idea!"

Isabel turns red. "I loved it in the moment. But then I called my therapist and realized it was a terrible idea."

The air goes out of the room. Louis and I can't help but share a look for a moment.

"Don't look so shocked. I already told you that I asked Todd to see a counselor," Isabel says to me.

"But I thought he wouldn't," I reply.

"I went anyway."

"Oh, Izzy," I say, "I'm so glad you're getting yourself some support. But you're right. Coming here like this was a terrible idea."

"I've been seeing a therapist, too," Louis interjects, leaning forward. "I'm really understanding why I behaved the way I did. Rebecca's encouraging me to find compassion for myself."

I roll my eyes. "That's touching, Louis. Does she know that you came here unannounced? Does she know that you took all of the money from my new bank account?"

"It was a spontaneous decision," he says defensively, before adding, "Half that money is mine."

I feel fresh rage surge through me, but it's Isabel who speaks first.

"You took Mom's money? What are you talking about?" She turns and looks at Louis with a shocked expression.

"Half of that is mine," he repeats.

"That was my jewelry. None of it was yours," I seethe.

"Jesus, Dad." Isabel looks sick. Louis has the decency to blush. "How could you do that to her?" she says, her voice sounding a little faraway.

Louis's mouth contorts as he searches for words. But I've had enough. "Isabel, Louis. I'm thrilled that both of you are in therapy. We can talk more about that and everything else at another time that is more convenient for me."

Isabel picks up her bag. "I'm really sorry, Mom. Let's go, Dad. You and I can talk in the car." Her voice is sharp.

Louis looks a little afraid. He turns to me. "You want Isabel to drive us all the way back to Connecticut? And then return to New York on a different day?"

"That's correct," I say.

"That's bullshit!" Louis cries out. "Why can't we just talk now?"

"Because I'm busy!" I yell back.

"Doing what?" he demands.

"Dad, stop," Isabel snaps. "We're being rude."

I nearly faint from shock.

Even Louis looks bewildered. "Did your therapist prescribe medication, sweetie?"

Isabel ignores him and turns to me. "When I went to see my therapist, I thought we'd talk about my marriage and how stressed I've been. But we talk about you."

I blink, speechless.

"I'm jealous," Izzy continues, words now tumbling out of her mouth. "I want to move to New York and start a new life. But I can't. I have kids who keep acting out, which is probably my fault for trying to make sure they have every advantage. And then my husband, without talking to me, quits his job and spends all day perfecting his downward dog in our living room. That is also probably my fault. Apparently I didn't 'listen' to him and 'notice' the signs that he was unhappy because I'm never home. Todd literally accused me of having an affair. Can you believe it? I told him that I would never use my free time to deal with another man. I'm cheating on him with hobbies. When I'm not working three thousand hours a week, I go to SoulCycle and knitting classes so I don't have to be home. Isn't that pathetic? Sometimes I just sit in my car in the Safeway parking lot and eat Twix bars and watch TV on my phone." Isabel finally lets out a breath. Tears pour down her cheeks.

I immediately put my arms around her. "Do you mean the Safeway off Helmdale Road? I used to sit in that same parking lot and eat M&M's when you were little because I didn't want to go home."

She cries harder.

I find Isabel's eyes. "It sounds like you're in a really tough place,

Izzy. And I'm sorry. But I'm so glad you're talking to someone. For what it's worth—and I'm not excusing his behavior—but it sounds like Todd's trying to get your attention. I hope you guys can find a way to talk to each other. And I'm always here for you. Just not at this particular moment," I add, tightening my robe.

Isabel nods, then takes a deep breath. "Come on, Dad."

Louis stands up. "Fine. But Sylvia, Rebecca and I've been discussing how unhealthy it is that you keep running from your problems. As they say, 'Wherever you go, there you are.'"

"Thank you for that gem of wisdom, Louis. Let me show you to the door."

I walk swiftly toward the front door when there's a banging from my bedroom. The noise reverberates through the apartment and I freeze.

Goddamn it, Frank.

"What's going on?" Louis asks, craning his neck, trying to locate the noise. "Raccoons," I say quickly. "There's trash cans in the alley out there. Okay. Off, you go."

I'm about to open the front door when the unmistakable sound of glass shattering fills the air.

"Jesus, Sylvia! Those aren't raccoons! You have a burglar!" Louis cries out.

"Oh my god!" Isabel shrieks. "Call 911! Do you have a bat?"

"Why would I have a bat? And it's not a burglar. Let's go." I physically pull their arms but they both shrug me off.

"I'll use this," Louis says as he grabs one of the clocks off the living room wall. It's about three feet long and made out of steel. He dashes toward my bedroom.

"Louis! Stop!" I cry desperately and race after him

"Dad! Wait for the police!" Isabel is right behind me.

But he's too fast. His hand is on the doorknob. He pushes it open and then holds the clock above his head as all three of us tumble inside, where Frank is trying to pick up the pieces of my bedside lamp. While naked.

Isabel shrieks at the top of her lungs.

Louis's wields the clock above his head and lunges toward him. "I'm gonna rip your throat out, you pervert!"

Now Frank shrieks at the top of his lungs. I jump between Louis and Frank.

"Sylvia! What are you doing?" Louis tries to step around me but I don't let him.

"This is Frank!" I blurt out. "He's not a pervert. Or a burglar."

Isabel shrieks again. Louis, stricken, stares at me as though I've just told him the world is flat. "What do you mean, 'this is Frank'?"

"Hi," Frank says, his voice shaking. "I'm really sorry, Sylvia. I was trying to get comfortable on the bed and accidentally knocked over the lamp."

There're shards of glass on the floor, right under Frank's feet.

"Hang on, Frank. I need to get the glass away."

I kneel down and pick up the large pieces of glass while Frank, mortified, holds a pillow over his penis.

"Isabel," I call over my shoulder as I place the glass into a trash can. "Grab the Dustbuster from the kitchen. It's mounted on the wall. I don't want anyone to get cut on these tiny shards."

Isabel doesn't move. She just keeps staring at Frank.

I turn to Louis. But it's no use. He paces in little circles, mumbling to himself.

I sigh and look at Frank.

"Just stay here a moment while I see my husband and daughter out."

"Should I get dressed?" Frank asks quietly. He then looks at Louis and Isabel. "I'm sorry to have given you such a scare. I hope to meet you under better circumstances one day."

Louis's head snaps up. His eyes are wild. "Better 'circumstances'? You're naked in my wife's bedroom, you motherfucker!" He springs like a lion onto Frank and pulls him to the ground.

Frank's pillow falls away as they tumble around, wrestling and yelling and punching.

And maybe a little biting.

Isabel screams and I stare, helpless. And also flattered. Like Cleopatra. Or Helen of Troy.

Of course, this would be so much more enjoyable if Frank and Louis were lotharios in their twenties rather than grandfathers—or soon to be grandfathers—in their sixties.

I worry about Louis's tendinitis when he elbows Frank in the face.

And I know Frank's lower back must ache when he arches his torso to push his thumbs into Louis's eyes.

Isabel is now trying to pull Louis off Frank. "Stop hitting my dad!" she yells.

"He's the one hitting me!" Frank yells back.

I turn off the lights. Everything goes black.

"That's enough!" I say breathlessly. "No more fighting. This is ridiculous. Isabel, Louis. I'm sorry you're meeting Frank this way. But you should have called before coming. And so, without another word, I want both of you to get up and follow me to the door."

I turn back on the lights. Louis blinks a few times. Then, as if on autopilot, he gets up off Frank and straightens his clothes.

He stares at me a moment. "How could you?" he finally demands with the most wounded expression.

I roll my eyes. "Oh, for heaven's sakes."

Louis looks like he wants to say something else, but instead turns to Izzy. "I'll wait for you outside." He marches out of the room and I hear the door open and close.

I then motion for Frank to stay and for Isabel to follow me.

We walk out into the living room. She picks up her bag. We stop outside my door.

"I don't know what's worse," she says, looking dazed. "That I just saw an old-man fight or that I'm, again, a little jealous."

As she leaves, I watch her walk down the hallway a moment before shutting and locking my door for what I hope is the final time tonight.

As I stand there a moment, Frank walks into the room. He's again covering himself with my pillow. His glasses are crooked and I can see a bruise forming under his eye. He rubs his jaw gingerly. "Sylvia, I don't know where to begin. That was not how I pictured this evening going. You must be so angry."

I blink. "Two men going to battle over me? It was . . . intoxicating. Do you need ice?"

Frank stops massaging his face. "Intoxicating?" he asks, his gaze growing dark. "That's a good thing, right?"

"A *very* good thing." I step closer to him. We lock eyes.

His gaze travels down my robe. I can feel my chest rising and falling.

Frank lets the pillow fall away. He's covered in scratches and has a few teeth marks on his bicep. I run my fingers over a particularly bad scrape by his rib cage. "Are you sure you're okay?"

"Never been better," he says and pulls at the knot on my robe.

The kimono slips down my back and lands on my feet like a soft wave crashing. Frank bends forward and cups my breasts. His tongue is on my nipples. I gasp with pleasure as he pulls me gently onto the floor and slides on top of me.

Oh my god. It's happening so fast.

I close my eyes and arch my back to meet him, clutching him with my thighs. I didn't know I could even still arch my back. Or clutch my thighs.

Oh my god. Oh my GOD.

This is nothing like it was with Louis. I'm slick with sweat. Frank is all the way inside of me and I want more and more and more. Our bodies rock back and forth. I cry out and Frank groans into my neck.

I have no idea how much time goes by as I lie there, shocked with pleasure, and Frank finally rolls off me. We lie next to each other and stare at the ceiling.

Frank picks up my hand and holds it above his head. He kisses my palm. "That was amazing."

I nod, still staring at the ceiling, and replay the evening's events through my head like a tape recorder. "So amazing," I agree. "How long until we can do it again?"

Frank turns to me. "How do you feel about twenty minutes?"

I climb on top of him and start kissing his neck, careful to avoid any sore spots. "Twenty is my lucky number."

Twenty-Seven

I'm not trying for any kind of record. But Frank and I have had sex every day for the last five weeks. Sometimes twice a day. And naturally there are the in-between sex acts that aren't officially sex. Like this morning when we . . . Actually, I'm not sure what that was called. But it was nice. Very nice, I think to myself, as I look across the table at Frank as he sips coffee and reads the paper. It's Sunday, late morning. Frank and I are having brunch at Perrine, the restaurant at The Pierre. It's all heavy white tablecloths and sleek mirrors on the walls. But there's also an old New York vibe. Not old-fashioned. But timeless. A restored elegance. Kind of like Frank and me, I think to myself as we smile at each other across the table.

"I like your legal pad. It's a brilliant disguise," he says as he takes a bite of his high-protein scramble and hands me the travel section of the Sunday *Times*.

I take a bite of toast and rearrange my legal pad on the edge of the table. "What if Ashton comes to find you? We need to have a story. We're working."

"Exactly. Very savvy."

I know he's teasing me, but carrying this legal pad everywhere we go together has given me a sense of freedom. Plus, I feel professional. When it's not on the table, I like to put it in my tote bag that's just two inches too short so it sticks out the top.

Louis looks at me over his coffee. "Nina and I never had brunch. She liked to sleep in. You and me? We're the same. Daytime people."

"It's true. We're very compatible," I say as I help myself to the fruit on his plate that I know he won't eat.

He puts down his cup. "I'm serious. I have never in my life met a woman more suited for me than you. I don't have to hide my family from you because you already know our dirty secrets. You get along with my daughter. Jesus. You're more like a mother to her than Nina. And I'm excited to meet Isabel with my clothes on. Do you think she'll like me?"

"Well," I say thoughtfully. "Seeing you in a naked brawl with her father was probably the worst-case scenario. So things can only improve."

Frank grins. "This is why I love you, Sylvia Fisher. Your everlasting optimism."

A hunk of honeydew lodges in my throat. I cough and hit my chest to get it down. I gulp water as Frank stares at me.

"I know. I said, 'I love you.'" He takes off his glasses and looks me in the eye. "Does that freak you out? Because I was kind of hoping you feel the same way."

I stare back at him helplessly. "I think so. I mean, you're lovely. Absolutely lovely. I'm sorry. I'm just . . . thrown."

I wince as Frank's temper flares. "So this is what? A bit of fun? A convenience? While you plan my daughter's wedding?"

"Are you kidding? This is incredibly *in*convenient. I'm risking my job, Frank. But I'm doing it because we have something special. I care about you. A lot. So no. This is not just 'a bit of fun.'"

We stare at one another for a long moment. Frank puts back on his glasses and speaks quietly. "Are you going to leave me once the wedding is over?"

"How could you even ask that?"

"I'm trying to understand—are we on the same page? Is this a real relationship?"

I reach across the table and grab his hands. "Frank. I love being with you. I love the way you clean your glasses with a special anti-microbial cloth. I love the way you got me fourteen thousand legal pads when I told you that they make me feel safe. I love that you have an addiction to sneakers. It makes me feel better about my own shopping habits. It's just that I haven't gotten to the place of saying 'I love you' or thinking too much about the future because we're both in the midst of an unpleasant separation. And, technically, I work for both you and your wife. So needless to say, things are complicated. But I'm trying to keep my anxiety in check and not overthink things because this is such a special relationship."

He finds my eyes. We hold each other's gaze as I lace my fingers through his.

"Are we good?" I ask.

"Yes," he says as he lets go of my hands and takes a sip of water. "We're good. I just needed to make sure you were serious about us. Because I'm man enough to admit that I do want to get married again. Some people might even say that I'm a catch."

He winks at me and I can't help but laugh. And then, after a quick glance around the restaurant to make sure the coast is clear, I lean across the table and kiss him.

He kisses me back.

All is right with the world.

Twenty-Eight

O h, fuckity fuck-fuck-fuck," Evie says breathlessly as she picks up a panama straw hat by Janessa Leone and pops it on her head. "He basically proposed."

"He did not! He just wanted to make sure I was serious." I flip through a clothing rack for the fifth time but can't concentrate despite the stunning inventory.

Evie and I are at a pop-up consignment shop in a loft on Spring Street. Reese texted us the address and a QR code to gain access. Very exclusive. And so after brunch, another round of kissing, and then a quickie in Frank's hotel room, I hopped on the bus and met Evie in SoHo, one of my favorite parts of New York. I love the cobblestone streets and fire escapes zigzagging across the buildings.

When we entered the loft, it was like walking into someone's enormous private closet. Exposed brick, high ceilings, all the clothes displayed on various racks or folded in antique trunks with little side tables showcasing vintage handbags in clear acrylic holders. We've been here for about thirty minutes and there haven't been more than a dozen other shoppers present. We all shop quietly and move around without elbowing one another over some treasure. It's much different than those sample sales I'd heard about where women—and men— basically dismember one another trying to get their hands on a be- loved Ulla Johnson dress that's seventy percent reduced. I love that Reese is so in the know about these secret sales. He understands how desperate I am to buy something new for the wedding. I sift once again through a rack and try to concentrate.

Evie takes off her hat. "So he didn't propose. But he said that he loves you."

"Yes."

"Do you love him? What do you think of this? For the ceremony?" She holds up a gray silk A-line dress.

I shake my head. "I need something more structured. That won't show sweat stains. And I don't know if I love him. It's too soon."

"Too soon or he's not the one?"

"Oh, Evie. This is preposterous. How could he love me? He doesn't know me well enough. You can't just go around telling people you love them. It's very confusing. Is that Celine?"

Evie's holding a skirt. "It's Ungaro. And it's seven hundred dol- lars. I'm putting it back. And I agree. You can't just go around telling people you love them. Unless, of course, you love them."

I give her a look and rationalize. "I don't understand why we're obsessing over this. Everything is fine. He understood what I meant by taking it slow. I love being with him. But I just got out of a relation- ship. We both did. It's not healthy to think about getting married again. Or even moving in with someone. I just got my own apartment. And I'm loving *our* life together—mine and yours, Evie."

Evie puts the hat back onto her head and looks at her reflection in a mosaic wall mirror. "I appreciate that, Sylvia. Because, for what it's worth, if you move into The Pierre with Frank, I'm coming, too. Now, focus. We're not leaving without a perfect wedding-day outfit."

Twenty-Nine

We didn't find the perfect outfit. Everything suitable was still out of budget. But then, as if by magic, a package arrived at our apartment a few days later. It was addressed to me. I tore it open. The card read, "Good luck, working woman. X, Isabel." I then lifted out a shift dress in a gorgeous navy hue. It was almost the same dress—just an updated version— of the one I had passed on years ago when shopping with Isabel.

I couldn't believe she remembered. I called her and cried.

She got a little embarrassed. "Relax, Mom. It's just a dress."

"It's more than a dress. It's Armani."

We hung up and I felt so good. Not just because I had a beautiful dress to wear to my first wedding job. But because my daughter had seen me.

Evie and I continued hitting every pop-up consignment shop

Reese sent us invites to. Now that it's December, there are all kinds of special holiday sales, and I found a fabulous faux Sherpa coat that was missing two buttons and therefore very affordable. Thank goodness for the old-fashioned home economics classes women were required to take once upon a time. I turn up its collar now as I step into the wintry December wind and head to the subway.

It's Friday morning—the day before the wedding—and I've just had an early breakfast in bed with Frank. I'm leaving The Pierre and heading directly to BarUp Lounge & Game Room to make sure everything is perfect for this evening's rehearsal dinner. A knot tightens in my stomach. I can't believe the wedding festivities are set to begin and am, truthfully, relieved. Not just because I want this trial period as Verena's assistant to be a triumph and to have full-time employment. But also because it'll be a relief to date Frank independent of work. Thankfully, Frank and I moved seamlessly past any awkwardness from that day at brunch. He doesn't say he loves me outright anymore, but he does little things to tease me, like saying, "I just love . . . everything about you, Sylvia." And I smile and say, "And I love everything about you, too." It's our little inside joke. Evie says it makes her want to barf, but I take that as a compliment since she says it with such affection.

Frank and Evie have become fast friends. He joined me at Wild One to watch her play the piano for a special holiday event last week. He was blown away. In fact, it was his idea to hire her last minute to join the band for the wedding. Evie loved this idea—she can make extra money and get to see the event I was living and breathing come to fruition. Plus, I love knowing that she'll be with me for my very first Manhattan job.

As I tighten my coat once more, I leave the subway station and navigate the streets of Manhattan's garment district. I forgot how much I missed the holiday season on the East Coast. I catch a glimpse of my reflection in a store window and barely recognize myself. Partly because Verena took me to her fabulous but criminally expensive hairdresser who declared my beachy highlights "cute" and then gave me streaks of caramel and cinnamon. I was hesitant at first. But now I realize I was born to be a brunette.

It's a cold day, but the sky is brightening into a glorious blue. The air is crisp and smells like ginger cookies as I duck into a café to buy biscotti and coffee for me and Verena. She's meeting me at the rehearsal venue, and although she rarely asks me to do the typical assistant grunt work of fetching her beverages and food, I do it anyway. She's become a mentor and a friend over these last weeks. Sometimes we stay late at the office and chat about life and love. She's so confident and strong that I was stunned when she started crying just a few evenings ago.

"I'm going to die alone," she declared as we ate take-out sushi in the conference room. Her face was dark and she wiped away the few tears that escaped down her cheeks.

"That is absolutely not true," I replied.

"Mark and I broke up. He's not leaving his wife."

She had mentioned Mark before, but this was the first time I was hearing about a wife. I put down my chopsticks and looked at her. "Did you know he was married?" But as soon as I asked, I already knew the answer.

Verena met my eye. "I've come to think of us as friends, Sylvia. And so I'm going to be honest with you. Not only did I know he was married, but I preferred it. It started as a fling. I just ended up really liking him. More than I've liked anyone in a long time."

I felt myself stiffen and spoke carefully. "I'm sorry. This must be very disappointing."

"Please don't be so fucking formal. You can be honest back. I deserve to be unhappy if I'm going to date married men. That's what you're thinking, right?"

I sighed. "I'm not judging you. I'm just surprised. You're a good person."

"I'm a good wedding planner. I'm a good boss. But I'm not a good person." Verena looks away from me.

I didn't know how to respond. And so I said nothing as she popped a piece of sushi in her mouth and continued staring at the ceiling. "I hate traveling alone. I hate the pitying look from hotel workers. Two weeks ago, when I went to Bermuda for that destination wedding, I lied to the person checking me in at the front desk."

I scrunched my brow. "But didn't they know you were the wedding planner?"

"Of course. But I still said, 'My boyfriend so wished he could join me for this. But he had too much work.' Mark was supposed to come. But he couldn't sneak away that weekend. Something with his wife's cousins in town, he said. I'm pathetic, I know."

I shook my head. "You're not pathetic, Verena. But if you want me to be honest, I think you're selling yourself short. You're too good to be someone's mistress."

"You have to say that. I employ you."

"You know me well enough to know that I never say things I don't mean. You're an amazing woman who deserves an honest relationship."

She looked at me for a moment before nodding. "Tell me more."

I smiled. "You're generous and fun and smart. You're such good company and always a pleasure to just be around. You can do so much better than a married man who lies and cheats. He's pathetic, Verena. Not you."

Verena's voice was unusually quiet. "You really think all that about me?"

I stared at her. "Verena. I think the absolute world of you."

Her cheeks flushed at the compliment, and I smile now thinking about that moment as I balance our drinks and biscotti and head down the sidewalk toward the restaurant. Truthfully, I'm too jazzed up to feel hungry, but the first rule of wedding planning is to keep blood sugar levels even. For the brides *and* the planners. I need to stay sharp and calm. I've been reciting my mantras and downloaded the *Rocky* soundtrack onto my phone. I listen to it every day and my breath quickens just thinking about what it will feel like if the wedding is a success. I have no doubt that Verena will keep her word and hire me full-time. And even though I no longer need to prove something to Isabel or Louis, I want to prove something to myself. And pay my bills, of course. But six months ago, I lived in a Florida retirement community. Today, I have a job in Manhattan. That means something.

That means something, I repeat again as I enter BarUp and feel a glow of pleasure for finding such an interesting venue. It's a former factory that's been stripped to the bones and remade into an airy but intimate space with rich, dark wood and aquariums built into the walls where exotic fish dart by. For the dinner this evening, we've arranged to have two rectangular tables in the center of the room that each seat forty people. Around the perimeter, there are cozy booths and highboy tables for those who prefer to sit and chat after their meal rather than go downstairs to the underground game room, where there are vintage arcade games, pinball, and bowling.

Despite living in Chicago, Dan's family wanted to host this event. When it came time to choose a venue and coordinate plans, I asked if they might be open to something a little less traditional. Initially, they were wary.

"But what's wrong with a nice French restaurant?" asked Dan's mother, Kathy, when we first spoke on the phone.

"We don't want to look cheap," added her husband, Tim. "We can certainly keep up with the New York folks."

"It's not possible to be cheap in Manhattan," I assured them. "And Ashton and Dan want to use this evening as an opportunity to relax and enjoy. The Plaza will be beautiful. But it's so formal, so traditional. Why not do something fun? Is there a kind of food or music you love? Anyone sing karaoke? Enjoy throwing axes?"

After a perplexing moment in which I explained ax-throwing bars—and quickly backtracked from the notion of arming a bunch of relatives with deadly weapons—I learned that Dan and his family are competitive bowlers. It was kismet, as I had just read a review of BarUp in *New York* magazine the previous week while in the waiting room at Ashton's gynecologist's office.

Dan's parents couldn't believe that it was possible to combine bowling with an upscale dinner. But as soon as I explained that the menu would include items such as nachos with Wagyu beef and drinks featuring blackberry vodka and chili-infused tequila, they were sold. And Dan was especially enthusiastic about the bowling jerseys we would be giving away as party favors.

I look over at the coat check station and smile as a cleaning woman polishes the hangers. The manager, Devon, is a dream. He's twenty-nine. His parents are both high-ranking members of the military and have instilled in him the importance of attention to detail. In fact, I look over and see him standing in the dining room using a ruler to measure the distance between the appetizer plates, which have already been set.

"Hi, Devon!" I call out.

He nods without looking up. "The boxes of bowling jerseys are downstairs. Let me know how you would like to distribute them to our guests."

"Sure thing," I say and head down the stairs into the vast underground game room. I smile, feeling transported in time as I scan the retro arcade games: there's pinball, Pac-Man, and even Skee-Ball.

I put my purse, the biscotti, and beverages on the bar-top and shrug off my coat. I roll up my sleeves. There's at least eight shipping boxes to open. I need to unwrap the shirts and sort the sizes. I'm about to open the first box when I hear my phone beep.

I see the text and gasp: it's a close-up photo of a penis.

Of course, it's Frank's penis. But I just can't get over the shock of sex pics. Or whatever young people call them. I was initially too shy to reciprocate. But then I realized that no one was going to sensationalize nude photos of me. I'm a grandmother, after all. And so I started having quite a good time replying to Frank.

Obviously, I can't do that now. But I take another look at Frank's penis and admire his creativity. Today, for instance, it has a thought bubble above its head: "I miss you, my queen." I love when Frank calls me that. I feel so regal. In fact, even now I notice that I've pulled my shoulder blades together and am standing tall.

I sigh. I can't wait until Frank and I can truly, openly date. It's been hard keeping it a secret. Sneaking around is not something I enjoy. I'm just not a subtle person.

The sound of someone's footsteps makes me jump and I drop my phone. It skids across the floor to where Verena is now standing, looking very posh in a crisp navy suit and Celine flats. She picks up my phone and glances at the screen.

I want to die. Thank god she doesn't know whose penis it is.

"No wonder you're fucking Frank. For a skinny guy, he's very well endowed." Verena hands the phone back to me.

As though moving in slow motion, I shove it into my purse. "What do you mean?" My voice is high-pitched and dumb.

"Cut the shit, Sylvia. I know about you and Frank." Verena picks up the box cutter and slices open a box of bowling shirts. "I'm almost insulted you haven't told me. But I get it."

Blood beats in my ears. "How?"

"The way you looked at each other at the cake tasting? The fact that Frank even came to the cake tasting? This is a marathon runner who probably hasn't seen a carbohydrate since the nineties. And there he is shoving a pile of chocolate mousse in his mouth? And then, his suit fitting. There was a moment when he literally tilted his head ninety degrees to look at your butt as you bent down to pick up your handbag. These bowling shirts are fab, by the way."

Verena has unpacked nearly a dozen jerseys by now. She holds one up. It's adorable. Black with gold script across it—"Dan & Ashton, Forever."

I nod weakly and search for the right words. "Verena, I'm sorry. I hope you know that I would never let my personal relationship with Frank influence the quality of my work on this wedding."

"Obviously," Verena says with a lifted brow. "I would have fired you if I thought otherwise."

"But how come you didn't ask me to stop seeing him?"

"Because I don't give a shit what you do in your personal life. And Frank's a great catch. I'm envious," she says with a wink.

"Really?" I ask, feeling both shy and flattered. And also bad because of her recent breakup.

As if reading my mind, she smiles. "More like almost envious. I could never date a man who weighs less than me. I need someone who can handle a fatty."

"Don't say that!" I say fiercely.

"Again, cut the shit. I'm overweight. But I'm rich and can afford the best tailor. Besides, fat people's skin ages better."

I burst out laughing. "You're amazing. And you're not fat," I add, meaning it. "Zaftig, perhaps. Which is very sexy. How are you feeling about Mark? Also, Bunny mentioned you the other day on the phone."

"I'm feeling very 'over' Mark and his marriage. I now just feel bad for his wife. You were absolutely goddamn right. I can do better than him. Now, onto more important matters—Bunny, the French-kisser?" Verena asks, her cheeks brightening.

"Yep. She wants to invite you to a special dinner with her and her husband but asked for my approval."

"And what did you say?"

"I made it clear that the only reason she can contact you is if she wants to hire your services for a vow renewal ceremony."

Verena grins. "Well done. I've made a hustler out of you."

I smile, proud, and start unpacking the jerseys. Verena does the same. We work in silence for a few minutes when my phone rings again.

It's a number I don't recognize, but I answer with my most professional voice. "This is Sylvia."

A woman's throaty voice echoes in my ear. "Sylvia, darling! This is Nina. I'm trying to check into the Plaza Hotel and there isn't a room for me. I'm sure this is an oversight, seeing as how I'm mother of the bride. Be a love and call the manager. I'll go have a latte while you sort it out."

"Nina!" I gulp. "I didn't even know you were back in town! There must be some mistake—"

Nina hangs up.

Verena stares at me. I swallow and explain. "Nina has returned to town and is trying to check in at the Plaza. They don't have a reservation for her."

"Did you not make one?"

"Of course I made one. She said she'd return for the wedding and a woman like her would never miss a social event."

Verena gestures at my phone. "They why are you not speed-dialing Fredrick at the Plaza?"

I nod, already on it. I dial the Plaza.

An operator picks up. "The Plaza Hotel. How may I direct your call?" I start to pace. "Fredrick Watts, the manager, please. This is Sylvia."

The operator puts me on hold. Generic music fills my ears. I blank it out and imagine I'm hearing the opening bells to Bill Conti's "Going the Distance" instead. I steel myself. This is the job. Of course something has gone wrong. That's why I *have* a job. For these moments.

A man's deep voice cuts in my ear. "This is Fredrick."

"It's Sylvia," I plunge in, my voice sharp. "Ashton's mother just called and apparently there's no room booked for her. What happened?"

Fredrick sighs. "Mrs. Levinson has a room. A lovely suite, in fact.

But she's requesting one with a different view. Unfortunately, it's unavailable."

I grit my teeth, furious with Nina for being such a diva. Verena looks at me. I roll my eyes to indicate that there is no emergency. I take a breath. "Fredrick, I'm sorry. But is there any way to give her the room she's requesting?"

"It's the room her husband is staying in," he says, his voice neutral.

"Her *ex*-husband," I say too quickly. Verena lifts a brow. I redden as I finish up with Fredrick. "Sorry. This must be some sort of marital issue. Switch their rooms if it's not too much trouble. I don't think Frank will mind."

"Very well," Fredrick says crisply. "I'll make the switch and then locate Mrs. Levinson myself. I have her cell number."

"Thank you, Fredrick. You're a doll." I hang up and let out a breath.

Verena takes a bite of biscotti. "So Nina wanted Frank's room?"

I nod and roll my eyes.

Verena laughs. "I love it. Wedding drama is the best. I like to think of it as job security."

I shake my head, firm. "The service we provide is not dependent on people behaving badly."

She takes another bite. "My career took off because a bride set your lawn on fire."

My throat tightens. *Laura Eliot.* I feel Verena's eyes on me and straighten up. "You would have made it anyway. Don't give Laura all the credit."

"I was giving *you* all the credit." Verena puts a hand on my arm. "Thank you for my career, Sylvia. And please take this for all the good I intend: may Ashton's wedding bring you terrible pain and terrific success."

Now I laugh. "Thank you, Verena. I appreciate the sentiment. But Ashton's wedding has already had pain and drama. She's fired me, locked me in a bathroom, and regularly takes me to her gynecologist. So Nina doesn't scare me. She's not even the bride. What's the worst she can do?"

Thirty

The worst Nina can do is give a spectacularly inappropriate toast at the rehearsal night dinner. Which is what she's doing. Right now.

I try not to worry. They're just *words*. They don't have to mean anything.

But my mouth is dry as I stand at the back of BarUp's dining room and stare at the crowd of people seated around the tables. The rehearsal dinner is in full swing, but now all chatter has died down and the guests hang on Nina's every word of her toast. I have to admit, she looks resplendent in her bohemian ensemble of caramel-colored leather pants and a floral blouse. All at once, my blazer and slacks feel institutional.

Her eyes glitter with emotion as she gazes at Frank. "I've been so stupid, Frankie. Selfish and dishonest. Weakened by desire." She pauses a moment to gaze at her rapt audience before putting a hand on Ashton's shoulder. "My darling daughter. When I woke up yesterday morning in Paris, I felt like I had come out of a dream. On my flight back, I wrote this speech. It is the best wedding present I could give you: your father and I will get back together. May your union be our reunion. May your wedding be our wedding renewal." Nina bends down and kisses the top of Ashton's hair, which has been swept up into a high ponytail with small wisps framing her face.

Ashton tucks one of those tendrils behind her ear and looks up at her mother. She's about to say something, but Nina raises her martini and sweeps it grandly through the air and declares, "To love! To family! To marriage!"

Everyone breaks into applause and Nina, beaming, sips her drink and walks around the table until she's standing directly beside Frank's chair.

Frank looks shell-shocked as he scans the room. I'm sure he's looking for me. But I press my back against the far wall by the kitchen—completely out of sight—and swallow tears. Nina hijacked Ashton's wedding. It's despicable. And yet I also feel a burning rush of humiliation because my personal feelings are tangled up in all of this.

I rub my temples and take deep breaths. I look out into the room and try to see if from a purely objective perspective: The guests are cheering. The mood is uplifted. And, most importantly, Ashton isn't glaring at her narcissistic mother with open hatred. In fact, she dabs her eyes and Dan rubs her back and the two of them smile as Nina stands next to Frank and taps him playfully on the shoulder.

"Frankie," she says in singsong. "I'm waiting."

Frank's face is red and he cleans his glasses on the hem of his black polo shirt. He's wearing graphite jeans, his new bowling shoes, and looks like he wants to crawl under the table. But after a glance at Ashton, he slowly stands up and faces Nina, who towers over him by nearly a foot in her stilettos.

They stare at each other for a few seconds before Nina caresses his cheek with her hand, her wedding band twinkling beneath the overhead lights. It's a familiar, warm gesture. She then wraps her arms around Frank's neck and kisses him passionately on the lips.

The room erupts again in hoots and cheers.

I put a hand on the wall to steady myself but then see the manager, Devon, peering at me from behind the bar. I immediately straighten up and grab the walkie-talkie off my belt clip. "Devon, first course," I choke out. "Let's roll."

Devon responds. "Roger that, chief."

I reclip my walkie-talkie and let out a huge breath. That's god-damn right. I'm the chief. The captain of this ship. The general of this brigade. These military metaphors are very helpful right now as I feel my blood pressure start to even out. I channel my inner Patton and use hand signals to direct the servers as they start carrying out the first course of family-style Wagyu beef nachos, butternut squash baked with brown butter, and tender green salads. The air smells like roasted garlic with a hint of lime and the guests chat happily as they pick up their forks.

I look back at Ashton, who is still whispering to Dan. I should go over and see how she is. And congratulate Frank and Nina. It would be the professional thing to do. And so I tug down my blazer, narrow my eyes, and start walking toward the happy family.

It's simple. I'll pretend that Frank is barely more than a stranger. I have not seen him naked. I do not have photos of his penis wearing sunglasses stored on my phone.

Just as I get within inches of them, I hear Nina's voice tinkle through the air. "This is going to be such fun! I picked up a little white dress at an atelier in Paris. We can exchange vows at the same time as Ashton and Dan. And then we must discuss you moving back to the house. My assistant can pick everything up from your hotel. And then we'll . . ."

I don't make it over to them. Instead, I take a sharp right and head down the side corridor toward the ladies' room. I push open the door. It's all textured wallpaper and concrete floors. I beeline for a stall and lock myself in before collapsing onto the toilet. I unbutton my blazer and put my head between my knees. I can't help but admire my black pumps. They're a smooth black leather. Italian. Another consignment shop purchase. While my head is between my knees, I check to see if anyone else in the bathroom. It's empty. I sigh, but then, as if on cue, I hear the door open. The sounds of the happy crowd echo into the bathroom for a moment before the door swooshes closed.

It's silent for a moment. And then a voice calls out, "Sylvia? Are you in here?" It's Ashton.

I gulp and stand up. "Hang on!"

I flush the toilet and come out of the stall. Ashton stands in front of the sink. I try to smile. "Well, that was something. How's the food?"

"I don't want to share my wedding with her!" Ashton bursts into tears and throws her arms around my neck.

"It's okay," I soothe. "You don't have to."

"But she thinks we are! And I was too mortified to say no in front of everyone! She manipulated me!" Ashton lets me go and wipes her eyes, which now flash with anger. "And my dad should not take her back. After everything she did to him? I mean, would you take Louis back?"

"That's a different situation."

"No, it's not." Ashton crosses her arms. "Louis cheated on you. My mom cheated on my dad. Why would anyone take back a liar and a cheater?" Her voice is so ferocious that she's practically spitting.

"I wouldn't take Louis back. Not because he cheated. But because I don't love him anymore. Do you understand the difference?"

"Not really."

"Your dad might love your mom enough to take her back." I swallow what feels like a knife lodged in my throat. "Only he can know in his heart how he feels. But it's okay to not want to share your wedding."

Nina strides into the bathroom. She looks at Ashton's tearstained, angry face and rolls her eyes. They stare at one another for what feels like the world's longest, most awkward moment.

I clear my throat and choose my words carefully. "Nina, I think it's perfectly reasonable that Ashton would like to keep this day about her and Dan."

Nina ignores me. She goes over to the vanity and takes a lipstick from her purse. She applies it, keeping her eyes on herself the entire time. "Seriously, Ashton. Why can't you be happy for your father and me?"

Ashton looks up at the ceiling.

I try again. "Nina, perhaps you and I could speak privately? Discuss an alternative plan for—"

"This is a family matter," Nina interrupts. "Be a love and fetch me another martini. I'm parched."

I start to back up toward the door when Ashton puts her hand up to block me. "Don't you dare listen to her."

"Ashton! Watch your tone!" Nina admonishes.

Ashton lets out a scream. Both Nina and I jump.

Nina then looks at Ashton's baby bump. "Hormones?"

Ashton screams again. "I HATE you!"

Nina's mouth drops. Even I flinch. "Ashton," I say, quietly. "Let's get some air."

I reach for her arm just as the bathroom door opens yet again. Dan and Frank rush in. Dan looks at Ashton. "Did you just scream?"

"I did," she says.

I pick up my walkie-talkie. "Devon," I say softly. "The main floor ladies' room is off-limits. Direct guests to the downstairs option. Code red."

Everyone looks at me. I reclip my walkie-talkie. "I don't want anyone interrupting this private moment. Perhaps I should leave now."

"Don't!" Ashton cries. "I need you." She then turns to her family. "I screamed because words don't seem to work. You guys can't renew your vows or do whatever the hell she's talking about at our wedding. It's so obnoxious, I can't even think about it."

Frank shakes his head at Nina. "You have a lot of nerve springing that on me in front of everyone." He turns to Ashton. "I went along with it because you looked so happy. I didn't want to ruin the evening."

Ashton nods. "Same! Dan's parents worked really hard with Sylvia to make this dinner special. I wasn't going to let Mom ruin it."

Nina's face burns.

Dan cuts in. "So it's decided: Ashton and my wedding will remain our wedding. Come on, hon."

They leave the bathroom holding hands, as a couple, united.

Now, it's just me, Frank, and Nina.

"Seriously, Nina," he begins, his voice no longer strained but, instead, straightforward. "You can't just fly back to town and decide that everything is okay again. What happened, happened. I've moved on. I'm happy now."

Nina's mouth drops. "You met someone?"

My breath stops. I don't dare look at either of them. I can feel the blood in my ears as Frank responds. "I have. And she's great. She's taught me what it's like to feel joy again. And she's also taught me that I don't want to hate you anymore. We have a daughter together and soon a grandchild. So if you'd quit acting like such an narcissist, I think we could enjoy some really nice family moments together. Like this wedding. It's Ashton's day. So could you please think about her happiness first? It would mean a lot."

Frank doesn't wait for a response. He turns and leaves the bathroom. Now it's just me and Nina.

She stares at the wall. I feel light-headed from Frank's speech about me and want to slip out of here as invisibly as possible.

"Sebastian left me," Nina whispers. I freeze.

Nina turns to look at me and continues as though this were a totally appropriate conversation. "He changed his mind and wants to have children. Obviously, I can't provide that for him. I'm not a vain woman, Sylvia. I have my quirks. But I haven't had a single cosmetic procedure. I don't dye my hair. I am committed to aging honestly," she says, her voice tinged with pride.

"That's marvelous," I say, trying to lighten the mood. "I, on the other hand, benefit greatly from a little intervention at the beauty salon."

"I'm sure that's not true," Nina says generously.

"Oh, but it is. And that's okay."

Nina looks away a moment. "How am I supposed to leave this bathroom and face all those guests? They think Frank and I are getting remarried."

"My advice would be to pretend nothing happened and just move on."

Nina stares at herself for a few seconds before nodding. "I can do that."

Thirty-One

The rest of the evening was, thankfully, uneventful. It's now nearly eleven o'clock and I've just dropped Ashton off in the Plaza's most splendid suite with her best friend and maid of honor, Tati, who arrived at the tail end of the rehearsal dinner. She came straight off her flight from Japan. Ashton was so excited that she told Dan to sleep in his own room, which I think was less about being traditional and more about Ashton getting some much-needed girlfriend therapy. I can relate—I'm rushing down the hotel's hushed hallways to my own room, where Evie is waiting for me.

For hotel venues, Verena insists that her wedding planners stay overnight the evening before should anything go sideways. Naturally, I invited Evie to join me for a free night at the Plaza. We've been packed for days. Even the lowest-tier rooms are called "deluxe king." It's funny—in our former lives, Evie and I both enjoyed luxury hotels. And even though I've stayed overnight plenty of times by now at The Pierre, there's something different about having a fancy hotel room registered under my own name.

"Hello?" I call out as my feet sink into the plush carpet. "Just freshening up!" Evie's voice echoes from the bathroom.

I take off my coat and drape it over the back of the chair at the antique writing desk. I look over and see that my suitcase has been laid out for me on a luggage rack. I open a complimentary mineral water and pluck a chocolate macaron from a tray that's set on the coffee table. A small note reads, "With compliments of Management."

"Are they as good as look?" Evie asks as she comes out of the bathroom, ensconced in the fluffiest robe I've ever seen. She points to her shower-capped hair and explains, "I'm deep conditioning. The bath products are from Paris."

I grin and head to the bathroom as Evie takes a macaroon, settles herself onto the rolled-arm sofa, and picks up a magazine.

Forty minutes later, I emerge in my own fluffy robe. I took a bath and then a shower. I exfoliated, lathered, luxuriated, and moisturized. I find Evie relaxing on the bed watching television. She's still in her robe and shower cap. I lie next to her and sink my head into the feathered pillows.

Evie sighs. "This is a long way from the Airbnb."

"And yet it's probably only fifteen minutes by cab," I grin.

"Seriously, Sylvia. We went from washing our armpits in a Starbucks lavatory to bathing in a room that features inlaid earth-stone mosaics."

I burst out laughing.

Evie raises a brow and turns off the TV. "I know nice bathrooms are not a novelty. We both have had very fortunate lives. We raised families in upscale homes and vacationed at lovely hotels. But this, right here, is different. We've come a long way in so many ways. And I will never again take for granted handcrafted, solid white marble vanities." She sees my face and grins. "That's right. I read the entire description of this hotel room on the internet while you were in the shower."

I laugh again. "Tell me more. Make it a bedtime story."

"Once upon a time," she begins, her voice tinkling with music, "two ladies of a certain age stayed in a room that featured a large, wood-paneled luxury closet with built-in drawers and storage. There was white-glove butler service upon request. It worked by picking up a magical phone, pushing the number zero, and asking for whatever it is they might have dreamed of . . ."

I FELL ASLEEP to the sound of Evie's soothing voice telling me all about complimentary shoe shining. When I wake up the next morning at six o'clock, it's now Evie who is asleep, her body rising and falling against the Italian percale sheets. I tiptoe out of bed and slip into the bathroom to get ready. This time, I don't take long.

I apply my makeup and slip on a flattering but comfortable bra and panty set. I zip up my new dress and do a little twirl. I have never felt so fabulous. I add an extra bobby pin to secure my now go-to chignon and make sure my ear mic is fully charged.

Satisfied, I leave the bathroom, tiptoe back through the hotel room while carrying my pumps and a small duffel bag, and open the door. Once outside, I slip on my shoes, close my eyes, and do a mental checklist: ear mic; hotel keys; duffel bag containing an emergency sewing kit, duct tape, clear nail polish, superglue, two hundred dollars in cash, an Ace bandage, Neosporin, safety pins, baby wipes, a roll of Life Savers, travel-size hairspray, a switchblade, a mini bottle of Jack Daniel's, and a prescription bottle full of Tic Tacs but labeled "Ativan."

I make my way down to the lobby, where I eat half a muffin and drink a quick cup of coffee before meeting up with the hotel's in-house coordinator to ensure that each detail has been executed to perfection. I'm blown away. The florist has transformed the gilded Terrace Room into a countryside, complete with soft lighting and floral archways. Midsize evergreen trees are placed around the perimeter of the room and it's all so fresh and serene.

I then take the elevator up to the Grand Ballroom, which is a masterpiece. There's more trees and bouquets of flowers spread throughout to emulate a botanical garden on the grandest scale. For an indoor wedding, this feels as close to the great outdoors as possible. The bronze centerpieces modernize the opulence of the room and the cheerful fairy lights give it a sense of humor.

I feel breathy with anticipation as I return to the elevators and head to Ashton's suite.

Once outside her door, I take a deep breath and knock. Tati, wearing red flannel pajamas, opens it and gives me a hug.

"Ashton told me everything you've done for her," she says as she squeezes me. "I love you already."

I flush and hug her back. "Ashton is so delighted you could come," I reply with a smile.

"I wouldn't miss this for anything!"

"Where is Ashton?" I ask, looking around the one-bedroom suite. The space is perfect. There's an expansive living area with a powder-blue couch and several upholstered chairs. There's a separate dining area as well as a cozy library down the hall if anyone needs privacy.

"She's getting her nails done. I think she'll be up in a few. Her mom wanted to do it together. Can I help move anything?" Tati gestures to the hotel staff that's just arrived and is moving tables and chairs in order to make space for hair and makeup stations.

"I think they've got it," I say as another round of people wheel in carts to set up bagels, spreads, muffins, fruit, and finger sandwiches on the enormous dining table along with coffee, tea, water, and bottles of sparkling juices.

"So Ashton is with Nina?" I repeat.

"Don't worry," she says, watching my face. "Nina didn't seem to think she was getting married today, too."

I sigh. "I take it Ashton filled you in?"

Tati nods, then giggles. "Sorry. I know it's not funny." I feel my lips twitch when we hear a knock on the door.

We turn and see Reese and his two assistants enter the room carrying what can only be the gown.

"Sylvia, love! The day has arrived!" Reese air-kisses me as he leads his people toward the bedroom. I quickly open the door for them and then open the large closet. Reese hangs up the gown, which is covered in a zippered bag.

Once he places the gown, Reese properly kisses me and then Tati. "I am so thrilled beyond thrilled for today's event. You'll show me photos, I'm sure."

"Of course. Reese, I don't know how to thank you. You're my hero." I hug him.

He hugs me back and we make plans to meet for lunch next week. He then leads his team out of the room. I can't help but laugh—his two assistants, one girl and one young man—follow him like ducklings.

I turn back to Tati just as the door opens again. This time, Nina and Ashton come in.

Ashton looks a little pale, but Nina is beaming.

"Sylvia!" she cries as though we're best friends reunited. "So happy you're here. Is there any way you can order me a chai latte with coconut milk?"

Nina then collapses onto the couch and puts her large, elegant feet, still clad in paper thongs, up on the coffee table. She's chosen a dark purple, almost black polish and wears a short, bubble-gum-hued silk robe that barely covers her tush.

Ashton is wearing a matching robe and keeps trying to yank it down. She hands a third robe to Tati. "My mom bought us these," she says with a straight face.

I notice that Ashton has thankfully chosen a soft pink polish.

"Isn't this what all the girls do these days?" Nina cuts in as she flexes her vampy toes and lets the robe ride all the way up her thighs. "Wear slutty robes and talk about boys as we get our makeup done? Speaking of," she breathes as she takes out her phone. "Sebastian keeps texting me. First, he breaks up with me. Now, he realizes that he misses me. What do you think, girls? Do I keep him around? He had such a beautiful body. And could do the most amazing things with his tongue."

My cheeks flame as I picked up the house phone to order Nina her chai.

Ashton looks ill and says nothing. Instead, she picks up a bagel and bites off a large hunk.

Only Tati considers the question. "There's no such thing as a casual ex-boyfriend. He's a goner," she says firmly.

Nina nods and leans back against the couch. "Very wise, Tati. Ashton, darling. Could you make me a fruit plate? The pineapple looks divine."

Ashton looks at Tati, who raises a brow and shrugs. She then turns back to her mom. "You want me to make you a fruit plate?" she repeats, her voice thin.

"That would be marvelous, sweetheart." Nina smiles.

"Shouldn't you be offering to make me a fruit plate, Mom?" Ashton asks, her voice starting to shake.

Nina scrunches her brow. "You're standing right by the food, dear. Is everything all right?"

"Everything is terrific," Ashton says slowly. "My mother woke me up on my wedding day and took me to a nail salon where she talked all about herself for an hour. She's now lounging on a couch and asking me to wait on her. And she *still* hasn't asked me when my due date is for her grandchild."

Ashton's voice is rising into the hysteric range. Tati shoots me a look.

I clear my throat and put down the phone. "Nina, your chai is on its way. And the hair and makeup team will be here in half an hour. I'm happy to grab you some refreshments. You said pineapple?"

"Thank you, Sylvia. But I've lost my appetite," Nina replies coolly. "I'm going to meditate now." She leaves the room and heads to the library.

Thankfully, for the rest of the morning, I'm able to keep Nina away. She thought it was a splendid idea when I suggested she remain in the private library to get her hair and makeup done with the stylists I had hired specifically for her because I had anticipated the need to keep her someplace else.

"This way, you'll get to surprise us with your entrance," I said, as though she were the star of the day.

"Fab idea, Sylvia."

That was two hours ago. Nina hasn't emerged once. She dispatched the makeup artist to get her more chai, but otherwise, she's been invisible.

Ashton and Tati have had a grand time getting dolled up. Their hair and makeup are finished, but Ashton is in the bathroom yet again. She's in that pregnancy stage of needing to urinate every thirty minutes and wants to wait until the very last moment to slip on her dress.

Tati, meanwhile, is ready. She wears a strapless silver cocktail dress. She's elegant, a perfect complement to Ashton, who now emerges from the bathroom with a braided wreath around her head. She's left her long hair flowing down her back and looks gorgeous, despite the hideous pink robe.

I realize that this is the first time I've seen Ashton wear makeup. We went with a look that the makeup artist called "bride having an orgasm on an abandoned beach." She blended all kinds of cream blushes and bronzing powders and charcoal liners.

Ashton brings a hand self-consciously to her lips. "Is the lip gloss too glossy?"

"No," I say firmly.

Tati agrees. "You look amazing. Time for the dress? I'm dying to see it."

She claps her hands together. But Ashton shakes her head. "I feel like I need one more pee trip."

"You have time. Don't worry," I say, soothingly, as we hear a knock at the door.

I open it. It's Frank. We lock eyes. He looks so handsome in his tuxedo. I feel a desperate urge to pull him in for a kiss. But, instead, I smile a polite hello and step aside so that he can come and see his daughter.

He walks into the living room and stops short. "Ashton," he says jokingly. "Did you change your mind about the dress again?"

I can't help but laugh as he stares at his daughter in full makeup, a hair wreath, and a ridiculous robe.

"Don't you love it? I thought it was very bridal." Ashton does a mock pose.

We all smile and Ashton's about to say something else when we hear the library doors fling open. Nina strides into the living room wearing a white sheath dress that covers about a quarter of her lithe body. Her hair is gathered in an updo of curls and she's draped in lavish emeralds. Her nails and dark purple lipstick are fabulous and sexy and totally inappropriate for a mother of the bride.

All of us are speechless for a full minute. Nina draws her shoulders back. "Well?" she demands, and does a little twirl.

I swallow. My mind races through the rack of backup gowns I've brought for Nina in the event that this occurred. I'm trying to figure out which one to suggest when Ashton's voice cuts into the silence.

"Well," she says with an even voice. "I suppose someone should wear white at this wedding."

We all freeze for a moment. Then, Frank laughs.

Tati giggles and Ashton smiles wickedly.

Nina slowly turns in a circle, her face a bit blank. "Are you all making fun of me?"

"Mom. You're basically wearing a naked dress to my wedding. Of course we're making fun of you. But go for it. Whatever makes you feel good. I honestly don't care anymore. My due date is May twelfth and now I have to go pee again."

Ashton walks out of the room. Frank and Tati try to swallow laughter as Nina looks honestly confused.

"Did I do something wrong?" she asks me.

I shake my head. "Everything is perfect. In fact, why don't the three of you head to the Terrace Room right now."

"Without Ashton?" Frank asks.

I nod and tap my ear mic so that I can communicate with the crew waiting by Dan's hotel room. "The train is leaving the station." I turn back to Frank, Nina, and Tati. "You all head to the elevator. Dan, his best man, and his parents will meet you there. I'll bring Ashton down to the Terrace Room in five."

The mood shifts. Even Nina follows my commands as I usher everyone out. I watch for a moment as Frank leads them down the hallway before shutting the door. I hear the toilet flush from inside the bathroom and clap my hands together. This is it.

Thirty-Two

I have never felt so proud. I can't believe we made it to this moment. Ashton is standing in her wedding gown. Her small baby bump is so delightfully feminine as the bodice gathers below her bustline and hugs her new curves with just the right amount of sensuous glamour. She looks like a living portrait as she stands by the window in the hotel room and gazes out below at Fifth Avenue.

"It's funny," she finally says, breaking a long silence.

"What's funny, dear?"

"All those people down there." She presses her hand against the window. "They all have lives. None of them know or care that I'm about to get married. It's just another day. Do I sound crazy?"

I smile. "You sound existential."

"Is that weird?"

"Probably. But you've been a bit of a weird bride," I tease.

"You mean a bridezilla?"

"Not even a little bit," I say firmly. "Except for the beginning, of course. But after that, you've been a dream. Truly, Ashton. I am so impressed with you."

"Even though I still can't mash a banana?"

"I bought you a banana masher."

"Ha ha," she says with an eye roll.

"I'm serious." My eyes glint. "I already ordered it. It's your baby shower gift."

"They make banana mashers?" she asks, incredulous.

"They make mashers, honey," I explain. "You can use them for bananas, avocados, sweet potatoes. I can't believe this is the conversation we're having."

Ashton takes my hands in hers and squeezes them. "Thank you, Sylvia. For everything."

"You are most welcome," I reply.

And we stand there for a moment, our hands intertwined, until my ear mic crackles. "All set. Green green green."

I answer back, "Roger that. The bride is on the move. Repeat, the bride is moving."

Ashton shakes her head. "You really love that ear mic."

"I won't lie. I could wear it all day. Are you ready?"

Ashton takes a deep breath and runs her hands down the bodice of her dress. "I am."

I gesture for Ashton to walk ahead of me while I carry the hem of her dress. We pass hotel guests and staff. I see little goose bumps on Ashton's arms as people smile and tell her how beautiful she is. She smiles shyly back.

We get into the elevator and ride silently down. When we get off, we walk to the entrance just outside the Terrace Room. From outside, we can hear Evie playing a sonata by Beethoven. The music is romantic and full of emotion. My eyes tear up for the hundredth time when I see Verena approaching us with Ashton's bouquet. I notice that she's wearing a snazzier suit than usual—a violet tweed Chanel skirt and blouse ensemble that accentuates her curves. I say a prayer of thanks to Isabel for my Armani. I feel professional and bold. Perhaps a bit conservative. But considering I'm sleeping with the bride's father, discretion is a good thing.

"You take my breath away," Verena whispers to Ashton.

Ashton smiles a *thank you* and takes her bouquet of cascading orchids, garden roses, lilacs, and tulips. The colors range from blush to deep magenta, and the ombré effect is dazzling. I help her step into the Jimmy Choos and then motion for her to wait a moment while I peek through the doors.

I watch Frank and Nina walk down the aisle together. Somehow, despite everything, Nina has managed to be a star. She's linked her arm through Frank's and smiles at the rows of well-dressed friends and relatives, waving as though she were Lady Di. And just like a glowing celebrity, she transcends her ridiculous dress and somehow seems magnificent, like a rare and beautiful creature you'd see on safari.

I nearly laugh when I see Frank's stoic face. I can practically feel the vein in his neck throb as he escorts Nina down this endless candlelit aisle strewn with rose petals from Ashton and Dan's "flower girl" grandmothers. When they finally reach their seats, Frank snatches his arm from Nina and nearly dives into his chair. Nina, meanwhile, offers the crowd one last wave before slowly settling herself into a seat beside Frank.

I take a deep breath and scan the room. Everything is in place: Dan stands at the altar next to his best man, a studious-looking young man named Milan. Tati is across from them. The officiant—

Dan's sister, Annie—stands in place expectantly. She's a lesbian rabbi. Not that her sexual orientation is relevant. I just love how the whole occasion has become a family affair.

I glance to the left of the altar and see Evie place her hands on her lap. There's a moment of complete silence as the guests shift in their chairs.

I touch my ear mic and speak in a low voice. "Operation Let's Get Married is set to commence."

Evie touches her own ear mic and replies in a low voice. "Roger that, captain."

She then motions to the string quartet seated across from her. They lift their instruments. Evie flexes her palms and then, together, they begin the opening chords to the Beatles' "All You Need Is Love."

Ashton's face breaks into a smile and she steps forward. She insisted on walking down the aisle alone. Apparently a lot of young people these days don't like the idea of being given away. I can respect that. I smile as I watch her eyes meet Dan's for the time. His face blooms with joy. This is the moment I love most. My heart swells as Ashton takes her first steps down the aisle. She goes slowly at first but is then enveloped by the sway of the music and picks up the pace. Everyone is smiling and I catch quite a few people pressing Kleenex to their eyes.

I sneak into the back aisle and watch as Ashton finally makes it to Dan. They look at each other for a moment and then Annie steps forward and begins the ceremony.

"Today, we celebrate the love, commitment, and friendship of Ashton and Dan. We come together as family and friends to witness their devotion to one another."

As Annie continues, I begin to relax and can't help but remember my own wedding day.

Louis and I did get married outside. It was the summer of 1980. His grandparents had a beach house in Delaware with a beautiful backyard. All rolling hills and endless grass. It was the most romantic setting. Except, of course, for the mosquitos. And the heat wave. It was over a hundred degrees and the air was thick and humid. I cringe thinking about my Barbie-doll dress with its yards of suffocating crinoline and long sleeves that felt like sausage casings. I had wanted something lighter, more beachy. But my parents were conservative and would've died if I'd worn something that showed even the slightest inch of skin. After somehow making it down the aisle without fainting, I missed everything the rabbi said because I was too busy silently cursing Louis for standing in the shady part of the chuppah. We laughed about it later that evening when the sun went down and the temperature dropped to a more manageable ninety-two degrees. I was punch-drunk from heatstroke and dehydration. I remember sitting at the table chewing ice while Louis danced like John Travolta. Everyone kept telling me how lucky I was to have such a handsome, charming prince. I bobbed my head, sure that they were right. I hadn't even thought to feel insulted. I now wish that I looked those people in the eye and declared, "Actually, he's the lucky one. And let me tell you why . . ."

I'm shocked out of my memory by the boom of the piano. Evie has begun playing the Beatles again. The joyful tune lurches me into the present and I realize that the ceremony is over. Dan and Ashton have been married and are now making their way back down the aisle together. The crowd is on their feet dancing and it's a real concert in here. Feeling almost shaky with joy and disbelief, I, too, get onto my feet and start clapping along until . . .

That's odd. The young woman across the aisle can't be Isabel.

Sheesh. That trip down memory lane really shook me.

I rub my temples and start singing along with the crowd. This is all going so well.

I really wish that Isabel look-alike would stop staring at me. And why is she mouthing what looks like *Mom*?

I feel prickles of shock all over my body but keep on singing as Dan and Ashton pass me by. They're followed by Tati and Mark, Dan's parents, and finally Frank and Nina.

As soon as Frank and Nina make it out the door, Isabel turns back to me and sneaks across the aisle. She grabs my hand. "That was so beautiful," she whispers. She's wearing a simple black dress and looks like one of the guests. She's smiling so hard at me that I can't help but squeeze her hand back, despite feeling thrown. As Evie and the musicians play an encore for the guests, I quickly exit the room and turn down a side hallway. Isabel follows me.

"Sylvia," Verena's voice crackles into my ear mic. "The wedding party is en route to pictures. The photographer is standing by. We're going to do a few outside."

"Excellent," I respond, trying not to sound dazed as I keep my eyes focused on Isabel's beaming face. "I've already set up heat lamps at the north entrance."

"Roger that. When we're finished, I'll escort them to cocktail hour and meet you there."

As soon I click off with Verena, Isabel claps her hands lightly. "Bravo, Mom. You really did it. And you look amazing."

I square my shoulders. "Yes, I did. And thank you once again for this dress. But, Isabel. What on *earth* are you doing here?"

She flushes. "Ashton said it was okay if I crashed—I wanted to surprise you. See you in action."

I let out a breath. "I suppose that's very sweet."

Isabel looks at the ground. "I thought if I told you I was coming, you'd get nervous. I just wanted to support you and tell you how great a job you've done. And also to give you this."

She opens her purse and takes out an envelope. I take it from her and peer inside. It's a check for sixty-five hundred dollars.

"It's the money Dad owes you," Isabel explains quietly. "He told me what he did. I'm giving you this on his behalf."

"Izzy, you don't need to get involved."

"Dad owes you this. He understands. He apologizes."

"No, he doesn't."

Izzy looks contrite. "Okay, fine. He doesn't apologize. But he does know he has no choice but to give you this back. And I promise that this is as involved as I'm getting. I have to focus on my own life. Watching Dad fight with your naked boyfriend was a real turning point for me. Todd calls it rock bottom."

"And how is Todd?"

"He says that was rock bottom for him, too. Bunny overheard us talking about it and asked way too many questions about both of your bodies before suggesting we hire a prostitute to fix our marriage. As soon as she left, Todd said he'd join me for therapy. Both of our parents cannot have better sex lives than us."

I look at Isabel for a moment. Her face is softer, her voice less severe. "It looks like therapy agrees with you," I finally say.

"It's hard but good. And Todd is back to work. Well, sort of. He set up a consultancy firm and works from home, which is actually nice. He's already got one client. We do yoga together in the morning. And he makes me breakfast. He's actually teaching the girls to cook, which is a really interesting way for them to learn math."

I can't help but laugh. Izzy blushes, then looks down. "Look,

Mom. I'm sorry I ever doubted you. You are an amazing wedding planner. An amazing person."

I open my mouth to respond but nothing comes out. Instead, it's like something inside of me releases. Like a boulder I didn't even know was strapped to my back has just now tumbled free. I let out a breath and turn to look at Izzy's familiar face. I tilt her chin up so I can see her eyes. "You have no idea how much that means to me to hear. And I want you to know that you're also an amazing woman. And I see you, too. You're in 'it' right now—having young kids and juggling work, marriage, and life is hard. But you're doing it."

I throw my arms around her. She hugs me back. We stand there for another moment when Verena's voice cuts into my ear mic. "Outdoor photos are complete. We're headed inside for cocktail hour. Over."

I touch my mic and respond. "Copy that."

Isabel watches me and smiles. "You really are a professional."

I smile back. "That's goddamn right. See you soon?"

She nods. "You bet."

We both turn and head in different directions.

Thirty-Three

If only I believed in drinking on the job, I'd ask one of the mixologists to make me a celebratory drink. I'm still basking in the Isabel interaction as I weave my way around the happy guests. They're drinking raspberry-infused vodka and gold-flecked martinis. I take a deep breath. Everyone loves cocktail hour. My mouth waters as the servers bring out trays of mini taquitos, risotto balls, and fresh albacore sashimi with crispy onions.

I see Ashton pop a piece of bruschetta in her mouth and look longingly at a guest's pink champagne. Dan rubs her back and immediately refills her pregnancy-friendly sparkling juice in a special goblet he bought her for today. He then takes a bottle of mineral water for himself and winks. She laughs. I smile as I watch her take his hand. They float around the room, looking as happy as any couple I've seen.

Even Frank is smiling, despite the fact that Nina keeps dragging him from guest to guest. I suppose she knows it's their duty, as hosts of this wedding, to make people feel welcome. And I have to say, watching her is inspiring. And knowing Frank the way that I do, he's probably relieved that she's doing all the talking.

Verena comes up beside me and gestures toward Nina. "That woman is a piece of work. But you've handled her perfectly. I admit, I was worried."

"About what?"

"That she'd throw a tantrum. We'd have to escort her out."

"The night isn't over."

Verena raises a brow. "So you do think she'll throw a fit?"

"I think she'll seduce someone totally inappropriate."

Verena laughs. "Another young stud?"

"Not necessarily. Just someone to cause drama." I narrow my eyes and watch Nina carefully. "She's not a big drinker, which is a pleasant surprise. So perhaps I'm paranoid. I just need to watch her."

I reach into my pocket and take out an index card. I've jotted down names—the people in Frank's family who are at war with one another, along with some of Dan's relatives that Ashton flagged for me. I show the list to Verena and scan the crowd, pointing out each person.

Verena puts a hand on my shoulder. "I was going to wait until after the reception, but I've never been good at delayed gratification. Welcome to the big leagues, Sylvia. I'd like to offer you full-time employment at my firm effective immediately. All the bells and whistles. Health care, an expense account, and a salary that will, at the very least, cover the cost of replacing your futon with an actual bed."

My stomach buzzes and I almost burst into tears. But instead, I straighten my shoulders and force a calm smile. "Thank you, Verena. I accept."

She smiles and squeezes my arm. "We are going to have such fun working together. Now, let's go and finish this wedding."

She walks off, making her way around the guests, noticing little details and directing the bussers to ferry away empty glasses or plates with just the slightest nod.

I stand there a moment. I did it. I really did it.

Thirty-Four

I was wrong and Ashton was right. The high-top Golden Goose sneakers that she insisted upon changing into are perfect. She lasted about thirty minutes in the Grand Ballroom before begging to make the shoe swap. And so I crouched by the side of her table and discreetly removed her Jimmy Choos. The party was already in full swing.

That was nearly four hours ago. My own feet are swollen and heavy in my pumps as I stand at my post against the back wall near the service entrance to the ballroom. I shift my weight. Thankfully, I'm too high on adrenaline to feel my feet throb. I must remember to borrow Evie's Hogans for the next wedding.

The next wedding.

My chest balloons with delight. I'm going to have another wedding. And another. And another. I have a career. I allow myself one huge smile before refocusing on the present. This wedding isn't over. But things are looking as good as I could have hoped. The guests enjoyed cucumber-rolled greens, lobster ravioli, and pork loin. I heard people swoon over the cake. In fact, Ashton and Dan have four different plates' worth of cake at their private table and I am under explicit orders not to let anyone clear it. They are both stuffed with chocolate and happiness and I can't help but smile as I watch the two of them dance to a Johnny Cash song, "You're the Nearest Thing to Heaven," that always makes me cry.

Evie and the band have been brilliant. I feel my hips sway along to the music and can't help but mouth the lyrics as I scan the room for Frank. He's still sitting at his table. The seats on either side of him are empty, but Nina is several chairs down and engaged in what appears to be a deep conversation with Dan's sister, Annie. Nina leans forward and has one hand on Annie's forearm. Hmm. Maybe they're discussing theology. Of course, most rabbis don't blush during discussions of Judaic history.

I think about intervening. But at this point, it doesn't matter if Nina sleeps with Ashton's sister-in-law. The wedding was a success. There's no damage left to be done. And so I watch them for another beat and even wonder if they might make a nice couple before turning my attention back to Frank.

I see that he's also watching them what an amused expression on his face. He shakes his head. God, he's so different than Louis. He's not nearly as broad and conventionally handsome. But I love his hands. His fingers are thick and manly and his palms are always warm. I stand there, just looking at him. I can't wait to run my lips down the back of his neck.

As if he can sense me watching him, he turns his head. His eyes widen. He winks at me from across the room and takes out his phone.

My phone beeps from inside my pocket. I check the text. "Almost free." I text back a heart emoji.

He texts back two heart emojis and cartoons of cats having sex. I laugh aloud.

He's in the middle of texting me something else when Verena approaches him. She lightly taps his shoulder. He puts his phone away and stands up. I can't tell what they're talking about, but Verena is smiling warmly and keeps glancing in my direction. I feel a little glow—they must be talking about me. In fact, I'm sure of it. Verena shakes Frank's hand, then quietly interrupts Nina and Annie and shakes their hands as well. She then heads toward me.

"Sylvia," she says with another warm smile. "I think you can handle the closing of this magnificent evening. I'm going to take off."

"Sounds good," I reply. "Enjoy your evening."

She squeezes my shoulder once more, then leaves through the service entrance.

I lean back against the wall and try to savor the success. Everything is just perfect.

Thirty-Five

Things are still perfect. Dan and Ashton were the last to leave the wedding—I didn't want to rush them. Even when the custodial staff came in with vacuums. But eventually they took the hint. Evie and the band had already packed up. Evie offered to wait for me so that we could share a cab back to the apartment. But I told her I wanted to surprise Frank in bed.

As I walk down the hotel's sumptuous hallway, I feel giddy. It's nearly midnight but I'm not the least bit tired. In fact, if my feet weren't so crippled, I'd be sprinting toward Frank's room.

I feel a little thrill as I round the corner. Frank is probably dead asleep. We last texted over an hour ago. He'd already gone up to his room and said we'd have a special evening tomorrow. But I have an extra room key. And I love the idea of surprising him. In fact, as I limp over to his room and put the key in the reader, I'm already imagining the things I'm going to do to him. I push open the door and nearly trip over a pair of shoes.

I roll my eyes. Frank is so messy. I pick up his loafers and, along with my duffel bag, put them in the spacious hallway closet before walking into the living room.

I glance across the room at the bedroom door and see that it's closed and the lights are off inside. A shiver goes through me. I stand by the couch and take off my pumps. My feet sink into the velvety carpet and my entire body sighs. Hmm. Maybe I'll take off all my clothes out here and surprise Frank in bed by slipping against his lean body and waking him with light, feathery kisses.

I start unbuttoning my dress and walk toward the bedroom when I trip over another pair of shoes.

I look down and see a pair of high heels.

As if in slow motion, I bend down and pick up the stilettos. They're classic black suede Christian Louboutins with the telltale bloodred soles. The tip of the heel is silver and looks like a dagger. I slowly turn in a full circle, now taking in every inch of the living room. It's like reliving that day with Belinda and Louis back in Boca. Only this time, I see everything: Frank's socks kicked off by the drapes. Nina's bra hanging off the antique desk chair. A large, half-full bottle of Acqua Panna sits next to empty tumblers on the coffee table. I close my eyes. I'm such an imbecile. How could I possibly think they wouldn't get back together?

From across the room, behind the closed bedroom door, I hear a woman moan, "Oh, Frank . . ."

Frank grunts and I want to die.

I have to get out of here. I quickly button my dress.

I pick up my shoes and go to grab my things from the closet when I hear Frank's voice: "That was incredible, my queen."

I stiffen.

Did he just call her *his queen*? The same thing he calls me? Rage rockets through me and I nearly turn and march into the bedroom.

But I don't. My shoulders sag as I realize that Nina has been his queen for much longer than me.

I need to go. I finally grab my things from the closet when I hear the bedroom door start to open.

"I just need some water," Frank says. Shit!

I don't have time to run to the door. Instead, in a blind panic, I jump into the closet and pull the door closed. It clicks.

"Hello?" Frank calls out.

I hold my breath as tears sting my eyes. This day has been too good. It was not supposed to end with me hiding in my lover's hotel room closet like the worst kind of cliché while he reunites with his estranged wife. I'm still holding my purse and duffel bag and can no longer keep the tears at bay. They roll down my face with abandon.

I hear Frank padding around the room until he sees the bottle of Acqua Panna.

"Got it," he calls out as he hums and takes a swig from the bottle.

He's happy. The thought hits me like a bulldozer. Of course he is. Nina is his wife.

She may seem like a lunatic to me, but he's known her for nearly forty years. They built a family together. My tears dry up and I start to breathe. I feel another stab in my chest but this time it's not anger. It's just the pure ache of sadness. Their daughter got married today.

I remember the night Izzy got married. Louis and I crawled into bed and sobbed like babies. Our little girl was in someone else's home, and all of a sudden, it felt so final. She wasn't coming back. Of course, she and Todd bought a house three blocks away. But still. I felt so empty. Like I poured my whole life into someone only to watch her leave. It's the closest I ever felt to Louis. We made love that night, clinging tightly to one another. Louis lit an oregano-scented candle.

I let out a breath. This closet is starting to feel a bit cramped. And I can't exactly hide in here all night. I peek through the slats in the wood. Frank is now sitting on the couch with no clothes on. Go back into the bedroom, I silently order.

He puts the water bottle back down but then puts picks up the remote and turns on the TV. Oh, for heaven's sake. I hate men.

"Are you hungry?" he calls out as he flips channels. "I'm starving."

"Shall I call in-room dining. What are you in the mood for?" That's not Nina's voice.

Blood pounds in my ears and the entire world seems to pivot on its axis as I peer again through the slats and watch Verena walk into the living room. She's wearing one of the hotel's robes and holds the cordless room phone. Her normally sleek bob is a wild nest of sex-blown hair.

She perches on the back of the couch and strokes Frank's neck. "Just tell me what you want. Burger and fries? Or something lighter?"

He closes his eyes as she starts to really massage him with her free hand. "That feels so good," he sighs.

"How dare you!" I burst out of the closet and hurl my duffel bag at them. It lands with a thud on the coffee table and knocks the Acqua Panna onto the carpeted floor. Nothing shatters. But over-priced mineral water leaks everywhere.

"Jesus!" Frank's face blanches.

"Oh, crap." Verena closes her eyes. "Sylvia."

Frank bends over to scoop up the bottle. "Sylvia," he stammers, his voice hoarse. "I thought we decided to meet tomorrow. What are you doing here? Why were you in the closet?"

"I came to surprise you. Then I heard . . ." I redden and clear my throat. "I thought you were with Nina and . . ." My voice trails off again and I look around, not sure what to do.

Verena seems to take this as her cue to disappear back into the bedroom.

Now it's just me and Frank.

He grabs a throw blanket from the back of the couch and wraps it around his waist. He walks toward me. "Christ, Sylvia. I don't know what to say."

I stare at him, dazed, and can't help but think about all the times he's been caught without clothes on. I almost laugh. But none of this is funny. I finally find my voice. "Well, thank you for not saying, 'This isn't what it looks like,' or 'I love you,'" I add.

He speaks quietly. "I do, though. Love you, I mean. And in the spirit of always being way too honest with each other, I really wish I didn't. Because I know you don't love you me back."

"Is that your excuse?"

"Yes. But it's a shitty one. A hackneyed song you hear on bad radio. 'Hurt the one I love before she hurts me first,'" he says sadly.

He looks so wounded that it takes me a moment to remember he just betrayed me. Epically. I almost try to make him feel better.

But I don't.

Instead, I pick up my bag. "I'm fond of you, Frank. We had such fun together. But I don't have time for this. I'm a sixty-three-year-old woman, and I've got my whole life ahead of me."

He gives me a small smile. "I'll miss you, Sylvia."

"You bet your ass you will."

I turn to leave when Verena reenters the room now dressed. She walks over to me and Frank and shakes her head, at once both admiring and contrite. "You both are so fucking civilized. I'm inspired." She turns to face me directly. "Sylvia, I'm sorry. I know this is no excuse, but I've been to enough AA meetings and psychotherapy to understand that I have a history of wanting what other people have. It's almost like its own addiction. And god knows, I've taken enough from you. I'm ashamed of myself."

I look at her and resist the urge to roll my eyes. "Thank you for that lovely and introspective speech, Verena. I believe every word of it. I also believe that you're a raging narcissist. I quit, effective immediately."

"Sylvia, seriously? You're going to throw all this away over some guy? No offense, Frank."

"None taken." Frank goes to stand next to her and looks at me. His face is so earnest. "She's right, Sylvia. Don't give up your job— your dream—because I screwed up."

I look back and forth between them. Frank's still holding the blanket around his waist. Verena, despite being fully clothed, still has her wild sex hair.

"I don't know whether to punch you both in the face or give you hugs. But I suppose that's my own issue." I turn to Frank. "Frank, we've said our goodbyes. I wish you the best. I hope to keep up with Ashton and see a picture of that beautiful baby when it arrives." I look at Verena. "Verena, as you say, cut the shit. You claim to be a bad person. I don't believe that. But I believe that *you* believe that. And so I'm getting out of the line of fire. You gave me a chance, and I will always be grateful. But I really need to leave without either of you saying another word or making this about you. I'm exhausted. We're all grown-ups here. Let's leave it at that."

I turn and walk out the door. I hear it shut behind me. I don't dare turn back as I make my way to the elevator. All I want to do is go home.

Thirty-Six

I feel numb. It's just after six in the morning and I'm sitting on the little sofa in our living room. Evie is making tea in the kitchen and has been talking nonstop since she woke up and found me asleep on the couch, still in my dress.

After I left Frank and Verena, I came straight to the apartment. As soon as I made it up the front steps and opened the door, it was like my legs stopped working. My bedroom felt too far away and so I collapsed onto the sofa. When Evie came in, I woke up and gave her every detail of what happened. It felt odd—I didn't even cry. Even when she hugged me and my cheeks sank into her red silk pajamas, I had no tears. And not much to say.

Evie, on the other hand, had a lot to say. "Those bloody, fucking fucker-bitches! I'm going to murder them!" And off she went, exploding with expletives, on a rant about Verena and Frank. She's been going on like this for at least a full five minutes. I don't even hear everything she's saying. Her litany has become like gentle background music.

Maybe I'm not numb. Maybe I'm just incredibly zen. I do feel this sense of calm, like warm water from the bluest lagoon, wash over my body as I sit and watch Evie bang around the kitchen and curse with abandon.

"... Stupid Frank and his stupid 'I love you' bullshit! I knew that man was not mentally fit. And Verena? What a lousy excuse for a person. I'm going to go online and skewer her business. She messed with the wrong fucking woman."

I can't help it. I burst out laughing.

Evie puts down the kettle and looks at me, her face breaking in concern. "Sylvia, love. Are you okay?"

I throw my head back and laugh harder.

She hurries over and grabs my shoulders, her eyes wide. "You're in shock, dear."

I breathe in Evie's expensive moisturizer. "Oh, Evie. I'm not in shock. I'm in control. I found your elegance very soothing, by the way."

Evie lets me go reaches for her phone. "I'm calling a doctor."

I stop her and smile. "Evie, just listen. In the last few months, I've moved to a new city with my best friend, set up an apartment, gotten a job, had some outstanding sex, and planned a fabulous wedding. I have a new relationship with my daughter. And so I refuse to think that this is the end of me. I've had my life turned upside down before. But I don't scare so easily anymore."

Evie starts to nod. "You've done a lot."

"As have you, my friend. So let's not let Verena and Frank be the end. We're just beginning here."

Now Evie smiles. "Yesterday was certainly a triumph. I was a big hit. People came up to me and asked for my contact information."

"Evie! That's so exciting!"

She tilts her head. "You know, I told them that I work exclusively for Sylvia Fisher Weddings."

"You didn't!"

"Of course I did. Quite psychic, now that I think of it."

I laugh again. Evie joins me. We're laughing and smiling and it feels like we might even start dancing if my phone didn't ring.

I glance down and see an international number.

"Who could be calling so early?" Evie asks as I reach to pick up.

I just shrug and answer the phone. "Hello?"

A man with an Italian accent lets out a breath, sounding relieved. "Good morning. Is this Sylvia Fisher's assistant?"

I see Evie in my doorway, a curious expression on her face.

I clear my throat and am about to answer yes, but then sigh. "No. This is Sylvia. I mean, I'm Sylvia."

"Ah, so happy to speak with you. My name is Lorenzo Cascio. I'm sorry to call at such an inappropriate hour but I'm desperate. My fiancée, Elena, and I are about to board our plane back home to Italy. We were at Ashton and Dan's wedding. Elena is begging me to call you. We're getting married in Tuscany this summer and things have gone sideways. Our parents had wanted to plan the wedding but that, as you might have guessed, has caused great friction. Things are now in chaos. Ashton said that you were the only person who could help us."

My heart is beating so fast that I force myself to take a long breath. "I'm sorry," I finally manage. "Did you say Tuscany? As in Tuscany, Italy?"

"Yes. Might you be available? Would you be open to traveling? All expenses covered, naturally."

At this point, Evie is standing right next to me. She's heard every word. She grabs my hand and clutches it.

I squeeze back and clear my throat. "I would be very open to traveling. And you happen to have perfect timing, Mr. Cascio. My schedule has just cleared."

"You have no idea how happy I am to hear this. And, please. Call me Enzo. As we are already friends." His voice is warm and musical.

"I very much look forward to meeting you, Enzo. And Elena. Please call me as soon as you land and we'll make arrangements."

After a flurry of "grazies" and a final "ciao," Enzo hangs up.

I clutch my phone to my chest and look at Evie, whose eyes are as wide as mine. "Italy," she breathes.

"Italy," I confirm. "I'll be needing my best pianist, naturally."

I'm not sure who squeals first. But soon the two of us are clutching each other and dancing around the room.

Thirty-Seven

There is no blue like the Mediterranean. The shades of turquoise and aquamarine that blend into a deep sapphire are enough to make me believe that heaven is truly a kingdom found here on Earth. At least, that's what Gabriella, my new bride Elena's best friend and cycling instructor, says. She also says, "Breathe into what's burning," which isn't nearly as inspiring. Particularly since every one of our "Tour de France" sessions sends me dangerously close to cardiac arrest as we climb the punishingly steep hills of the Italian countryside.

But I'm not complaining. It's shocking how different I feel these days. Not only have I gained some wonderful muscle tone, but I feel more relaxed, stronger, more in control of my life. Evie and I have moved into an apartment on the grounds of Castello di Vicaro, the magnificent estate that has been in Elena's family for generations. This is where the wedding will be. There are olive groves and vineyards and a cliffside garden that overlooks the jeweled sea. Our apartment is located at the edge of the property, which makes for an easy ride into town. It's all stone and whitewashed walls. When we sit on our little patio and enjoy a morning coffee, the air smells like salty bread and grapes.

Everything feels blissful. Now that the work of planning a wedding has been off-loaded to me, Enzo and Elena's parents are once again getting along fabulously. And Elena is a dream bride. Joyful, easygoing, not the least bit stressed. Even her enthusiastic exercise habits are a plus. I'm the fittest I've ever been and it's a nice way to bond and get work done.

The wedding isn't for another three months. But it's going to be the biggest, most lavish production I've ever pulled off. Both Elena's and Enzo's families are enormous. And rather than a single celebration, this wedding is more like a weeklong festival with everything from a sunset party on a yacht to an all-day cycling excursion where guests will visit local wineries.

I wake up every morning full of energy. Like today, for instance. It's not even seven o'clock and I'm sitting on the patio with my trusty legal pad making a list of the vendors we'll need to service the various parties. I'm so busy that it's hard to be in touch with my old life. But I do talk to Louis occasionally, mostly about practical matters like our divorce. And Isabel and I chat at least three times a week. She loves to hear the latest about my work and I love to hear about the girls. She and Todd seem to be in a good place, which thrills me. I even miss Bunny. She recently sent me a photo from Mykonos. She and Marty look so happy. Of course, it would have been nice if they weren't naked. But I tried to only look at their smiling faces. Frank and Verena have disappeared from my world like traces of smoke after a fire.

Of course, I still have fantasies. But I don't even think of them as fantasies. They're more like "vision board" ideas. If I were to make a list of what would be on my current vision board, what pops into mind is the following:

Luxury Brides does a huge spread on Enzo and Elena's wedding. They write about my big comeback in an emotional, heartwarming piece that catches the eye of a *60 Minutes* producer. I can just imagine my interview. I'd be wearing a serious but elegant suit and discuss what it's like to reinvent oneself later in life. *Sylvia's Second Act.*

And naturally I think what it would be like to live abroad forever. I thought New York was my new home. But maybe I'm destined to be a citizen of the world. For now, it's Italy. And then London. And then . . . Well, as they say—more will be revealed.

Hmm. I like that. I'm going to jot it down in my journal, which I've started to keep just in case that *60 Minutes* interview really does happen. I'm writing down a few more thoughts when I hear someone calling my name. I look up and see Elena running down the hill toward me. She looks unusually stricken.

"Sylvia! I need you!" she says, breathless, as she approaches. She runs a hand through her dark, glossy hair. "I don't know what to do!"

"What's going on?" I ask.

Elena plops down in the chair across from me and practically whispers. "When I came downstairs, I saw her. Coming out of a taxi. With luggage!"

"Who?" I ask, confused.

Elena, her normally sweet face now dark, fires off a flurry of Italian profanity before grabbing my hands. "Luciana," she finally utters.

My stomach clenches. *Luciana.* "You mean Enzo's ex-girlfriend?"

"Yes. And she is not alone."

"She came with a man?"

"She came with a baby."

Elena bursts into tears. I immediately get up and start to rub her back. I see Evie standing in the doorway off to the right. She's heard everything and meets my eye. I raise my brow and let out a breath. Weddings. They just never get boring.

I suppose that's life. Or *la vita*, as I now say.

Acknowledgments

I would not have written this book if I hadn't signed up for UCLA's extension program. Thank you to Paul Witcover, my wonderful instructor. And thank you to Lynn Hightower, my wonderful instructor, mentor, and now friend.

Receiving the Allegra Johnson Prize from UCLA in May 2020 is also a part of how I finished this book. Thank you, Roberta and Alex Johnson, for making this award available and for being such generous champions of writers.

I also want to thank all of the wonderful teachers, instructors, and professors I have had over the years.

I must say a special thank you to Professor Yusef Komunyakaa, my undergraduate mentor and advisor, for his encouragement, his knowledge, and his kindness.

Thank you to Team Sylvia. To the team at WME—to Danny Greenberg for introducing me to my incredible agent, Erin Malone.

Also, thank you to Florence Dodd, Laura Bonner, Carolina Beltran, and Alexandra Figueroa. And to the team at Pamela Dorman Books/ Viking Penguin—Pamela Dorman, you are one of my heroes. It has been an honor to work with you and Marie Michels. Also at Penguin— thank you to Brian Tart, Andrea Schulz, Patrick Nolan, Tricia Conley, Tess Espinoza, Matt Giarratano, Nick Michal, Diandra Alvarado, Nicole Celli, Jason Ramirez, Paul Buckley, Claire Vaccaro, Kate Stark, Mary Stone, Chantal Canales, Lindsay Prevette, Carolyn Coleburn, Yuleza Negron, Lauren Monaco, and Andy Dudley. And a special thank you to Charlotte Mursell at Orion for your wonderful input as well.

I also must thank all of my dear friends (and cousin, Rachel!) who listened to me talk about this story and came along on this journey with me. I am blessed to have you all in my life. Thank you to my walking buddies—you know who you are—and also to my long-time friends from Highland Park. And to my "sister," Kelly, for always being up for listening to me talk shop.

I am so deeply grateful to all the people in my life who support my family. Without you, I would never have found the time to sit in front of the computer. Kim Hanke, I told you that if I ever published this book, I would mention you in the acknowledgments. I meant it. And a very special thank you to Dr. Clarissa Armstrong—for everything.

And, finally, I need to thank my husband, Dean Georgaris, for his unyielding support and love. You never doubted me. And you gave me the best possible advice a writer could have: finish. Thank you, Dean. You are my favorite writer, my favorite person.